STRING CITY

AN INTERDIMENSIONAL THRILLER

GRAHAM EDWARDS

SOLARIS

First published 2019 by Solaris
an imprint of Rebellion Publishing Ltd,
Riverside House, Osney Mead,
Oxford, OX2 0ES, UK

www.solarisbooks.com

ISBN: 978 1 78108 567 7

This is a work of fiction. All the characters and events
portrayed in this book are fictional, and any resemblance
to real people or incidents is purely coincidental.

10 9 8 7 6 5 4 3 2 1

A CIP catalogue record for this book is available
from the British Library.

Designed & typeset by Rebellion Publishing

Printed in Denmark by Nørhaven

STRING CITY

For Pete

See a penny
Pick it up
All the day
You'll have good luck

The Tartarus Heist

1

They stormed my office brandishing clubs. Some carried torches, burning despite the torrential rain. Orange flames flashed off sulking puddles but the body of the mob was a mass of shadows, more like ghosts than people.

Here in String City, they could have been either.

I checked the locks: six down each side of the door, all singularity-bonded. Each lock had internal gravity equivalent to a dwarf star and the door itself was quarter-inch glass. With two extra dimensions woven into the panes, it rated an effective thickness of three miles. More than enough to stop a crowd of angry citizens baying for my blood.

Like any good private detective, I make security a priority.

A thunderbird swooped low, gold wings obliterating the jagged city skyline with a shadow the size of six city blocks. The torch flames jostled in the darkness. When the thunderbird climbed again, its hurricane slipstream opened the clouds. Watery sunlight splashed down over distant neon-crusted towers and soaked the street in an uncertain glow.

The mob reached the door and stared in at me. There was

a round man in a square stetson carrying a battered leather satchel, a tall woman with her arm in a sling, a dockside worker in greasy overalls. I watched as the anger drained from their faces—all faces that I recognised. I didn't like what was left when the anger was gone.

It looked too much like hope.

As soon as I turned my back on the door, the anger of the mob came back. The glass might have been three miles thick but I could still hear the shouts. Someone screamed for my blood.

I hurried to the big walnut desk at the back of my office. To get there, I had to weave through the piles of case folders stacked from floor to ceiling. It was like a maze. I wondered how many hundreds there were. I must have been crazy to take on so much work, but times were hard. I'd have been crazy to turn it down.

Nobody knew what had started the financial collapse, and even the quantum economists could see only a single downward spiral ahead. Folk trudged the streets with their heads down and their hands stuffed deep in their pockets, and talked grimly in bars about the end of the world. It was nothing you could put your finger on, but it was also everything. If life was a symphony, it had suddenly started playing in a minor key.

You might not think a city-wide depression would be good for business. But I'm a private investigator. When money's tight, decent folk will burn down their homes just to get the insurance and who do the loss adjusters call in to rake through the ashes? Gumshoes like me. Then there's the hopeless unemployed who cheer themselves up by cheating on their wives. There's nobody more ready to pay a shamus his fee than a jilted dame. Need I go on?

Think of them all. A whole city full. All those poor saps who figure that, with the world going to hell in a handcart, they've got nothing to lose. Like the man said, it's an ill wind blows no sucker any good. For the first time since Laura died—geez, had it really been ten years?—I was making good money and the sun was shining down on my shabby little office. Could you blame me for making hay?

I took a sheet of paper from the desk and wrote a single word on it in black pen. I picked up a roll of sticking tape. Dragging my boots back over the frayed carpet, I returned to the door.

The mob held its collective breath. Expectant faces bobbed like buoys in the ocean. At the back, a hooded man loitered. His features were lost in shadow. Had he been there before?

I took a breath, made ready to tape the notice I'd made to the glass. The notice that read:

CLOSED

The city exploded.

I saw it over their heads: a spear of dazzling purple light shooting straight up out of Tartarus, String City's gambling quarter. A dozen gaudy nightclubs tore themselves apart and the ring of tower blocks surrounding them folded to rubble. Cars flew skyward on jagged arcs of electricity as all the neon in the district shorted out, big colorful volts that stabbed the clouds before arcing over and down into what was left of the neighborhood. Bricks and bodies flew clear of the epicenter, riding the lightning. Dust billowed into a seething black mushroom that ate the sky. The thunderbirds scattered.

The ground bucked like a mule and in my office stacks of case files collapsed like the statues of dictators on revolution night. Outside, a crack tore down the middle of the street. Asphalt strips unrolled like clocksprings, tossing hapless pedestrians into the air. A big one tipped a municipal garbage truck on end and ejected its golem operators into the gutter.

The people outside my door clung to each other, screaming.

Something was tumbling out of the dust cloud, turning end over end: a rectangular chunk of debris thrown up by the explosion, trailing sparks and showering rubble. It reached the top of its trajectory and started to fall. It looked about the size of a railroad carriage. It was tumbling this way.

I screwed up the paper and tossed it aside, then swiped my hand down the row of locks. One by one the singularities inverted and I yanked open the door. Wind howled in, laced with the last of the rain; with it came a rumble like the bellyache of the gods.

"Get inside!" I yelled.

The mob poured through the open doorway, a liquid, terrified throng. The chunk of debris bore down on them like Armageddon.

"Hurry!" I hauled the woman with the broken arm over the threshold. "You all in?"

I looked for the hooded man, but he was nowhere to be seen. Maybe he'd run away, or been swallowed by one of the sinkholes opening up in the street. Outside, a hundred more folk were running and bleeding. There wasn't anything I could do for them.

The rectangular missile was rushing straight toward my office.

I slammed the door and engaged the locks a second before it hit. One corner of the thing hit the sidewalk like a pile driver, embedding itself six feet deep in the exact spot the mob had been standing. The rest of it crashed against the door, buckling as it tried to smash its way through. It was like someone had dropped a whale on the world. A crack split the glass from bottom to top, but the door held. Everything shuddered. The mob and I waited, shuddering too. Ash from the distant explosion rolled over the street and smothered the glass and everything went black.

Everything except the neon lettering still spitting fitfully on the broken slab of steel that had flown halfway across the city to fetch up against my door. The letters flickered electric red, dying one after the other before my eyes. I had just enough time to read them before they went out altogether. The words they made filled me with dread:

TARTARUS CLUB

2

WE EYED EACH other across the office, the mob and me. The light from the burning torches picked out my desk, the couch, the stacks of case files.

"What in the halls of Hades was that?" said the round man in the stetson. Sweat beaded his chubby upper lip.

"Death throes," said the docker. "This whole town's going down. Time we all got out."

"Out where?" said the woman with the broken arm. "There's nowhere to go."

"You can still get a Greyhound out over the Scrimshaw Bridge. They're saying the Gates of Gehenna have opened."

"Yes," said the round man. "But at what price?"

"A heavy one." The docker took a step toward me. "Which is why I want my money back, gumshoe."

His words spiked the mob like a cattle prod. Shock from the events outside drained away. The anger was back, and in force.

"Yes." The round man smeared the perspiration from his lip. "I paid you in good faith and you're not a step closer to finding my son."

"You promised me I'd have my insurance money within a week," said the injured woman. "I haven't worked in two months and the rent's due tomorrow and..." She broke down.

They came toward me. I retreated until the backs of my legs hit the desk. "Wait up, folks. We can work something out."

"Don't jerk us around, buster."

A new voice. I looked for its owner, saw nobody. Then a lens of air advanced through the little crowd. It was shaped like a woman. My nostrils caught an unmistakable ozone tang.

"It's cash or blood," said the sylph. "Your choice."

I held up my hands. The dame might have been made of fresh air but experience told me the fist she was waving could still pack one hell of a punch.

"You'll get your money." It was a promise I couldn't deliver on, but I was desperate to buy time. I cursed myself for taking their cash up-front. In the past I'd always played a no-win, no-fee game with my clients. The depression might have made these poor suckers desperate, but it had made me something worse.

Greedy.

"I've got a safe in the cellar," I said. They didn't need to know it was empty. As fast as the money had come in, the spiraling rent had sucked it back out. "I can give you the readies right now or—" I sucked in a breath "—or I can give you my signed guarantee that your cases will be solved by the end of the week. All of them."

"Cash or blood," snarled the sylph, floating nearer. The air inside her carried its own weather systems. Tiny black clouds told me a storm was brewing.

"Then I'll open a vein and sign in whatever comes out." I scanned their faces, looking for the hope I'd seen earlier. It wasn't there.

"I say we take the money," said the docker. "Then burn this place to the ground."

There was a rumble of assent. I considered stretching over the desk to the drawer where I keep my gun. I figured they'd take me apart before my fingers reached the handle.

"No," said the woman with the broken arm. "I didn't come here for this. I want answers. I want the evidence I need to survive."

"False evidence for a dodgy insurance claim?" said the round man. "My son is missing—do you have any idea what...?"

"He's supposed to be investigating my workforce for fraud," called a woman from the back of the crowd.

"My son-in-law's been fooling around." This came from a shifty-looking satyr with scruffy legs and double recurved horns.

"Like my wife," growled the docker.

They pressed closer. The heat from the torches baked my face. Smoke coiled against the ceiling.

"And you?" I said, staring at the sylph.

"You don't remember, do you?" she replied. Her words crackled like lightning. She waved her transparent arm toward the maze of heaped files. "You've taken on so many cases you've lost track. You've lost touch, gumshoe. Lost touch with the whole world. Time to burn."

She grabbed the docker's torch. The flaming brand seemed to float in her heat-haze grip. How exactly did sylphs interact with the physical world? I had no idea.

The telephone on the desk rang.

3

"I'M GOING TO take this call," I said slowly. "Then I'm going down to the cellar to the safe. You want your money, you'll get it. You want me to stay on your case instead, just say the word. But you set this place burning, you'll burn with it. And so will the cash."

I stopped, mouth dry. As gambles went, it was a poor one. But it was all I had.

I held the sylph's gaze for two more seconds while the phone continued to ring. Tiny thunderheads roiled behind her smoky eyes.

Slowly, I moved my hand to the phone. Nobody stopped me. I picked the receiver off the cradle, licked my lips.

"Hello?"

"We got trouble," said a voice like a road grader.

My eyes went to the neon sign lodged outside the door. My heart imploded.

"Hyperion," I said. "It's been a long time."

Meanwhile, the sylph was lowering the torch toward the nearest stack of files. At the last second, the round man with the missing son stayed her hand.

"Let him take his call," he said. "Maybe somebody else needs him."

A sound like an airstrike came down the phone line. I pulled the receiver from my ear. When a Titan coughs, you make space in a hurry.

"You should gargle, Hyperion," I said when the detonations had died away.

"It's the dust. We got one Hades of a mess down here."

"The explosion?" It figured. Hyperion owned the Tartarus Club. Whatever calamity had hurled that neon sign halfway across the city, he was sitting in its aftermath.

"Yah. I want you to come down here. Take a look."

"Why? I thought you Titans cleared up your own messes."

"Usually we do. This time we got a big mystery. Too big for us."

I wondered what kind of mystery could be too big for guys who used trees for toothpicks. I also wondered if it was possible to turn down a Titan and live.

I hadn't done business with the Titans since the affair of the dead wolf in the hat. That debacle had resulted in Hyperion's brother Iapetos vanishing into a stray dimension and a very nasty stain appearing on my carpet. Iapetos hadn't been seen since. That stain sure lingered though.

"That explosion must have taken out half a block," I said. "I'll bet the cops are all over it. Why not let them handle it?"

Hyperion laughed. My fillings sang like church bells. "When did a Titan last call the cops? You kill me, gumshoe!"

I sighed. "Well, all right. But I'm kind of busy right now. Maybe I could stop by tomorrow?"

Six octaves fell off Hyperion's voice. He sounded less like an airstrike, more like mutually assured destruction. "You will be here in five minutes."

There was a click and the line went dead.

I studied the faces of the expectant mob. If patience was gasoline, they were running on fumes. Jump ship now and there'd be no ship to come back to.

Snub the Titan and I'd end up in hell. Literally.

What I needed was a way to be in two places at once.

4

LIKE MOST CELLARS, mine's dark and damp. The plaster is cracked and warped, but that's just the dimensions, jostling for space. String City's full of dimensions.

A little light drips down from the street grille and makes long shadows on the walls. The only other source of illumination is the boiler. It's an old-model ZZ-Redstream Tokamak Afterburner, big as a bus and ugly as Frankenstein's pineapple patch. It was built to power an airport. It serves to keep off the chill.

Just as I reached the bottom of the steps, the tokamak's plasma burner kicked in. A small volcano hit the cellar with fusion light. The extra brightness picked out the shape of the doorway in the corner that some previous tenant had bricked up, long before I'd arrived. It also showed me what I'd come down for: the crate in the corner.

The crate was one of the things I'd inherited when I took over the business from its former owner—an old friend called Jimmy the Griff. I'd been in a bad way—two weeks previously, my wife Laura had died. I was drowning. Jimmy threw me a lifeline.

"They're just gumshoe gadgets," Jimmy had said when he'd pointed out the crate. "Disposables. You use them once, you throw them away. I got them at this trade show. Most are just gimmicks, nothing any self-respecting detective would ever use. But some... well, they might come in handy."

He'd shown me round the place, told me how this was the oldest brownstone in String City. "There's a foundation stone buried somewhere," he said. "You wouldn't believe the date. The dimensions are tight here—the tightest I've ever known. I'll bet you can feel it. There's more than three hundred ways in and out of the cellar, and I've tried them all except one. I reckon you'll feel right at home."

He said all that, and then he left. Jimmy knew how hard it is to steer your whole life on to a different compass bearing, and he knew I had to turn the wheel myself. I'd already signed the lease and taken the keys; what else was there to say? Besides, Jimmy had always been a restless soul, even when we were kids.

As soon as I was alone in the cellar, I sat down and cried.

Not long after Jimmy sold me the business, he turned to crime. First he was arrested for holding up one of the mail trains headed out to the Unknown Worlds. After breaking out of Wulan Penitentiary he started a run of bank heists that sent him straight to the top of the Most Wanted list. Got himself a hobby too: playing chess with the gods. Then he lost a game to Cronos and everything changed, and I mean everything. When you lose to a god, you pay one hell of a forfeit.

Ten years had passed since then. Another time. Another story.

I pushed back the past, opened the crate and rummaged inside. Doing so made me think of Laura. I think of her a lot, even now. The mob's low murmur drifted down the stairs from the office. I ignored it.

At last I found what I was looking for: a brass disc the size of my palm, a bit like a dame's compact. I flipped it open. There was a mirror in the lid. Below the mirror was a button marked *ON*. I punched it and the thing powered up with an almost imperceptible whine.

Below the button was a toggle switch and a digital readout. On the edge of the case was a much smaller button marked *STANDBY*. On the back of the compact was a tiny label that read:

WHEN COUNTER REACHES ZERO, THIS DEVICE WILL SELF-DESTRUCT.

I flicked the toggle switch. The mirror clouded over. The air shook. The brass case jangled like Christmas and got so hot I dropped it on the cement floor. The lid snapped shut and it fell silent. I picked it up. It was cold again.

A red light blinked slowly on the front, and then someone spoke behind me.

"Okay." The voice was eerily familiar. "This is kind of weird."

I dropped the compact in my pocket and turned to look at myself.

* * *

5

You think you know who you are. Every time you shave, the mirror throws back the face that's always been there. Oh, that face changes over time—more wrinkles and stiffer stubble and those nasty shocks of grey at the temple—but it's all still you. But when you come face to face with yourself—your *real* self—you discover you didn't know diddly.

He was shorter than I'd imagined, with a stoop to the left. Heavier too, especially in the gut. But me, without a doubt.

"So what's the deal?" he said.

"You're a doppelganger." I pulled out the compact and waggled it. "I just created you."

"So what are you now? A god?"

"No, just a guy in a spot."

"So what's new?"

"Look, I don't have much time. I need you to mind the office while I check out a case at the Tartarus Club. It won't take long."

"Tartarus Club? You getting mixed up with Titans again?"

"Not by choice."

"How's business?"

"Don't you know?"

The doppelganger's brow creased. "I remember last year, and before. Anything more recent, I'm kind of fuzzy." He pointed to the compact. "Maybe that thing works off an old backup."

I had no idea how the device worked at all, but the idea that something was constantly backing me up sent needles down my spine.

"So how's business?" he repeated.

I shrugged. "Good and bad."

"Which is it today?"

"Mostly bad."

"Figures."

The conversation trickling down the stairs was getting louder. The doppelganger cocked his head. "How many folk up there?"

"Enough."

"Mood?"

"I'll give you one guess."

He plunged his hands in his pockets. "So you get to ride the range while I clean the shit from the back porch."

"You're me. What's the difference? Like I said, I won't be long."

"That's not what bugs me. What about me? How long do I get?" He pointed to the compact.

"I don't know what you mean."

"Check the label."

On the back of the compact was a small white panel printed with minuscule text. I scanned it, mouthing the words.

"See your reading hasn't improved," said the doppelganger.

"Shut up. It says here that, once activated, you've got a lifespan of two hours. Putting you on standby stretches that out; it pauses the countdown until you're reactivated. Means you're unconscious though." I looked him square in the eye. It should have been like looking in a mirror, but it wasn't.

He studied the tokamak's pressure gauge. "This thing always runs hot." He nudged the dial down two degrees.

"Clock's ticking," I said. "You going to help or not?"

"I get a choice?"

"We all get a choice."

"Save the platitudes, buddy. This is you you're talking to."

"What can I say? You know me too well."

"Too right I do." The doppelganger started pacing up and down the cellar. He kept to the shadows, carefully avoiding the dust motes. Just the way I do. "Only, a guy gets to thinking... what's in this for me?"

"What's in it for any of us? Look, you get to do what you do. What I do. Hell, up until two minutes ago you didn't even exist."

He stopped in a pool of shadow. Under the brim of his fedora, his face was invisible. "The folk up in the office. They're mad at you?"

"Put it this way: if you can't talk them down, this place goes up in flames."

"Hell of a responsibility to give someone you only just met."

"You know, I already feel like I've known you my whole life."

The doppelganger's hand jumped out of the shadows. Tentatively I shook it. It was creepy, like kissing your sister. "Okay, buddy," he said, "you got yourself a deal. One condition though."

"Name it."

"I get to choose a new brand of coffee. That crap you drink tastes like donkey shit."

He vanished up the stairs. A few seconds later I heard the rumble of his voice as he spoke to the mob. I wondered if I'd done right. It felt like big things were on the move, things I couldn't see.

Bottom line was this: I didn't trust myself an inch.

I grabbed my leather coat from the peg at the foot of the cellar steps, turned it inside-out three times until it was made of oilskin and shrugged it on. I took two steps backward until my left heel lodged in an interbrane rift, and twisted both my feet to the right. Smooth as a symphony the dimensions opened up. I knelt down, closed my eyes and sniffed hard until I caught the scent of ramspeed lavender. I folded myself in half, in half again, and posted myself sideways through a slot in the world-wall, letting myself fall and fall until the westwise wind caught me up and blew me away between the strings.

6

A WORD ABOUT the cosmos.

Some folk say it's like one of those souvenir jars you can pick up by the ocean, all filled up with layers of colored sand. This layer's icicle blue; this one's envy green; this one shimmers with the fool's gold of false promise. The layers are called branes, and they contain just about all the things you can imagine, along with plenty you can't. Stars and comets, rocks and trees, crystal deserts, electric gods, lost souls, forgotten trinkets, worlds broken and whole—they're all sandwiched inside that jar. There are lifetimes in there, and more besides.

Now look closer. Just like the branes make up the cosmos, there's something else makes up the branes. It's what ties everything together, the stuff that lies coiled at the heart of it all.

String.

The trouble with string is that it's forever getting tangled. Turn your back for a second and it sprouts more knots than your grandma's knitting basket. Each knot is unique and each one warps the universe that surrounds it, sometimes a little, sometimes a lot. Some knots wind themselves so tight that the dimensions get twisted completely out of true, all eleven of them. Others rear up like coral cathedrals only to collapse under the weight of their own impossibility. Big or small, that's the one thing these knots have in common—they never last.

Except one.

Nobody knows why this one knot lingers. Maybe it's bigger than the rest, or older, or stranger, or all three or neither. In this one special place the cosmic string tangles into more of a knot than you ever saw before in your life. It's more than a cathedral, more than a coral reef.

The folk who live there call it String City.

One more thing about the strings. Whenever they move, they vibrate, and when the strings vibrate, the cosmos *sings*. I've heard folk claim the whole cosmos is one gigantic violin. Others reckon it's a twelve-string steel guitar, rocking out the middle-eight of space-time. Me, I've got a tin ear, but I can hear when the song of the strings is so out of key it sounds less like music and more like the contents of a ten scrapyards dropped from five miles high. Trust me, it's not a tune you can hum.

When I stepped between the strings that day, it was more than just listening to city life in a minor key. The chainsaw screeching told me at once that something was wrong.

Badly wrong.

7

Blocking my ears as best I could, I unfolded myself just enough to get my bearings.

I knew straight away that I was off course. String City was nowhere in sight. Below me was a waterfall-growl that could only be the River Styx. As for the strings themselves... they were rolling like a typhoon ocean. They cracked like whips, lashing me with their atom-frayed ends. I sped through them like a shooting star, burning up.

I tried to stop. Couldn't. Tried to change direction, find some kind of beacon in the black. No dice. I was lost in the slash of the strings and the endless rumble of the underneath.

Worse than that, I could hear the rising howl of the boundary wolves.

I tried again to change course. The strings fought me all the way. I opened the tails of my coat, attempted an Immelman Turn around the bow wave of a passing brane. Still no luck. I tried dumping myself back into the nearest reality, even risked a dive through the corona of a wayward sun.

Nothing worked.

I began to panic.

What had started as a routine interdimensional hop from my office to the Tartarus Club was rapidly turning into a life-or-death struggle. Actually, given what lurked inside some of the seedier dimensions, I could easily end up neither alive or dead, but something a lot worse than either. I spent three more seconds wondering what the hell was going on, then turned all my attention to the only thing that mattered.

Getting the hell out.

Risky as it was, I let myself fully unfold. At once, hard wind battered me from all sides. Including inside. I flipped forward, snatched another look at the Styx. That river's bigger than most oceans—hell, bigger than most *worlds*—and it's all made of faces.

A billion lost souls fixed me with white dead eyes and begged me to pull them free.

I looked the other way. Far in the distance, the lights of String City flared, no bigger than dust motes. So small I could have eclipsed them just by holding up my thumb. I didn't, just in case they didn't come back.

Instead, I took off my coat.

We'd been through a lot together, that coat and me. All the same, I wondered if this was set to be our last adventure. One thing was for sure—this wasn't the time to be undressing.

But I had no choice.

Working fast, I turned the coat inside-out four times until it was made of interlaced darning needles. Painful to wear, but useful if your intention is to thread cosmic string. Wincing, I put the coat back on. A thousand tiny pin-points jabbed my flesh as I waved my sleeves through the nearest skein of string. The needles slithered like shrimps through a fishing net.

The Styx rose up beneath me. On the far shore, hairy shadows were gathering: the boundary wolves. They'd already sniffed me out and now they were looking for a taste. Boundary wolves think they're guardians of the cosmos, but answer me this: would the guardians of the cosmos really lick their own ring-a-dings?

Something yanked my arm. One of the darning needles had threaded itself into a loose strand of cosmic string. I allowed myself a small sigh of relief.

Grabbing the string's free end—making sure it didn't take my fingers off in the process—I fed as much of it as I could through the rest of the needles. Once I'd threaded the coat with the cosmos, all I had to do was hang off the strings and glide my way down the braneway to the nearest dimensional snag.

And hope the strings didn't snap.

The Styx fell behind me as I shot past. The ultimate zip wire. The howling of the wolves died away. Before me, String City blew up like a balloon.

At last I was close enough to reality to open a fresh slot in the world-wall. I pulled it wide, shut my eyes and folded myself in half, in half again, until I was small enough to fit through. The song of the cosmos snapped into silence and I hit the deck, hard. As I rolled, I whipped off my coat—trust me, when you're wearing a coatful of needles, gymnastics hurt—and turned it inside-out twice until it was made of shalloon. I threw the coat on again, came out of the roll and fetched up against something big and unyielding.

I opened my eyes.

I was standing in the shadow of something as vast as the Himalayas. The something bent down, bringing horns like cathedral spires to within inches of my face. I looked up into a face too epic for even the widest screen.

"What kept you?" said Hyperion.

8

Giving me no time to reply, Hyperion turned and lumbered up the steps into the casino's main lobby. I felt the dimensions groan as he squeezed a body the size of a small moon into a building built mostly for regular folk.

I followed, amazed that the Tartarus Club was still standing. All around was devastation, yet through the clouds of smoke and dust the casino's marble columns still towered, though many were cracked and askew. The roof was a mess, and the neon sign that had once adorned it... well, I knew exactly what had happened to that.

Hyperion led me deeper inside. Every step he took, I took two hundred. You never get over how big Titans are. We reached the main gaming floor and found it deserted. Abandoned cards lay strewn across empty tables; chips stood in piles beside stalled roulette wheels; slot machines beckoned, but there was nobody to take them by the arm. Empty of people, the casino was full of dust. I remembered how Hyperion had been coughing on the phone. I looked up and saw he'd put on a respirator. It looked capable of recycling enough air for a small city.

I was about to speak when a huge mirror fell from the wall behind a bar and smashed on the floor. As the shards of glass flew toward me, I folded my coat collar round until it was made of tungsten plate and flipped it up to make a hasty shield. The glass bounced off it and landed in a sea of torn green baize.

"I can't believe the place is still standing," I said, turning my collar down again. "I saw the explosion. It looked like a nuke."

"Not a nuke."

The Titan sounded confident he knew what he was talking about. I thought back to what I'd seen. For all its devastating effects, the fireball itself had been relatively small. Less a ball than a spear, in fact, a line of purple flame heading straight up like a scratch on the filmstrip of the world.

"Still, some kind of bomb?"

"Yah. But the blast, it was kind of funky."

"Why would someone want to blow up the Tartarus Club?" I realised that was the wrong question. "Who would *dare*?"

My head was spinning. The Titans are the biggest crime lords this city—or any other—has ever seen. You hardly dare breathe near a Titan... and you certainly don't light a fuse under one.

Hyperion led me up a huge staircase and into the security suite, a vast room packed with antique furniture and hi-tech surveillance equipment. An array of sixty-four monitors covered one entire wall. The remote cameras had been angled to show every corner of the casino, but most of the screens were obscured by smoke. Facing the monitors, sprawled on a megaton Chesterfield, was Hyperion's brother, Oceanus, and two of their sisters, Rhea and Tethys. Like Hyperion, they looked more like geological phenomena than living beings.

I shivered. Titans solo are bad enough. Titan families are something else. They take the notion of sibling rivalry and make it a life's work. And Titans live a long time.

"So here's the gumshoe," said Oceanus. The Titan dames said nothing, just allowed scowls like sinkholes to demolish their faces.

"So what's the deal?" I said.

Oceanus stood. Beneath the Chesterfield, hydraulic rams moved to redistribute the weight.

"We was robbed," he said. "Take a look."

They took me into another room. It was even bigger than the first and full of rubble. The back wall looked like an upturned battlefield and the ceiling was open to the sky. In the center of the room, poking up from the middle of the devastation, was a safe. The door to the safe—a slab of dull metallic stuff as big as a football pitch—looked intact.

"They started with drills, bangers, seismic bungs, everything," said Hyperion, flicking a chunk of plaster off the door handle. "Lucky the safe's charm-steel."

"Only luck we got is bad," growled Oceanus.

Trying to ignore the fact I had an angry Titan at each elbow, I made a quick circuit of the room, picking my way through the wreckage and looking for anywhere the safe might have been breached. Apart from a few scratches, all four sides seemed undamaged.

"Is anything missing?" I asked.

"The safe held," said Hyperion. "Anyway, we have a suspect. One of the security golems. We found it just outside the blast radius, missing an arm."

"Suspect?" said Oceanus, glowering at Hyperion. "It's open'n'shut. I say we strings the clayboy up and watches it stretch."

"That's not how this is going to work," said Hyperion, returning the glare.

"Because why not?"

"Because you are not the boss!"

I held my breath.

"The golem done it," growled Oceanus. "Don't tell me you don't know it."

"Maybe it did. But we need an independent investigation. The gumshoe is here to prove it really was the golem—so that there is no argument."

"Who's arguing?"

"I just want us all to see eye to eye."

"I'll *poke* your eye!"

"As if you could, *little* brother!"

The two Titans were nose-to-nose. Their lips had curled back to reveal teeth like civic sculptures. The ground shook.

Rhea and Tethys walked up, and the shaking got a whole lot worse.

"What do you want?" said Hyperion to the dames.

"To put you two chumps straight, as usual," said Tethys, the taller of the sisters. "Golems, they ain't smart enough to set explosives, you know that, I know that. It was that guy in the hood, like I'm telling you. The one showed up on the security camera."

"That's a steaming crock, Tethys," said Rhea. She was bigger than both her brothers put together and spat out words like cannon shells. "What's on the camera is horseshit. It was the electrics set things off, I tell you. They've been shorting for months. If I was running this dump I'd have fixed them up by now." She glowered at Hyperion.

"Keep out of it, sister!" snapped Oceanus.

"It's the wiring!" Rhea retorted. "Cut and dried!"

"I'll cut and dry you, you little squirt!" snarled Tethys.

"I'd like to see you try!"

Taking a deep breath, I stepped between them. It was like walking the alley between a bunch of battling skyscrapers.

"Say, folks," I said, "it looks like you've already got some leads for me to follow. Relax. Let me see what I can dig up."

Four horned heads descended to my level, twisting space and forcing perspective.

"You think you got the answers, little man?" said Rhea.

"It's not about what I think, ma'am. It's about what I do."

She sneered. Before I could go on to deliver my standard speech about seeking truth in a world built of lies, Hyperion stepped in.

"What I say goes, and I say the gumshoe's hired," he said, "His fee comes out of my personal allowance. Now, let's give our private investigator some space."

Another pause, during which four pairs of Titan eyes narrowed and four sets of Titan breaths were drawn. I fought the suction until, without warning, they lost interest and left the room. All except Hyperion.

"You have a sack of guts, boy," he growled. "Do not let me down."

9

I WISHED I carried better equipment in my coat than just a Sherlock glass. But it was too late to go back to the office for proper forensics. When a Titan puts you in the yoke, he keeps the reins tight. Besides, I was nervous about making the return trip, given the chaotic state of the strings.

"You know the dimensions better than most," I said to Hyperion as I studied the safe door up close. "Have you noticed anything weird going on out, you know, out in the strings?"

"Mostly the strings get out of the way for us," he rumbled. His huge face creased. "Lately though... yah, moving through the dimensions is like moving through treacle."

"I don't know about treacle," I said. "It's more like swallowing swords. What's happening? It's like the whole cosmos is coming apart."

Hyperion shrugged. "Bad times coming." He waved a colossal hand at the rubble. "Maybe this is the start of it."

"You believe what people are saying? About the end of the world?"

"Who doesn't?"

I picked what looked like a grain of salt off the edge of the safe door and pulled out the Sherlock glass. Through the lens, the salt grain stopped looked less like a salt crystal, more like something out of a factory. A very tiny factory. Its jagged surfaces were etched with little swirls; on one side I swore there was a serial number. I dialed up the magnification, but I was damned if I could get it to focus.

"What have you found?" said Hyperion.

"Don't know. I never saw anything like it. It could be a designer drug, only it goes all quantum round the edges. The closer I look, the more blurry it gets." I dropped the grain in an evidence pouch. "I've got kit at the office might pin it down. Meantime, let's take a look at that camera footage."

Back in the security suite, Hyperion adjusted the chair so I could sit at the surveillance desk. It took a lot of adjustment. I wound back the tape, found the segment I was looking for and pressed *PLAY*. The monitors flickered, then flashed up multiple views of the casino from earlier that day: the big gaming floor; the back office where the books got cooked; even the rest room cubicles.

One screen was blank. No picture, no static. Nothing. The label under the screen read *BASEMENT*. The hairs on the back of my neck prickled up.

"What's this?" I said, tapping the black screen.

"Loose wiring."

"Enough to cause an explosion?"

"Do not believe everything Rhea says."

I scanned the rest of the screens while the video played. Folk came and went, shooting craps, playing blackjack and Roentgen

Roulette. I was surprised how few people there were. During most of the hours before the explosion, the casino had been barely a quarter full.

"Where did all the punters go?"

Hyperion shifted uncomfortably. "The place warms up after dark."

"Since when? As long as the doors are open, the craps are flying. I've never seen Tartarus so dead."

The Titan seemed about to argue. Then his massive shoulders slumped. "This city—it is not what it used to be. Nothing is. Bad times coming, like I said."

I decided not to mention the boom in the private investigation sector.

When the tape reached the moment of the explosion, sixty-three of the surveillance screens lit up like the day of creation. The camera trained on the basement stayed dead black. Bright fire erupted through the casino. The cameras shook and showed smoke, dust and punters running for the doors. At the emergency exits, a line of security golems stood ready to frisk them.

"So that was the bomb," I said, freezing the tape.

"I can see why you are a detective."

I nudged the tape back then crawled it forward again, frame by frame. Debris flew in slow motion, disappearing off one screen to appear on the next. People fled like bad animation. Dust settled.

I wound back again, inched the tape a third time. Froze it as a shadowy figure loomed, briefly, from the chaos. A tall figure, hooded, face hidden in shadow. It was there for just one frame, on just one camera. Then it was gone.

"Is this the character your sister was talking about?"

"Looks like a glitch, right?" Hyperion sounded eager.

I looked again. This time it didn't look like a person at all, just a shadow in the smoke. I punched out a hard copy. On paper, it looked like a Rorschach blot.

"Tethys has an overactive imagination," said Hyperion. "Time to stop chasing shadows. We have the security golem chained up in the store. I want you to interview it. Then we can put this whole thing to rest."

Getting hired by a Titan is careless. Defying his orders is plain dumb. But I never claimed to be careful, or smart. Just curious.

"Don't take offense," I said, "but you're kind of cramping my style."

Hyperion's face clouded over. It was like a lunar eclipse.

"What I mean," I went on quickly, "is this: you brought me here to conduct a fair, impartial investigation, right?"

"Right," the Titan said with measured menace.

"Okay. One reason you want me to do that is to keep the peace and stop your family tearing itself to pieces arguing over who set off the bomb. Seems like Oceanus buys the golem theory—Rhea and Tethys not so much."

Silence from the Titan. I took a deep breath.

"But the main reason I'm here is to prove that you're right and your sisters are wrong. That way, you get to keep your hand on the tiller and your sibs in their place. Am I wrong?"

Thunderstorms crackled on Hyperion's brow. "Your point?"

"My point is this: how does it look if we get too cosy, you and me? If this is going to work, you've got to make it look like I'm a free agent. Otherwise your brother and sisters will just figure I'm your stooge and you'll be back where you started."

Another silence, this time much longer. "How long do you need?"

I'd left the doppelganger with just two hours on the clock. I'd already been here for nearly half an hour. "Thirty minutes?"

"Don't push your luck." His extended forefinger hit me like

a freight train. "You got five minutes to sniff around on your own, then you tell my sisters you found evidence to prove it was the golem. After that, you're out of here."

When he'd gone, I took a minute to catch my breath. It's not every day you challenge a Titan and live. I checked my watch. Five minutes was nothing. Still, worlds have turned in less time. At least I had a hunch about the best place to start.

10

I'D EXPECTED THE basement of the Tartarus Club to be dingy—something like my cellar, only Titan-sized. Instead it was kind of beautiful, with fluted columns, fancy drapes. Mostly columns. You're supporting a floor walked by Titans, you need a lot of columns.

There were pool tables too, hundreds of them, all different sizes. The smallest would have served most airports as a runway. I remembered how Hyperion used to run Tartarus as a pool hall. Made good money, so he'd told me. Then the neighbors started complaining. Turned out Titan pool balls are so big they mess with the tides. So he retired the tables, reinvented the place as a casino and never looked back. Until now.

I walked between the tables, disorientated. I wondered how I'd know when I'd reached the part of the cellar that was underneath the safe.

It turned out to be easy, on account of the big hole in the ceiling. That and the gigantic corpse lying underneath it in a pile of shattered oak and crumpled blue baize.

I pulled a flashlight from my coat, shone it up through the hole. The hole went right through the floor above and into the bottom of the safe. As I'd suspected, it had been blown from beneath. But why hadn't the Titans thought of looking down here?

I moved the flashlight beam around. Inside the safe were thousands of shelves stacked with charcoal and smeared with gold. Burned notes and melted coins. Whoever blew the safe wasn't after the money.

Wind gusted down from the hole. It smelled like hot desert sand. Strange. As I stood there it died away.

I turned my attention to the corpse. He was a giant, twice my size. Lying flat on his back in the ruins of the pool table, he wore a leather apron, torn open to reveal a big hole in his chest. Most of his insides were on the outside. His gaping eye stared up through the hole in the ceiling.

His one eye.

The dead guy was a cyclops.

I clambered through the wreckage, checked the body. The apron was more than just leather—it was meshed with chain-link. Must have been one hell of a bang to mess up the poor sap like this. The rest of his clothes had been shredded in the blast. There was something, though: tucked under his shoulder I found a scrap of fabric, like burlap only heavier. It was charred almost black, but I could just make out letters printed on it:

SCAT

It meant nothing to me. I dropped it my pocket for later.

In the cyclops's apron pocket, half-covered in gore, I found a business card for an outfit called *Single Vision Forge*. The address was some industrial unit on the east side, a real shabby part of town.

On the back it said: *Brontes*. His name, I guessed.

The card was slippery with blood. When I turned it over again, it dropped from my fingers. I picked it up, and that was when the gigantic hand descended on my shoulders. I looked up into a pair of hurricane-sized eyes.

"Time is up," thundered Hyperion. Then he spoke into a walkie-talkie the size of an electricity substation. "The investigation is over. String up the clayboy."

11

BY THE TIME we got back to the security suite the lynching was well under way.

"Pull it tight!" shouted Rhea. "If we have to go through this charade, let's do it properly."

"What d'you think I'm doing?" said Oceanus.

"You're a big galoot!" said Tethys. "Give it here!"

The three Titans were fighting over one end of a steel chain slung around a ceiling beam. The other end of the chain was wrapped round the neck of the golem. The golem's feet were waggling, six feet off the floor.

I stood in the doorway, drowned in Hyperion's shadow.

"Looks like they started without us," rumbled the Titan crime lord.

"Only because you told them to," I said. "Did you know about the dead cyclops in the cellar?"

Hyperion glared at me. "You didn't find a cyclops. You found golem clay. Precisely the evidence we needed."

"What? It wasn't clay I found down there, and you know it."

I was about to argue further when Hyperion pinched my head between his finger and thumb. "Do you want me to squeeze?"

I ducked free and called to Tethys: "What about that hooded figure you saw on the surveillance screen?"

She waggled the chain and shrugged. "Maybe it really was a glitch in the system. Like Hyperion said, you can see the Messiah in a potato if you look hard enough."

Desperate, I turned my attention to Rhea. "You said it was the electrics."

"Hyperion pointed out you can't lynch faulty wiring," she replied.

I didn't bother challenging Oceanus, whose eyes were awash with an ocean of bloodlust.

"I don't get it," I said, turning back to Hyperion. "Why bring me all this way just to...?"

"Just to what, little man?"

I watched helpless as the golem's neck turned to paste. I curled my fists. It may just have been an automaton, but it was an innocent automaton.

"You know you can't lynch a golem?" I said suddenly.

Tethys blinked. "Why not?"

"No spine. Also no windpipe. Not much anatomy at all, truth be told. No, there's only one way to carry out a golem execution."

Rhea bared her teeth. They looked like icebergs, only I'd never seen icebergs filed to points before. "And what's that, gumshoe?"

What else does a guy do in a casino except gamble?

"I'll tell you. But first let me interview the poor sap," I said. "Clay in the cellar is just circumstantial. You all want concrete proof, right?"

They took the golem down and used the chain to tie it to a chair. The chain bit deep into the soft clay round its gut. Golems don't feel pain, but this one sure looked sore.

"What's your name?" I said.

The golem didn't reply, just sat sullen and quiet. I'd given it time to mould its neck back to something resembling normal. It still looked lop-sided. I asked the question again, but the golem kept its mouth shut. Behind it, the three Titans cracked their knuckles, making sonic booms. Still the golem said nothing. Finally, Oceanus reached forward and clipped it on the ear.

"Talk, clayboy," he hissed. "Or I starts making mud pies."

The golem mumbled something I couldn't hear.

"What was that?" I said.

"Ain't got no name. I's a golem. I's got a number."

"Okay. What's your number?"

"Nine-eight-one-two-slash-seventeen-twelve."

"Mind if I call you 'Slash'?"

The golem didn't respond.

I was considering my next question when the golem started pulling chunks of clay off its forearms. It slapped them on its chest and moulded them into a startling pair of pecs. It swapped its thighs for its calves. Then it fell still again.

"What was all that about?" I said. Again, no answer.

"I told you it was acting up," said Rhea. "Didn't I tell you? Last week it broke off all its fingers and stuffed them up its..."

"All to pieces!" shouted the golem. "All of it! Smash it up, all to pieces!"

Rhea gave me an "I told you so" smile.

"Smash what up?" I said. "What do you want in pieces, Slash?"

The golem had fallen silent again. It lolled forward, ticking over.

"S'obvious," said Oceanus. "It wants to ice Tartarus. Like I says all along—it's the clayboy done it. Let's string 'im up again!"

"I'm not so sure." I went over to the golem, prodded the chunks of clay he'd been moving around.

"What do you mean?" said Hyperion.

"Blowing a vault—that takes imagination. Not much, but some. Golems—they're not known for blue-sky thinking."

I plucked a bead of clay off the golem's leg, rolled it between my fingers. There were some golems that claimed to have souls. Hell, I'd met one of them once—called itself Byron. But most were still just machines, slaves to their programming.

I pressed the clay back where it belonged.

"You know how a golem works?" I said, addressing all four Titans. They exchanged uncertain glances. "No? Okay, I'll tell you. Buried in this poor sucker's chest is a roll of parchment covered in Hebrew binary code. That's its operating system. Quite a thing, that code, given the Hebrew number system has no zeroes. The programmers get round that with fractals, which means the code's full of all these tiny holes. The holes in the code mean they can..."

"This going someplace?" said Oceanus. "Only I really wants to mash something."

"Cut to the chase, gumshoe," said Hyperion.

Tethys and Rhea said nothing, which was somehow scarier.

"My point is," I said, "this golem isn't a crook. It's just got a virus."

"A what?" said Oceanus.

"A virus. All those fractal holes in the binary code? Sometimes those holes get infected—fill up with stuff that shouldn't be there. Like when you catch a cold and your sinuses fill up with fluid. It's just the operating system that's infected, but to the golem it feels like its whole body's out of whack, like nothing fits together. So it starts taking itself apart, rearranging its limbs, to try and get back into shape."

"And that fixes it?" said Rhea.

"No. Nothing works. Eventually the golem tears itself to pieces. Literally. That's why your golem's been acting up. It's not bad. Just sick. I've seen this a lot lately. The whole municipal workforce is affected—garbage collectors, street sweepers, the whole shebang. It's like an epidemic. No cure."

"Bad times," said Hyperion, in a voice surprisingly quiet for a Titan.

After a pause, Oceanus said, "Can we hang it now?"

"But I don't believe Slash—I mean the golem—had anything to do with the heist," I said.

"Says you," said Oceanus.

"It's my professional opinion."

The golem jerked back into life. Behind its empty eyes, a strange white fire was burning. It raised one grey hand and plunged it deep into its chest. The hand emerged in a shower of clay holding a tattered scrap of parchment. With the other hand, it started ripping more lumps of clay from its belly, its legs, its face. Soon the marble floor was splattered with sizzling gobs of clay. Meanwhile, the golem was shrinking, fast.

"That's gross," said Tethys, turning away. For a big girl, she sure was squeamish.

"Spoils our fun, is what it does," said Oceanus.

Soon there was nothing left of the golem but one twitching hand. Its last act was to crush the parchment in its fingers. Then the whole hand hardened and shattered to powder. Slash was no more.

"Guess that means he's off the hook," I said, and I turned to face Hyperion.

Here's the thing with gambling: once you start, it's hard to stop.

"Why don't we all go down to the basement?" I added. "Take a look at what's really there?"

Hyperion smiled an earthquake smile. "Think you're clever, don't you, gumshoe?"

"Just doing my job," I replied.

The Titan spread his arm out into the corridor. "After you."

12

"So what are we meant to be looking at?" said Tethys.

I surveyed the cellar in amazement. The broken pool table was gone. All the blood was gone. The floor was clear and the ceiling was back in one piece. In the far shadows, another Titan was lurking. He was carrying a bucket big enough to hold two of the Great Lakes, and a very large mop.

The dead cyclops was nowhere to be seen. In the middle of the patch of floor where he'd been lying was a single blob of grey golem clay.

"He was right here," I said. "I swear."

Hyperion made a show of looking round. "These old pool tables bend the light," he said. "Funny what you think you see."

"There was a dead cyclops here and you know it!"

The dimensions creaked as Hyperion's hand shrank small enough to clamp me round the throat. He lifted me off the floor, all the way up to his face. My feet dangled. I could see the curvature of the earth.

"Get this, gumshoe," he said. "The golem did it! See the clay there? That proves it. Right, Oceanus?"

"Right, boss," said his brother.

"Rhea? Tethys?"

"The lynching was fun," Tethys allowed.

"I'm prepared to believe you," said Rhea. "This time."

"You didn't need me at all," I said to Hyperion, making a point of not looking down.

"You served a purpose," said Hyperion as he lowered me—none too gently—to the floor. "Now you're finished here. Go back to your office, send me your written report, and don't give this so-called mystery another thought. Savvy?"

None of this added up. In fact, the whole thing stank. But I knew when *not* to challenge a Titan. The tell-tale is when all the other Titans back away.

"Sure thing," I said, brushing dust off my coat. "No problem. I'll just take my hat and leave. Nice doing business with you again. Kind of."

"Before you go," said Hyperion, "Tell me this: are you a gambling man?"

"I bet both ways on the big Derbies," I said. "Roll the dice once in a while."

"Let me give you a word of advice." He leaned close enough for me to see the jackdaws roosting in his pores. "Never gamble your life on a Titan's fancy. You will lose. Every time."

He rose abruptly and marched his siblings up and out of the basement. "Don't forget that report, gumshoe," he called. "Oh, and mind the strings on your way out."

I thought about hanging around, but what was the point? The case wasn't shut—hell, I'd barely got it open. But it seemed my work here was done. Plus I'd been away from the office longer than planned. I was worried about the doppelganger. I was so keen to leave, I didn't even register Hyperion's remark about the strings. My head full, I automatically opened a snag to the first available dimension and folded myself into the void.

The angry strings swallowed me whole.

13

It was worse than before. Far worse. The strings bit like vipers and the boundary wolves chased me all the way from one side of the bulk to the other. I barely made it through alive. By the time I landed back in my office, I'd used up half the seams in my coat and lost all the hairs on the backs of my hands. I was black and bloody, dripping sweat. It was a wonder I hadn't soiled my pants.

I clambered to my feet, checked the snag had closed behind me. You leave a dimensional doorway open, you'll get more than just a draught coming through.

The office looked just as I'd left it: coffee bubbling in the corner, case folders piled high. My own self sat in the chair with his feet on the desk. Okay, so that part was weird. Then I saw what was different: the mob had gone.

I turned my coat inside-out until it was made of flannel and used it to towel myself down. Then I tossed it on the couch. It didn't feel right to sit in the client's chair, so I just stood there and stared myself in the face.

"How did you get rid of them?"

The doppelganger slugged down coffee. "Who?"

"The crowd of clients I left here. You know, the ones who wanted to burn the place down?"

"Them. Right. I talked them down."

"You did what?"

"I apologised for screwing up, told them to come back next week."

"What else? Their cases would be solved? They'd get their money back?"

"Both. I made them a special offer. One week only. The truth: free of charge."

"They bought that?"

He tossed his empty coffee cup in the trash. "I talked sweet. You should try it. So, we going to get to work?"

"There is no 'we'."

"Whatever you say. You're the boss." The doppelganger spat a wad of tobacco on the carpet. I hadn't chewed tobacco in years. He leaned back in the chair. It creaked just like it does when I'm sitting in it. "So what happened at the Tartarus Club?"

I glanced at my coat, lying where I'd thrown it on the couch. The brass compact was in the inside pocket. One push of the button and he'd wink out of existence. I weighed the option against planting my knuckles on the bridge of his nose.

Instead, I sat down heavily in the client's chair, grateful for someone to talk to.

"It was a bust," I said.

"A bust?"

"A weird bust at that. Hyperion really gave me the runaround. First he wanted me to prove this poor sap of a security golem blew up the casino, just to get his sibs off his back."

"Figures," said the doppelganger. "Titans do family feuds like the rest of us do intercontinental ballistics."

"Only I don't think that's what was really going on."

"The golem was innocent?"

"Totally. Not guilty, just badly programmed. The whole thing was a smokescreen to distract Hyperion's sibs from what really happened."

"Which was?"

I stretched my back and heard a castanet click. After two trips through the unfriendly strings, my whole body ached. "I don't know. I got a sniff of a proper lead, but by then it was too late."

"It all sounds deeply hokey to me."

"You win some, you lose some."

The doppelganger snatched up a sheaf of case folders and waved them in my face. "Right now we're not winning anything, buddy. You see all these? Not one of them solved. You might think we're busy but I'll tell you this for nothing: unless we start ticking some of these boxes, busy don't mean diddly!"

"And I keep telling you there is no 'we'!"

Sneering, the doppelganger strode over to the door and stared at the neon sign still resting against the cracked glass outside. The ash from the explosion had cleared. The street was mostly craters and wrecked automobiles. The sidewalks were empty.

"Was it a good lead?" he said.

"Maybe. Probably."

"What was it?"

"Dead cyclops in the cellar."

"Clues on the body?"

"Some. What's it to you?"

"Just interested."

"Don't be. Leave me alone."

"Any reason I should?"

"Plenty."

"Like what?"

"Like you're not real."

He rushed me, fist drawn, and socked me on the chin. I can't believe I didn't see it coming. I fell off the chair, my jaw ringing like a bell.

"That real enough for you?" he said.

I was up twice as quick as I'd dropped, my own fists clenched. He came at me again. I feinted left but he read me and ducked. He tried a gut punch, but I saw it a mile off and dodged. I unleashed a haymaker that whistled through thin air. We went at each other like that for sixty seconds and neither of us landed a single punch. In the end we just stood there, glowering.

"I can read you like a book," he panted.

"You telegraph your every move."

I shot another glance at the couch. His gaze tracked mine.

We both ran.

I got to the coat a fraction of a second before he did. I thrust my hand in the pocket, pulled out the compact, flipped it open. The digital readout showed the number 1:08. As I hovered my thumb over the little button marked *STANDBY*, it changed to 1:07.

"So that's it?" said the doppelganger. "An hour to live and you're just going to wipe me out?"

"You can't wipe out what's not real."

"I'm more real than you, buster. If anyone should be running this joint, it's me."

"I don't think so." My thumb hovered over the button.

"At least I remember what this business was built on. At least I know why we do what we do."

"I told you, there's no 'we'."

"I thought you had a motto. Have you forgotten?"

"Of course I haven't forgotten."

"What is it?"

"You know as well as I do."

"Tell me!"

I almost pressed the button then. I was sick of his sneer, his whining voice. His foul familiarity.

"'First the client'," I said through gritted teeth, "'Then the truth'."

The doppelganger nodded. "Hyperion hired you. You walked away."

"He was playing games. Screwing me around."

"Still comes to the same thing."

"Which is what?"

"Unfinished business. A stinking, Titan-sized heap of it."

"I got fired. What do you want me to do?"

"Accept help. You're sinking fast, buddy. What you need is an assistant."

"And you're it? With an hour left on your clock?"

He smiled a smile I didn't care for. The worst of it was, the smile was mine.

I pushed the button and the doppelganger vanished.

14

I SPENT THE rest of the day reviewing the case folders of the people who'd coming knocking on my door. I should have felt grateful the doppelganger had bought me time—that was why I'd activated him, after all. Instead I just felt a sullen hatred. What right did he have to remind me of the principles on which my own business was founded? Who was he to preach to me about integrity? Then, as I realised the scale of the mountain I had to climb, I felt something close to despair.

I kept looking at the compact. I felt like a murderer. But what could I do? Like most of the gadgets in the cellar, the compact was single-use only. Reactivating it wouldn't bring him back to life. It would condemn him to death.

What would they call it, I wondered? Fratricide? But he wasn't my brother. It couldn't be suicide—even when he was all played out I'd still be walking and talking. The paradox clogged my head like sourdough. I worried at it until my teeth ached. I drank neat bourbon to dull the pain.

By the time the sun went down, all I'd done was move the case files from one side of the desk to the other. The doppelganger was right. If I was going to climb this mountain, I needed help.

Traffic was moving on the street again. A thunderbird had made a late pass and filled up enough of the craters with guano to make a passable carriageway. Municipal sweepers cleared the debris, opening the way for a procession of soft-tops with Rottweiler engines and lenticular paint jobs. Party animals gathered under the neon. Party people too. A pair of hamadryad hookers took root on the corner, shaking their gourds, bark peeled right back to the forks in their lower branches.

I opened another bottle of bourbon. As I downed the first slug, my stomach growled and I realised I hadn't eaten all day. I checked the clock. Persephone's Pizzas would be open and I was in the mood for chorizo.

Before leaving the office, I checked my coat pocket for my wallet. Instead I came up with a folded piece of paper. I flattened it out. On the paper was printed a murky view of a smoke-filled casino. Half-hidden by the smoke was something that might have been a man in a hooded cloak, or the Messiah in a potato. It was the hard copy I'd printed off Hyperion's surveillance camera.

I went through the rest of my pockets and found the scrap of cloth, the business card and the evidence pouch carrying the grain of stuff that wasn't salt. Also my wallet, with just enough cash in it to buy the pizza I was craving.

I hesitated in the open doorway, rain clattering off the brim of my fedora, wallet in one hand, evidence from the Tartarus Club in the other. A pair of hot rods raced past, spraying water over a crowd of cosmophysicists. Across the street, one of the hamadryads popped her seed pods at me.

I looked up, read the stitching on the needlework sampler that hung over the door:

First the client. Then the truth.

My stomach rumbled.

I closed the door, took off my coat and went to work.

15

I STARTED WITH the grain of white crystal. Curious about that miniature serial number, I hauled the baryonic rasteriser up from the cellar and plugged in the macro lens.

The rasteriser's a clever piece of gear. It crosses a stream of left-handed muons with a optophobic laser to turn whatever you put on the slide into a Moebius hologram. That's just like a regular hologram, only it unwraps at least five extra dimensions. Put your mother under the lens, you'd see sides of her you never knew existed. Probably wish you didn't, too.

Two nanoseconds after the muon stream started up, the grain burst into purple flame.

The detonation cracked the rasteriser's casing, sent the lens spinning across the room like a supersonic frisbee. It clipped my ear and sunk itself in the opposite wall. The rasteriser collapsed to the floor in a million pieces. A mushroom of silvery smoke billowed against the ceiling. If that really had been salt, you'd have been wise not to shake it on your salad.

I was pleased to have discovered a fragment of the explosive used to blow the safe. I was mad that, in the process, I'd destroyed it. I kicked the chair across the room, thumped the couch, poured coffee, spilled it, poured it fresh and chugged it down. I glared at the hamadryads—by now they'd shed most of their leaves and were attracting quite a crowd.

After I'd calmed down, I turned my attention to the surveillance photo. I didn't need fancy equipment for that—just my eyes.

At first I favored Hyperion's opinion that it was just a phantom image; if Tethys hadn't put the idea of a hooded figure in my head, I wouldn't have seen a thing. But, the more I looked, the more I thought that maybe Tethys had something. Was that trail of smoke an arm? That shadow a hidden face? Maybe it was a man after all, someone stealing through the chaos while everyone ran for the hills. The real perpetrator.

When I used the Sherlock glass to look closer, the image collapsed back into a heap of pixels. The hooded man vanished. I took the glass away and he didn't come back.

I stared at the picture a minute longer, willing my eyes to catch him. It was like looking in an empty pocketbook, wishing it full of bills. But it didn't happen. The ink blot was just an ink blot.

Disgusted, I tossed the picture aside. Another bust.

More coffee, then I set the two remaining pieces of evidence on the desk. These I had real hopes for. No phantoms these, but actual physical things, recovered with my own hands from the scene of crime. From a corpse that Hyperion had for some reason seen fit to sweep under the carpet.

I ran the scrap of cloth through the Planck scanner but it came up blank. Just regular burlap, badly charred, squid-ink lettering stamped by hand: *SCAT*. Well, scat is animal dung. Poachers track scat through the wildwood. It's also that thing jazz singers do when they can't remember the words. Not to mention the acronym used by the String City Association of Tulip-Fanciers, but I couldn't see that crowd planting anything at the Tartarus Club. Least of all a designer bomb.

Which left the business card.

Even with the blood cleaned off, the card didn't show me any more than what I already knew: the name of the dead cyclops was Brontes, and he worked at Single Vision Forge. The address put the forge in a small industrial park near Carr Industries, the biggest power station complex in String City. It's a grim place, hot and smoggy. I'd been there a few times and didn't relish a return visit.

I dropped the card on the burlap scrap. I rubbed my eyes and listened to my belly grumble. Outside was all darkness and neon. Why the hell was I bothering with this when I had a hundred other cases lined up?

A voice echoed in my head. It was my own voice. Only it wasn't. It was the doppelganger's.

"First the client," it said. "Then the truth."

Ignoring the hunger pangs, I picked up the stuff from the desk and went to the Feynman globe.

The globe is one of my favorite gadgets. It's really eleven globes in one—one for each dimension, all of them contra-rotating through this fancy metaball gearbox. The machine has an integrated brane-space that warps the surface geometry of the individual globes so when they all turn together they look like beads of mercury doing the please-excuse-me. Anyway, the point of the thing is to isolate the coordinates of any given point in space-time to the nearest semi-electron. When you walk the dimensions as much as I do, coordinates matter.

I'd bought the globe as a basic route-finder, but soon discovered you can also use it to access the strings. The metaballs fend off the worst of the dimensional debris so it's a smooth enough ride, and the manufacturers even claim resistance to leviathan attack. On the down side, they amplify the background branewave radiation to the kind of level that melts gonads.

In other words, to actually use it to travel around, you've got to be desperate.

I spun the three primary space globes. They caught the neon light from outside and sprayed dirty rainbows up the office walls. As they jostled against the time globe, it stole their momentum and started to turn itself. From there, the seven nested subdimensional globes began spinning, one after the other.

Hypnotising me a little, all that contra-rotary motion set me thinking how everything that happens affects everything else. How everything *matters*. Once upon a time that thought would have made me nervous. Not any more. You fret too hard about consequences, you never get out of bed. Trust me, I know. Oh, don't get me wrong. I'm not saying *nothing* matters. It's just that some things matter more than others. It all depends on your point of view.

Truth matters. That much I do know. As the years roll on and the worlds turn tighter and faster, I'm getting to believe truth is *all* that matters. It's that thought alone keeps me behind the desk of this two-bit private investigation business, keeps me facing down angry Titans and sulky gods, keeps me grinding down the leather on the soles of my shoes in the hope that the sucker I'm following might just lead me to an answer.

I opened the globe's scanner slot and dropped in the business card. The globe's got any amount of fancy interfaces, but if you have hard evidence the scanner works best. It read the address on the card, sniffed the varnish for residues and cross-referred the two. Ten seconds later, all the globes locked in place and a screen popped up displaying a schematic of String City. The east side, to be exact. Right in the middle, pinned by a set of crosshairs, a little yellow light was flashing.

I had my coordinates.

I used the globe's remote bladderwrack plug-in to check the weather on the east side: freezing smog and acid sleet. A normal day for that part of town. I turned my coat inside-out five times until it was triplex titanium foil with a lead-lined codpiece. Then I folded myself in half and posted myself into the globe's outbox.

16

A SMALL METAL plate on the side of the Feynman globe promises "a smoother ride through the cosmos". For once, the blurb was right. The dimensions are riddled with potholes—using the globe is like graduating to air suspension. In the early day I used the globe pretty much all the time. I'm a natural stringwalker, but working the dimensions is still a pain in the ass. The globe made it easy.

Later I found the safety warning on the inside of the power box. The one about the gonads. After that I retired the globe as a journeymaker and just used it to verify coordinates. Actually it was a relief to go back to riding the dimensions raw. After all, it's what I was born to do.

But now, scooting between the strings, surrounded and protected by a metaball shield projected by the globe's remote tracker, I remembered what I'd been missing. I also remembered how the metaball amplification could work like a set of nutcrackers and checked my codpiece. Everything was intact, so I relaxed and took in the view. Trust me, it was worth it.

String City was laid out below me. The streets looked like a billion diamond necklaces tangled on black satin sheets. Way to my left was the finance quarter. The twin towers of the Silverlode loomed over the regular banks like a chromed victory sign. Next door was the bunched neon of the Hot Hub, String City's entertainment district. You go to the Hub at night, you can sample most anything, from crowd-pleasing 5D movies to illegal syren song. Beyond the Hub was a vast sprawl of malls and condos, cut through by the snaking River Lethe. Beyond that the dockland with its wharfs and warehouses and big quarantine fence, and from it all the countless roads and railtracks cutting out across the town.

From out here in the dimensions, String City looked just like it always did: big and gaudy and unlikely as all hell. But the high viewpoint and the clarity of the globe's metaball lens revealed things I'd never seen before. Changes. Like the way parts of the river had started to flow uphill. Like the way some of the streets had three ends. Like the way whole districts had shrunk, or got bigger, or disappeared altogether.

Like the way the cosmic string binding up this whole place in one gigantic cat's cradle had got frayed, and how those frayed ends had started slashing at reality like a cat o'nine tails, making stripes across its back.

"Bad times coming." That's what Hyperion had said. Maybe he was right.

Safe in the metaball, I realised how lucky I'd been when I'd walked the strings earlier that morning. I remembered something else Hyperion had said, that these days working the dimensions was like moving through treacle. The kind of treacle that wants to peel off your skin and cram your bleeding muscles down your own flayed throat.

Then the metaball began to stutter as the rogue strings started cutting into it. At this rate, I'd be lucky if it lasted the journey.

I came to a decision. As soon as this trip was done, I'd turn my back on the dimensions altogether and go back to pounding the streets. Maybe take the occasional cab, expenses allowing. My stringwalking days were over. Leastways, until the cosmos got its act together.

Or came to an end.

It was a big decision. I'd been walking the strings for as long as I could remember. It helped with the detective work but it was more than that—it was in my blood. The idea of giving it up was painful. But what could I do? Seeing the strings all snarled like this was like coming back to the pool you'd swum in every day for years, only to find some joker had swapped the water for sulfuric acid and shipped in a school of piranhas.

A pack of boundary wolves appeared over a nearby event horizon. They snapped at a crease in reality and earthquakes shook all the tenement blocks on the south side of the city. The quakes bled beads of dark matter into the void; the beads settled on the strings like dew on grass. The strings hissed, gave off clouds of recombinant plasma that attacked the wolves, turning them to living stone. Howling, chewing at their own petrified limbs, the wolves spiraled back into the aether.

The strings continued to lash.

On the south side of String City, the earthquakes deepened. The turmoil in the strings was soaking through the branes and shaking up the many worlds they contained. The knots of the cosmos were tightening.

I crossed my hands over my codpiece, closed my eyes and waited for the journey to be over.

17

I FETCHED UP in a square flagged yard. The weather was as bad as the bladderwrack had predicted. The sleet burned hard and the smog glowing livid yellow under the thick night sky. The six cylindrical towers of the Carr Industries power complex marched across the skyline. Fueled by nuclear syren song, they shook with a fury that, were it ever to be unleashed, would make the explosion at the Tartarus Club look like a party popper. I pulled my coat tight and tried not to breathe the toxic air.

At the end of the yard was a concrete blockhouse with a waterwheel on the side. The architecture was gulag meets country cottage. If I hadn't known the sign over the door read *Single Vision Forge*, I'd never have guessed, there were that many letters missing. The roof sagged and the windows gaped. The whole place had been all the way to the dogs and back again.

As I crossed the yard, a musclebound giant in a leather apron shambled out of the doorway. He was carrying a holdall as big as my desk. When he saw me he stopped and blinked his single eye.

"We closed," he said. He looked about to say more. Then he decided that was enough, put down the holdall, closed the padlock on the door, picked up the holdall again and started toward me. His head was down and his eye refused to meet either of mine.

When he drew level with me, I pulled the business card from my pocket.

"This look familiar?" I said.

He stared at the card. "Where you get that?"

"Off the body of a guy who looked a lot like you."

The cyclops extended a hand big enough to swallow mine whole and leave room for several more. With surprising delicacy, he took the card. His face crunched up. Tears dripped from his eye into one of the yellow puddles littering the yard.

"You saw his body?" he said. I nodded. "How he look? He look... peaceful?"

I thought about the corpse in the cellar. About how most of it had resembled raw steak.

"Very peaceful. You worked together?"

"Work together. Live together. Brontes—he my brother. We do everything together."

"Does that include blowing up the Tartarus Club?"

The cyclops delved into the pocket of his apron and brought out a hammer even Thor would have thought twice about lifting. "You want I turn you into horseshoe?"

"Calm down, buddy. What I want is to ask a few questions."

His eye narrowed. "You cop?"

"Do I look like a cop?"

"If you not cop, that big guy send you?"

"Big guy? You mean Hyperion?"

"I guess."

"Nobody sent me, buddy. I'm just trying to get to the bottom of things." I paused. "Trying to make sure your brother didn't die for nothing."

That did it. The cyclops's massive shoulders twitched, then collapsed. He dropped the holdall in a puddle, sat on it and started to sob.

I raised my collar against the sleet and waited. Eventually the cyclops dried up. I was about to prompt him when, to my surprise, he started talking all of his own accord. That happens more times than you'd think. Sometimes you have to push; mostly folk just want to tell you their story. Either way, I'm always ready to listen.

"It Brontes," he said. "It his idea. He always with the ideas, my brother. 'Hey, Steropes,' he says, 'why we isn't making something else than horseshoes?' So we starts make thunderbolts for Aeolus."

"The wind god?"

"That him. Anyways, those Thanes up on the Mountain, they starts breed thunderbirds and nobody want regular bolts no more." He jerked his thumb over his shoulder. "I got heap of regular bolts out back, you know anybody wants."

"Nobody springs to mind," I replied. "So after the thunderbolt business dried up you went back to making horseshoes?"

"S'right."

"How come you got mixed up with the Titans?"

"Titan and cyclops, we goes way back. We cousins, only those Titans, they say we runts of family. S'pose we is, you put us against Hyperion."

"You put anything up against a Titan," I said, "it comes out looking small."

Steropes scratched his nose. "S'right. Anyways, we always had—what you call—feud? Yeah, that it. Family feud. We get together, we fight. Titan and cyclops. Fighting cousins. Only, cyclopses so small they always lose. So we stop. Just make us honest living, you know?"

"So what went wrong?"

"It got so folks they don't want horseshoes no more. Time was there was loads of horses. Now they most in boneyard. Or in cans. Last year we scrapes by—this year, nothing. Bad times, mister. Real bad. So Brontes, he figure we got one choice."

"Which is what?"

"Crime," said Steropes matter-of-factly

I gazed through the sleet at the neighboring industrial units. Hundreds of little businesses, all desperately trying to turn a profit. Printers and packers and makers of lace. Little businesses all folding up, one after the next. I wondered how many others had crossed the line of the law to make ends meet.

"So let me guess," I said. "Brontes figured he'd blow the safe at the Tartarus Club and steal whatever he found inside. Plus get one over on the family to boot."

Steropes nodded miserably. "We went together. Brontes steals us big rig. Makes me drive. Makes me wait outside while he does job. Says he doesn't trust me to... mister, you see, I not too bright..." His voice trailed off, leaving empty air. He gave me a plaintive look. "Anyways, he come out with stuff he heisted and loads it in rig. Then he goes back for rest. Then there's big bang, and I waits and waits, but Brontes, he doesn't come out. I know he's dead 'cos my heart makes little stabs, but I waits. Then those Titans start busying and I get scared and drives big rig down to river and I jumped out before it hit the water and it rolls under those waves and sank down and down and down. Nearly I didn't jump, 'cos they say you go under Lethe that water makes that you forget everything and I thinks maybe that not so bad. My brain, mostly it don't remember much too good anyways, but I get to feeling it never forget that how Brontes is dead. Not ever. Feelings like dead family, they don't go away, and it gets so how you just want to wipe them out, you know?"

"I know," I said, because I did. "So what happened next? Did you come back here?"

He sniffled, wiped his nose on his apron, nodded. "Walked home. Sits me down. Wait 'til I forgets what I waiting for. After while I remembers all over Brontes is dead. That's when I couldn't bear it no longer and I packs my undershorts and brings my hammer and... and here's I talking to you."

"This 'stuff' that you stole," I said carefully. "What exactly was it?"

His brow furrowed over his single eye. "Dunno."

"Was it gold? Diamonds? Bonds?"

"What's bonds?"

"Never mind. Was it shiny?"

"Dunno. It in sacks." He started crying again. "I so stupid! I forgets everything! If I jump in that River Lethe, you wouldn't know difference!"

I felt like putting an arm round his shoulder. It would have been easier to hug a rhinoceros. "Where will you go?"

"Dunno. This city, it all I ever know." He picked up his hammer and started pounding the ground with it, over and over again. The whole yard shook. "I just walk 'til I stop, I guess, then walk some more. Walk 'til I stop for good."

I'd heard worse plans. If you'd asked me in the first year after Laura's death, I'd have said I'd heard few better.

Steropes put the hammer down and looked round in puzzlement.

"What that?" he said.

Even though Steropes had stopped pounding it, the ground was still shaking. Everything was shaking. The puddles bounced like drumskins; the forge's water wheel turned against the flow;

electric light pulsed like muzzle flashes through the smog.

Someone was coming through the dimensions.

Reality unzipped. A freshly-cut snag opened from the end of the canal path all the way up to the top of the nearest cumulus cloud, lighting up the night. A Titan stepped through, wearing a halo of lightning.

"Hyperion," I sighed. "I was wondering when you'd show up."

18

The snag that Hyperion had opened was vicious crimson, like a knife wound. Round its edges, torn strings spat like cobras. The Titan battered his way through all the same, muscling back the dimensions. For a second he swelled to full-size. I felt the whole world creak beneath my shoes.

Then the snag snapped shut and there was just steaming smog and a shadow as big as the night. We cowered under it, me and the cyclops. So did the rest of the city.

Hyperion took a deep breath and dropped a dozen sizes. The dimensions protested but he elbowed them aside. Soon he was no bigger than a department store. He squatted, dipped his head, planted his horns on the ground, massaged the back of his neck.

"Why did I pick such a small world?" he groaned. His skin was flayed and his eyes looked like baked eggs.

"Don't let him thump me," said Steropes, backing away.

"Out of my way, gumshoe," said Hyperion. "The cyclops is mine."

And there I was, caught like the world's smallest bratwurst between two mountains of rye. I considered getting the hell out, but where could I go? The yard was closed on three sides and Hyperion blocked the fourth.

"I'll strike you a deal, Hyperion," I said. "You tell me what's going on, I'll tell you where the stolen gear is."

Hyperion's eyes turned crimson. The cyclops gasped.

"'Deal'?" said Hyperion. "'Gear?'" His voice was calm. Not necessarily a good sign.

"Sure." I was already drowning—why not shout for sharks? "How else am I gonna close this case?"

Those crimson eyes disappeared behind eyelids like garage doors. When the doors opened again, the eyes were smoking. "You are off the case, gumshoe. Or did you forget?"

"Sorry, buddy, it doesn't work like that. You hire me, we've made a contract. Contracts work both ways—you're a businessman, you know that. Two to make one, two to break one. And I never said I was finished."

"Oh, you are finished all right." Hyperion smiled, revealing several thousand teeth. The journey here had stripped them of their enamel, and his gums were bleeding.

"I see you had trouble with the strings too," I said. "Reckon it cost you to get here. Why bother?"

"Tell me, gumshoe," said Hyperion, "what is to stop me squashing you now, like a bug?"

"Nothing," I replied, "except this. You ran yourself in circles trying to hide the truth, but here you still are, and here I still am, and here's this case still open. So why not help me close it? When that's done, if you still want to, you can kill me. If you do I'll die happy, because I'll know the answer to your damn mystery. You'll be happy too, because I'll take whatever secrets you've got to my grave."

Hyperion's fingers closed round my neck and I went up like an express elevator, the Titan's chin speeding past like the side of a cliff. A second later I was staring him straight in the eye. I tried to breathe and couldn't.

"You have a fancy tongue on you, gumshoe," said the Titan, "but you forget one thing."

"What's that?" I gasped.

"I do not care."

"So why are you here?"

Another long, slow blink. "To end this."

"So I was right."

"Right? About what?"

"Loose ends..." Hyperion's fingers gripped my neck like the forks of a front-loader. I was fading fast. Summoning the last of my strength, I croaked, "Let me... help you... tie them..."

A great growl rose in his throat, like he'd swallowed Africa. His fingers tightened; my vision tunneled. My head fell forward and the sleet slithered down the back of my neck. I must have blacked out, because the next thing I knew I was back in the yard, face down in a puddle.

I tried clambering to my feet, got as far as my knees. Something like an avalanche crashed to earth in front of the forge, but it was only Hyperion sitting down.

The Titan began to speak.

19

"What I said about business at the casino being slack," he said, "that was not the half of it. The Tartarus Club has been struggling all year. You saw the security footage, gumshoe—you saw how empty the place was."

"You've got other sources of income," I said. "Fall back on them."

"I cannot. Everything is going south in this city. Time was we could have got by on protection money alone. These days nobody pays their insurance. We turn the screws, they just show us their empty wallets and take their punishment. The bottom has even fallen out of the moonshine market. And with inflation at a billion percent we cannot even print our own bills any more—Hades, even the Mint cannot keep up. You know the score—do not tell me your business does not suffer too."

This wasn't the time to disagree. "Times are hard," I agreed. I decided to play a hunch. "Is that why you had something valuable stashed in that safe? Your own insurance to protect the Titans against the fall?"

"Could be," said the Titan. "Could be a certain client made a certain deposit—security against gambling debts. Could be that deposit had a certain extraordinary value."

This was getting interesting. "What client?"

"A shipping magnate, name of Pyx. Suffice it to say he lost to the house and I was forced to retain his deposit. He died the next day, trapped in the cargo hold when one of his ships went down. A tragic accident."

"House always wins, right?"

"Of course."

"So that's what was in the safe? Mr Pyx's deposit?"

"Yah."

"How much money?"

"Not money."

"What then?"

"High explosives."

Beside me, the cyclops whimpered. I had a hunch I knew the rest of the story, but I wanted to hear it out loud. I had another hunch too: as soon as the story was done, I was a dead man.

"Explosives? What kind of gambler pays his bills with—well,

whatever it was, it sure wasn't nitroglycerin."

"No, it was not nitro." Hyperion hesitated. "It was scathefire."

"*Scathefire?*" I swallowed hard. I thought about the single grain of what looked like salt that had blown my baryonic rasteriser into a million pieces. I thought about the size of the Titans' safe, and imagined it packed full of the stuff.

"Scathefire was banned centuries ago," I said. "The Thanes put out a Universal Order and had it all railroaded out to Oblivion."

Hyperion nodded. "How Pyx got hold of it I do not know. All I know is sixteen sacks of scathefire ended up in my safe."

I was reeling. I looked at Steropes. "So the explosion... Brontes didn't blow the safe at all, did he?"

The cyclops shook his head miserably. "Brontes, he knew the... what it called? Combi... combi..."

"Combination?"

"S'right. He say Titans ain't got no imagination and they always uses a birthday. So he tries all the birthdays and he in."

Hyperion scowled.

"So he wasn't planting the explosive—he was stealing it!"

"I guess," said the cyclops.

I tried to picture it: Brontes cracking the lock and opening the safe, climbing inside, carrying out the scathefire one bag at a time. Toward the end something must have gone wrong. I imagined the safe door swinging shut accidentally, the cyclops dropping one of the bags in surprise and learning the hard way that scathefire is volatile as all hell. It probably exploded on impact and blew a hole right through the floor of the safe, killing Brontes instantly and dumping his body down into the cellar. Not to mention throwing a plume of purple flame into the skies over String City and launching the Tartarus Club's neon sign on a hyperbolic trajectory that finished up smack against my office door.

"What I don't get," I said, looking Hyperion square in the eye, "is how the cyclops got past your security in the first place." Sometimes hunches are like itches. They burn so bad you've just got to scratch. "So why don't you answer this for me, my old Titan buddy—when exactly was it you hired Brontes to rip off your own casino?"

Steropes's jaw dropped open, all the way to his chest. Hyperion swelled like a pufferfish. I wondered which fist he'd use to mash me into the ground.

Then, suddenly, the Titan deflated like an empty blood bag. His shoulders sagged. I've never seen something so big look so spent.

"Last week," said Hyperion quietly. "I set the whole thing up last week. Only thing I could think of. I thought—and I guess you already figured this out for yourself—I thought if I could stage a fake heist I could claim on the insurance, get the casino liquid again. Then maybe downsize, consolidate, restructure..."

"Downsize?" I exclaimed. "Consolidate? You're a *Titan*! Holy Mother, have things really got this bad?"

Without a trace of sarcasm, Hyperion said, "Yes."

"And what about the poor cyclops brothers? What did they get out of it? Steropes—how much did you know about this?"

"Don't know much of nothing," said Steropes. "Brontes—he was the brains."

"That much is obvious." Hyperion barked out a bitter laugh. The forge he was leaning against trembled. "You did not even know that your brother had a habit—the kind of habit the Tartarus Club was built for. Brontes had been throwing his profits across our craps tables for years."

"I get it," I said. "Brontes agreed to do your dirty work, you agreed to clear his gambling debts?" Hyperion tipped his horns—a rare Titan gesture of respect. "So what did you tell

Brontes to do with the scathefire? Dispose of it? Was that part of the deal?"

"Dispose of it?" said Hyperion. "Dispose of something as valuable as scathefire? Are you insane? You never know when you might need to make a big bang."

I scrunched my eyes and worked my brain. "So as soon as the insurance claim goes through, Brontes brings the scathefire back? You wipe his slate clean, maybe slip him a small bonus if all the bags are intact? Is that how it was going to work?"

"More or less."

"Why bother bringing me into it?" I was running out of things to say. With Titans, when the conversation stops, the action starts. And with Titans, the action mostly hurts. "Was it really just to pacify your siblings?"

"Partly. Once you helped me finger the golem, I was going to use your report to butter the insurance boys."

Hyperion stood up so fast a whole new weather system formed around him. The sleet turned to snow, peppered yellow by the smog. The snow congealed around the forge like sick clotted cream.

"Talking is done," said the Titan. "Time I collected what I came here for."

Something was making a banging sound. At first I thought it was Steropes's hammer. Then I saw it was the cyclops's knees knocking together.

"And what exactly did you come here for?" I said to the Titan, my heart sinking.

"The scathefire, of course," said Hyperion. "It is my property, after all. And I want it back." He winked a huge, hideous wink. "Like you said, gumshoe—the time has come to tie the loose ends."

Just as I began to wonder what Hyperion would do when he

learned his precious explosives were at the bottom of the River Lethe, the dimensions split open again.

20

The other Titans came through all in a rush: Oceanus and Rhea and Tethys and half a dozen others whose names I didn't know. Between them they opened a snag that ran from the Carr Industries power complex all the way down to the elevated highway. Even as they materialised they were tearing into each other. Whale-sized arms swung haymaker punches while screaming jaws belched foundry fire. Pocket hurricanes whirled around them, turning the air into an electric cocktail. Lightning struck three of the six Carr plants, which went critical instantly, nuclear fuel belching out on screaming waves of syren song. The three remaining cylinders kicked into overdrive to cope with the surge. The acid snow went from yellow to red. The ground began to melt.

The newly-arrived Titans rampaged through the industrial park, kicking over factories, spearing warehouses on their horns, punching aside the cranes and derricks of the railroad loading stages. They were barely managing to keep control of their scale—one second they were as big as hillsides, the next they were vast like stars. Oceanus squashed himself small to squeeze under the aqueduct, but as he closed in on the forge he started rising again like bread in the oven of the gods. His eyes were fixed on Hyperion. All their eyes were. If they were fighting each other, it was only in competition to be the first to reach the brother who'd betrayed them.

As his furious siblings approached, Hyperion swelled up, ready to take them on. I looked for a bolthole, but Steropes was one step ahead. He picked me up, ran me out of the yard and across the tracks. We huddled in a coal heap and watched the fireworks.

They fought like dogs, the Titans. Dogs bigger than ocean liners. For a while the night sky was all horns and teeth and crimson blood splashing down through acid-yellow storm clouds. Everything they trod on, they pulverised. The industrial park turned to dust and flying bricks. The chaos spread. Soon the whole east side looked like crushed toast. Sewer pipes burst, sending high-pressure muck ballistic. One of the Titans picked up a bridge, used it to smash another into the ground. The sky filled up with fighting; the ground went dark with the fallout.

We watched in silence, me and the cyclops, as the industrial heart of String City was systematically demolished.

Even Titans can't take a beating forever. Tethys died first, speared by a sibling wielding a makeshift sword that looked like it was once a radio mast. It's something to behold, the corpse of a Titan. When they die, they revert to natural size. Natural size for a Titan is too big for this or any world. They unfold like origami, all kinds of hidden pleats popping into existence—dimensions you never knew were there. They get big in so many directions you can't keep track, so you just look away. When you look back, they've expanded all the way out of sight. That's when you cover you ears, to stop the sonic booms liquefying your brain.

The carnage continued. One by one, the Titans bit the dust. Eventually only two remained: Hyperion and Rhea. Brother and sister faced each other across the wasteland that used to be the energy capital of String City. Under their feet, a single remaining power plant bravely squirted its juice to as much of the metropolis as it could.

"You betrayed us," said Rhea in a voice like thunder.

"How did you find out?" said Hyperion. He was bleeding from more places than he had skin left. The blood made a lake that was badly in need of a dam.

"We managed to reboot the cellar CCTV. You were caught on camera, brother. Following you here was easy—you left a trail as wide as my ass."

"But I zipped the dimensions behind me."

"Your flies came open."

They faced each other in silence. Rhea was holding something behind her back. I couldn't see what it was; the smoke from the ruined factories was too thick. Hyperion reached out, touched his hand to her cheek. It was like watching worlds collide.

"Where did it all go wrong, sister?"

"When we started trusting you."

She brought her fist round like a prizefighter. It was bunched around something she'd picked up off the street. It was one of Theo Carr's power stations.

The cylinder's thermonuclear core cracked like an egg on the point of Hyperion's jaw and a sonic beam of pure syren song jetted out. A black mushroom cloud burst from the top of the Titan's head. Two seconds later he was radioactive dust from the waist up.

It took a while for his legs to fold. By the time they did, Rhea was long gone. Last I saw of her, she was stepping over the horizon and into darkness. She was the last of the Titans, and she never came back.

As for me and Steropes, we stayed in the coal heap a while, watching things fall down. The cyclops sobbed like a baby until he was all out of tears. I asked him what his plans were. He said he didn't know. I asked him what Brontes would have had him do.

He said: "Who's Brontes?"

Poor sap. Barely enough brain to keep his head from caving

in. On the other hand, maybe—just maybe—that made him the luckiest guy in the world.

"Too bad you lost the scathefire," I said. "You could have sold it. Set yourself up."

His face brightened. "I forgot. That what I done!" He delved in the pocket of his apron, came out with a fistful of bills.

"Where did those come from?" I said. I'm used to surprises, but this one made my gut turn over.

"It was when big rig sank in the river. I gets out and waved it bye-bye. Then this man—he comes up out of the water holding all the bags."

"The scathefire?"

Steropes nodded. "He asks me do I want it and I says he will keeps it but only just so long as he pays me some money. So he pays me some money and he takes the bags away." He waved the cash excitedly. It would keep him in cheeseburgers for about a week.

"Let me get this straight," I said. "A guy walked *out of the river*? The River *Lethe*?"

"Yeah."

"Who was he?" I said. "What did he look like?"

Steropes looked puzzled. No surprise there—he'd forgotten his brother; what chance he'd remember this?

"Dunno," he said. I sighed. Then he added, "Just some guy with a hood."

I pumped him some more, got nothing. This last twist worried me. Worried me badly, actually. But, as far as this witness was concerned, I knew I'd reached the end of the road.

"You need to get out of here," I said. "I suggest you head north. When you reach Oblivion, hang a right. You'll go a long way before you hit trouble." I scribbled a list of motels he could use where the roaches were clean and the management didn't care how many eyes you had. "Can you read?"

"Dunno. I's stupid, me."

"Just keep walking," I said. "Keep walking 'til you stop for good."

He thought about it, frowned, said, "I heard that somewhere. Who told you that?"

"Smartest guy I know."

21

By the time Steropes had gone, I was up to my knees in acid snow. I could feel it burning the legs of my pants, so I turned my coat inside-out three times until it was alkali tweed and stretched it down to my ankles. I waded through the snow to the highway, figuring I'd thumb a lift, but the highway was just a mess of ice and broken asphalt, studded with Titan toe-bones. The traffic was as flat as cardboard. Nothing moved, all the way out to forever.

The entire east side of String City was dead, flattened by the Titan showdown. And I was stuck there.

The snow drifted round my waist. Behind the devastation, the sun was coming up. The light felt good; it was the only thing that did. The loose radiation from Hyperion's remains was sparking random pockets of evolution, and the shadows were starting to move of their own accord. So was the smog. The weather was growing teeth.

Suddenly I didn't want to be there.

But how to get back to the office? The road I'd set Steropes on was a one-way street straight out of town. A last resort for no-hopers. Well, that wasn't me. Not yet, anyway.

That just left the strings.

The snow buzzed at the level of my chest. The shadows

multiplied. The smog grew claws.

Luckily I had a last resort of my own.

I shoveled my hand down into my coat pocket and pulled out the Dimension Die. The Dimension Die was another of the gumshoe gadgets I'd found in Jimmy the Griff's crate. I'd never seen another one like it. To me, it was more precious than scathefire. It looked like a regular die, only without any spots. Just a small blank white cube. Six sides, each side no bigger than my thumbnail.

A Dimension Die does a simple thing: when you roll it, it creates a disposable reality you can hop through to wherever you want to go, instantly. It avoids the strings altogether, leaves them right out of the equation. In short, it cheats.

A simple thing, but powerful as all Hell. And where there's power, there's a catch. Which is this: the die's got six sides, which means you get to use it six times. After that, there's nothing left. You might as well roll it down a craps table at the Tartarus Club for all the good you'll get. Six sides, six rolls, six clean trips through time and space and most of what surrounds them.

Six last resorts.

Five of the die's faces were black obsidian; the sixth was white ice. That was because I'd used it once already. Lent it, actually, to a couple of friends who'd needed a fast exit from a semi-dimensional self-reticulating oubliette inhabited by an insane spider queen. But that's another story. I turned the die in my fingers. Did I really want to use up another of its sides? But it was my deus, and I sure was stuck in a machina.

The acid snow closed like a Titan's fingers around my throat.

I rolled the die.

* * *

22

MY OFFICE LOOKED just as I'd left it.

At the same time it felt utterly *wrong*.

I checked the singularity latches on the door, counted the walls, rooted around in the cellar. Nothing missing. Then it hit me.

The place felt empty.

I took the brass compact out of my pocket, brushed my fingers over the controls. Did I want to reactivate the doppelganger? It would give me company for an hour. An hour and seven minutes, to be precise.

Outside, the sun was climbing over the city. For a second, bright rays punched in through the window and filled the office with gold. Then the clouds sank down and the rain started up.

I tried to pour coffee but the machine was jammed. I wrestled with the filter, yanked the spout. Nothing gave. I remembered the doppelganger saying he'd changed the beans. Seemed to me he'd spannered the works.

Fighting caffeine withdrawal, I dug out the crisp new case folder I'd marked *Tartarus Heist*. In it were the scraps of evidence I'd collected from the casino. No paperwork—there hadn't been time. I knew I should type a report. Instead I just shut the folder and scrawled *CASE CLOSED* on the cover.

As an afterthought, I put a tick in the *Solved* box. Closed and solved aren't even kissing cousins, but in this case both applied. I'd dug up the truth—well, as much truth as was there to be found.

Pity there was nobody left to pay the bill.

I tossed the folder in the filing tray. The piles of unsolved cases looked more daunting than ever. I wondered where to begin.

Someone tapped on the glass.

Glad of the distraction, I opened the door. Outside was a woman: young, scrawny, wet, shivering. The rain had molded her hair to her scalp.

"Is the job still going?" she said. She pointed to a card stuck to the inside of the window. I hadn't noticed it before. I peeled the card off the glass, turned it over. It read:

HELP WANTED

The handwriting was mine, but I hadn't written it. I cursed the doppelganger, and thanked him, all in a single unspoken breath.

"Could be," I replied. "Why? You interested?"

"Yes. Can I come in?" Her eyeliner was as black as the hair plastered to her head. The rain had smeared mascara down her face. She looked like she'd been weeping oil.

"Sure," I said.

The girl scuttled in like a mouse, black eyes wide. I wanted to throw my coat round her, warm her up. But I don't give that coat to just anyone.

She shook her head and squared her narrow shoulders. "So, what's it all about?"

I wondered why she was asking such a big question. Then I got it. "You mean the job?"

"Yeah. What d'you want me to do?"

"Do? Honey, I haven't hired you yet. Hell, I don't even *know* you."

She was strolling round, the mouse-act over. Now she was a cat, into everything. She kicked a stack of folders, riffled the address book, stirred the trash. "No," she said brightly. "But you will."

"Why would you think that?"

"Is this coffee machine working?" She pulled the lever. Black tar hit the hotplate and sat there sizzling.

"You didn't answer my question."

Now she was round the back of the machine, pulling wires, flushing valves. A brown bubble burst from the vent, floated up, popped on the ceiling. From inside the machine came a gurgle, then fresh coffee started running from the spout. She was already there with the jug. Soon the smell of java filled the office.

"Where'd you learn to do that?" I said.

"I used to work in Starbucks." She danced to the desk, perched on the corner. "Well?

"Well what?"

The girl smiled. White teeth shone like shots of sunlight through black mascara streaks. "Am I hired?"

"What's your name, honey?"

"Zephyr," she replied.

"Cute name."

"My brother was called Hurricane."

"Let me guess—you've got a sister called Gale."

"Now who's being cute?"

"You think you can just walk in here and start calling the shots?"

"You're the one who opened the door."

I looked her up and down. "'Zephyr', huh? One gust of wind and you'd blow away."

"I'm tougher than I look."

Behind her, a stack of folders teetered and fell, spreading six months of filing across six square feet of grubby carpet. I felt my shoulders sink. How had it come to this?

Zephyr picked up an armful of papers and held them out toward me.

"Look," she said, "you don't have to tell me whether I got the job or not. Just tell me where these need to go."

I sighed. "Is that coffee hot?"

"I guarantee it."

"Right. Pour us both a slug. You're on a week's trial. Let's get to work."

Wharf and Web

23

At first I was wary about the whole assistant thing. You work ten years alone, all your spaces get personal. But Zephyr somehow fitted right in.

By the end of her first day, she'd split the case folders into two piles: *Solved* and *Unsolved*. There were more in the first category than I'd realised. Discovering that gave me a boost. We bagged these up and piled them in the cellar, next to the tokamak. Zephyr spent the next few days working through the *Unsolved* folders, filing them alphabetically and cross-referring the dates. She spent an hour learning my handwriting then checked all the contact reports. She indexed evidence. She even worked out this neat color code to show how close to resolution a case was: a blue tag meant cold as a Jotun's jockstrap; yellow meant we had a trail to follow; red meant the trail was hot and the truth was close enough to smell.

I hauled up a spare filing cabinet from the cellar, set it next to the coffee machine. I already had a cabinet in the office, but I'd never considered using it to keep files in. The top drawer leads to a deep and distant dimension. It's a dangerous place, crisscrossed with railroad tracks. I've ridden its Search Engine from time to time. Each time I do, I swear I'm never riding it again. The middle drawer holds my arsenal. As for what I keep in the bottom drawer—well, that's a story best left for another day.

While Zephyr was doing all this I was doing what I do best.

Sleuthing.

I started with the mob of angry clients who'd come beating on my door. My doppelganger had promised them I'd solve their cases; it was a promise I intended to keep.

First off was the shaggy-legged satyr. He'd hired me on behalf of his daughter, who suspected her new husband was a philanderer. After an hour on the young goat's tail I discovered he was rubbing his horns on one of the hamadryad hookers who'd taken root across the road from my office. Talk about under your nose. I took a roll of pictures to the daughter as proof and left the two of them to butt it out.

I worked steadily through the rest of the cases, not once questioning my good fortune. Not only had the doppelganger written a recruitment ad on my behalf, but the first applicant for the job had proved to be some kind of administrative genius.

It was only later I got to wondering if it was all too good to be true.

I tracked down the stetson-wearing man's missing son in a Hot Hub whorehouse and exposed the woman with the broken arm for the insurance scammer I'd always suspected she was. Neither client thanked me. The docker's missing wife I found in a back alley, covered in bruises. I informed the poor dame her husband had accused her of adultery. She informed me how many times he'd raped her. I took her to a refuge and left them to call the cops.

Between times I caught up on penny-ante jobs for Japheth, Japheth, Pegasus and Jones, a firm of disreputable uptown solicitors. I served writs, collected a little debt. I also gathered evidence for a civil liability case—that meant taking pictures of a broken flagstone in Nephilim Square. The flagstone was about four hundred yards across and stuck up sixty feet. No wonder folk were tripping over it.

The rain stopped toward the end of the week, and fog rolled in off the river and smothered the city. By then, Zephyr had the paperwork as straight as a unicorn's horn. Me, I'd knocked seventeen case folders off the *Pending* pile. For the first time in months I felt like I was moving forward.

The only member of that mob still unsatisfied was the sulky sylph. She dropped by late one afternoon to chase me up. She was calm, a complete contrast to how she'd been on the day of the Tartarus heist. Hers was a weird case; she claimed someone was messing with her internal weather.

"When you're made of air," she said as she breezed through the office, "climate change is a big deal."

"I need a few more days," I said. "Maybe a week. Have you seen a doctor?"

"I don't need a quack. I need whoever it is to stop tweaking my jetstream." Inside the sylph's aerated body, the skies looked clear. But you never knew when a storm might be brewing.

"Leave it with us, ma'am," I said. "We'll get to the bottom of it."

"'Us'?" said Zephyr after the sylph had left. "Does that mean my probation's over?"

I surveyed the office. It still looked decrepit, but it was tidier than it had been in years. Maybe since forever.

"You do a good job, honey," I said. "You can stay. We're nearly out of coffee though."

She held up a tin of grounds. "Way ahead of you, boss."

While Zephyr was messing with the urn, the morning papers arrived.

The front pages were running stories about the fog (thickest for six hundred years), the regular brownouts caused by the recent implosion of the power district due to a Titanic brawl, political scandal up on the Mountain, where the Thanes who supposedly ran String City hadn't been seen for days, latest rumors about the end of the world... the usual mix. The *Herald* had an exclusive shot of Medusa's latest hairstyle and the *Standard* led with an op-ed piece about how the explosion at and subsequent closure of the Tartarus Club had unbalanced the economy so much the whole city was about to tip sideways. The scary thing was it sounded plausible.

Right below the Tartarus article was a two-liner reporting sightings of strange hooded figures throughout the city.

I thought back to what I'd seen on the Titans' surveillance camera. Or thought I'd seen. Then I remembered the character lurking at the back of the mob that had crowded my door. I scanned the rest of the papers and found four separate reports about hooded strangers. Somewhere at the base of my skull I was getting, if not a hunch, then certainly an itch.

Zephyr parked a cup of coffee on the desk, breaking my concentration. I stopped myself shouting at her. It was hard, getting comfortable with company. She must have sensed it, because she backed away.

"I thought you said this was working out..." She left a blank space at the end of the sentence for me to fill.

I folded the papers, gave her a long, hard stare. "Where are you from, kid?"

"I already told you: a long way from here."

"I'm a private investigator. You think I'm going to accept an answer like that?"

"It's the only answer you're going to get."

"Now you're just weaving."

"I can weave all day."

"I'll just bet. At least tell me where you're staying. You turn up every morning, tip out every night. Where d'you go?"

"Why should I tell you? It's not as if *you've* got a home to go to."

"Meaning?"

"Meaning I've seen the bunk down in the cellar, tucked behind that noisy old boiler that looks like a rocketship."

"So I sleep at the office—so what?"

"So I was right: you have no home."

I found some sports results in the paper that looked interesting. "Trust me, I've got a home."

"So why don't you ever go back there?"

"You see that clock on the wall? Says it's time to change the subject."

"Suit yourself." Pouting, Zephyr dropped on the couch. "Anyway, where I'm living is no secret. It's just a hostel down the road. I tried it on the off-chance, happened to mention I was working for you and the man behind the counter set me up a tab. I couldn't believe my luck."

"The big brownstone? Guy who runs it has a pet salamander?" When she nodded I said, "That's Tony Marscapone's place. Tony's a good guy. I did him a favor once—showed him where his wives were buried."

"Where his... how exactly was that a favor?"

"Tony was wanted by the cops. Multiple homicide. Tony had a house full of four wives and zero affection. He kept saying how, first chance he got, he was putting them all on a train to Oblivion."

"Oblivion? Where's that?"

"You think you're from far away? Trust me, Oblivion's further."

"Why did he hate his wives so much?"

"They were banshees. It was an arranged marriage—actually Tony was duped; the poor sap just found himself in the wrong bar at the wrong time. He got drunk and entered a karaoke tournament, only he accidentally checked the box on the entry form that put himself up as the prize. These four banshee sisters won the tournament on sheer volume, moved into his house and just carried on shrieking." I held up my hand. "It's a long story—all you need to know is one day there was no more noise from the Marscapone place and the cops fingered Tony. When they found he'd bought four train tickets to Oblivion the day before, well, that clinched it."

"How is sending someone to Oblivion murder?"

"The fact you ask the question proves you've never been to the place. Anyway, after he got the death sentence, Tony got his one phone call. He called me, told me he bought the train tickets but never used them, couldn't go through with it. I believed him. He hired me to save his neck. Thirty minutes before they were due to wire him up I was digging holes in the back yard of Tony's next-door neighbor, a noise abatement officer called Jenkins. Turned out Jenkins had been filing complaints about the banshee decibels for weeks. When the sisters ignored his court order he went postal and silenced them for good. Buried them in his own cabbage patch and went right back to work without breaking sweat. Lucky for Tony, Jenkins forgot one vital thing."

Zephyr's black-rimmed eyes were wide. "What?"

"Echoes. You wait long enough, sound always comes back. Especially the death cries of a banshee."

I broke off. Zephyr's hands were trembling so hard the coffee was slopping on her blue-jeans. I took the cup before she scalded her legs. As soon as I'd set the cup down, she grabbed my hands. She was shaking like Pompeii.

"I'm sorry," she said. "I thought I was coping with all this, but..."

"Coping with what?"

She shook her head. "It's not like I haven't seen my share of strange things. Before I came here, I had this... oh, never mind. It's just that I thought this place was starting to make sense. But hearing you talk about... about *banshees* and *Oblivion*—I don't know, it just... and last night I could hear this couple in the next room at the hostel—"

"What did you hear?"

"It sounded like they were *eating* each other." A tremor ran through her. "This place, this city, it makes no sense but somehow—"

"It hangs together?" She nodded, leaking tears, dumb. "You get used to it." I put my hand on her shoulder. "You sure you don't want to tell me how you got here?"

Before she could answer, the office door swung open. Fog billowed in, followed by a tall, slender woman snug in glistening mink. Purple lips tightened round a black cigarette holder, then parted to leak blue smoke into the room.

"My name is Kisi Sunyana," she said, "and I want to hire you."

24

I TOOK THE dame's mink coat, sat her in the client chair. Her eyes were hot like the end of her cigarette, like the ruby on her wedding ring. Her silk dress was yellow, split and wrapped to reveal stripes of black skin. She looked like a wasp.

Zephyr scowled at me as I hung the mink on the stand.

"I thought we weren't interested in new clients," she hissed. "Not until the backlog's cleared."

"Who said I was interested?" She scowled and returned to her filing.

"Do you have anything to drink?" said the dame.

"Coffee?" I took my seat behind the desk.

"I was thinking of something stronger." She crossed her ankles; the diamonds on her shoes flashed like sun on water. Her cheeks worked the cigarette like bellows.

I took a bottle of bourbon from the drawer, poured us each a double. Zephyr made a show of riffling papers. I ignored her.

When the dame's silence didn't stop, I said, "So, Mrs Sunyana, what's all this about?"

"Please, call me Kisi. I'm here because of my husband."

"What's he done?"

"What do men always do? He's cheating on me."

"You're sure about that?"

"Of course I'm sure! Why else would I be here?"

"You'd be surprised. There's plenty of folk hire a detective hoping things aren't what they fear. What they don't realise is, most of the time they are."

"Believe me, I'm sure. The only reason I need you to prove it is so I can crucify him in the divorce court. Then everyone will see what a louse he is!"

I sat back, the bourbon burning the back of my throat. "So you still love him." I stared at her through the smoke.

She draped her arm over the back of the chair. "Whether I love my husband or not is irrelevant."

"If you still love the guy, why throw him to the wolves? Yourself too, for that matter."

"Have you ever been married?"

"Twice."

"Did you love your wives?"

"More than they knew."

"Then you know what I mean."

I opened my mouth to snap something back, then changed my mind. On the couch, Zephyr was peering at us over the top of a case folder; when she realised I was watching she buried her head.

"So," I said, downing the rest of the bourbon, "what have you got?"

Kisi Sunyana reached inside her bag, handed me an envelope. I skimmed through its contents. They looked like contact reports from another detective agency. I checked the letterhead: *Scrutator Inc.*

"What's this?"

"I've had my husband under surveillance for some time now. I went to this place because it was new in town. They had an opening offer."

"Two stake-outs of the price of one?"

Kisi raised one immaculate eyebrow. "You know the outfit?"

I jerked my thumb at the door. "Hell, lady, we're practically neighbors. The Scrutator moved in a month or two back. Talk about close competition. Lucky for both of us there's more than enough work to go round."

"Well, despite all the assurances, I'm afraid the Scrutator failed to live up to its sales pitch."

I parked my boots on the desk, thought better of it and dropped them to the floor again. "Let me guess," I said. "Scrutators are robots, right? This one spun you some line about how truth is logic and the universe is all made of cogs and ratchets and pinions, which means everything can be fixed in time and space and proved to eleven decimal places? The whole cosmic watchmaker thing?"

"I do seem to recall something of the sort. How did you know?"

"It's my business to research the competition. Scrutators are your basic standard issue adding machines—the Thanes use them up on the Mountain to wrangle the city budgets, plan political campaigns, that kind of thing. But Scrutators are also built to learn, so every now and then one gets ideas above its station. Each year the Thanes let a few Scrutators set up in business, just to see what happens. Mostly they go bankrupt and end up back on the Mountain, crunching numbers. That's robots for you—all hard edges but inside soft as cheese."

"Perhaps. But actually it was the hard edges that put me off."

"Meaning?"

Kisi Sunyana leaned across the desk. Her dress gaped. I tried not to. "I got my free stake-out. I even got evidence that my husband was conducting secret liaisons with someone—I have no idea who. But I soon realised that there's one thing a mechanical man will never understand."

"Which is what?"

She ground her cigarette into her glass. The bourbon sizzled. She seized my hand, pulled it to her, pressed it against her exposed ribcage. Her skin smouldered. Her heart hammered against my palm.

"This!" she said. "This, gumshoe, this! Because, yes, I do love my husband, I love him enough to want him back, whatever he's done. But before I forgive him I want to see him dragged screaming through burning coals, see his lights drawn from his belly and the living skin flayed from his back! I love him enough to hate him and ruin him and see him lose everything he's ever worked for and hoped for, including me, especially me. *Especially* me. Only then will I let him have me again. The asansa are powerful but I am a woman, and more powerful still. No robot could ever understand this, only a man. I need a man to seek me out the truth. I need a man. Are you that man, gumshoe? Are you?"

25

TWO HOURS LATER I was crouched in a wrecked railroad caboose, staring through a spyglass at the biggest freezer in String City.

Eight years had passed since the Big Tusk Railhead had closed down. These days it looked like more a scrapyard. Some would-be sculptor had heaped all the rolling stock in the downside fiddle yard and called it art. Nobody came to look. Which made it the perfect place for a stake-out: the junked carriages made good hideaways and I knew I wouldn't be disturbed. Big Tusk is the highest outcrop of the ivory ranges flanking String City's river plains. Sure, it's weird to get mountains made of ivory but, when cosmic string gets tangled, geology takes a sharp turn into left field.

The railhead overlooks the warehouses south of the Lethe wharf. The tracks—all rusted now—snake out over the river via the Scrimshaw Bridge. Time was most of the city's trade came through the railhead. Then things changed. Container ships started bringing in cheap goods from the Unknown Worlds and suddenly the steam trains weren't running any more. The wharf grew itself a dandy set of monster cranes; behind the docks a whole new warehouse district sprang up. For a while, String City groaned under the weight of foreign imports.

Now even the container trade was drying up. The ships were growing barnacles, getting too heavy to sail. Entropy everywhere. The cranes were rusting quicker than the rail tracks. The warehouses were beyond shabby.

All except one.

The headquarters of Sunyana Enterprises was a squat silver slab. Even in the fog it shone. The yard was full of gleaming automobiles; busy figures swarmed behind polished windows. Seemed it wasn't just the private investigation business that was booming.

The building was mostly one giant freezer. The silver cladding was insulation; criss-cross refrigerant pipes made the roof look like a huge waffle iron. The offices were bunched at one end, including the big one with the widescreen window where my client's husband spent most of his days.

I zoomed the spyglass, saw a tall man through the tinted pane, pacing the boards. The fog made the image murky; I adjusted the optics to sharpen things up. The man was talking into a voice recorder. The spyglass gyros stopped the lens wobbling as I zoomed in on his tie pin, read the name engraved there:

Kweku Sunyana.

There he was. The biggest meat mogul in the city. Slaughterhouses, sausage factories, burger joints... Sunyana owned them all. That was why the name had sounded familiar. He was one of String City's rich and famous.

I lifted the lens to his face. Ladykiller face, all soul and jawbone. Luscious hair. Iron teeth like a mako shark.

Just what you'd expect of a man-eater.

26

"Asansa?" Zephyr had said after Kisi had left the office. "What's that?"

"One of the old city families," I said, flicking through the notes I'd made on the meeting. "Kweku Sunyana is chief. He handles meat. Not literally: he buys and sells carcasses, makes burgers and sausages, owns the city's biggest restaurant chains. Call it an extension of his natural urge."

"Which is what?"

"To drink human blood."

"*What*? He's a vampire?"

"No. The vampires left String City a couple of years back. The zombies too. Time was it was fashionable to be undead. Not any more. With the apocalypse coming, death's the new black."

"Apocalypse? Are you serious?"

I shrugged. "It's what the front pages say. Me, I just keep breathing."

"So this Sunyana character..."

"Kweku Sunyana."

"... he's just a guy who likes to drink blood?"

"All his family do. It's their thing. But habits like that make for bad PR. And if there's one thing an asansa craves more than human flesh, it's respect. So they focus on fresh food and good wine and keep the blood baths to a minimum."

"So is this Kweku Sunyana some kind of celebrity?"

"Not so you'd recognise him in the street. But everyone knows his brands. I'll say this about the asansa—they know how to get the best out of a raw steak."

With Kisi gone, Zephyr was relaxing again. She bunched her legs on the couch, grinned at me over her knees.

"So," she said, "when do we go and check him out?"

I went to the filing cabinet—the one without any files in it. I opened the middle drawer, pulled out a spyglass and a seven-shot Colt. "*We* don't," I said, checking the chambers on the gun.

I holstered the Colt and grabbed my coat off the peg.

"Wait a second," said Zephyr, leaping off the couch. "I thought we were partners."

"Honey, you're my assistant. That means you assist. So far it's working out. Don't push it."

"But what will I do while you're gone?"

"Same as you've been doing. Push some paper, get the place straight."

She planted small hands on bony hips. Her cheeks turned crimson. "The place *is* straight! Thanks to me! I've spent half the morning pushing paper, planning your day, only to have you take off on a wild vampire chase just because Kisi-with-the-yellow-dress Sunyana let you squeeze her tits!"

"I didn't touch her... she just wanted me to feel her heartbeat. And they're not vampires."

"Look, you're the one who wanted an assistant. I'm here to help, to learn. You could train me up. I could be of real use to you, if you'd let me!"

She took a step toward me. Small as she was, somehow she filled up the office. I almost backed away.

"Honey," I said, "it's sweet of you, but..."

"Don't patronise me!" Her cheeks were as red as Kisi Sunyana's eyes. "Are you going to take me or not?"

I turned my coat inside-out three times until it was black leather, slung it over my shoulder. "It could be dangerous. Riverside's not safe these days, not since they cordoned the wharf."

She pouted. "'Stay at home, little girl'? Is that it?"

"That's not what I said."

"How long will you be?"

"Don't wait up."

She coiled like a prizefighter. I steeled myself for the blow. Gradually she relaxed again. The color drained from her face and her shoulders dropped. "I suppose I could start work on the cellar. It's still a mess down there."

"Sounds like a plan. Watch the roaches. They move in gangs."

"I'll be careful. Make sure you are too."

"I didn't know you cared."

"I don't. It's just that you haven't paid me yet."

"End of the month. Like I said."

"Whatever."

I left her scowling on the cellar steps and set off on foot for the river.

27

I SPENT THE morning watching Kweku Sunyana through the widescreen window of his office. He dictated letters, held meetings—standard CEO stuff. At one-fifteen the fog broke and he took lunch on the roof terrace with another city bigwig: Theo Carr, the fusion king. I wondered if Carr had come for a loan. He was badly in need of one, ever since the Titans had unplugged his power plants.

After lunch, Sunyana went back to business. More dictation, more meetings. Occasionally he went to a cage in the corner of the office, fed whatever was inside. It looked like some kind of bird: a parrot, maybe. Between times I read the Scrutator's reports on the guy. Nothing remarkable—I could have written them myself, based on what I was seeing today. One odd thing stood out though: mid-afternoon the previous Wednesday, Sunyana had answered the phone. Immediately after the call he'd canceled all his appointments for the rest of the day and jumped in a cab. The Scrutator had tried to follow but lost him. The last thing the Scrutator recorded was that the cab had been headed toward the wharf.

Nobody went to the wharf.

The sun dropped behind the dockside skyline. Cranes jabbed it like rusty scalpels. The daylight went away and the fog came back. I paced up and down in the caboose, stretching bunched muscles, waiting.

At six-seventeen, Sunyana's window went dark. I swung the

spyglass down to the white Cadillac in the car park. It was a convertible with six legs and sentient brakes. Very chic, very expensive.

Time passed. Sunyana didn't show. I rewound the lens and flicked the bloodhound switch. The gyros pulled the spyglass sideways to a catwalk on the side of the freezer building. A dark figure was hustling along it. I let the lens zoom in, saw sodium light glint off iron teeth.

At the end of the catwalk, a set of steps led down to the service yard. Sunyana slipped between delivery trucks, moving with that weirdly fishy gait all the asansa have. Soon he was through the perimeter and headed across the wasteland behind the yard.

Beyond the wasteland was the wharf.

I stowed the spyglass and jumped out of the caboose. The fog scoured me like cold steel wool, but there was no time to turn my coat around. Sunyana had two hundred yards on me, and he was moving fast.

The railhead steps took me straight past the service yard. From there I crossed a culvert and cut a diagonal on to the wasteland. The open ground behind the Sunyana freezer was nuclear swamp, hard to build on. There was nowhere to hide, but the fog was thick and Sunyana wasn't looking back. The mud sucked my boots. I hoped the isotopic alligators weren't awake yet.

Sunyana stepped up the pace. Where was he going? You sneak away to meet a lover, you don't want to turn up with radioactive ankles. Besides, there was nothing out here. Pretty soon he'd fetch up against the wharf cordon fence. End of the line.

I jumped an open sewer grate. The stench was shocking. A voice floated up, calling me back. I kept running. In String City, the sewer system has a mind of its own. Trouble is, it's the mind of a serial killer. Near the fence, Sunyana slowed down. I ducked behind what looked like a wrecked automobile; it turned out to be an alligator's ribcage. All that radiation means the swamp critters grow *big*.

Sunyana pulled some kind of tool from his jacket. He thumbed a toggle and the dusk lit up with pink maser light. He swung his arm in a circle and the fence grew a hole. He stepped through the hole and took off across the swamp again.

Astonished, I came out from behind the alligator bones. Cutting the cordon fence was a major felony. Crossing it was suicide. Worse, Sunyana had left a hole in the fence big enough to ride a pony through.

It wasn't exactly ponies the fence was built to contain.

I approached with caution. I couldn't believe what I was doing. I should have been running, alerting the cops. Mostly running.

When I got near I saw the hole was closing up of its own accord. Sunyana's maser must have had a synchronous disjunction field. Attachments like that are expensive, but then so are six-legged Caddy convertibles.

I gauged the distance between me and the fence. I tried to gauge how crazy a guy would have to be to do what Sunyana had just done. Was I that crazy too?

I checked the Roentgen counter on my boots. Radiation was low this evening; I could afford to stay out here another couple of hours. The question was, did I want to?

The hole was halfway shut.

I ran for the fence.

Six yards short of the hole, my shin cracked on something hard. I went down, face-first into the swamp. I spat mud, rolled on my back. A figure rose up and loomed over me. I reached for the Colt; my hand barely touched the grip before something like a carpenter's vice closed on my wrist and hauled me upright. The mud tried to suck me down, but whoever was doing the lifting was strong.

I swiped mud from my face and cursed. The mud might have been low-gamma, but with this much on me I'd need more than just a wipe down. I yanked my wrist free, made ready to shout at my assailant. But the dude spoke first, in a voice like an old-time radio broadcast:

"Forgive me for tripping you, but I could not let you follow our quarry into the quarantine zone."

A face resolved itself: burnished and bronzed and almost human. Its cheeks were scarred with fretwork; through the perforations I could see about a billion tiny gears spinning around each other.

"Scrutator!" I said.

The robot bowed its intricate head. "At your service."

"In your electric dreams." I looked at the fence in time to see the hole close up completely. "See what you did? You just lost me his trail!"

"An alternative analysis suggests I have saved your life."

"It's my life, buddy. I'll do with it what I please."

"All is not lost."

The Scrutator pointed with a slim, hydraulic arm. I peered through the fence and the fog. Sunyana had reached the water's edge, where floodlights washed a stepped pyramid surrounded by cranes. A big sign stood before it carrying a picture of giant gold feather and the words *Quetzal Imports*. The cranes moved like herons, fishing for loads and hefting them skyward.

As we watched, Sunyana disappeared inside the pyramid.

"There," said the Scrutator. "We now possess information we did not possess before. We have pushed back the tide of entropy. The cosmos is a more ordered place."

I resisted the urge to poke out its whirling eyes. "Less of the 'we', buddy. You just queered my pitch."

"I cannot parse that sentence."

"Don't get funny with me."

"The case is one step closer to being solved. Is this not progress?"

"The only progress you're making is toward the breaker's yard. Don't you get it? Kisi Sunyana fired you. You're off the case, pal. Go home and wind up your clockwork, or whatever it is you do to keep yourself busy."

"I cannot. The truth is not yet established. Order has not yet been restored."

"Not your problem, pal."

"I do not disagree: the truth belongs to no one individual. Nevertheless, truth exists, and must be found."

I took a breath. Inside the robot's chest, cogs whirred. No heart there. I remembered how Kisi Sunyana had held my hand to her breast.

"Look," I said, "The lady came to me. So it's up to me to see this thing through. Let it go, buddy. Find yourself some nice fat writs to serve. Work like that—it's what you were built to do."

A purring sound came from inside the Scrutator's head. It stood still so long I thought it had shut down. Then it said, in a small, still voice:

"Do you hear that?"

Something tingled down the back of my neck. "Hear what?"

The robot raised its finger, cocked its head. "Something. Everything." Then some widget clanged in its chest. The strange moment passed. "There is nothing more to be done here. I will return to my center of operation."

"First smart thing you've said." I scraped my boots clean on an alligator bone.

"Can I assist you with an offer of transportation? I have an automobile parked not far from here."

I took my coat off, turned it inside-out six times until the radioactive mud had turned to vanilla.

"Thanks," I said. "I'd rather walk."

28

By the time I got back to my office it was full dark. Across the street, the hamadryads were painting their leaves vivid scarlet; greasers in hot rods cruised the corners, looking for trouble. Beyond the tenements, smoke still rose from the wrecked eastside. The streetlights were out across approximately half the city. At least the garbage collectors had taken away the neon sign that had flown here from the Tartarus Club.

Kisi Sunyana was waiting for me in the doorway.

"You're soaked," I said.

"You smell good," she said. "Have you learned anything?"

I hesitated. "I don't discuss cases in progress. A lead's one thing—the truth's another."

"So you have a lead?"

"I didn't say that."

Her eyes burned like coals. "Could I at least come inside?" she said. "I've grown terribly cold standing here, waiting for you. And I am, as you observed, wet."

I pulled out my key. "I guess I could find you a towel."

Once we were inside I flicked the light switch. Nothing. Outside, the streetlamps had died. No power for six blocks in any direction. I lit a candle.

The office was empty; Zephyr hadn't waited up. I shucked off my coat, dropped my boots in the electron soak, tossed Kisi a towel from the washroom. While she dried her hair, I poured us a couple of bourbons. My hand shook. Maybe it was the radiation. I steadied it by scrawling a hasty note on the pad by the phone.

Quetzal Imports—pyramid—Sunyana connection?

Kisi came over and I quickly closed the pad. She took the glass, her fingers brushing mine. We both drank.

"So," she said, pressing the towel to her throat, "did you see my husband today?"

"Like I said, I can't discuss the case."

"Please. I'm not asking for details. You told me yourself you were going to check out his offices. I just wondered what you saw."

"There's something got me wondering," I said, dodging the question. "What does a dame like you see in a guy with teeth like one of his own mincing machines?"

She smiled. "Ah—the problem of flesh."

"If that's what you want to call it. So spill: how does it work? I mean, really. The guy's hobby is biting people; you just look like a regular dame. What's the deal?"

She put down her glass. Her eyes were kaleidoscopes in the candlelight. "It's very simple. The asansa have different kinds of bites. Have you noticed how their teeth are arranged like sharks' teeth? Several sets, nested one behind the other?"

"Hard to miss."

"Well, they use whichever set is appropriate for the occasion—and the mood. All the families are different. The Sunyanas, for instance, have five sets of teeth. Kweku calls the first his 'social set'—the basic teeth he uses for talking and smiling and so on. He has two sets he uses for eating: one for public meals and another for private. When an asansa eats in private, things can get... messy. The fourth set looks like what you'd expect to see in a vampire's mouth, only they're made of metal. Kweku calls them his 'high-day irons'. If he bites you with those, you become asansa yourself. I can't remember the last time Kweku used them. He's very civilised, you know."

"That's four sets of teeth. You said there were five."

"The fifth set he keeps just for me." She turned away, letting the straps of her yellow wasp-dress fall loose. "Dry me, would you?"

When I'd toweled her shoulders, she asked me would I dry the rest of her back. She even unwrapped the dress for me, all the way down to the seventh stripe of silk. Very obliging.

"Thank you," she said. "You'd make a wonderful masseur."

She faced me and the rest of the stripes pooled on the floor.

29

"I MET THE Scrutator," I said afterward. The power was still out and the candle flame was wavering, on the verge of dying. Kisi Sunyana was black on black. So was my mood. "Damn heap of sentient scrap, stealing my trade!"

"The robot? I thought I'd fired it?" said Kisi. She'd warmed up all the way through to hot. My kind of radiation.

"That's what I said. Maybe it went to the union."

"Do you mind if I move? My leg's gone to sleep."

"Feel free." She moved. I moved. Parts of us both found new places to be. My mood lightened. "One thing's got me puzzled."

"What's that?"

"If you love your husband so much, how come you're here with me?"

"I told you. He's hurt me. So I need to hurt him back. This is as good a way as any. Wait while I turn over."

"So you're just using me?"

"I don't hear you complaining."

"You don't know for certain Kweku's having an affair."

"He's doing something behind my back. Hold still a moment... there."

"There?"

"No... *here*."

"Doesn't mean he's cheating. Trust me—when a guy visits the wharf after hours, it's unlikely to be for pleasure."

"Speaking of pleasure... how does that feel, gumshoe?"

"Dandy. All I'm saying is, if he isn't cheating, and finds out you are, what's he going to do to me?"

"Are you worried about his teeth?"

"They are a factor."

"Don't worry. I can handle Kweku."

"Seems to me he can handle himself. Hey, how are you doing that?"

"I practice martial arts. Give it a moment—you'll like it. Yes, Kweku is very self-assured. The Sunyana are very proud, very honorable. Kweku isn't just a businessman—he's the head of an ancient family. Most people just see the meat he puts on their plate. To Kweku, meat is his life's blood."

"Your husband's business is booming. He's one of the few to escape the recession. He must be doing something right."

"Yes, profits have been up the last three years running. I don't know how he does it. But I never did have a head for business. Only love. Hold me here."

"Here?"

"No, *here*."

"How are you *doing* that?"

"I can also do this."

"Holy mother of..."

"I just wish I knew what my husband was doing hanging around that wharf. It's so dangerous. I mean, that's why they put that fence up, isn't it? Because of the quarantine and everything?"

"The fence wasn't his concern. He just took the shortest route to the pyramid."

"It's time to stop talking."

"Why do we need to...? Oh..."

The candle went out. Down in the basement, the tokamak was roaring. Laura's face filled the darkness, watching me with her dead eyes. Was she judging me? No way to tell. I waited for the guilt to roll in but it didn't.

I was glad she was there.

30

When I woke, Kisi was gone. Laura too. The cushions were on the couch backward. So was I. Outside, the fog had returned with a vengeance, thick yellow with a hint of dawn. Too late for night owls, too early for mail. I got dressed, fired up the coffee machine. Kisi Sunyana had played me like a fiddle, in more ways than one. My strings were still twanging.

I pulled my boots out of the electron soak, checked the Roentgen counters. They were clean. I checked my coat; it still smelled of vanilla. I turned it inside-out twice until the scent was gone, then hung it back on the hook.

I drank coffee, stroked the small hairs on the back of my neck. Something still prickled there, still not quite a hunch. I leafed through a few reports, watched the fog bubble, tried to work out what was wrong. Eventually I saw it.

If it was too early for mail, why was there a letter on the mat?

I picked it up, opened it, expecting it to be from Kisi. I read:

I was still here when you came back last night. I'd spent the day tidying up the cellar, like I said I was going to, and when I'd finished I made cocoa and sat on the cellar steps, only I must have fallen asleep, because the next thing I was hearing voices. It was you and that woman. I didn't want to eavesdrop so I stayed down here, turned up the boiler and just listened to it roar. Later, after she'd gone, I came upstairs. You were asleep on the couch. I saw the notepad on your desk and opened it, and saw what you'd written there. That's when I decided.

Here's the thing. I want you to take me seriously. The only way that's going to happen is if I prove to you what I'm capable of. So I'm going to check out that pyramid, whatever it is. Heck—maybe I'll even solve the Sunyana case for you!

Don't come after me—I want to do this by myself.

Zephyr

I read it twice, then screwed it up and hurled it across the room. The girl was crazy! By now she was probably dead.

Outside, a municipal cleaning truck crawled past on grimy millipede tracks. Roving suckers vacuumed trash from the gutters. Also chunks of asphalt and a couple of hobos. The fog bulked out, eclipsing the early light.

I turned my coat inside-out three times until it was a life preserver, pulled what I needed from the middle drawer of the filing cabinet and headed for the river.

31

THE RIVER LETHE runs right through the middle of String City and out the other side. Nobody knows what its source is, but once it gets past the wharf it joins the Acheron and together they head out for the ocean. Time was, boats packed the river like beans in sauce. Not any more.

Acheron Lock is the only place still busy, mostly with tourists; everyone likes to see water defy gravity. It's not such a great trick once you learn there's anti-matter in the lock gates. Downstream you can take a fishing trip; the salmon there claim to have knowledge of the secrets of the universe, but most of them don't even know the alphabet. The occasional swimmer still tries to doggie-paddle across the Acheron, even though they know they'll come out in tears. Nobody dares swim in the Lethe. That's because the water wipes your mind clean of all its memories. In the Lethe, you keep your waders on at all times.

Waders I didn't have. But I still had no intention of getting my feet wet, so I let my boots take me down the crumbling pier to where the *Argo* was moored. I knew the *Argo* of old. Her skipper and I went back a long way.

As I stood at the end of the pier, I hoped we went far enough.

"Jason!" I shouted. "I need a favor."

The door to the *Argo*'s wheelhouse jerked open. Blue eyes stared out from a face that was all beard and wrinkles. "I knew it was going to be you," Jason said. "Did I say that already?"

"Hello, Jason."

"D'you want to come aboard? Or were you just leaving?"

"You got a gangplank?"

"I knew you were going to say that."

I waited while he fussed with the plank. Halfway through he forgot I was there and greeted me all over again. Jumbled memory's a side effect of working years on the Lethe. Mostly Jason just suffered from *déjà vu*; today he seemed particularly mixed up.

We drank hot syrup in the wheelhouse and I let Jason talk. I didn't like wasting time, but if I wanted his help I needed him sweet.

"Business is bad," he said, sipping the sickly brew. "Dredging's a lost art. Dredging's a lost art. Did I say that already?"

"They still paying you to move silt around?"

"Naw, these days I salvage. Ever since I lost that fleece. Gold sinks. Bicycles too. You'd be amazed what people throw in the river. Bicycles, dishwashers, even automobiles. And bicycles. Amazing what I pull up. You'd be amazed. I sell on enough to cover my costs. Bicycles too. Did I say that?"

"You might have mentioned it."

"Also, the Lethe being what it is, I do a fair trade in lost souls."

"You dredge up lost souls?"

"You'd be amazed what you..."

"Look, Jason, about this favor..."

"Can I get you a drink?"

I waggled my mug. "You already gave me syrup, Jason. One cup's more than enough."

He grinned; his beard parted enough to show where his teeth had once been. "I like syrup. Did I ever tell you that?"

"Worked it out for myself, buddy."

He stood up, an ancient hairy barrel of a man. The wheelhouse was small and between us we filled it. He wiped the window, peered outside. "I feel like I've been here before," he said, suddenly plaintive. "Have I? Or did I just arrive?"

"You're on the river, Jason," I said. "It's where you live. You're always here."

"I know, but..." he shook his head. His beard rustled like cellophane. "Never mind. Did you tell me what it was you wanted?"

"I was just about to."

A look of infinite sorrow shadowed Jason's face. "You may have to tell me more than once."

32

THE FOG MADE for slow going. It took the *Argo* an hour to cut its way through the shallows and round the curve to where the docklands began. I could have used the footbridge—I guessed that was what Zephyr must have done—but its deck is exposed and I worried Sunyana might have spies. So Jason it was.

As he steered his beloved *Argo* away from the jetty, he started singing a shanty from the old days:

So steady me hearties and buckle up tight
Protect yourselves front and behind
For the waves they do wetten, and if you should let 'em
You're sure to be losin' your mind

"The water's calm today," I said, peering cautiously over the bow rail.

"The Lethe's always calm," Jason called from the wheelhouse. "Sunshine or storm, she'll never try to drag you down. Safest waters I ever worked, and that's a true fact."

"Really? I always figured it was dangerous."

"Danger's down to you. The Lethe—she'll take you readily enough, but only if you give her no other choice. She'll look after us, don't you fret."

He turned the wheel to starboard. The bow swung to port. The *Argo* still had her original reverse tiller. Jason liked her that way.

Out on the water, he was more like his old self: the Jason I'd come to know during the long years of war preceding this time of relative peace. Sadly, the coming apocalypse—if that was what it was—was proof that these quiet days were just a lull before another storm.

As for the war, well, I did my best not to think about that.

The boat turned, cutting through a shoal of selkies. The seal-women kept pace with us for a while, surfing our bow wave and singing in their high voices. Their silvery faces were pretty and mindless. They kept catching my eye and looking startled, like they'd never seen a person before. Still, they looked happy. Maybe attention span isn't everything.

The fog thickened like gravy.

"Are you sure you know where you're going?" I said. "I can't see a thing."

"I get soundings off the bottom. You'd be amazed what you can do with an echo. Plus I get soundings off the bottom. Did I mention that?"

I shivered: the strident selkie song made me think of Tony Marscapone's dead banshee wives and nuclear syrens.

It also made me think of Laura.

Cranes loomed in the fog and the edge of the wharf came into view. Jason goosed the throttle. The gunmetal water grew choppy and the selkies scattered. Under the waves I caught glimpses of ghostly faces, staring up at me with dead, blank eyes.

"Lost souls?" I edged back from the rail.

"Some," said Jason. "Most are just folk. Nothing rots in the Lethe, and the water keeps you fed, and keeps you down. When you fall in the river, it wipes your memory, but it doesn't just do it once—it does it over and over, so you keep waking up with all your past on the tip of your tongue. See how puzzled they look?"

He was right. The faces looked lost, confused. Like they were about to speak, but had forgotten what they wanted to say. Truth was, they'd forgotten everything. A thousand times over. All because of the water. One drop was all it took.

The waves were beginning to splash over the bow. I stepped back from the rail.

"So how are the lost souls different to these poor saps?"

"The souls run deep. In the still waters. Dredging them up brings good money—there are folk think lost souls make great hood ornaments. That's my trade. I hate it, but it pays. But you've got to watch the Maelstrom."

"The Maelstrom?"

"Where the souls gather. You get caught in the Maelstrom, you're fishbait. Did I mention they make great hood ornaments?"

"You said they prefer still waters. Isn't the Maelstrom a whirlpool?"

"Only round the edges. Round the edges it's like some crazy polka. But in the middle it's still. That's where the lost souls are, right in the eye of the storm. Did I mention the fishbait?"

My eyes plumbed the depths. My thoughts circled back to Laura.

"Sometimes I wish they never found her body. That way, I could convince myself she was still alive."

"Finders keepers," Jason replied. "You lose, you weep."

Faces bubbled up, burst, fluoresced and folded, dead leaves drenched by the tide. They were strangers all, unfamiliar spirits.

Now I'd started thinking of Laura, I didn't want to stop. But thoughts are a curse and Jason had said something.

In the middle it's still.

The short hairs on my neck were prickling again. Why did that sound familiar? Was it the river, playing tricks?

"The eye of the storm," I muttered. "The still center of the dance."

Not déjà vu, I thought. Presque vu: *the feeling like everything's about to make sense.*

Something wailed in the fog. The sound was raw and mournful, a leviathan's moan. The waves surged. Jason lashed the wheel and leaped down the steps to the deck. He started coiling ropes, pulling chains, turning capstans.

"What's happening?" I said.

"Bow wave. There's another ship out there. A big one. Headed our way."

The river bucked like a mustang. The *Argo*'s keel left the water. She flew, tipped on her nose, crashed back into foam. I dodged behind the wheelhouse to keep dry. Jason was there before me; he looked like a barrel but moved like an eel.

An iceberg appeared out of the fog. A second look told me it wasn't an iceberg but a huge, glass-walled container ship, splitting the river like Moses. Its lower hull was caked with barnacles the size of truck tires. The *Argo* was a gnat in its shadow, all set to get swatted.

Jason scampered back up the stairs to the wheelhouse and spun the wheel hard to port. The *Argo* lurched starboard, straight toward the wharf. For a second I thought we were going to make it, but the container vessel was turning too, as slow as seduction. The ship's transparent sides thundered past and through the glass I saw crates stacked high, row upon row. All the crates were stamped with the same two words: *MUSCAE MORTUUS*. There was no time to puzzle what that meant because two seconds later the *Argo* smashed straight into it.

The impact tossed me all the way to the *Argo*'s stern. I landed in a snake pit of tangled ropes. The whole port side of the *Argo* caved in. She rolled like a dead dog, lethal water climbing the deck.

I ran to the mast. The water chased me. The container ship glided on as if nothing had happened. I found rungs, started to climb the mast. The *Argo* heeled over; I felt like bait on a rod. The waves snapped like hungry crabs at my heels. The stone wall of the wharf loomed before us, tantalisingly close. The container ship had slowed to a crawl, ready to dock. I reached the crow's nest. Beneath me, the *Argo* was sinking fast.

"Jason!" I shouted.

He was clinging to the wheelhouse roof. When he saw me, he found a rope, swung on it like a monkey. He eeled up the mast toward me. The water pursued him. I reached down.

He was three feet away when the water splashed his foot.

Something like moonlight crossed Jason's face. He opened his mouth to speak, forgot what he was going to say. I tried to stretch down but the nest's ropes had me hamstrung.

Jason screamed.

I snapped my spyglass to full extension, held it out.

"Grab the glass!" I shouted.

Jason lunged, snagged the rim of the lens, lost his grip.

Fell into the river.

There was a single second before his face went completely blank. Just one second. I thought he was going to call my name. Then the moon-look settled over his features and Jason went away, all of him, forever. Next minute he was just another face under the water.

The dockside was just five feet away. I jumped from the crow's nest over open water to dry land, hitting hard and jarring my ankles. I tucked and rolled. The mast smacked down beside me, splintering to matchwood. I staggered to my feet, shaking all over. I looked back at the river. With a groan like whalesong, what was left of the *Argo* disappeared beneath the waves.

33

I LIMPED THROUGH the fog to the base of the pyramid. The huge structure rose into the murk in a series of gigantic steps, each ten times the height of a man. The blocks it was made from were smooth marble, coarsely veined. Instead of mortar, some kind of sticky black liquid oozed from between the joins. It smelled like corpses.

I walked along the side of the pyramid until I found a door marked *NO ENTRY*. I tried the handle; the door was locked. High overhead, a crane jib hefted crates from the hold of the docked container ship. The crates flew in silence, vanished into a cavity high in the pyramid's side. The crane came out empty, went back for more. Cold wind gusted the fog. I shivered.

Poor Jason. All those years at sea searching for the Golden Fleece, only to end up as a two-bit dredging captain lost in the boondocks. Once he'd been mighty; he sure had fallen.

I thought of his face, all moonstruck and empty.

And again I thought of Laura, her face. How must my wife have looked as she'd shed her clothes and walked into the waters of the Lethe? Had she looked like Jason? Had there been a single second of doubt? Of despair?

A gang of mudlarks saw her go in, and they were the ones who sounded the alarm. To this day I don't know why they did that. It wasn't like there was any hope for her. As soon as the phone delivered the news, I hurled myself riverside. While the cops steered their dredging boat over the spot she'd gone under, I found the shapes of her feet, still pressed in the mud. The S-shape of the glass-cut scar on her right heel. Professional as ever, I took a plaster cast. After that, my memories go to mush.

The cops found her body somehow, hauled it up from the deeps. They called it suicide, even though it wasn't. Laura hadn't wanted to drown herself—she'd wanted to wipe her memory clean. Death was just a side effect.

That was the hardest part. That was what kept me awake in the small hours, shivering in the cramped cellar bunk of a two-bit mid-town detective agency while the roaches played craps and the tokamak ticked. Even in waking hours, the thought could stab me any time, any place: a cold, rotten knife in my heart. A question like an icicle.

What was it my wife had wanted to forget?

Was it me?

I turned my coat inside-out until it was made of zibeline. Zibeline keeps the damp out and the warmth in. I felt in the pocket for my skeleton key, then remembered I didn't have it any more. Pity—that key and I had been through a lot together. It was an old acoustic model, with a voice that could vibrate the tumblers loose on any lock in a twelve octave range. Now it was singing soprano in the Vaderkvarn Orchestra. Talk about a career change.

I rattled the door handle, frustrated. I could have used the dimensions to translate myself from one side of the door to the other. But short hops are especially hairy—it's easy to get straddled on the strings. And, given the uproar I'd been experiencing lately in the deep dimensions, there was every chance I'd flip straight into the jaws of a boundary wolf.

Besides, I'd made myself a promise: from now on, everywhere on foot.

There was a low-relief symbol on the door: an ear of corn packed with kernels. On an average day, most of String City's maize supply was stacked in this pyramid. Time was the grain was guarded by a dread serpent with gleaming metal wings. These days, Quetzal Imports made do with CCTV.

The corn kernels were painted gold, except for the outer ring which was picked out in copper. I counted the copper kernels: there were twenty-four of them. When I tapped one, it depressed: a button. The gold kernels were all fixed in place. Interesting. It struck me the corn stalk looked a bit like a handle. I tapped a few more of the copper kernels at random, and pulled the stalk.

There was a dull clunk, then all the buttons popped back out again. A cheerful automated voice said:

"Failure. You have three attempts remaining."

The ring of copper kernels was a keypad. All I needed was the code. I waited, fearing my failed attempt might have triggered an alarm. Nothing came running.

The crane swung overhead. I watched as it carried more crates into the pyramid. Through a break in the fog, I spotted the big Quetzal Imports logo painted on the side of the crane's control booth: a giant golden feather. The feather was patterned—spotted, actually. I counted twenty-four copperey spots arranged in a ring. Nine of them had a tiny black dot in the middle.

Surely it couldn't be that simple.

I punched the nine copper kernels corresponding to the pattern on the feather. I held my breath and pulled the handle.

"Failure. You have two attempts remaining."

The buttons popped out again. I looked harder at the feather painted on the crane, let out a curse. I'd got the pattern wrong by a single button. I pushed the kernels again, double-checked. When I was convinced it was right, I tried the handle again.

"Failure. You have one attempt remaining."

It figured. What corporation would display a security access code in its logo? It was a tease, probably intended to make schmucks like me punch in the wrong code and set off the alarms. I was back at the start with just one chance left.

I released the handle, and saw that the end of it was shaped to look like a dragon—the dread serpent Quetzalcoatl, to be exact. Once upon a time, Quetzalcoatl had been the guardian of the dawn. Must have been quite a sight, those big gold wings popping up over the horizon every morning. One hell of an alarm clock. Then Ra and Apollo had muscled in with a time-share operation. Unable to compete, Quetzalcoatl had given up on light-bringing and gone into the import/export business: mostly cheap stationery, diaries, calendars, that kind of thing.

I held the thought. Back in the distant past, before Quetzalcoatl had hit on the old wings-over-the-horizon trick, there had been no day, no night. Time had just oozed along in an indeterminate river of sludge. Quetzalcoatl had brought order to chaos, inventing routine. Inventing the twenty-four hour day.

I counted the buttons that ringed the keypad again. Twenty-four.

"Midnight," I muttered, stroking the button at the top of the circle. I moved my finger to the bottom. "Midday."

That morning, with winter fast approaching, the sun had risen over String City just a whisker after six. I counted six kernels round the ring and pushed the button. Just one button. The time of today's dawn.

I gripped the corn-stalk handle. Steeling myself for the alarm. I pulled the handle.

"Thank you," said the automated voice, with just a hint of disappointment.

The door hissed open.

34

THE PYRAMID INTERIOR was hot and dank. I snuck down corridors, following my nose. That black goo was everywhere, pooling in the cracks where walls met floor. The deeper I got, the worse the stench became.

Whenever I reached a fork I turned left. Most architects are right-handed. They put all the stuff they want you to see on what they think of as the good side. Everything else—air-con and plant rooms and garbage chutes, all the secret spaces—they park on the left. Trust me, if you want to get under the skin of a building, make yourself a southpaw.

I passed a garbage chute and the stench got worse. The corridor narrowed, darkened, got grimy. Then I hit a ramp that took me up toward a shaft of light. I stepped out on to a catwalk. Steel mesh flexed under my boots; smoke bit my eyes. I looked out and down, into the heart of the pyramid.

The first thing I thought was that I'd flipped into the dimensions without meaning to. There was string everywhere, all stretched and knotted and braided, a thousand cats-cradles trying to do the Peppermint Twist in a triangular hangar big enough to hold two dozen thunderbirds. The catwalk I was standing on hung halfway up the wall. Above me, the pyramid's stepped sides converged to a point, hung all the way with platforms and bridges of string and all manner of cradles and ziplines, the kind of adventure playground that nightmares are made of.

Then I blinked and saw it wasn't string; it was silk. I wasn't in the dimensions. I was in the biggest spider's web this world had seen. Any world, for that matter. I suddenly knew what the black goo was.

Ichor.

I shouldn't have been surprised. Everyone knew who lived on the wharf: Arachne, the spider queen. She'd retreated here after besting her old rival Pallas Athene in a street brawl. Their feud went way back, and it was me who'd brought them together to finish it. Under duress. It had been quite a sight, watching a giant spider beat seven bells out of a goddess who wore a Gorgon on her chest.

Soon after Arachne had holed up on the wharf, she'd started making babies. Word was the father was a tarantula who came in on one of the last banana boats from the Unknown Worlds. She'd had her way with the poor eight-legged sap, eaten him, got on with the business of laying eggs and never stopped. When her children reached the millions, the Thanes built the perimeter fence and put the whole dockside into quarantine. Everyone knew Arachne wanted to rule the cosmos. No sense making it easy for her.

Arachne's web filled the lower half of the pyramid like cotton candy. It seemed like there was more silk down there than air. But the silk was sheer; you could see right through it. Clinging to an enormous knot in the middle of the web was Arachne herself. She was really just a giant spider but she'd worked some kind of charm, faking up parts of her body to look like a woman's. Some of it was halfway to being convincing, but mostly she resembled a butchery victim recovering from a road traffic accident.

Behind her, slung upside-down in a hammock of silk, was the corpse of Pallas Athene. The goddess was a giant, ten times the size of a normal woman, and someone had embedded a fire hydrant in her neck. Beneath the spout was a pool of faintly glowing liquid—ambrosia. Why would someone want to drain a goddess of blood when she was already dead?

Cocooned in the shadows beneath Pallas Athene, tiny in comparison to the dead goddess and the spider queen, was Zephyr.

Covering the floor were millions of spider eggs.

Swarming on the web were millions of baby spiders.

I backed into a shadow. Zephyr was alive—I could see her cocoon moving as she breathed. Unconscious though. Why hadn't Arachne eaten her already? More urgently, how I was going to get her out? I wouldn't get ten yards across the web without the spiderlings taking me down. Again I considered a dimension-hop. But I could sense that Arachne's silk was messing with the local cosmic geometry. Well, she did used to be a spinner of worlds.

I made inventory of the weapons I'd picked up from the filing cabinet: the Colt, also an abseil pistol and a pocket flamethrower. I guess I'd had some crazy notion of swinging off a ceiling, torching everything in my path—the whole hero bit. Now I was here I could see that was a bust. If I started spraying fire the whole web would go up like knitted kindling. The resulting flames would light the fuse on several million angry spiders.

Something was happening down on the floor. A battalion of spiderlings was making its way toward the pyramid's far corner. Perched on her knot of silk, Arachne turned to watch. A door opened, throwing pale light up one wall. The light glanced off a ledge directly opposite the spot where I was crouched. Leading from the ledge was a short passage, beyond which I could just make out a second chamber. It was dark and full of big square shapes: the stacked crates from the container ship.

I turned my attention back to the door. Someone was walking in.

The spiderlings swarmed around the intruder. They scrabbled under his feet, lifted him up and swept him up the web to Arachne's lair. I recognised him at once.

It was Kweku Sunyana.

35

SUNYANA WAS TALL—taller than me. Still he was dwarfed by Arachne. He didn't seem scared though. When the spiders dropped him at their queen's many feet, his face broke into a smile as wide as the Styx. He was sporting teeth different to the ones I'd seen through the window of his office. Still made of iron but bigger, sharper. Serrated.

Arachne leaned her crude woman's torso over her swollen spider's abdomen. She blinked a few eyes. She had a mouth, mostly human. When she spoke, it didn't move an inch.

You are wondering why I have called you back to my palace, she said. Her words seemed to come from everywhere. They made the web hum like a tuning fork.

"Always a pleasure to be in your company, Arachne." Sunyana sounded suave and confident, but I could see he was seething underneath. His long fingers kept clenching and unclenching. When he spoke, his teeth moved with a life of their own.

You are a magnificent liar, said Arachne. *Nevertheless, you are wondering.*

"I am curious, I'll admit," said Sunyana. "Last night you made it quite clear you didn't need my services any more."

Do I detect a note of resentment?

"Not at all. I'm just sad we'll no longer be doing business together. We made a great team."

Arachne threw back her head and laughed. Her voice bounced round the web, triggering laughter from her children. Soon the whole pyramid was filled with cackling spiders. Then, as abruptly as she'd started, Arachne stopped. Silence gripped the web.

We were useful to each other, for a space of time. Now that time is over.

"It doesn't have to be," said Sunyana. "I've had some ideas."

Arachne folded her arms across her chest. Arms and chest were mostly human, provided you ignored the broom-bristle hairs. She smiled, revealing big black teeth made of chitin. I wondered if she and Sunyana shared a dentist.

I have a keen appreciation of ideas, she said. *Tell me yours.*

As Sunyana spoke, I understood what was bubbling under his

suave exterior. It was desperation. "Look, Arachne. A year ago you agreed to supply me with all the raw meat I needed to keep my factories running. When I came to you, the city livestock business was in bad shape. Last month it collapsed completely. Every last cow carcass has been stripped to the bone. The poultry farms can't scratch a living any more. Mad-tail has decimated the swine herds. I'm the only trader left with stocks in his freezers. If the people of String City want meat, they have to come to me. But I'm down to just one supplier: you."

A sorry tale. Tell me, does the population know what it is really eating?

"Are you kidding? All the meat I get from you I process—and I mean, *process*. I don't do steaks or chops or joints any more, just hamburger and sausage, reconstituted loaf. Anything to disguise what it's actually made of."

One might take offense at such a statement.

"I don't mean to be rude, Arachne, but if I told people the entire city had been eating spider meat for the past three months, there'd be a riot. Or worse."

There is such narrowmindedness in the world. They should be grateful for my generosity.

My stomach flipped. I'd picked up a Sunyana burger from a kiosk on the way over. Wolfed it down. Now I knew what was in me, I wanted it out again. Worst of it was, it had tasted good.

Ignoring my rising gorge, I thought it through. Spider meat! For Sunyana it made a sick kind of sense. I wondered what was in it for Arachne.

"So please," Sunyana was saying, "can we renegotiate? I know I'd have to reduce the order, but it's just that... Arachne, the city will starve."

You overstate your case, Arachne replied, *and thus betray your true fear. Let your precious city eat cake. What really concerns you is loss of trade. The collapse of your business empire.* She leered, tarry ichor drooling from the corner of her mouth. *Bringing shame upon your family.*

Sunyana sank to his knees. "Please. I'm begging you. I've never let you down. Surely my loyalty has earned some reward?"

Loyalty is not the issue, only the simple law of supply and demand. For a full year now I have been preparing my spider troops for the invasion of String City. In all that time my frankly remarkable fecundity has meant that my army has been growing faster than I can contain it. Therefore I have required what you might call a "safety valve". This is how I have been able to supply you with all the spiders you have needed to keep your meat processing plants running at full capacity. As my children have grown, so I have made regular culls in order to save the majority from the threat of overpopulation.

Now the day of the invasion is close, caution is no longer part of my strategy. On the contrary, I need all the spiders I can spawn. Therefore, I no longer need you.

The burger was doing more than just turn in my gut. Now it was trying to climb up through my throat. It was one thing to know—like everyone knew—that Arachne wanted the city. To hear her say it out loud was something else.

As for learning the invasion could happen tomorrow... that was enough to stop your day in its tracks.

Sunyana felt it too. His black skin went grey; his iron teeth crashed like surf.

Arachne went on.

However, in one respect you are right, Kweku Sunyana. You have *earned a reward. This is the reason I invited you back to my palace this morning. I regret I may have dismissed you somewhat sharply last night. Today I wish to make amends.*

"I don't understand," said Sunyana. In a flash he'd switched from despair through suspicion and all the way to calculation. I wondered who I'd trust least with my mother's ashes: the asansa butcher or the spider queen. It was a tough call. "What kind of reward?"

An opportunity to indulge an urge your wife prefers you to suppress. I have a gift for you, Kweku. Behold!

On cue, a team of spiderlings opened a skylight. A fog-wracked sunbeam refracted through the web, illuminated the spot where Zephyr was cocooned. The light hit her face, made her screw up her nose. She came round, opened her eyes, saw where she was.

Kweku Sunyana swiveled awkwardly toward her, his movements weirdly like those of a puppet. Swiftly he advanced, metal teeth clacking like a bear trap. He looked out of control, as if his body was doing all the things his mind didn't want it to.

Zephyr began to scream.

36

I GRABBED A strand of the web, tested it with my weight. The silk sang like a violin. There were words inside the song, barely audible.

... glory... girl...

The music drilled into my teeth. I snatched my hand away and saw the palm was laced with tiny cuts—the silk was full of splinters, like grated glass. If I tried to traverse it, Arachne's web would cut me to ribbons.

Words in the web? No time to dwell on it now. Instead I traced the route of the catwalk. It ran all the way round the inside of the pyramid to a point directly above the chamber entrance, right beside the upside-down corpse of Pallas Athene.

Immediately over the spot where Zephyr was lying.

Not stopping to think, I ran. The catwalk's metal mesh bounced and rattled, but the spiderlings were too busy enjoying the floor show to notice me up there. As I neared the upturned goddess, I primed the abseil pistol and fired it into Pallas Athene's right heel. The piton bit deep, the cable snapped taut and I threw myself off the catwalk, swinging out wide and slamming back against the goddess's tree-trunk thigh. I let out the line, jouncing off Pallas Athene's hips, off the broken shield that concealed the decaying wounds in her chest, off her throat, off her lifeless face. Snarled up in the lank forest of her hair, I finally ran out of cable.

Below me, Sunyana was bending over Zephyr and using his iron gnashers to snip away the cocoon. Shrugging off her weak punches, he scooped her up, held her tight to his chest. His eyes had rolled over white like a shark's. A whole new set of teeth thrust forward from his jaw, buzzing like ripsaws.

I let go of the abseil cable, slithered down through the goddess's greasy tresses. I steeled myself for a twenty foot fall to the floor.

His teeth inches from Zephyr's neck, Sunyana stopped. There was a commotion near the door. Spiderlings were rushing to intercept someone who'd sneaked in unnoticed. They surrounded the interloper. Sunyana turned to look. His hideous jaw dropped wide.

I guessed the last person he'd been expecting to see was his wife.

"What are you doing here?" Kweku Sunyana demanded. The buzzsaw teeth didn't do much for his diction. "How did you find me?"

"I hired someone," Kisi replied. She shot me a single glance. "You think I didn't see your notebook, gumshoe?"

"This isn't what it looks like," moaned Sunyana. His teeth

jittered, like they were trying to say something different to the rest of his mouth. His body twitched, drawn by his compulsion to feast.

"Oh, I rather think it is," said Kisi. The spiderlings clustered round her legs.

Climbing down from her knot of silk, Arachne lumbered across the web toward where Kweku Sunyana stood.

This is an unexpected entertainment, she said. *However, it is unwanted. I will not be interrupted in my own domain. My children: the intruder is yours to do with as you please.*

Instantly the spiderlings swarmed up Kisi's legs. She tossed me a weird look—something between plaintive and furious. Directly below me, Kweku groaned and jerkily lowered his teeth to Zephyr's neck again. Then, suddenly, the spiderlings were flying through the air. When they landed they were all curled up. Dead. I remembered Kisi mentioning something about martial arts.

Arms and legs flailing, Kisi Sunyana drilled like a dervish through Arachne's front guard. Dead spiders started backing up, making a dam that prevented the others from rushing in. I wondered how Arachne thought her invasion plan could succeed, if one woman could cut such a swathe through her soldiers. Then I saw the millions swarming down the web to avenge their siblings. Arachne would win this battle by maths alone. Not to mention any war she cared to wage.

As a side order, Kisi was doomed.

But not just yet. Using her limbs like scythes, she slashed through the sea of spiders all the way to her husband's side. A second before Kweku's teeth opened Zephyr's carotid artery, Kisi shoved him backward into a wall of silk. Then she grabbed Zephyr and threw her to the floor. Free of the cocoon, Zephyr came up fighting. Kisi kicked out, caught Zephyr on the side of the head. Zephyr went down again, hard. Kisi reached behind her back, unsheathing the katana I'd totally failed to spot. The samurai sword spun in her hand, stopped with its point against Zephyr's breastbone. Zephyr froze.

Kisi glared at her husband, who was struggling to free himself from the sticky web.

"I'll start with your lover," she said. "And I'll finish with you."

She drew the katana back.

I let go of the goddess's hair.

I fell in slow motion, watching the katana circle back, hold, swing forward, round, down... and then the laws of physics finally crashed me on to Kisi's back.

For a horrible second I thought the impact had driven the blade right into Zephyr's chest. Then I rolled sideways and saw that Zephyr was rolling too. The sword bounced on the floor. So did Kisi.

She came up screeching. Her human mouth poured out more venom than ever came from a spider's. She ran at me, stopping with her face inches from mine. Her fists were clenched; hell, by the look of her, everything was clenched.

"You're good with the truth, gumshoe, I'll give you that," she snarled. "Just not so good with secrets."

"Truth's not what you think it is," I said. "Your husband's been faithful. More than I can say for you."

"Then who is she?" She snapped out her hand and grabbed Zephyr round the throat. Her face contorted with rage.

"She's with me," I replied. I drew back my fist and delivered an uppercut that closed Kisi's mouth with a crack. I felt bad about doing it, but I figured it was either her or Zephyr. When I thought of it like that, turned out there was no contest.

Kisi's rage turned to abject surprise. She teetered and let

Zephyr go. Arachne dropped down from the web behind her. Kisi fell right into the spider queen's clutches.

I was of the understanding that you and I had struck a bargain, gumshoe, Arachne said. As she spoke to me, her spinnerets squirted silk cords round Kisi's neck. *After our last encounter, you told me that you never wanted to see me again.*

"Want doesn't always get," I said.

How true. However, in my case, it usually does.

Arachne opened her mouth wide. Huge mandibles scrambled up and out of her throat. Human arms and spider legs lifted Kisi off her feet. Kisi screamed right up to the moment Arachne bit off her head. After that, she just hosed out blood. Arachne crunched her and swallowed her. A few seconds later she spat out a long ribbon of yellow fabric, splashed with red.

I never eat silk, she said. *That would be just too peculiar.*

Meanwhile, Kweku Sunyana had freed himself from the web. He made a lunge for Arachne, yelling incoherently. I thought Arachne would kill him too, or at least fend him off. But she didn't. Instead she spread her arms wide, retracted her mandibles and bared her pale human throat.

It is about time, she said, and allowed Kweku Sunyana to sink his iron shark's teeth deep into her neck.

The asansa are known for subtlety and seduction. They like the finer things in life, and pride themselves on being able to suppress their hunger. What happened next was neither fine nor seductive. It was butchery and greed, pure and simple. Within two seconds, Arachne's throat looked like raw hamburger and Kweku Sunyana was fleeing for the door with mad eyes and black ichor dripping from his jaws.

I was tempted to just stand and watch. Some sights just grip you, you know? Instead I edged around the shuddering Arachne to where Zephyr stood, dazed. Her jeans were torn and her face was streaked with spider blood.

"You came after me," she said.

I thought about all the things I wanted to say. Mostly I wanted to shake her until all the bones rattled in her scrawny body.

"Save it for later," I said.

"I'm sorry. I guess I've got a lot to learn."

"Every day's a school day."

The spiderlings were frozen. Like us, they couldn't take their eyes off Arachne. All those spiders—that's a lot of eyes.

"We've got to get out of here," said Zephyr.

Easier said than done. Between us and the door was a wall of spiders. The goddess's hair was way out of reach. There were no trapdoors, no hidden exits.

Arachne swiveled in our direction. Incredibly, she was grinning. Her face was covered in bits of Kisi.

I knew if I asked him back he would bring his favorite teeth! The holes in her windpipe laced her voice with toots and whistles. *I also knew he would be angry with me for terminating our contract, that he would be ready to lash out. Therefore he would come prepared. The arrival of your little friend here just made it easier for me to set my trap.*

"You *wanted* him to bite you?" I said. "Why?"

You saw how easily his woman cut down my children. They are many, but they are weak. Nobody likes a spider, but everybody is ready to step on one. So I needed to advance their evolution.

"That doesn't make sense," said Zephyr. "How does killing you make them stronger?"

Arachne didn't reply. Her body was jerking. Her feet rattled on the ground.

The holes in her throat started closing up. The human parts of her jumbled up with the spider parts. She healed. She merged.

She *blended.*

Her teeth *grew.*

In spasms, Arachne's legs curled up underneath her. They stopped, jerked a little longer, became still. Her body looked clean and restored. But it was utterly still. Was she dead?

Too much to hope for. Her legs uncurled, one by one, spider-perfect. Her torso was lithe and fully human at last; her face was gaunt and gorgeous. She had the mouth of a great white shark and eyes like diamond dinner plates. She was far more than what she'd been, but there was no word for what she'd become.

Except there was. It tickled the back of my mind, an ancient name from long before the dawn...

One by one, Arachne's eight legs reached out, each touching a different strand of the web. The web hummed. The spiderlings tried to run but the web had got sticky—really sticky. The humming coursed through them. Arachne's spider army rang like cathedral bells. And all the little spiders grew sharks' teeth also. Every last one of them.

"Anansi-asansa," I murmured.

"What?" said Zephyr.

"It's what she is. What all of them are now turning into."

"Anansi-asansa? It's quite a mouthful."

"So will we be, if we don't get the hell out of here."

Arachne's babies opened their altered eyes and fixed on their prey.

Time to jump the dimensions. I had no choice. It was fifty-fifty I'd survive the journey. With Zephyr on board the odds were a lot worse.

I gathered her to me. "Hold tight."

Something slapped my face: a length of rope. The end of the rope was looped. I looked up, saw a shining bronzed face staring down at me from the open skylight.

A voice like an old-time radio broadcast said, "Please insert your feet into the loop and hold tight."

"Who the hell is that?" said Zephyr.

37

I DON'T KNOW how the Scrutator hauled us up so quick. Maybe it had a winch in its belly; robots pack all kinds of hardware. All I know is five seconds later we were standing outside on one of the highest steps of the pyramid. The air was clear, the sun bright. We were above the fog.

"The spiders are coming!" said Zephyr.

I peered down through the skylight we'd just scrambled out of. Several million ravening anansi-asansa spiders were climbing toward us. The web whined like all the string sections in the cosmos mashed up together, each playing slightly out of key. The sound set off nasty harmonics and I heard those words again: *girl... glory*. The whole pyramid started to boogie.

"I will deal with them." said the Scrutator.

The robot unlatched its right hand. A welding gun slid from its wrist. I turned away just as an arc of dazzling blue light fused the skylight shut.

I found myself staring straight down the side of the pyramid. The huge steps descended in a series of vertiginous drops; jump just one of them and we'd break our necks. Below was a rolling bank of grey vapor, thick as molasses. There were no ladders, no ropes, nothing to help us descend.

"Shame there's nowhere to go from here," I said as the Scrutator stowed its welding torch. "Still, thanks. For the rescue."

"I had decided to pursue my own investigation into the pyramid," said the Scrutator. "However, it soon became apparent that you and your assistant were already here and in perilous circumstances. Immediate extraction was a requirement."

"Why bother? I mean, why the heroics? I thought your programming was all about the truth and nothing but."

The Scrutator froze. For a minute I thought it had shut down. Then the gears in its head started whirring again, this time real fast. Behind the fretwork in its cheeks, ratchets caught on pinions, capacitors discharged with great crackles of fire, belts spun so fast they started to smoke. A high pitched whine rose in its chest. I wanted to back off, but the only way was down.

The Scrutator cocked its head like a big bronzed bird. The whining stopped; the gears wound down.

"I believe I must have rescued you because it was... the right thing to do. This is... interesting. I calculate that there may be something beyond truth. However, I do not know its name."

I slapped its mechanical shoulder. "Buddy," I said, "welcome to something that resembles the real world."

"I hate to butt in," said Zephyr, "but we're in trouble."

Above us, near the apex of the pyramid, a ventilation grille flew open with a bang. Spiders boiled out of the exposed duct like black lava and poured down the steps toward us. At the same time, the crane loomed up out of the fog; a gang of spiderlings had hijacked the control booth. The crane swung its load of crates at us, a squared-off demolition ball aimed to scrape us off the side of the pyramid. We ducked. The crates missed the back of the Scrutator's neck by six inches, reached the end of their arc, swooped back again and smashed into the crane's supporting tower. The crates disintegrated, shedding vast clouds of tiny black granules into the fog. The stench was appalling.

"Ugh," said Zephyr, holding her nose. "What *is* that stuff?"

"Dead flies," said the Scrutator. "Rations for Arachne's spider invasion force."

"*MUSCAE MORTUUS*," I said. "Remind me to brush up on my Latin."

The sea of fog boiled with black shapes. For a second I thought maybe the flies were zombies, coming to eat us alive. But there were no more zombies in String City. It was yet another battalion of horribly mutated spiders, climbing up from below to intercept us. We were cut off.

"Did you bring your vehicle?" I said to the Scrutator.

"Yes," the robot said. "My automobile is legally parked on a meter at the perimeter of the wharf zone, and is not therefore within easy reach. I have no further contribution to make to this escape."

"Sweet," I said.

"There's only one thing left," said Zephyr. She seized my arm. "You're the only one who can get us out of here. Fold us up. Do your dimension thing! Hurry!"

I hesitated. Spiders above, spiders below. Chances were they wouldn't kill us right away, just cocoon us and take us to Arachne. I tried to imagine what kind of torture would amuse a psychotic flesh-eating spider queen. The bad kind, I decided.

Zephyr's eyes implored me. They were black with fatigue and mascara. She looked at me with an absolute trust I'd never seen in anyone before. Not even in Laura.

"I can't carry the robot too," I said at last. "The way the strings are right now, they'd earth on its metal chassis. We'd all get superconducted."

The Scrutator seemed about to protest. I waved it silent: there was no way I was leaving it behind. I reached in my pocket and brought out the Dimension Die. Two of its sides were white, four dark. Four rolls left. Four more narrow escapes at my fingertips.

The spiders were close enough to see the blacks of their eyes.

"I can't keep doing this," I said. "There'll be a price."

"We'll pay it!" said Zephyr.

"That's what I'm afraid of."

"I am willing to make an appropriate contribution to any fee that might be levied," said the Scrutator.

I tightened my hand on the die. "Put your arms round me." My companions obeyed. Zephyr looked at me with that same terminal trust.

"Wait," said the Scrutator. It raised a finger, cocked its head. "Do you hear that?"

"What?" I said, exasperated.

The robot held its pose for a second, then relaxed. "It is of no consequence. I believe the time has come for us to depart."

"No kidding!"

I rolled the die across the surface of the pyramid step. It bounced, spun, came down white side up. The white snapped to black, and the black ate us up.

38

The Dimension Die works by sucking on your intentions. You could say it's a little like a vampire, only instead of blood it draws subconscious thoughts. Oftentimes it fixates on desires, which is why it works so well as an escape hatch: the place you really want to be is usually somewhere safe. Especially when there's a spider army at your back.

But your subconscious doesn't just contain desires. There's other stuff down there too. Stuff like dreams and secrets and unspoken guilt.

Stuff like hunches.

If it had just been down to desire, the die would have

transported us back to my office. Instead we landed in the middle of a busy street. A klaxon blared—an omnibus was bearing down on us. Its eight mechanical legs were too much like a spider's for my liking.

I grabbed Zephyr and the Scrutator, hustled them on to the sidewalk a second before the omnibus turned us into groundmeal. Passers-by gave us a wide berth, but no special attention. In a city like this, you get used to strangers materialising at random.

"Where are we?" said Zephyr.

"It would appear that we have performed a translatative interbrane manoeuvre," said the Scrutator, "resulting in our emergence on to the Street of Plenty in String City's central financial district."

Zephyr looked up the street, down the street, at me. "It looks safe enough to me. But why did we end up here?"

"Search me," I replied. My feet were aching; my hands stung from where the web had slashed me. All I wanted was coffee and bourbon, preferably at the same time. Plus a chance to empty out my pounding head.

"Why didn't you flip us back to the office?"

"Does it matter?"

"Don't get snappy."

"I'm not snappy!"

"What's wrong?"

I rounded on her. "In case you hadn't noticed, I almost got minced by one of my least favorite spiders, and all because you thought you wanted to play detective. A woman died, and we only got out because a goddam machine fancied itself as a hero—no offense, Scrutator..."

"None has been taken," said the Scrutator.

"... and to cap it all I've wasted another roll of the die."

"'Wasted'?" said Zephyr, folding her arms. She was getting

cross too. I was too worked up to care.

"The die's a cheat. A cheap trick. It's not something you can keep on doing, over and over again—it's too convenient. The debt mounts up, and sooner or later it's got to be cleared."

"We're alive. That's all I care about."

"As if all that's not enough, I end up here, in a street full of banks and business exchanges, right across the street from the Birdhouse—which happens to be where I spent one of the most miserable days of my life—instead of back in my office where the chairs are soft and the liquor's hard. You want more?"

"What's the Birdhouse? What do you mean, 'miserable'?"

"I don't want to discuss it."

"Is it some kind of aviary?"

The Scrutator was pointing. "Miss, please direct your attention to the small building resembling a bunker situated in the center of that otherwise empty lot. That is the entrance to the Birdhouse, which is the popular name for String City's largest underground security facility."

"That's enough!" I said. "It's time to go."

"So what happened to you in there?" said Zephyr.

I was already walking away. I set a blinding pace and didn't care if neither of them kept up. I held my mouth shut the rest of the walk back to the office. It was a long walk.

At the door, I turned on Zephyr.

"You got any stuff inside?" I said.

"A few things. Why?"

"Get it and go."

"What?"

"You're fired."

"*What?*"

"You heard me."

"But why?"

"I haven't given you enough reasons? Try this: because of you, my client got killed."

"Kisi Sunyana was just using you. I saw..."

"I know what she was doing. Doesn't mean she deserved to die."

"I know, but..."

"Also, it means I don't get paid."

"If I may propose a counter-argument," said the Scrutator. "Regardless of the present condition of your client, the truth has been established. The case has been solved."

"Didn't you hear me the first time?" I said. "There's more things to life than just the truth."

"You would be surprised by the things I am able to hear. And yes, I am prepared to believe that your statement about truth may be correct. However, I also believe that you are not always right."

My head ached. I rubbed it. It went on aching. "You want to explain that?"

"You have chosen to relieve yourself of the services of your assistant. This is a mistake. It is also... beneath you."

The robot had started shaking. Its clockwork whined like a scramjet. I thought its gears were going to blow out of its face. Exhausted as I was, I was fascinated.

"Go away," I said. "Both of you. Just go away and leave me alone."

"I'm sorry," said Zephyr. She tried to take my hand. I snatched it away, but she grabbed it and held on. "Look—I was angry, okay? When you wouldn't let me work on the case, it made me feel like I was invisible, like you refused to see me for who I was. So I decided to ... I don't know—"

"Prove yourself?"

"Yes! And I was wrong, it all went wrong and... but the

Scrutator's right, we *did* get to the truth. Isn't that what this job's all about? A case like this, maybe it was always going to end in a mess. At least we got out alive, all three of us. And maybe Kisi Sunyana got no more than she deserved." She stopped, bit her lip.

The sky picked that moment to throw us some rain. The fretwork on the Scrutator's face closed up. Zephyr stood there waiting for me to open the door, getting wetter and wetter until she looked just as bedraggled as she had the first time we'd met.

I put the key in the latch, turned it.

"You'd better come in, before you catch your death." I looked at the robot. "You too, else you'll rust."

"I am robustly proofed against all forms of oxidisation," said the Scrutator proudly.

We all went inside.

39

"The Birdhouse is where they keep something very special," I said. My coat was off, my feet were on the desk. There was bourbon in the glass and the glass was in my hand. "It's a vault, like the Scrutator said. I got wrapped up in a case there once, fell in love, fought some zombies, got trapped in a labyrinth with a monster as big as a moon."

"Just a regular day in String City?" said Zephyr. She was reclined on the couch, head propped on her hand, steaming as she dried. The Scrutator was ticking quietly on the other side of the room.

"Funny girl. After all that, I faced an even worse monster and lost my best friend and escaped. It's a long story—maybe I'll tell it you sometime."

"You won't get the chance. You fired me, remember?"

"Case like that," I went on, "you never forget it. The memory works in you like a splinter, never gives up. It grows. You get to thinking it's more important than it really is—the most important thing ever, maybe. But it's only a memory."

Zephyr stared at me through her weeping mascara. "That's not really what you think, is it?"

"I guess not. When we turned up at the Birdhouse just now my first thought was, 'Hey, that's a coincidence'. I told myself some cosmic thorn must have snagged us as we flew past and just dumped us there. Chance in a million. Only that can't be right. Because there was something else."

"What?"

I gulped down the bourbon. My hand was shaking. "That first time at the Birdhouse, I met a hooded man, only he wasn't really a man. He was a Fool."

"You mean like an idiot?"

"No, I don't mean that at all. I'll tell you all about Fools another day, but here's the thing: the day the casino blew up, I saw a hooded man outside my office. And the cyclops, Steropes, said he saw one too. Factor all that in, it's too much to be coincidence. So, I got to thinking there was some other reason we'd ended up back at the Birdhouse today. Something like, oh, I don't know..."

"What?"

"Fate," I said quietly.

"Is there such a thing?"

"Depends on the weather. Anyhow, 'fate' isn't quite right either. I think the Dimension Die found something in my head and used it to redirect us."

"What do you think it found?"

"A hunch. Biggest hunch I ever had. One that's been creeping up on me these past weeks. It must have been waiting until I was wide open just now, flying between the branes out of the jaws of death, just waiting so it could drop me in the middle of exactly where I needed to be."

"The banking district?"

"Yes. No." I rubbed my face. I wanted to sleep. "Hell, I don't know. I feel I should understand, but I don't. I feel it, but I can't explain it. You know when you wake up from a dream, only the dream's gone? Or you see someone you know and can't remember their name..."

"... but it's on the tip of your tongue?"

"Right. All I know is, something's brewing, and it ain't coffee."

"If I may correct you," said the Scrutator, "The coffee has in fact brewed. Would you like me to pour you a cup?"

"Why not?" I stretched the ache out of my arms. The day was a country mile from over—I needed something to keep me awake.

The Scrutator brought us both paper cups, stood back to watch us drink.

"Hey," said Zephyr, "That's not half bad."

"Where'd you learn to make coffee like that?" I said. It was more than just good: it was the best coffee I'd ever tasted.

"I have never performed the operation before," said the Scrutator, "but it would appear to be a straightforward chemical process. I trust I have combined the ingredients in a satisfactory way?"

"I'll say!" said Zephyr. "Pour me another, Bronzey. Hey, do you actually have a name? There's a lot of you guys, right? You can't all be called 'Scrutator'."

"My given name is pronounceable only in machine code. 'Bronzey' is a satisfactory alternative."

"Okay—Bronzey it is. What do you think, boss?"

"I think you should ask the robot why it's rifling through your filing cabinet," I replied.

"Forgive me," said the Scrutator. "Efficient as your system of record-keeping appears to be, I have taken the liberty of punching code-slots in the corners of your paperwork."

"Code-slots?" said Zephyr.

"The slots will enable me to read, index and cross-refer any report against any other report in a matter of seconds. It will greatly improve the speed at which your business can process information."

"Provided I keep you around to scan the slots?" I said.

"The presence of a Scrutator will allow the system to operate at maximum efficiency."

I finished my coffee. Damn, it was good!

"What do you think, Zephyr?" I said. "You're the one who set the system up. Are you ready to hand it over to a machine?"

She shrugged. "Since you fired me, you'll be wanting someone else to do your filing."

"Right," I said. "Scrutator—you're hired."

"Thank you, sir," said the Scrutator. "I am glad to be relieved of the responsibility of running my own business. It was an interesting experience, but not one for which I am well adapted. I am first and foremost a public servant."

"Well, I ain't the public, and you ain't my servant. You'll get a fair wage and a share of the profit. If we make any."

Zephyr stood up, smoothed out her damp clothes. "I'll be off," she said. "Good luck, Bronzey. I think you're going to need it."

"Hold up," I said as she opened the door. "Where are you going?"

"Back to my apartment," she said. "I'll collect my things, move on. Without a job I won't make the rent at the end of the month. As landlords go, Tony Marscapone's a good sort but he won't let me live there for nothing."

"I know," I said. "So I'll say it again: where are you going?"

She stood in the doorway. The rain gusted in, soaking her all over again. Her face made a quizzical shape. "What are you talking about?"

I picked a case folder off the desk.

"Got an interesting one here. Someone's hawking pirate movies out of Harry's Holodeon. Harry reckons it's the projectionist. Sounds open and shut. A great case to cut your teeth on."

"Cut my... you mean I'm not fired after all?"

"Sounds like."

The quizzical look turned to fireworks. Any last doubt I was doing the right thing went away as she turned on the sparkiest smile you ever saw. She threw herself across the desk, wrapped her arms round my neck, planted a hot, damp kiss full on my lips.

"Thank you! Oh, thank you! I won't let you down, I promise! I really won't!"

"Okay, doll," I said. "You convinced me. You want to stop dripping on the paperwork?"

She climbed down, still popping that grin, then kissed the Scrutator on the cheek. Its gears revved; it smoked a little.

"You know something?" she said with her arm draped around the robot's neck. "I think we're going to make one hell of a team!"

The Last Dance

40

THE CASE OF the movie pirate looked like a great way for Zephyr to properly learn the ropes. Plus I'd get to show her the Hot Hub. The girl had been with me over a week, but she was still a stranger in town. Time for a little orientation. You want to learn what makes a town tick—*really* tick—you need to see how the residents let off steam. You want steam in String City, hit the Hot Hub.

"So, how far is it?" said Zephyr.

I'd rigged the Feynman globe to project a map of the city on the wall. I traced the route with my finger.

"Some miles," I said. "We could take a cab, but it eats into the overhead."

"What about the dimensions?"

"Still a no-go."

I'd hoped the storm in the strings would blow itself out. But every time I dipped my head into the dimensions I just saw it getting worse. I hadn't realised how much I'd relied on stringwalking as a way of getting around. Like the man said, you don't miss it 'til it's gone.

"Then we'll have to walk," said Zephyr.

"Guess we got no choice."

"There's always that dice thing."

"Strictly emergency use only. I told you that."

"I don't know why you make such a big deal about walking. I thought being a gumshoe was all about pounding the streets. If you ask me, all that folding yourself in and out of the cosmic string or whatever it is—all that hopping across the dimensions in the blink of an eye—I think it's made you lazy."

"More to it than blinking an eye, honey."

"Don't be pedantic. You know what I mean."

I stared morosely at the map. "It sure is a long way."

"Then we'd better make a start."

The Scrutator looked up from its desk. The movement made me jump. After ten years solo I suddenly had two assistants and it took some getting used to. The office felt crowded: three desks instead of one; two filing cabinets—one even had files in it, alphabetised and everything. There was barely room for the couch.

"If I might interject, sir," said the Scrutator. "Only this morning I retrieved my automobile from its parking place near the wharf. It is currently garaged at the Marscapone building at the other end of this very street. If you wish me to, I will recalibrate the vehicle's insurance status to enable its use as a company vehicle."

"You'll drive us?" I said.

"You have divined my intention with admirable ease, sir," said the Scrutator. "I will be ready to undertake the mission in approximately eleven point eight three minutes."

It stood up, a tall bronzed machine in the mould of a man. The night before I'd found a can of wax in the cellar. The robot had spent the whole night buffing. Now it gleamed.

I surveyed the office again, tried to imagine it from a client's perspective. To my surprise it looked pretty good—borderline professional, just as long as you ignored the stains on the carpet. Neat desks, the globe looking fancy in the corner, a bookshelf stacked with all the detective's essentials. The rich smell of hot java. And the three of us. The private investigator and his faithful assistants: the shining robot with all the facts at its mechanical fingertips; the trainee investigator who looked like a waif and behaved like a bull terrier.

"You got out of that one," said Zephyr, punching my arm.

"Huh? Oh, the automobile. If you'd rather walk..."

"No, it's okay. I was just checking the scale on this map. You're right—it's all the way through the financial quarter and out the other side. I say we let the robot drive us. Agreed, boss?"

Boss. I liked the sound of that.

41

SEEING AS HOW the Scrutator was state-of-the-art, I'd figured he'd have fancy wheels to match. Some new hybrid off the Mountain, with chrome fenders and perturbation brakes. Turned out the robot's car was a vintage VW half-track in camouflage red. It was actually cool.

When the car pulled up outside the office, Zephyr stared at it with her mouth open.

"It's got tank tracks on the back," she said. "And legs on the front."

"Most String City autos run on legs," I said. "You've been here long enough to learn that."

"I know but... it's just that every time I think I've got the hang of this place, I see something even weirder."

"Trust me, that feeling doesn't ever go away."

We ran through the rain to the half-track. A storm was raging and the forecast was for worse. Still, at least bad weather meant the lights would stay on. Following the collapse of Theo Carr's fusion grid, Aeolus the wind god had picked up String City's power contract and, with hurricane season imminent, it looked like the old deity was set to make a killing.

We climbed into the car. Rain pounded the canvas roof. The Scrutator engaged the gears and the four front legs engaged the asphalt. The tracks rumbled. The VW lurched forward.

"It isn't exactly kind to the environment," said Zephyr, peering at the black cloud chugging from the snorkel exhaust.

"Or the street," I said. The tracks were tearing the asphalt into neat chunks. "Those ain't breadcrumbs."

"My apologies," said the Scrutator. It flipped a toggle on the dash. The rumble dropped to a whisper. "I neglected to remove the parking cleats. This vehicle's controls are somewhat rudimentary. However, it is a joy to drive."

"A what?" I said.

"A joy to drive."

"That's what I thought you said."

"What exactly do you mean by 'joy', Bronzey?" said Zephyr, grinning.

There was a pause. The Scrutator's gears clicked and whirred. "The word presents itself as being appropriate to the situation. As to its precise meaning—I confess I am uncertain."

"Let us know when you get it," I said.

Zephyr had been hoping for a grand tour, the whole tourist bit. But the Scrutator took us the quickest route, which meant dark alleys one minute, bland freeways the next. The torrential rain turned the view to mush. All we saw were grey facades and flinching umbrellas, and the only clue we'd reached the Hot

Hub came when the neon signs got brighter and the passers-by wore fewer clothes. As the Scrutator turned into Vaderkvarn Street, the clouds lifted and the downpour turned to drizzle.

"We'll walk from here," I said.

"Harry's Holodeon is at the other end of the street," said the Scrutator. "I calculate you will each be exposed to at least seventeen litres of rain before you..."

"That's all right," said Zephyr, kissing his cheek. "I need to stretch my legs."

"You go back," I said. "We need someone at the office. You can pick us up when we're done."

"I am, of course, at your service, sir," said the Scrutator through the window as it pulled away.

"No, you're not," I called. "You're on the team."

Zephyr didn't have a coat, so I'd picked her one off the rack in the cellar. Long blue leather, big buckles. As I'd handed it over, it struck me she'd been wearing the blue jeans and white blouse she'd had on all week.

"Is this all you've got?" I'd said, plucking the sleeve of the blouse.

Zephyr shrugged. "It's all I need. Tony lets me use the laundry room whenever I want. Most evenings I spend wrapped in a towel in front of the washing machine, watching my clothes go round."

"You should shop."

Her mouth turned down. "I don't like shopping."

"That's something for a dame to say."

"Thanks for the coat. Is it... can it do what your coat can do?"

"You mean, like this?" I took my own coat off the peg, turned it inside-out twice until it was swanskin.

"That's amazing. So can mine do that?"

"No, honey. It's just a coat."

She pouted. "When you've finished training me up—when I'm a real private investigator—will I get a coat like yours?"

"It isn't a uniform."

"But where did you get it? Who made it?"

"Long story," I said. "Maybe I'll tell you one day." I hunched up my collar, pulled down my fedora. The rain turned Zephyr's hair into a black skullcap. Maybe I should have picked her out a hat too.

We set off down the street.

"You think String City's a melting pot?" I said as we passed a line of pinball arcades. "This here's the fondue."

A bunch of donkey-headed winos brayed at us from the kerb. We hustled past, found our way blocked by a long queue lined up outside the opera house. Most of the folk waiting were human. Plenty weren't.

"The *Vaderkvarn*," I said. "See the neon windmill on top? One of the city's oldest landmarks. Place used to be a strip joint, then it climbed the scale. The house band is famous in most of the known worlds. I could get tickets."

"I prefer rock and roll," said Zephyr.

Past the opera house we hit the adult boutiques. Time was the windows were opaqued; then the law relaxed and everything went on show. Zephyr took it in without flinching.

"You said the Hot Hub would show me what String City's all about," she said. We'd stopped outside an exotic lingerie store. The troll in the window was striking all kinds of poses. The only thing it proved was Chantilly lace and rhino-skin don't mix. "Either I'm getting used to the place or..."

"Or you're not easily shocked?"

"Maybe that's it."

The rain hammered hard. We ran the last fifty yards to Harry's Holodeon, huddled together under the canopy. Zephyr pulled a folder from her inside pocket and we reviewed the case notes.

"The proposition is simple," I said, scanning the contact report. "Harry Arriflex runs the movie house, has done all his life. This is a guy who lives and breathes the silver screen. Harry's a straight arrow, always has been. I'd trust him with most folks' lives."

"Not your own?" said Zephyr.

"I never go that far. Anyway, Harry came to me last week saying a pair of municipal agents had come sniffing round his theater. The municipals showed him pirate copies of all the movies he's been running this past six months. The tapes were rough—shaky, dark, like they'd been filmed from the back row by someone with a cheap camera. Harry wanted proof that the back row in question was his. The municipals said they didn't need proof. Harry threw them out and came straight to me. If he doesn't button this up, he'll be out of business before the month's out."

"But he thinks the municipal agents could be right? Someone really could be ripping off these films in his cinema?"

I nodded. "He's got his eye on Saul Flowers, the projectionist. Saul's a creature of habit. Every afternoon he runs the projector; every night he picks a penny arcade and drops the coins he just earned down the chute. When he gets home he drinks four bottles of rum. Mornings he spends throwing up."

"Why does Harry keep him on?"

"Harry's a good employer. There was a time when Saul steered straight. Then his wife died and he took his hands off the wheel. My guess is he met some guys at the arcade who made him an offer he couldn't refuse. Now he's a pirate."

"The poor man."

"The poor man's a crook, and Harry's a friend of mine. It stinks, but it's the job."

Zephyr scrunched her nose and pulled her coat tight. "I suppose it's like being a doctor," she said. "You have to detach yourself. Emotionally, I mean."

I looked down at her. "The day you do that," I said, "is the day you hit the showers."

Her distaste turned to puzzlement. "Really? But you always struck me as... I mean, you're always so cold and distant."

My gut collapsed. She'd bowled me that one from nowhere. I waited while rain dripped from the brim of my hat; I needed a minute to wind up my bat.

"I do what I do," I replied at last. "How I do it is my business."

She made a face like she was about to throw me a sassy retort. Instead she went over to the movie poster in the Holodeon's lobby window.

"'*Forbidden Liaison*'," she read. "*A torrid tale of passion without limits*. Sounds juicy."

"Yeah." I went to join her. "Harry specialises in movies like that."

"Like what? There's no picture on the poster. How are you meant to know what it's about, apart from the words?"

"Folk know," I said. "The law says you can't put still frames on the street. Says it's not the kind of thing ordinary folk like to see. Go figure."

"How bad can it be? After what I saw in those shop windows, I'd have thought anything goes in this town."

"Mostly it does. But there are still taboos, just like anywhere. Although I guess you'd consider this one odd, considering what else goes on here."

"So what's the movie about? Is it sex?"

"No. Romance."

Zephyr laughed. "*Romance*? They don't allow romance in String City?"

"Not when it's between two different species."

"What did you say?" All the bull terrier went from her voice. Suddenly she sounded like someone had socked her in the gut.

"You okay?"

"I'm fine. Ignore me."

I eyed her for a minute, then went on.

"Romance between one species of person and another falls under the obscenity laws. I don't mean sex—that's tolerated. I mean true love. In reality, it happens all the time, of course. But the municipal charter holds it's offensive to put stories like that in a movie theater, unless you got a special license."

"It happens all the time?"

"Sure. Take the Sunyanas: human and asansa. Perfect example."

She shuddered. "The way that marriage ended, maybe the authorities are right. Maybe inter-species romance should be banned altogether."

"Live and let live is what I say." I couldn't fathom why she was reacting so badly to this. "Zephyr—are you all right?"

"You should handle this case alone." Her mascara was running again. "I'll wait out here. I'll be fine. I'll help with the next case, I promise."

I had a lecture ready, something about how truth was supposed to transcend prejudice. I wish I'd got to deliver it—it would have been a doozie. But I didn't get the chance, because two blocks over from the end of Vaderkvarn Street, just past the line where the Hot Hub butts up against the financial quarter, a cataclysmic bang split the sky right down the middle. It was bigger than the explosion that had rocked String City, the same way a planet is bigger than a peach.

Everything shook, from the bedrock right up to the stratosphere. Out beyond the skin of the world, all the dimensions trembled.

The effect on the city was brutal. Skyscrapers flew like javelins. The whole financial district reared up; entire boulevards cracked down the middle. That was all I saw; a split-second later a cloud of ash came boiling toward us, eating everything in its path.

Already deaf from the blast, I grabbed Zephyr and hurled us both through the lobby doors and into the foyer. We tumbled down the stairs that led to the auditorium while the rest of Harry's Holodeon came apart around us. Our heads cracked together. Everything went black.

42

I OPENED MY eyes. Immediately they filled up with dust. I blinked it away, sat up. Shards of masonry slid off my shoulders. Harry's Holodeon was all smashed seats and plumes of smoke. The movie screen drooped like a punctured parachute. A forest of glass spikes surrounded the remains of the projection booth; the diced-up body inside could only be Saul Flowers. Guilty or innocent, it didn't matter any more; the poor sap was dead.

I heard distant screams, muffled. I clapped my hand against the side of my head and most of my hearing popped back.

"Come and look!" Zephyr was standing on a pile of rubble. Her coat billowed like a blue spinnaker. Strong wind to make leather float that way.

I climbed the rubble, reached her side, looked out across the city.

The entire Hot Hub district looked like a war zone. Most of the buildings were felled like trees; fires raged everywhere. Upturned cars lay heaped like drifts of steel leaves. Hundreds of people wandered bleeding and moaning. Hundreds more weren't wandering anywhere.

Beyond the Hot Hub, almost nothing was left. The financial

quarter was razed, a wasteland. All the big banks were flattened, tall concrete towers knocked down like ninepins. They lay in a radial pattern, centered on the biggest crater I ever saw.

"That must be where it went off," said Zephyr. "You know this city like the back of your hand. What was there that anyone would want to blow up?"

I shook my head. Not because I didn't know. I knew only too well. I shook my head because I couldn't believe it.

"It's the same place we were yesterday," I said. "Right after that business at the wharf."

"You mean that place with the funny name? What was it? The Birdcage?"

"Birdhouse. Strongest vault in all String City. Looks like someone finally decided to crack it."

"But why? You still haven't told me what they keep in there that's so special."

My ears cleared further. Klaxons were screaming all over town: emergency services converging on ground zero.

"Let's go see," I said.

43

By the time we got to the Street of Plenty, the cops had everything fenced off. Time was I knew how to deal with cops. Not any more.

"Are these really the police?" whispered Zephyr. "Tony Marscapone told me they were all zombies. This lot looks more like they're off to a carnival."

A riot van had pulled up, spilling a squad of half-naked people decked with flowers and grass and sporting straw hats. Most were human, though a couple looked like ambulatory snakes. Several carried brightly colored bullwhips.

"The zombies have moved out," I said. "These guys are the radaloa. It's a long story."

"Tell me." Zephyr squeezed my arm. "I'm trying to understand this city, I really am. I *need* to understand it, or I'm going to go crazy."

I scanned the ranks of the cops, looking for a face I knew. Unless I saw it, we were going nowhere.

"Okay, here's the short version. Years ago, the cops weren't radaloa or zombies—they were just regular folk like you and me. But things went sour. For some reason a culture of violence grew up in the force. It started with cops beating perps for no good reason. That's bad, though you could say nothing new. Then it escalated. Racial profiling, species profiling, an unjustified armed response killing once a month, then once a week, then every day. Finally, this one cop shot a guy just for parking in the wrong zone. Blew his face off, then shot his wife in the passenger seat and his kids in the back. There was a riot. Citizens took up arms. A mob torched the precinct house, melted all the cops who were holed up inside. The riot got worse. Times were bad already; I guess folk were just looking for someone to blame."

"A mass depression?"

"I guess. Anyhow, things got so bad the cops were practically wiped out. The municipals got desperate and fixed up this deal with the Obeah brothers."

"Obeah? Isn't that like voodoo?"

"Exactly like it. The Obeah brothers were small-time hoodlums who were big on folk magic. They raised up a whole new police force of zombies from the graveyards behind the Bayou. It worked out well. Zombies are hard to kill and relentless when it comes to pursuing the perps."

"What did these Obeah brothers get out of the deal?"

"What do you think?"

"A fat check?"

"The fattest. So they say."

Zephyr nodded. "So where are all the zombies now?"

"They were taken out last year by the radaloa."

"And what exactly are they?"

"Radaloa. Voodoo spirits."

"I thought that's what zombies were."

"No. Zombies are just something the Obeah boys thought up to make a fast buck. The radaloa are the true guardians of voodoo lore. They're big on morality and justice. They like to do the right thing. Also, they have this thing about straw hats."

"So, what, they just took over?"

"More or less. The radaloa rewrote the magic that kept the zombies... well, 'alive' isn't the word. But you get what I mean."

"So what happened to the zombies?"

"Apart from one, they all fell apart. Literally. Took weeks to clear the gutters. Caused one hell of stink."

A shadow fell over us. I turned to see a neat midriff cinched tight by uniform blue. Six feet above the midriff, framed by wide tattered wings, was the face I'd been looking for.

"Deliciosa," I said. "Glad to see you again."

"It's been a while," the giant cop replied.

"Who's this?" said Zephyr. Given it was the first time she'd ever been in the presence of a twelve foot zombie angel, she was holding it together pretty well.

"An old friend of mine," I said. "I met her when she fell from heaven. After she died, she joined the force. It happens."

Deliciosa knelt so as to bring our faces together. A gust of wind fluttered her wings. She smiled, giving us a glimpse all the way through her head to the back of her skull.

"You're looking good," I said.

"Not as good as I used to," the undead angel replied. "I may be the only zombie left on the force—the only one left in String City, probably—but the power of the divine won't hold me together forever. I'm afraid my days are numbered."

"Cheekbones like yours," I said, "they never go out of fashion."

Deliciosa raised decaying fingers to the holes in her face. "The new look suits me just fine. I always said beauty was skin-deep."

"Real beauty's deeper, and you know it."

Deliciosa let out a sigh. Given the state of her, her breath should have smelt like rotting meat. But the aroma I caught was warm cinnamon. "We could have made one heck of a team, couldn't we?"

"Guess we'll never know." I gave her a what-might-have-been kind of look, then returned her sigh. "So what happened here anyway?"

"Someone blew up the Birdhouse."

"That's so crazy it's off the scale. How did they manage it?"

"That's what we're trying to find out."

"Any way you can let us down there?"

"I'm sorry. The whole area's sealed off. Pick any cop you like and they'll tell you the same thing: go home."

"But you're not just any cop, are you?"

Throughout the conversation, Deliciosa's face had been drawing closer and closer to mine. Her peeled lips parted, her jawbone grating with the movement. I remembered how once we'd kissed, and hoped she was remembering it too.

"I knew you'd show up again," she said. "It was only a matter of time."

"Time is something I don't have a lot of. Please—can't you let us through?"

She considered this for a long time. At last she stood tall and spread her wings wide. Firelight glowed through torn feathers, turning them to brilliant orange flames. She drew in a single breath and lit up the day. Onlookers gasped. If Deliciosa hadn't been undead, they probably would have screamed. Seeing an angel up close... it gets to you in ways you never knew existed. Trust me, I know.

She stood like that for ten seconds, the ultimate diversion. By the time she lowered her wings again, Zephyr and I had snuck deep inside the blast radius of the explosion that had cracked String City's toughest vault like an egg.

44

"What was all that about?" said Zephyr as we clambered down into the crater.

"Long story," I said.

She grabbed my shoulder and pulled me up short. "You say that every time I ask you about anything. Well, it's not good enough! Not any more. Not if you want me to follow you into somewhere that looks like the jaws of hell!"

"The jaws of hell you have to pay admission," I said. "This is different. Probably worse."

"There you go again. What is it with you? You're always hinting at things you never actually talk about. Everything's always 'another story'. Well, I'm sick of it! If you want me to be your partner you've got to come clean. No more secrets!"

"Everyone's got secrets." I stared her down.

She dropped her eyes, briefly, then fixed me again. "All right. Okay. Maybe I haven't told you everything about myself either. But can't you at least tell me what we're doing here, and why that angel-thing bothered to let us through?"

Wind pounded us. It was blowing down into the crater from all sides, blowing hard. That bothered me; I wasn't sure why. The smoke inside the crater was thick. The ground was littered with gold coins and silver bills, badly charred. Everything was tilted. The air felt spiky.

"Okay," I sighed. "Maybe it all connects. The angel's name is Deliciosa—you probably caught that much. We met inside the Birdhouse, a while back now. Back when she was alive and... well, beautiful."

"Did you fall in love with her?"

Dust caught in my throat, made me choke. "Hard to say."

"What were you doing in the Birdhouse?"

"Surveillance. The rumor was someone was trying to crack the vault where they keep the Still Point of the Turning World."

"Still Point of the what?"

"Turning World. It's what the Thanes built the Birdhouse to protect."

"You're losing me again."

The wind fired banknotes at us like paper bullets. Other things flew past too: scraps of fabric, scraps of flesh. A lot of folk worked in the Birdhouse. Or used to.

"Everyone's got their own idea what the Still Point is," I said. "Some say it's like a dance. Others say it's more like the *center* of a dance: without it, the dance couldn't exist. Me, I've got two left feet, so none of that figures. All I know is, the Thanes say the Still Point needs protecting at all costs. And I mean *all*."

I stopped. My mind had flashed back to Jason and the *Argo*. I remembered staring down into the Maelstrom. The eye of the whirlpool, the place where everything appeared to be at rest. I suddenly knew what it had reminded me of.

Zephyr was pondering what I'd said. "Are you trying to tell me somewhere in this city there's a safety deposit box containing the... what, the heart of the universe or something?"

"Not the heart. A heart's a thing. The Still Point's not a thing, it's... oh, think of it more like a container."

"A container for what?"

"For the only thing that matters."

"Which is?"

"It's got a name, but I don't think it means very much."

"Tell me it anyway."

"It's called the Glory."

Zephyr sighed. "Talking to you is like peeling an onion. Every time I think I'm getting somewhere, it turns out to be just another layer."

"Believe me, honey, if you ever saw the Glory, you wouldn't be able to hold back the tears."

"It's that bad?"

"Bad. Good. Everything between and beyond. Everything. The Glory is the lifestring of the cosmos. Without it, there's nothing."

"Okay. I get it. I mean, I don't get it, but I get it. The Glory is some kind of shining light. And the Still Point is what it's wrapped up in. And the Birdhouse is the vault where the Still Point is kept. It's like a set of Russian dolls."

"If you like. And right here is where the Birdhouse is. Or was."

"Until someone blew it up."

"I don't understand how they did it. The Still Point's got a lot of protection. Not least a guard dog the size of a small town. Actually, not so much a guard dog. More a behemoth. And the Still Point... honey, it's *big*. No, more than big. It's *everything*. Look, have you heard enough yet?"

"Not in the slightest."

"All the same, we have to keep moving."

"Okay. But I reserve the right to ask more questions as they occur to me."

"I never thought you wouldn't."

Further into the crater, things got raggy. Pits like shrapnel wounds leaked curled-up dimensions. Planck whirlwinds whipped out of nowhere, each one hiding a nasty dimensional snag at its core. A crack in the ground spewed cosmic string like an Indian rope trick. There was a background howl: boundary wolves on the prowl for anyone playing chicken with the edges of reality, and sounding far too close for comfort.

The Still Point of the Turning World.

Everything.

This had been no ordinary explosion.

Zephyr clutched my arm. "There's something not right about this. Not right at all. What *happened* here?"

"A bigger bang than I thought," I muttered.

A tiny tornado wiggled our way. Rogue laws of physics flew from its spinning edges, squeezing demon faces from the air, transforming the rocky ground to crumbling chalk, to hard diamond, to spitting lava. I pulled Zephyr out of its path.

"You don't want to get caught in one of those."

"It only comes up to my knee."

"Small is worse."

"What happens if they get you?"

"You get sucked out of this world and into another. No telling which."

"Like *The Wizard of Oz*?"

"Not much."

The tornado zipped past, leaving a trail of altered terrain. Pale powder flew in its wake. Something slapped against my ankle; I grabbed it, held it up. It was a strip of hessian, ripped, burned. Letters were stenciled on it:

THEFIRE

"'The fire'?" said Zephyr.

"Not 'the fire'," I said. The back of my neck was crawling up under the brim of my hat. "'Scathefire'. Second time I've seen it in as many weeks. There are way too many coincidences stacking up here."

"What's scathefire?"

"You heard of high explosives? This stuff will blow more than your mind. Now we know what they used to crack open the Birdhouse vault."

"Never mind the vault—it looks to me like they blew a hole in the whole *world*."

Something burst from the charred soil a hundred yards away. Teeth like fighter jets chomped the smoke. Dog-breath washed over us like industrial waste.

"What is it?" cried Zephyr.

"Boundary wolf! Run!"

We fled hand in hand, running downslope, heading deeper into the crater. Behind us the boundary wolf bayed. I looked back; its snout was right on our heels. I kicked dust in its eye. It snarled, fell back, came at us faster. Its shaggy mane crawled with fleas the size of housecats. Its shoulders pumped like beam engines. We hurdled a shattered wall. The bricks were melting, running together. The wind pushed us on. The wolf howled again, a sound like ten thousand elephants being drawn through a mangle.

Without warning, a quantum tornado swept right between us and our pursuer, collapsing five of the eight local dimensions. Pure good fortune. The howl of the boundary wolf went supersonic. The wolf itself folded up, vanishing into a space the size of my fist. The emptiness burst like a balloon and the ground closed, clanging like a gong.

"What happened?" said Zephyr.

"We got lucky."

We ran on.

The deeper we went, the bigger the crater got. The dimensions were definitely misbehaving. Riemanian anomalies kept opening up around us, spilling out string and fine slices of brane before snapping shut again. It was like crossing an icefield, feeling it break under your feet, just waiting for the ocean to reach up and drag you under.

All around us the ground was splattered with enormous chunks of flesh. We passed a heap of intestines resembling a freeway interchange. Zephyr screwed up her face.

"What kind of creature did that come from?"

"Behemoth." I looked sadly at the carnage. "He used to guard the Still Point. For a big guy, he was a real softy."

"Let me guess: another story?"

I shrugged, too sad to speak.

Eventually the ground leveled. We'd reached the bottom of the crater. Ground zero. The place where the Birdhouse used to be.

The wolf-howl undercurrent died away. The smoke smoothed to a haze. The dimensions stopped trying to break through, contented themselves with bubbling round unseen corners. We slowed to walking pace. We didn't stop holding hands.

Something loomed out of the mist.

I peered, trying to make it out, which is why I didn't hear what was coming up behind us. If it had been a boundary wolf, our tale would have ended there. But it wasn't.

Deliciosa landed beside me with a flutter of feathers and rotting flesh. My arms grew goosebumps. In a place like that, it was comforting to have a twelve-foot angel at your side. Even if she was coming apart.

"What are you doing here?" I said.

"I thought you might need some help." She pointed. "Have you any idea what that is?"

"It looks like a man," said Zephyr.

"Yes, it does," said Deliciosa.

Zephyr stared at her, then me. "But it isn't a man, is it?"

"No," I said. "It isn't."

"Then what the hell is it?"

45

CROUCHED ON THE ground in the middle of the crater was a hooded figure. My arms must have got a taste for the goosebump thing, because they were doing it all over again.

"It's a Fool," Deliciosa told Zephyr. "I did a quick flypast before the barriers went up. Stupid of me really, but I had a lot of friends who worked in the Birdhouse. I wanted to see if any of them had survived."

"Had they?" I was resisting the urge to run. I'd sparred with a Fool once before and didn't relish a return bout.

"What do you think?" The angel bowed her head before going on. "We've been getting reports of hooded figures for months now. They've been coming in from all over the city: appearing in witness statements, on CCTV footage, anywhere there are shadows. It's almost as if they've been waiting for something."

"I know exactly what they've been waiting for," I said.

"You do? What?"

I told Deliciosa about the Tartarus heist. How a mysterious hooded figure had duped a couple of cyclops saps into emptying the Titans' safe, and especially how the safe had been packed full of the most powerful explosive the cosmos had ever known.

"Scathefire?" said Deliciosa. "I thought that was just a myth."

"Trust me, it's real. And it's clearly what the Fools have been looking for all this time. They've dreamed of blowing open the Birdhouse for eons. Looks like their dream finally came true."

"I hate to sound like cracked vinyl," said Zephyr, "but what exactly *is* a Fool?"

I shared a grimace with Deliciosa. Talking about Fools is a dirty job. But someone's got to wear the rubber gloves.

"Fools are worse than bad," I said. "Literally. It's like... well, imagine light and dark. Now imagine neither. That's Fools. Life and death, good and evil, right and wrong... you take it all away, what you're left with is the Fools."

"So they're the bad guys?"

"Not exactly. More like... look, take the Thanes."

"The Thanes? Those are the people who run String City, aren't they? Sort of like the government?"

"Thanes aren't people, but that's close enough. Now the Thanes, most would say they're on the side of good. Thanes are... well, they *shine*. Am I right, Deliciosa?"

With tears in her deep, decaying eyes, the angel said softly, "Yes. Oh, yes."

"Thing is," I said, "while the Thanes might be good, the Fools aren't really bad, not as in evil. Fools are outside all that."

"So what do they do? What's their thing?"

"They meddle. What a Fool likes most is to take things apart. There's some say that's their right, since Fools can create things too, and that's a skill more rare than you might think. I don't mean create as in paint pictures or write computer code or think up new flavors of ice cream—I mean *really* create. Fools make things that never existed before."

"So they're like gods?"

"Not in the least. Fools do like to create, but for them it's just a hobby. What they *really* like to do is see how things work. You meet a Fool, the first thing he'll do is shake your hand. Next he'll strip your fingers to the bone to see how the joints work. Then he'll unpick the nuclear forces holding your atoms together. When he's finished, if you're lucky, someone'll sweep what's left of you into a bag."

"So what's this one doing here?"

"I think I know," said Deliciosa.

Before I could stop her, she'd marched right up to the Fool. She bent down, grasped his hood and ripped his cloak away. The wind snatched the cloak from her worm-ridden fingers and threw it into the sky, leaving the Fool naked and revealed.

Zephyr put her hand to her mouth. I heard her stomach trying to climb up inside her throat.

If Deliciosa looked bad, the Fool looked worse. Fools are neither dead nor alive. They're not even undead. They just are. Or aren't. It's a tough call which.

The Fool had all the parts of a man, in all the wrong places. There were bones on the outside. His skin hung like washing inside his ribs. His organs were anything but internal. His skull was smooth, faceless. His eyes were stapled to his fingers, the better to see his work.

There was something in the Fool's lap, nestled on a cushion of intestines spilling from his exposed pelvis. It shone like a small sun. His eye-capped fingers were busy with it, darting in and out of its light, constantly burning up before regrowing, like everlasting candles. Each time they dipped inside the little sun they came up carrying something random and bizarre: a peach, a haystack, a pocket watch, a cumulus cloud. Most of these surprises were impossible—either too big or too small to be really there, impossible even to handle at all. But the Fool handled them all the same.

Handled them, took them apart, then tossed them aside like orange peel.

Littering the ground at the Fool's gore-streaked feet—and gradually getting bigger—was a heap of golden dust. The fundamental components of all the things he was deconstructing.

"Is that sun-thing what I think it is?" Zephyr whispered. She didn't need intuition. When you get close to something like that, you just know.

"Yes," I said quietly. "That's it. The Still Point of the Turning World."

"He's taking it apart." Zephyr started backing away. "What happens when he's finished?"

"The Glory will be exposed."

"And then?"

"You ever build a house of cards?" Zephyr nodded. "You know the one card at the bottom—the one that, if you take it away, makes the whole house come down?"

"Stop! Don't say any more."

The Fool's fingers worked faster. More and more things were flying out of the Still Point. Most of them were things I didn't recognise, didn't even want to see. The Fool was dismantling cosmic secrets, and even the dust they were made of could burn your eyes from their sockets.

"Time to go!" said Deliciosa. Her wings were buzzing, ready to lift her off.

Planck tornadoes whipped up from the soil. Big ones.

"You fly ahead!" I shouted over the rising wind. "We're right behind you!"

I grabbed Zephyr's hand. Before I could close my fingers, a Planck tornado whipped up out of nowhere and started sucking her toward it.

"Help me!" she yelled. I tried to run, but the same wind that was pulling her was pushing me the opposite way.

Struggling even to stand, I took off my coat, turned it inside-out until it was made of buckytube monofilament and spun it into a lariat. High winds slip right past buckytubes. At least, that's what I hoped. I whirled the lasso over my head, tried to snag her. The noose missed, hit the ground steaming. I reeled it in, made ready to try again.

The Planck tornado spun itself into a frenzy. Zephyr flew toward it, her heels dragging grooves in the dirt just as if she was being pulled by an invisible horse. I threw the lariat again. It looped round her arm. She grabbed it with both hands. The lariat crackled like an electric eel.

"Don't hold on!" I yelled. "It doesn't like it!"

She let go and allowed the lasso to do the holding. Meanwhile, a dimensional snag had opened up inside the whirlwind, round like the mouth of a straw. Zephyr's legs lifted off the ground and plunged into it. I hauled on the lariat. There was panic in Zephyr's eyes. That was bad. You hit the dimensions with a head full of fear, fear's all you'll find in there.

"Look at me!" I shouted. "I've got you!"

Our eyes locked. But the lariat was slipping off her arm. I was losing her. "Don't let the dimensions take charge! You've seen what I can do. You can do it too. Just let them know who's boss!"

Her hips sank deeper into the tornado. Her body flattened out. She started to fade. She was slipping between the strings and there was nothing I could do about it. To follow her, I'd have to let go of the lariat. As soon as I did that, she'd be gone, and the snag would close before I could reach it. I'd be cut off from her, with no idea what direction she'd gone.

The lasso slipped off Zephyr's arm.

She gave a long, wailing, terrified scream. That's when the angel swooped in.

Deliciosa didn't try and save Zephyr—by that point the poor kid was beyond saving. Instead, the angel hung suspended on her zombie wings directly above the tornado, bent her head low and whispered something in Zephyr's vanishing ear. Zephyr listened, then her dwindling face calmed and she closed her eyes.

The dimensional snag snapped shut. I fell backward, the lariat limp in my hands. The shockwave knocked Deliciosa to the ground.

I clambered to my feet, dazed.

The Planck tornado was gone.

So was Zephyr.

46

"We have to go!" Deliciosa tugged at my coat. I shoved her away.

"Not yet!"

Planck tornadoes leave interference patterns in the dirt. If you take a mold, you can track them. It took me two seconds to switch my coat to sharkskin, another two to pull the atmospheric casting kit out of my pocket. The tornado tracks looked like a million chipmunks had been line-dancing. The tracks wouldn't last, not in this wind. I didn't have much time.

I dropped to my knees, ripped open the pack of self-hydrating plaster.

"Leave it!" Deliciosa took the plaster pack from me, tossed it away.

"What are you doing?"

"Look at me!"

Her angel eyes were wide and angry. That suited me—I was mad too and needed a target. I considered mulching her rotten nose into the empty sack of her sinuses. The only thing that stopped me was knowing that hitting zombies is like punching tripe. That, and I still remembered the good times.

"Do you want to save the girl?" Deliciosa said. I tried not to look at the beetle that was crawling out of her ear.

"What do you think?"

"Then save the girl! But not here!"

Zombie hands grabbed my head, swiveled it toward the view. The entire crater was rolling like an ocean. The Fool's hands were a blur; the Still Point of the Turning World was a sticky glow in his lap, shrinking steadily as he tore the fundamental core of the cosmos to pieces. Through the threadbare seams of reality, the boundary wolves bayed their favorite hunting songs. Everything was coming apart. Everything.

"Let's get out of here," I said.

47

DELICIOSA FLEW ME out. It was worse than a flight through Hell. Trust me, I'm qualified to make the comparison.

By the time we left the crater, the city streets were snapping like popcorn and the sky was boiling like the stroganoff of the gods. Tower blocks went over like dominoes. The sewers grew mouths and started chomping up the streets. Thunderbirds lost their sense of direction and hit the city parks like meteorites. Behind the sky, hulking things moved that hadn't moved in aeons, looking for ways to get through into next-door realities.

Tight around my ribs, holding me safe inside the chaos, were the decaying arms of a zombie angel.

Apocalypse. End of the world. Folks had been talking it up for years. Hell, I'd talked it up myself often enough. Underneath, had I really believed it would happen?

I believed it now.

We flew through wormholes and powder storms: the worst kind of flak. After a dozen close calls, we finally reached the end of my street. Deliciosa swooped low and dropped me like a sack. The carriageway was in two halves, each part jerking like a severed worm.

"I can't stay with you," she shouted over the battle-roar. "I'm still on duty."

"Law and order? At a time like this?"

"Now more than ever."

Duty I understood. But this was madness. "You'd be safer in my office."

"Safety is not a factor. Now get inside before the storm hits."

She pointed straight up. Gunmetal clouds had been chasing us like a herd of buffalo all the way from the crater. At last they'd caught up. It got dark, fast, then darker still. The sun fell off Sol's chariot and hit the river, hissing madly. Sol herself flew west on the end of Arvak's reins; the other horse, Alsvid, started grazing on the dead.

"Ra will be glad his contract ended last week," I said.

"Get inside!"

"Wait! You whispered something in Zephyr's ear. Just before the tornado got her. What did you say?"

Deliciosa didn't answer, just spread her wings and took off. Some second thought brought her briefly back to earth. She bent, embraced me, kissed me on the cheek. Her lips were cold, but her breath still smelt of cinnamon. I wanted to hold her. But she was already back in the air.

"Be careful out there!" I shouted.

A wheel flung from Sol's chariot took the wings off a passing thunderbird. The bird clipped the deli, its crippled body bowling the length of the street and knocking down nine of the ten pillars supporting the Temple of Isis.

"When they start getting strikes," Deliciosa called down as she flew away, "Then I'll be worried." But there was fear in her eyes.

I jumped the gap between the two sides of the street, ran to my office door. It was locked. I patted my pockets, searching for the key. Behind me, a sewer grate yawned, belching a black miasma across my back. I ignored it. I also ignored the Planck tornadoes forming on the corner where the hamadryads used to root. A dozen harpies shrieked past, human corpses clinging to the sticky hairs on their thighs.

I found the key. As I held it up, it slipped from my fingers. It was too dark to see where it fell. I bent, fumbled. I touched something hot and sticky that touched me back. I jerked my hand away, tried elsewhere. Behind me the sewer gaped, drooling slime.

My fingers brushed the key, snatched it up. Before I could reach the lock the sewer lunged... and the door clicked open. A mechanical hand closed on my collar, yanked me inside. I hit the carpet, rolling between the Scrutator's legs as it slammed the door shut. The sewer mouth struck the glass, smearing it with slime.

"Deadlocks!"

A tremor went through the floor as the singularity bolts crunched together.

"I apologise for having secured the latch," said the Scrutator, wiping raw sewage from its arm with a fair impression of distaste. "But I was apprehensive as to the security of the situation."

"No problem," I gasped. I tried to get up, found my ribs were hurting. I'd hit the floor hard. And Deliciosa's grip had been strong.

"It pleases me to discover you are still alive, however, I am curious as to the whereabouts of the young female, Zephyr."

"You and me both."

The Scrutator's cogs ground against each other. "Am I to conclude that Zephyr's location is currently unknown?"

"I lost her." I stood, holding my ribs, grimacing with pain. "But she ain't gonna stay lost for long!"

48

First I spun up the Feynman globe. The metaballs bounced over each other like chrome puppies. I zoomed the optics to wide, punched in a Boolean search algorithm. There was a clank as the pinions meshed with the local brane-space. I set my eyes on the scope, hopes high. But the optics stayed stubbornly dark.

I set my palm on the casing. The globe was hot, too hot. I tripped the diagnostics, saw red lights across the board. The globe had meshed with reality, but reality hadn't meshed back. The scathefire had sent a tsunami through the brane-space. It could be years before the interference subsided.

If it ever did.

I shut down the globe, turned to the bookcase.

On the top shelf I keep trashy novels. Westerns, mostly, the odd cheesecake romance. The rest of the books look smart but they're only there to impress the clients: Ichnuemon's *Dragon Baiting*, a rare hardback edition of *The Unlikely Almanac*, the Sakharov translation of *Searching the Bulk*... all detective defaults, but I only have to read a book once to get it in my head. My head's good like that.

There's one book that's different. Like most lexicons, *The Big Dictionary* is there to tell you what words mean. The difference is, every time you open it, the meanings change.

I picked the dictionary off the shelf, cracked the spine back and forth until the cover read *Q to U*, opened it at *T*. I flicked through to *Temporal Speleology* and ran my finger down the page. I found the section about Planck tornadoes—how they open up snags through the sixth dimension into a limbo where the laws of chromodynamics flower like a limestone cavern. It's a beautiful, deadly place. If you get sucked inside, you can end up anywhere.

The passage told me nothing I didn't know already.

I cracked the spine again. Soon the book was a schematic of the chromodynamic limbo. I scanned the ready reckoner of tornado silhouettes and found a match for the one that had taken Zephyr. This enabled me to track a theoretical path through the cavern system. But that place is a labyrinth where even the left-turn trick doesn't work. By page seven I'd lost the thread.

I shut the dictionary, rammed it back on the shelf.

I tried everything I could think of: the Mappa Mundi, the Clockwork Locator from the crate in the cellar, the Rhabdomancy Tarot. I even dipped into the top drawer of the filing cabinet and opened up the rift that leads to the interdimensional Search Engine. You can ride that iron horse most anywhere. But I found the tracks all torn up and the Engine nowhere to be seen.

Dead ends at every turn.

Outside, the rain had turned the color of blood. Thunderbird corpses filled the street to the rooftops. Nothing was moving but the weather.

I slumped in the chair, pulled a bottle of bourbon from under a pile of case notes. I drank it from the neck. Thought hard. Came up blank. I'd tried everything I could think of. There was nothing I could do.

I'd lost Zephyr.

All the time I'd been searching, the Scrutator had been parked in the corner, watching me operate, ticking quietly. Now it came forward.

"An excessive intake of alcohol will only inhibit your cognitive function," it said.

"Nuts." My ribs hurt worse than ever. I took another swig.

The Scrutator sat cautiously in the client chair. "May I?"

I slid the bottle across the desk. The Scrutator took a hesitant sip, the liquor sloshing past the ratchets in its neck. Its eyes wobbled. "The taste is pleasing."

"You can taste?" I reclaimed the bottle, found a pair of shot glasses, set up doubles. No sense being uncivilised. "Machines can taste?"

"What you define as 'taste' is merely the chemical analysis of substances passing through the corporeal threshold. It is a reproducible phenomenon."

"Since they tuned up your taste buds, you'd think they'd have greased your vocabulary."

"I cannot parse that sentence."

"Never mind." The bourbon was working on the pain in my side. I figured three more doubles, I wouldn't feel a thing. "So, you Scrutators—the Thanes built you, right?"

"That statement is correct."

"You ever see one? A Thane, I mean."

"Nobody sees the Thanes. Not even their children."

"Huh? I thought the Thanes couldn't have kids."

"I mean the Scrutators. The Thanes construct their children. I, and all my kind, are their offspring—that is how they regard us. They love us. That is why they saved us."

The Scrutator downed another shot of bourbon. You wouldn't think alcohol and androids were compatible, but it seemed to me the robot was slurring its words.

I was struggling with the idea of the Scrutators being the children of the Thanes—that a bunch of omnipotent entities more godlike than the gods had even felt the urge to get parental. And why, in order to scratch that particular itch, had they decided to head for the metalwork shop?

"So how did they 'save' you?"

"Last year, the Thanes recalled all the Scrutators to their origination plant, packaged them up and despatched them out of the cosmos to a location where..."

"Hold up, metal buddy. Rewind. Did you say, 'out of the cosmos'?"

"I believe those were the words I used. All my siblings have now been despatched. I am the last Scrutator left in String City. And, for the record, I am not made of metal."

The bottle was nearly empty. I had another one somewhere. My brain was too fuzzy to tell me where. "But... 'out of the cosmos'? Nobody goes *out*. There is no *out*—everything's *in* the cosmos. The dimensions, the strings, everything. What did the Thanes *do*?"

"They are the Thanes," said the Scrutator, as if it was an explanation.

I shook my head, bemused. "Why didn't they send you away too?" Another question occurred to me. "What do you mean, you're not made of metal?"

"I am what you might term an experimental model. All my siblings were indeed forged by metallurgists. I, however, was knitted."

"*Knitted*?"

"From cosmic string. On the macro scale, I give the impression of operating on straightforward mechanical principles; however, were you to examine me at a sub-nano level, you would perceive my weave." The Scrutator paused, the shot glass an inch from its gear-lined mouth. Its eyes trembled. "The weave of me is also the weave of the worlds. This is the reason I was forced to stay behind when my siblings left: because I am knitted from the cosmos, I am therefore part of the cosmos, and so cannot leave it by conventional means. I am the web and the web is me; I am attuned to the cosmos to such a degree that I hear all the sounds filtering down through the web of the worlds, all the echoes pouring in from the great beyond, everything that collapses into the distilling receptacle that is String City. This ability is a blessing, but it is also a curse, for it gives me the ability to hear everything that is going on, at all times, simultaneously, everywhere."

I put down the bourbon, grabbed the Scrutator's thin wrist.

"You can hear everything?" I said. "Everywhere?"

Eyes knitted from cosmic string and addled by bourbon struggled to focus on my face. "I believe that is what I said."

"Can you hear Zephyr?"

49

THE SCRUTATOR SOBERED up as quick as it had got drunk. Just flicked a relay in its belly, flushed out the booze. Me, I had to use strong coffee.

"Can you hear her yet?" I said for the fourth time.

"Ssh," said the Scrutator for the fifth.

It was inching on its mechanical tiptoes from one corner of the office to the other. Its arms were cocked at weird angles, like it was doing tai chi.

"What are you doing?"

"Triangulating. Please remain silent."

I swigged more coffee. My head felt like an anvil under a

cyclops hammer. I tried to imagine what the Scrutator was hearing. Everything? *Really* everything? Was that even possible? But this was String City, where all things collide, and a robot was a child of the Thanes.

I opened my mouth to ask what it was like, to have all the sounds of the cosmos filling your ears, every second of the day. The Scrutator's baleful glare closed it again.

Best leave the robot to it.

I carried my coffee down to the cellar. The street grille was leaking thunderbird blood down the corner wall. I mopped it clean, tossed the rags into the tokamak, then sat on the bunk and wondered what Zephyr's apartment was like back on her homeworld.

"You have no home," she'd said to me.

She was wrong.

Truth was, I owned a clapboard house on Nukatem Street. I'd gone back there just once since taking over the detective agency from Jimmy the Griff. A single visit in ten years. I wondered what the old place looked like now. Dusty, I figured. If it was even standing.

I closed my eyes, imagined the front door of the home I'd shared with Laura. Imagined slipping the brass key into the lock, hearing the slow creak of the hinges as I pushed the door open. The antique mirror in the lobby, the mahogany staircase. Downstairs would be dark, on account of how the house backed on to the elephants' graveyard. Those bones take out a lot of light.

I imagined opening the door to the front room. Seeing the hospital bed in the middle of the floor, the rest of the furniture pushed to the walls to make room for it, the bed that had held Laura for all the long months of her illness, until the day she decided to end it. Beside the bed, a small nightstand crammed with tablets and tonics. A jug that had once held water. An IV stand. A cheap novel with a bookmark in the middle: a novel that would never now be finished.

A dent in the mattress in the shape of my dead wife. The shape of Laura.

Lying on the bed beside the dent, a cardboard box.

I imagined walking over to the box, taking off the lid, peering to see what was hidden inside. Hearing the echo of her laugh as she said what she always said when I couldn't make sense of things:

You get too bogged down in the details, baby. You never see the big picture...

"I believe I have triangulated the position of your assistant in eight of the eleven dimensions," the Scrutator called from upstairs. "This should be enough to generate an optimal path for acquisition."

I took the steps three at a time. The office was nearly as dark as the cellar: another thunderbird had crash-landed outside, splashing the cracked windows with fresh blood. The Scrutator stood in deep red shadow balanced awkwardly on one leg, mechanical limbs extended at haywire angles, gears grinding against gravity.

"I should be grateful if you would hurry, sir," it said. "I regret I can maintain this posture for only another seventeen point four seconds."

"What can you hear?"

"I hear a rhythmic non-verbal vocalisation, concurrent with the reflexive intake of breath."

"Meaning?"

"I believe Zephyr is sobbing."

"Where is she?"

"Positioning coordinates are available on the surface of my retinas."

I looked into the robot's eyes. Numbers like tax bills scrolled behind its pupils. I memorised the sequence, not understanding—not needing to understand. Raw data was all I needed.

I grabbed my coat from the stand, turned it inside-out twice until it was moleskin. Not knowing where I was headed, I went for comfort. I reached in the pocket, took out the Dimension Die.

"I am afraid Zephyr's location is not stable," said the Scrutator, "due to disruption in the branes caused by recent cataclysmic events. The data you have absorbed will be invalid in nine point nine seconds."

I closed my fist over the Dimension Die. It bothered me how much I'd come to rely on it. Now there were only three rolls left. At least this time I wasn't using it as a cheap means of escape. I was using it to perform a rescue mission.

"Six point seven seconds," said the Scrutator.

I thought of Zephyr, and all the places she could have ended up.

"Two point five seconds."

I thought of home.

"Zero point six seconds. Sir, I advise you to..."

I filled up my head with the coordinates and rolled the die.

50

A WORD ABOUT worlds.

First you've got the strings, then you've got the branes. The idea that branes are like sand layered in a jar is good, but look at them another way and you'll see they're also like flesh—the deep, damp flesh of the cosmos. The thing is, flesh needs support, otherwise it's no better than egg custard. The strings help with that. They run through the branes like rebar through concrete. Or ligaments. But they're not enough. What flesh really needs is bones.

That's where the worlds come in.

Some folk think the worlds ride on the waves of the cosmos, like ships on an ocean. In fact it's the other way round. Every world's a bone, part of the unimaginable skeleton that supports the bulk. Like bones, the worlds are all connected. Toe-bone to skull-bone, and all bones between. There's billions of worlds, all joined up by the strings, each with its part to play. Billions of bones. You should see the anatomy chart.

Like bones, worlds do different jobs. There's all shapes and all sizes. Some move, some are locked solid. All have a part to play, some more important than others. Some are hidden, purpose unknown.

There's one world that's different. Plenty seek it; few find it. Not that it's hidden—it's just hard to grasp. It's a slippery world, small like a pebble. An unremarkable world tucked deep in the bulk, just another tiny link in a vast cosmic chain. It's a place I've been to many times, and go to whenever I can, because it's something special. Like all worlds, it has many names.

I call it the Wishbone.

51

I KNEW THE place at once. Worlds tug you down, each with its different pull; if you want to know where you are in the cosmos, just ask the soles of your feet. Last time I was in this world I went to help a woman whose baby had turned to wood. Another long story.

I knew as soon as I arrived that was something badly out of

step. It was like hearing an untuned piano, or a band playing five-four jazz while everyone danced the waltz.

I was in an alley. It was raining. No surprise there—weather joins worlds just like the strings. I took off my coat, turned it inside-out three times until it was seersucker, and stepped out into the street.

To my right rose a sheer rock face. On top of the rock was a Victorian mansion. Scaffolding held up the rock, which was crumbling like cheese, and behind it was a modest city skyline. A full moon lit up evening clouds; beneath it, a terrace of dark houses. Traffic clogged the street, the end of rush hour. The city looked familiar, but I couldn't quite pin it down. I see a lot of cities.

My key fob's got a built-in Kronechtomiser. Just a cheap plastic thing, useless for serious time-slicing, but what do you expect from a breakfast cereal giveaway? Still, it's handy when you want to glimpse the history of a place.

I used the Kronechtomiser to scan the rock face. Seen through the little lens, the scaffolding melted away. The mansion faded, was replaced by a Norman castle. Pennants flew, arrows too. I saw carts, a gallows, men in Lincoln green. One wore a hood, although I knew for a fact he was no Fool.

I put the key fob away. A police car punched a hole in the traffic. Blue lights flashed. Rain fell. I listened, but all I could hear was the police car's siren. Gradually it faded. The rain eased and I started to search. The moon was bright, nearly as blue as the traffic cop's flashers.

It didn't take me long to find Zephyr. She was crouched under a tree opposite the alley where I'd materialised; the Scrutator's coordinates had brought me more or less to the bullseye. She was sobbing, just like the Scrutator had said. The tree was in the front garden of a house with no glass in the windows. The garden looked like a scrapyard. Rats gnawed abandoned tires;

tarpaulins flapped over mangled bicycles.

Zephyr was balled up beside a broken washing machine, arms round her knees, crying into the rain. When she saw me, she opened her arms and let me hug her. We stayed like that for a while, cold in the drizzle. Eventually I pulled away.

"You ready to go back?"

She looked at me blank. "You came for me?"

"Who else?"

Thin shoulders trembled. "It's too late for that. I've been trying to save myself, ever since I got back here. But nothing works. Nothing makes any difference. You might as well go. Leave me here. There's nothing anyone can do."

I showed her the Dimension Die. "You know how it works. I roll this, we're out of here."

Zephyr shook her head. "That's not what I meant. I meant you *can't* save me. You can't change what I am, what I've done."

I put the die away, sat next to her, put my palms on the dirt, and let this world's broken rhythm soak up into them.

"What did Deliciosa say to you? Just before the tornado carried you off."

Zephyr wiped her eyes with her sodden sleeve. "She said, 'Think of where you want to be.' That's all."

It figured. Planck tornadoes are a little like the Dimension Die—they feed off your thoughts. If you enter one in a panic, you'll wind up in Mammon's mouth. Deliciosa had been smart enough to calm Zephyr down, allowing her to decide her own destination rather than let the tornado do it for her. Looked like the trick had worked.

Yet it didn't look like Zephyr was happy about the result.

"Is this your home?"

"Yes. Nottingham. England. I've lived here long enough to know it inside-out. Only..."

"Only it doesn't feel right? The place feels out of kilter? Like none of the angles fit?"

Her black-rimmed eyes were brilliant in the moonlight. "That's right! How did you know?"

"This isn't your world. Not quite. It's a parallel one. Planck tornadoes never move in straight lines—it's why they're called twisters. You aim at the gold and end up in the black. Happens all the time."

"So you're saying this might be Nottingham, but it's not my Nottingham?"

"Right. It's close, but nobody's smoking a cigar."

She nodded. "I knew it. I knew something wasn't right."

"Let me guess—the days are looping?"

"What?"

"Looping. Are you seeing the same events repeat themselves?"

"How did you know?"

"Just tell me what you've seen."

She smeared a rain-streaked hand across her face. "I've been watching myself, coming and going, over and over again. It's like I'm seeing history repeating itself, but I can't do a single thing to change it. Believe me, I've tried. I've been here for three weeks now, trying every single day to make things different, and nothing's changed."

The rain had stopped. A rat sniffed my boot. I kicked it away. The clouds peeled back from the moon, revealing a sky turned to night.

"Three *weeks*?" I said. "But you've been gone less than an hour." I shouldn't have been surprised. Time twists when you walk the Planck.

"How can that be?"

"Never mind. Just tell me what's going on. Start at the beginning."

Zephyr's eyes filled up with tears again. "There is no beginning. It's all just a great big circle turning round and round, over and over again."

"Tell me anyway."

"You see that house there?" She pointed across the street. "The one with the orange curtains? That's where we used to live, me and my boyfriend. Raymond, his name was. The house was split into flats; we had the top floor. It was pretty shabby but we didn't care. It was our place. Our home.

"We'd been together nearly a year, Raymond and me. We met when he came into the shop where I worked—one of the big department stores in town. He wanted to buy some fancy bath stuff for an aunt, so I helped him pick out a bottle. He asked me on a date, and I went, and that was that. He told me was a waiter.

"The first few weeks were great. We did all the usual things: movies and pizzas and, well, you know. He took me for a meal at the place where he worked. It was this fake medieval hall that did themed banquets. Every night he'd dress up like Robin Hood and carry great plates of meat about for the punters. We went there on his night off and had the most amazing time, eating suckling pig and greasy venison and, oh, it was wild! When all the punters had gone, we stayed behind, and Raymond got them to turn up the music and turn down the lights and we danced to this amazing minstrel music that was all lutes and harps and bagpipes. We danced and danced, and the funny thing was that the more we went round and round, the more it seemed like it wasn't us dancing at all. It felt like we were completely still and it was the room doing the dancing. The whole room turning around us. The whole world even. Isn't that strange?"

"It isn't strange at all, honey," I said.

"Anyway, toward the end of that first month, Raymond started working longer and longer shifts, so I ended up spending a lot of evenings alone in the flat. He got moody—I assumed he was just tired. I've never been good at staying up late, so I just used to go to bed and tell him not to disturb me when he came in.

"One night I couldn't sleep. I don't know—maybe the moon was too bright. I got up, made myself a drink of chocolate and waited for him on the couch.

"He came in around two in the morning. At first I thought he was drunk, because he smelt awful and couldn't keep his balance. He kept coughing, like he'd got something stuck in his throat. I waited for him to spot me, but the lights were out. I don't think he even knew I was there. He took a beer from the fridge and drank it straight down from the can. He'd just grabbed another when he suddenly doubled up with his hands clutched against his stomach. He dropped the beer, which started spurting all over the floor.

"I jumped off the couch, going to help him, thinking maybe he'd got a cramp or something. I stopped when these things sprang up and ripped open the back of his shirt."

"'Things'?"

"Quills. It was a row of quills, like on a porcupine."

Zephyr stopped, clamped her arms round her knees again. Her eyes were distant, unfocused.

"Go on," I said.

"There was this cracking sound. It was his bones. It was... appalling. He dropped to all fours and his whole body changed shape. His hands melted together into hooves. His shoulders grew taller and narrower, his neck got thicker. A snout pushed its way through the middle of his face, and these two enormous tusks came out of his mouth. I swear I heard his jaw breaking. You have no idea."

I'd seen more shapeshifters than she'd seen movies and eaten pizzas and, well, you know. "Go on," I said.

"He turned into a boar," she said. "My boyfriend Raymond turned into a wild animal by the light of the full moon. And there was me, watching, wondering what was going to happen next." She started crying again.

"So what did happen?"

"He saw me. He came toward me. He was sort of... snuffling. I backed into a corner. I was terrified. This great wild boar came right up to me, and when I looked into its eyes it was still Raymond. It was Raymond's eyes looking out. He looked just as scared as I did. I reached out and stroked his head. His back was all covered in those quills, but the fur on his head was soft.

"He only stayed that way for a few hours. The next morning he was back to normal—more than normal, really. He was relaxed, cheerful, happier than he'd been since I'd known him. He was... wonderful. I kept trying to talk about what had happened, but every time I was about to say something I just caught his smile and froze up. I just didn't want to do anything to burst the bubble. After a while, I even started to believe it had just been a crazy dream.

"The next month it happened all over again. And every month after that.

"I stayed with him through the transformations. After he'd changed, well, it wasn't like a werewolf movie or anything. He didn't go on a rampage or killing spree. It was just sort of sad and ordinary. He kept rooting round the flat, as if he was looking for something. Me, I'd just leave him to it and go back to bed. When I woke up the next day, he was in bed beside me, human again.

"Then, one morning, I woke to find that this time he hadn't changed back. I didn't know what to do. I called in sick at work and hung around the flat, waiting to see what would happen. After the second night he was Raymond again. Gradually it got worse. Each month, he spent more and more time as a boar, and less and less as a man. I had more and more time off work. The flat was a mess—his hooves ruined the carpet, and the smell... it was foul."

"You *never* talked to him about it?" It was a little hard to believe.

"Never. Talk about the elephant in the room." She barked out a laugh. "Okay—not exactly an elephant. It's crazy, I know, but it was like... we both knew what was happening, but neither of us dared to raise the subject. But it was taking its toll. I got depressed, couldn't sleep, started taking tablets. Soon Raymond was a boar most of the time. Whenever anyone came to the flat I sent them away, or just ignored the door altogether. It was a terrible time. And do you know what the worst of it was? Raymond hated it. Every single second of it. He never said it, but I knew he wanted it to stop. So I stopped it for him."

A thin cloud slit the moon. Silver light washed the giant rock that held the remains of Nottingham Castle. Even without the Kronechtomiser I thought I could see the ghosts of older times.

Zephyr went on. "I was back at work. I was trying to get my life back on track. I'd pretty much decided I was going to leave him, but I couldn't pluck up the courage. I got off the bus. I was carrying shopping bags—I'd been to the supermarket. I went up to the flat, found Raymond in his boar-shape, as usual. He saw me and ran at me. He took a swipe at me with his tusks. If I hadn't moved he'd have opened me up like a sardine tin. He stood there—the boar stood there—steam coming out of his snout, the quills erect on his back. He grunted, and looked as if he was going to charge me again, but then he stopped.

"He stopped and looked right at me. This horrible, giant, stinking animal looked at me with my lover's eyes. I could see right inside him, all the way inside to where my Raymond was trapped. He looked so sad. He was pleading with me. He couldn't say anything, but I knew he was pleading.

"I went to the bedroom, took my silver christening crucifix out of the drawer and went back into the living room. Raymond hadn't moved. I didn't say anything, didn't even think. I just drove the crucifix into his neck like a dagger. I must have hit an artery, because blood sprayed out, all over the place. He fell to his knees and started panting. I fell with him—my face was right next to those awful boar's tusks. If he'd wanted to, he could have taken my head off. But he didn't. Then I held him as he died, waiting for him to turn back into the man I'd loved. That's what happens in the movies, isn't it? Doesn't the werewolf always turn back into the man? But he didn't. He stayed a boar. I never saw Raymond again. And every day since that day, I've had to live with the knowledge that I murdered him."

Zephyr's tears had dried. I held her hand, got nothing back, let go.

"Raymond was a bosquadrille," I said. "Shapeshifter, from the wildwood. Time was this whole town was surrounded by deep forest. Just ask Herne the Hunter. Bosquadrilles are were-humans—that's why they remain as beasts when they die. My guess is he'd been walking the years, waiting for someone like you to come along."

"What do you mean, 'walking the years'?" She was all spent. She asked the question, didn't care whether or not she got an answer. I gave her one anyway.

"Honey, bosquadrilles live a long, long time. Chances are Raymond was here centuries before this city was. Before even the castle. He'd have seen some things."

"Like Robin Hood?" Seemed like she was listening after all.

"Maybe. Mind you, Hood isn't what folk think he is. Not at

all. When we get back to String City, maybe I'll take you to the wildwood. You can ask him yourself. Meantime, your story—it isn't finished, is it?"

Zephyr fetched up a long sigh. "You've probably guessed the rest. After I'd killed Raymond—once I came to my senses, I mean—I realised I couldn't stay in the flat. What on Earth do you do with a dead boar in the middle of Nottingham? So I ran.

"I ran through the streets, not caring where I was going. It was raining—pretty soon it had turned into a storm. I found myself up at the castle gates. It was night, so they were locked, but I squeezed through. It's a sad place now; there's hardly anything left of the original walls. But that night it was... different. Perhaps it was the lightning—all that flashing made things look strange and magical. I felt detached, in a kind of limbo. I kept seeing things out of the corner of my eye, catching glimpses of old buildings that shouldn't have been there—towers and battlements. I saw shadows, people running, orange light like flames. It was as if I was in two places at once."

I nodded. "Anomalistic interbrane entemporation. Extreme emotion can trigger it."

She glared at me, continued, "I kept walking. The castle was much bigger than it should have been. I went through gates that shouldn't have been there, down passages, through great halls. I could hear men fighting, but I never saw them. I went through another gate, under a portcullis, and suddenly I was out in a street—just a regular city street. It was still raining. I assumed I'd had some kind of hallucination and decided to go back to the flat. Maybe I could clear up the mess after all. Then I started looking in the shopfronts, and at the beggars in the gutters, and at the birds that were swooping overhead. The birds were as big as Airbuses. That's when I realised I wasn't in Nottingham any more. The weird thing is, I didn't question what was going on. I felt, I don't know... *energised*, more myself than I had for months. It was very peculiar.

"I walked the rest of the night and through into the next day, until I found myself at your office. Something made me stop outside your door. That's when I saw the 'Help Wanted' sign on the glass. And... well, the rest you know."

Forbidden love. No wonder she'd freaked when she'd seen that movie poster in Harry's Holodeon. It was a story I'd heard a hundred times before. Love between species. Love between worlds too.

Folk are always slipping between worlds. Emotion opens the doors, but the reason the doors are there in the first place is the wildwood. The wildwood's like fungus: it grows everywhere, and underneath it's all connected. Its roots run deep, go back a long, long way. The oldest forests of all lie north of String City. Folk still go there to hunt, gather berries, make voodoo. Occasionally they come back.

Thing is, the wildwood winds its roots into people too. Most folk don't realise we're all part sap. It's the sap that draws people across, when the weather's right, and the time's right. Draws them along the strings, through the roots of the wildwood, across the bulk. Plucks them from one unlikely place, sets them in another. That's what happened to Zephyr. She was just one more transaction on the purchase ledger of the cosmos.

Trouble was, the books weren't balancing.

Something made me stop outside your door.

That's what she'd said. It was the biggest of all the things she'd said, and she'd all but thrown it away.

The hairs on the back of my neck were prickling like boar quills.

"What exactly was it that made you...?" I began. But she put her hand on my mouth, pushed me back against the tree.

"Be quiet!" she hissed. "Look, over there. Here I come again!"

52

ACROSS THE STREET, a bus had pulled up. A small thin girl with short dark hair got off. She was carrying plastic bags full of shopping.

She was Zephyr.

Zephyr—the Zephyr who was with me—gripped my hand. "Please," she said. "Oh, please, let it work this time!"

I stared at her. "Let what work?" I said. "Zephyr, what have you done?"

"Just watch."

When I looked back, the bus had already pulled away. The parallel Zephyr was walking up the path to the house. She went inside and, a minute later, appeared at an upstairs window. She knelt; now we could only see her head. Something out of sight cast a big shadow up the wall. A shadow with spines.

The parallel Zephyr got up and disappeared through a door. The adjacent room lit up. She rummaged in a drawer, came up with empty hands, then ran her hands through her hair, looked puzzled. She rummaged again, in vain. Then she left the room.

Beside me, something glinted in the moonlight. I looked down, saw my own Zephyr holding up a silver crucifix.

"I went inside the apartment earlier," she said. "I keep going in there, rearranging things, trying to make things different. Trying to change my past. Trying to stop myself from killing him. This time I took the murder weapon."

In the flat, the parallel Zephyr reappeared in the living room. She bent again, lifted up one of the shopping bags. She drew out something long and shiny. Seemed she'd been shopping for silver candlesticks.

She bludgeoned the boar to death.

My Zephyr threw the crucifix in the dirt, buried her face in her hands.

"It never works!" she sobbed. "Whatever I do, she finds a way round it. I glued up the door locks—she smashed a window to get in. I herded the boar out into the garden—she bludgeoned it to death with a spade. I've spent three weeks trying to erase my crime from history, and nothing works! What am I going to do?"

"There's nothing you can do. History is history. You have to let it go." I took her arm; she shoved me away.

"Don't tell me what I have to do! I've been sent here for a reason! I know I have! I'm here to make up for my crime! I have to make things different! If I don't... I don't think I can live with myself!"

"You did what you did. Crime of passion. Who'd blame you?"

She thumped my chest. "*I* blame me! And who are you to call me a criminal?"

"That's not what I meant, honey."

She glared at me, her anguish just as bright as the moon. "Help me, please. Isn't there something you can do? I've seen you do things, incredible things. Isn't there some magic you can work? I'm not asking you to rewrite the whole history book, just wipe out one mistake. I'm begging you, please!"

I held her, feeling her sob. She seemed very small. I felt sorry for her. For Raymond too. Bosquadrilles are noble creatures, rare and old. It was wrong, what she'd done. Even though I knew I might have done the exact same thing myself, if love had pushed me that way.

"There's something," I said slowly. "It's not magic exactly, only a trick."

"I don't care what it is. I only care if it works."

"It's dangerous," I said. "It's nothing I've used before."

"You can make it work."

"I don't know."

"I believe in you." She put her head down, her eyes up. A small and vulnerable woman in the moon-shadow of a tree rooted deep in the place where outlaws once ran.

So help me, it was an offer I couldn't refuse.

53

THERE WAS ONLY one safe way back to String City: the Dimension Die. Even if the dimensions hadn't been screwed up, I'd probably have used it. Alternate realities are sneaky things: if you don't use the same route back you used to get in, everything can get redoubled. A parallel String City wasn't somewhere I cared to explore. A city like that, things could get *really* weird.

"Stand back," I said. "For this trick to work, we need to take something with us."

I took off my coat, flapped out the creases. I turned it inside-out seven times until it was a combination weave of white alpaca and six-dimensional twill. I spread it on the ground, unfolded it until it was twice its usual size. I let it settle, unfolded it again. Twice more and it covered the whole garden. I kept unfolding, doubling the coat's size each time until it was bigger than the street. Then I flipped it over and folded it back up with the street inside.

Zephyr watched me work, her mouth hanging open.

"That's a good trick," she said.

"You ain't seen nothing yet."

I put on the coat. It was heavier than usual.

I took out the Dimension Die, held it up in the moonlight. Two black faces left. If I used it now, it would be good for only one more roll.

"Zephyr..." I began.

The hope on her face shut up my mouth and made up my mind.

She held my hand.

I rolled the die.

54

We materialised in the cellar of my office. Above our heads the trapdoor was shut. The street grille was clogged with bloody thunderbird feathers. Everything was dark.

"Should we let Bronzey know we're back?" said Zephyr.

"Let's finish our business first. Then we'll rap with the robot."

I tripped the override on the tokamak, turned the dial to low. The fusion burners lit up then immediately damped down. A baleful glow settled on the cellar. I took an iron key from the run of hooks above the mattress. My hand brushed the smaller brass key hanging beside it, knocking it to the floor. Zephyr picked it up.

"What's this for?" she asked.

"Nothing important," I said.

"Is it for that?" She pointed to the vague outline of the bricked-in door in the corner.

"No. It doesn't matter. Like I said."

I hung the key to my empty house back on the hook.

Zephyr was staring at the bunk. "Don't you get lonely? Working upstairs, sleeping down here? I'd go crazy."

"It's what I do."

I went to the crate of gumshoe gadgets, popped open the secret plank in the side. A hidden lock shone in the light of the tokamak.

"Jimmy told me only to open this compartment in an emergency," I said. "I figure that's what we've got."

"You keep mentioning this Jimmy," said Zephyr. "You told me he was the detective who owned the business before you, but who actually was he? How did you know him? And don't tell me it's a long story."

I smiled. Felt like a long time since I'd done that.

"The short version is, Jimmy and I grew up together. Not here, someplace else. We were like brothers. Then we fell out, like brothers do, went our separate ways. Jimmy trained as an architect, ended up working as a short-order chef. We met up again during the Titanomachy—that was a big war between the gods and the Titans. And I'm sorry—that really *is* a whole other story. Anyway, after the war we got separated again. Jimmy fetched up in String City. That's when he set up the detective agency. Meanwhile I'd gone on the road, got myself married, eventually found my way here too."

"I remember you telling Kisi Sunyana you were married. What happened to your wife?"

"There were two. The first one cleaned me out. Not that I was rich. The second one—Laura her name was—made me rich in ways I hadn't known existed."

"What happened to her? To Laura?"

"She got sick and died."

"I'm sorry."

"Thanks." I held up the iron key. "We're wasting time."

There were two kinds of gadgets in the crate. First were the gimmicky ones—like the doppelganger compact that was still burning a hole in my pocket. One-shot devices, occasionally useful when solving really obstinate cases. Second were the ones in the secret drawer. These I rarely used, on account of how they all had hidden consequences. Prices to pay.

I opened the secret compartment. Brought out the quantum zoetrope. Gave it to Zephyr.

"It looks like a snowglobe," said Zephyr, turning it in her hands. "Only there's nothing in the globe."

"There will be."

I took off my coat, folded it in half, then in half again. I kept folding until it was the size of a postage stamp. Then I slipped it through the slot in the zoetrope's base.

The zoetrope shook. Workings whirred. Shapes condensed inside the globe. Snow started falling. When the snow stopped, there was a miniature street inside. The street I'd brought here from the Wishbone.

"This zooms it in," I said, touching one of the knobs on the side.

Zephyr turned the knob. The street got bigger. Now a single building filled the globe: a terraced house.

"It's my apartment!"

The zoetrope spat out my coat. I shook it out to normal size, turned it inside-out four times until it was calfskin, tossed it on the bunk.

I showed Zephyr how the zoetrope worked.

"These knobs on the side work the view: zoom, pan, so on. The rest of it's like your basic movie editing suite. These dials shuttle the timeline backward and forward. You can make selections, cut and paste. Edit."

"What am I editing?"

"Your past."

55

I LEFT HER in the cellar, went to join the Scrutator up in the office.

"I deduced you had both returned," said the robot as I came

up through the trapdoor. "However, I was reluctant to interrupt whatever activities you had chosen to undertake in the cellar. I am, of course, aware that there is a bunk down there."

"There was no funny business," I said, "if that's what you mean."

"Is Zephyr in good health?"

"She's okay, I guess. A little mixed up. I've given her something that might help. What's been happening here? Are the deadlocks holding? I still don't like that big crack in the door glass."

"The office is secure, despite increasing levels of violent activity outside. According to the police wavelengths—and based upon what I myself have observed through the windows—I can report that, while the municipal department has been clearing the streets of downed thunderbirds, String City's major residential zones have come under the occupancy of a substantial invasion force consisting of anansi-asansa."

"Arachne's spiders!" I said. "So she's launched her attack after all. I guess the explosion at the Birdhouse was the perfect diversion. Given what the scathefire did, I'm surprised there's any city left to for her conquer."

"String City is indeed experiencing severe dimensional disruption," said the Scrutator. "A powder storm is raging on an unprecedented scale. The strings are transmitting rumors of devastation through the bulk at unprecedented speed. Worlds are falling. I can hear it all."

"What are those?" I said, peering through the window. The sky was full of big silver shapes, flying high.

"I believe they are B29 Superfortresses, transported here through a convolutionary wormhole, possibly from an earlier age of the Wishbone, or a world like it."

"Let's hope *Enola Gay* ain't up there."

Out in the street, a mob was engaged in a running battle with a squad of spiderlings from Arachne's army. Mobs in String City are exotic affairs; this was more exotic than most.

Centaurs chased legless lizards. The lizards had coxcombs and spat brimstone. Golems blundered after the lizards; nymphs were driving the golems on, shouting in their ears. A trio of Gorgons went past dragging a cauldron. The snakes on their heads were feeding on their eyes. The street itself moved like it was alive; sewer grates popped open, spilling steaming gloop over the asphalt. Black feelers poked from the underworld, scenting for prey. Scurrying between the feet of the passers-by, everywhere you looked, were the anansi-asansa. Spiders with iron fangs.

"Any new clients?" I said. A two-headed hippo trotted past with half the Seelie Court on its back.

"I regret to report we have taken on no new cases today."

"It'll pick up later."

Zephyr came up from the cellar. She was carrying the zoetrope like it was the crown jewels.

"I've finished." She looked flushed, happy, like a child wanting to show off a painting. "Do you want to see?"

She set the zoetrope on the desk. We crowded round it. She pushed the button marked *PLAY*.

Inside the globe, a scene unfolded. A bus pulled up in the street. Zephyr climbed off. There was a jump cut, then Zephyr was in the apartment. Raymond was there. A couple more jumps and they were dancing. A waltz. Tinny music wafted up from the globe. The dance went on, jumped, repeated. It repeated over and over. In her man's arms, the miniature Zephyr was crying. She looked very happy.

"That's it," said the real Zephyr, the one at my side. "It doesn't look much—it was hard getting the joins right. I suppose it's a bit jerky."

"It's fine," I said.

"What I wanted to ask you was—well, these edits I've made in the zoetrope, do they... is this what's happening back in my world, back in Nottingham?"

She didn't seem to notice my hesitation. "More or less. The edits percolate out through the dimensions. Like music through harp strings. They set up harmonies in every parallel world they can find. In most versions of the Wishbone, you and Raymond are now together."

"So this new sequence of events I've made—it's true?"

"As true as you want it to be."

The blush spread from her face down her neck. She looked as happy as the Zephyr in the globe. "Then I've done all I can. Only, I was wondering—what should I do with these?" She held up a sheaf of little cards, like Polaroids. "These are all the bits I cut out. Like the, you know, the part where I stabbed him with the crucifix. Each time I made a cut, the zoetrope spat out one of these. They're like little moving pictures. I don't know what to do with them."

She held them at arm's length, nose wrinkled, like she didn't want to touch them.

I looked at the deleted scenes. I looked at the Scrutator.

I looked at Zephyr.

"Come with me," I said.

56

THE SCRUTATOR DROVE us to the crater in his automobile. It was a rough journey, but the robot was well acquainted with String City's back-alleys and the car had good legs. When we reached the Street of Plenty, we found the crowd barriers deserted. All the cops had either fled or been blown into the crater by the relentless wind. There were a few residual tremors, and the tornadoes had mostly blown themselves out. Zephyr and I left the robot with the car and descended into the crater on foot.

The Fool was exactly where we'd left him, sat at the bottom of the crater, still dismantling the Still Point of the Turning World. The pile of golden dust had grown to a small mountain. The SPTW looked smaller than ever. How long before it was nothing? Minutes? Days? Who knew?

"We can't stop it, can we?" said Zephyr, staring at the hooded figure.

"No," I said. "Nobody can. The clock's ticking."

We waited for a tornado. The first two that came looked big and nasty, the kind best avoided. The third was tiny, little more than a dust-devil. I brought Zephyr within throwing distance.

"Not too close," I said. "It may look small but it can still suck you down."

"You don't need to tell me."

I stepped away, so she could do what she needed to do.

One by one, she threw the deleted scenes into the tornado. Instead of swallowing them down, the whirlwind tore them to shreds.

I waited, wishing I felt good about what she was doing. It was a fine thing to see her happy. But it was hard to be happy myself with a Fool sitting right there, taking the worlds apart.

Besides, I couldn't stop thinking about crates and consequences. About prices that have to be paid.

Zephyr accidentally dropped one of the deleted scenes. An eddy snatched it up. She didn't notice. The scene skated over the ground, right toward me. I trapped it under my boot. I picked it up: a little square of card with a moving picture on the front. I started toward Zephyr. I was going to give it to her, so she could throw it away with the others.

What I saw in the picture stopped me short.

The scene was from early in the sequence. It showed Zephyr getting off the bus. When she reached the garden gate, she stopped to switch her shopping bags from one hand to the other. I didn't recall seeing her do that before. Then I remembered Zephyr distracting me when we'd been watching from under the tree. By the time I'd looked back, the bus had already driven away.

This was a moment I'd missed.

In the picture, Zephyr was about to set off up the path to the house when she spotted something on the ground. She bent her knees, picked it up. Moonlight turned it silver. Something gripped my chest. It was my heart, stopping. The hairs rose on my neck.

The thing Zephyr had picked up was a penny. Just a penny, lying in the street, lying there for anyone to find.

I waited for my heart to start beating again. For a second I thought it never would. When it did, it was thundering.

"All done!" Zephyr skipped over to me, clapping her hands. "And, do you know what? I feel *fantastic*!"

She wrapped her arms round me and kissed me full on the lips.

"I'm glad," I replied.

"Me too! Are you ready to go? Is there anything else you need to do here?"

"No," I said. "Nothing."

I slipped the deleted scene into my pocket and we climbed up out of the crater, and the Scrutator drove us back to the office. Zephyr was so happy she didn't remark on my distracted air until we were sat back in our chairs.

"Are you okay?" she said. "It's just... I thought you'd be pleased for me."

"I am," I said. "Really. It's peachy."

"No. Something's wrong. What is it?"

The deleted scene played over and over in my head.

"I've got a question for you," I said.

"Is it a hard question or an easy one?"

"Depends on you."

"Ask away."

"When you were talking about how you came to String City, you told me something made you stop at my office door. What was it?"

"I don't really remember. I just... no, wait a second, that was it. Something flew past my head. A bird. It startled me, it flew so close. I sort of jumped back, into the doorway of your office. That's how I saw the *Help Wanted* sign."

"What kind of bird? Was it big?"

"No—actually it was small. It flew really fast, like a bullet. I only caught a glimpse. I remember the color though. It was blue-green, electric."

"Like a kingfisher?"

"Yes! A kingfisher! That's exactly what it was like. Why are you so interested?"

"Bird spotting's my thing. Didn't I tell you?"

I rubbed my neck. It was hard to keep my tone light. First the penny, now this. A big part of me wanted to tell her everything these two things made me fear. But where to begin?

"You're a strange man," Zephyr said.

"It's a strange town, honey."

The Scrutator came in then, having got back from garaging the car at Tony Marscapone's place. The sun was going down; the street was quiet at last. No mob. No spiders. Still, I closed the deadlocks. It was probably just a lull.

We stood a minute, the three of us. Then Zephyr spread her

arms, hugged us together.

"We're quite a team, aren't we?" she said.

We both resisted, the robot and me. At last I relented, let her squeeze me close. The Scrutator made a resistant whirr before bringing his mechanical body in for the clinch. Then we broke and sat behind our respective desks. Zephyr was grinning. The Scrutator purred. Despite everything, I forced myself to smile.

"You know," said Zephyr, "I've come a long way today. I've seen this crazy city fall down about my ears, and seen my own past blow away like a cloud of dandelion seeds."

She kicked off her shoes, lifted her legs, dropped her little bare feet on her desk. The Scrutator planted his cleats on his. I raised my boots, assumed the position. It felt good. A ritual. Maybe even a rite of passage.

"The other thing I've learned," Zephyr was looking right at me, "is that it's okay to rely on other people. You'd probably call that 'sappy', but it's true. And true things are what matter. They're also our business. We're here to seek out the truth. That's our job."

The prickle that had been plaguing my neck was subsiding. So help me, it was my eyes prickling now.

"Thanks to you and your magical zoetrope," said Zephyr, "I made a new truth. And now the world's got to hold to it. Isn't that right?"

A note of pleading had edged into her voice. I ignored it. I ignored the trap in what she'd said and held on to what counted: the idea that truth was important. That much I could believe in. There was a truth in that office, right there, right then, one I kind of liked. Whatever else was happening out in the cosmos, well, the deadlocks would keep it from us. For a while.

Right now, a while was enough.

So there we sat with our feet up. We laughed. We drank coffee laced with bourbon.

For a time, things felt good.

Just as long as I didn't think about Fools and kingfishers.

And pennies.

Windy City

57

Seven days passed, during which I finally grew to understand why Zephyr and Raymond had never talked about the guy being a bosquadrille. "Talk about the elephant in the room," she'd said. Well, instead of a room I had the inside of my head, and in place of the elephant I had a shiny spinning coin and a bird with blue-green feathers.

I had little enough idea what they meant individually. Together, they signified nothing at all. Except they did. I just didn't know what. So I avoided them. Every time my thoughts strayed their way, I turned my mind to someplace else: an old case, a new case, the fact that none of our clients could pay us and we owed the bank a Thane's ransom, didn't matter what. I was in denial. If you'd asked me, of course, I'd have denied it.

On the morning of the seventh day, the sun rose bright as a tangerine. For all the rioting that had gone on the night before, and for all the devastation evident in the street outside, it sure was a beautiful dawn. I flipped over the calendar and immediately choked on my coffee. From the sublime to the mundane in a single swipe of the wrist.

"Tax inspector's due," I said.

I trudged to the coffee machine. My first visit from the tax department in ten years and I'd done nothing to prepare. I pulled the spigot with a shaking hand and ended up with more java on my shirt than in the cup.

"Let me do it," said Zephyr. She pushed me aside and drew us both a double espresso. "And stop fretting. They probably won't turn up, given the state of emergency and everything. I can't believe collecting taxes is very high on the government's to-do list right now."

"You don't know the municipals," I said, pulling a clean shirt out of my desk drawer. "They subbed out the whole tax business a couple of years ago. The new operators are keen as razors. They'll be here."

"You think so? Have you seen the state of the street?"

I had to admit things looked bad. The tangerine sun had already disappeared behind clouds, and the road outside the office was crushed like an accordion and littered with half a dozen fresh thunderbird corpses. Most of the surrounding buildings were rubble. Beyond, the String City skyline looked like a set of cancer-ridden gums. Gale-force wind blew grit and tattered newspapers in a horizontal stream. It had been blowing like that for days.

A single hamadryad hooker stood forlorn on the kerb. She looked like a lightning-struck elm, bent double by the wind. There were no passers-by to offer her trade. Looking at the state of her, I doubted anyone would have stopped anyway.

"It's like the whole city's dying," said Zephyr. She looked tired, and her face was pale.

"It's dead already," I said. "It just doesn't realise it yet. The minute that Fool started picking at the Still Point, the future was set. He's still picking at it now, and there's nothing anyone can do to stop it. It's only a matter of time."

"We have a saying back in my world, you know: 'Where there's life, there's hope'." The dead tone in her voice told me she didn't believe it.

"Folk say that here too. Doesn't stop the tax inspector calling."

"Money isn't everything, you know."

"It ain't the money, honey. It's what they do to you when you don't have it."

Together, we dug out the ledgers from the last decade and piled them next to my desk. Ten years of accounts stood nearly as tall as I did. I was about to start going through them when the door flew open. We both jumped, but it was only the Scrutator. Wind gusted past it, and for a second I thought the neatly ordered accounts books were headed to all seven points of the metacompass. But the robot was fast, managing to open and close the door quick enough to stop the gale wreaking havoc.

"Hey Bronzey," said Zephyr. "Did you sell the car?"

The Scrutator trudged across the carpet and slumped in its chair. "I did." The gears in its head were grating. Its shoulders sagged.

"You didn't have to do this, buddy," I said. "I know you loved that car."

"While I regret selling the automobile, I am glad to be of some small service. The agency's cashflow has suffered greatly during the current crisis." It held out a wad of battered bills. "This will at least enable us to trade for a little longer."

"Well, I'm grateful." It was a touching gesture, and I hated the fact I felt disappointed: the wad was thinner than Cain's alibi. Still, since the inflation curve had hit the stratosphere, most bread had gone stale anyway. "You want to put it in the safe?"

Head drooping, the Scrutator dragged its heels down to the cellar.

"Something's wrong with him," said Zephyr.

"The robot's just sore at losing its wheels."

"That car didn't have wheels. It had legs and tank tracks."

"The principle holds."

"He hasn't been right all week. I think he might be depressed."

"Machines don't get depressed. Maybe it needs a service. Anyway, you're hardly the life and soul this morning."

"I'm fine."

"Look," I said, tapping my pencil on the desk, "maybe the robot's just freaked. I know I am. For years folk have been touting the end of the world; now it's come knocking. But that won't stop the taxman. So please—can we get back to crunching the numbers?"

Before we could crunch anything, the biggest gust of wind yet stripped the street bare. Screeching like a banshee chorus, it carried off the bloated thunderbird corpses, scalped the asphalt and snapped off the poor hamadryad at the roots. I jumped up to snap the deadlocks, but I didn't even make it to the door. If I had, I'd have been dead, because right then a second gust hit the office building head-on. Cinderblocks flew like feathers. The glass in the window screamed. The wind dug in its claws, snapped sideways, and the whole office lurched a foot to the left. The front wall blew off like a champagne cork, leaving a gaping hole.

The wind stopped blowing and started sucking.

Zephyr grabbed me. I grabbed the desk. We hung out sideways like a daisy chain. I was glad the desk was bolted down. All the paperwork took flight. The Scrutator rushed up from the cellar, ticking fit to bust. Its arms went into some kind of overdrive, fielding the papers like some crazed baseball catcher. The cleats on its feet grew teeth—they bit the floor, keeping the robot from flying away. For several seconds, the entire office was full of flying paper.

At last the storm subsided. Zephyr and I crashed to the floor. The Scrutator stopped its dervish act. It stood, fists packed tight with ten years' worth of accounts.

The silence wasn't exactly worse, but it was still bad. Bad because you kept expecting another demon gust. We crept around, righting chairs, restacking shelves. Zephyr stopped to check her zoetrope was intact—the wind had taken it right off her desk. Luckily it had landed in the yucca. She peered into the globe, checked that she and Raymond were still dancing. They were.

She set the zoetrope back on her desk like it was the Holy Grail. Her face looked strangely slack; maybe both my assistants were depressed. Meanwhile the Scrutator was sorting the books back into order like a supercharged postal worker and good job, because that's when the tax inspector walked in. Zephyr looked up with a smile on her face. The smile was fake, but the scream that followed it was real.

The tax inspector was a giant scarab beetle.

58

A WORD ABOUT the Mountain.

The Mountain's where the Thanes hang out. The Thanes run things. Except they don't; they just tell the municipals what to do. It's the municipals who actually make things happen.

Except it isn't.

Truth is, String City mostly runs itself. But most folk like to believe there's order, and the Thanes know that, so they spend the taxes they collect on paying the municipals to keep house. That means employing the cops, the schoolteachers, the garbage collectors... all the same public servants you'd find in any city anywhere in the cosmos.

As for the Thanes—they keep themselves to themselves. Just as well, if the rumors about their powers are true. Don't get me wrong—they really are the good guys. No question of that. It's just that legend has it, if you look at a Thane, your eyes melt all the way through the back of your head. Then your head implodes. In a good way, they say—there's no pain, only ecstasy.

Doesn't sound like ecstasy to me.

As talk of the end of the world spread, every department on the Mountain started sub-contracting essential services. Word was the Thanes had long known what was coming. Devolution was their way of cutting loose. If you ask me, that smacks of cowardice—not that I'd ever say that to a Thane. By the time the beetle turned up in my office, nearly half the public sector had been privatised: hospitals, street maintenance—you name it. As for tax collection, they subbed that out to the sewer system. Strangely appropriate.

Sewer intelligence was a long time coming to String City; evolution runs slow in the dark. But there were a lot of drains down there. Some brought waste from extremely toxic places: the Carr Industrial Belt, the Cicatrix, the Nuclear Dustbowl... a real primordial soup. Over time, that waste started clogging, gelling. Having babies. The babies were... odd. Like most babies, they grew, and soon got too big for those cramped pipes. At that point they collapsed back into a single organism: the sewer-mind. The story goes its first words were, "I stink, therefore I am."

The sewer-mind spent years educating itself. Any literature that got swept down from the gutters, the sewer-mind read it all, from the tabloids to the complete works of Shakespeare. But while it got bright, it also got frustrated. Finally it understood why: it was unemployed. Waste disposal was a metabolism, not a career.

So it started looking for work. At the exact same time, the municipals started tendering for the tax collection gig. It was a perfect match—so good they turned over the entire Mountain bureaucracy to the sewers. The sewer-mind split into subdivisions and started running everything from social care to parking fines.

It never looked back.

I explained all this to Zephyr. She couldn't take her eyes off the giant beetle.

"I thought it was a spider at first," she whispered. "That's why I screamed."

"Don't worry about it," I said. "Nobody likes tax inspectors. Me—I'm just queasy with bugs."

"That's not very fair, is it? I mean, they're only human... well, you know what I mean. But why a beetle? I thought you said the sewer-mind was handling all this."

"Think of a regular brain," I said. "It's built from neurons. Neurons fire volts at each other. Some say that's all thought is: just electricity. But the sewer's brain is different."

"Why? What's it built from?"

"Dung balls."

I waited while she thought it through. "Are you trying to tell me this beetle is one of the sewer's thoughts?"

"Not quite. Look, here's how it works. You've got billions of scarab beetles rolling billions of dung-balls through thousands of miles of underground tunnels. All that traffic is what creates the sewer's thoughts. But the hive-mind still has to interact with the rest of the world. So it sends out individual scarabs as avatars. To do the dirty work. So to speak."

Zephyr came out from behind the desk, held out her hand to the beetle.

"Hello," she said. "My name's Zephyr. Care for some refreshments?"

The scarab's wing-cases vibrated in confusion. It wasn't used to folk being polite. It reared on its back legs, bringing its antennae level with Zephyr's face. Slowly it extended a feeler.

"Um, do you have dung?" said the scarab.

Zephyr's smile might have been false, but it didn't falter. "Sorry, no. There's a pot of fresh coffee though. Do you take sugar?"

"Twelve, please." The scarab pulled a pencil from behind one of its antennae and used its mouth-parts to sharpen it to a point. "Um, where would you like me to sit?"

59

TURNED OUT WE were the scarab's first ever assignment. It was twitchy, kept dropping its slide rule. When it moved, its shell creaked and my skin crawled, but at least it had manners.

"It's like a child on its first day at school," Zephyr whispered to me once it was settled. "I feel like I want to wipe its nose."

"It doesn't have a nose," I muttered back. "It's a bug."

The Scrutator tapped my shoulder. "I beg your pardon, but someone is calling for help."

"With ears like yours, can't you always hear someone calling for help?"

"Yes."

That brought me up short.

"However," the Scrutator went on, "this particular individual is within close proximity—directly outside the office door, in fact."

"There is no door." I pointed to the wall that wasn't there.

We went outside to look. The air was calm, the city quiet. Eerie. I almost preferred the storm. Almost. A cry came from above. I looked straight up and saw a skinny man hanging off the guttering, twenty feet over my head.

"Jump," I called.

"If I jump," he answered, "I'll break my legs."

"The robot will catch you."

The man considered this for a long time. Eventually he let go and fell. Sure enough, the Scrutator caught him and lowered him to the ground. The man brushed himself down, tweaking mustaches like yard brooms. Somehow he managed to grin around the wad of chewing tobacco that was filling his mouth.

"Obliged," he said.

"How'd you get up there?" I said.

"The wind. What else? That storm sure was a doozie."

"So where were you headed?"

"Here. You the gumshoe?"

"That depends who's asking."

"I'm asking."

"And you are?"

The man spat a black looger on the street. "Name's Jarrett. Pete Jarrett. Got some investigatin' needs doin'. You the man for the job?"

"Depends on the job."

"Don't want to say too much about that."

"Then I don't think we'll be doing much business."

I headed back inside. The Scrutator followed. The man loped after us.

"They said you were the best," he said to my back.

"I am." I continued to walk away.

"So how about I tell you a little bit?"

I stopped. "I'm listening."

"See, I work up at the Aeolus Corporation. Things up there—they ain't right. There's exploitation of the workforce—the boss, he's denying the folk their basic rights. Me, I'm buildin' a case. But there's places inside the factory I can't get. I need someone to dig, fella. Someone like you."

"What do you think?" I said to the Scrutator.

"My interest is not significantly aroused," came the answer.

Zephyr was right. The robot sure was in the dumps.

"Look, buddy," I said to Jarrett. "Labor problems—it's a noble cause. But this isn't a good time. I've got cases coming out of my ears, I've got the taxman breathing down my neck. And, in case you hadn't noticed, the front of my office just blew off. Then there's the end of the world..."

"I know some boys could help with that," said Jarrett. He chewed some more, spat some more.

"Help with the end of the world?"

"Nope. Your missing wall."

"Still no deal. Sorry."

"I'll pay up front. Cash is king."

I thought about the measly wad the Scrutator had got in exchange for its automobile. By now it was probably worth the price of a cup of coffee. Another day and it wouldn't buy the paper cup.

"In case you hadn't heard, Jarrett, the king just got guillotined. Now beat it."

"Might change your mind," said Jarrett, "when you take a look at this."

I ignored him. Nothing he could show me would make a difference. Then the Scrutator tapped my shoulder.

"It appears that Mister Jarrett has an interesting proposition," it said.

Jarrett was holding up a pouch no bigger than a pomegranate.

"Whatever coins you've got in there," I said, "would barely cover the expenses."

"Ain't coins," said Jarrett. "It's Schrödinger's Gold."

I gulped. "Say that again."

"Schrödinger's Gold."

I took the pouch from him. My hands were shaking. The pouch was ludicrously heavy, but that could have meant anything. I shook it. It sloshed.

"What's Schrödinger's Gold?" Zephyr looked up from her desk, where she'd gone back to staring at the zoetrope again. I didn't like the way she kept touching her fingers to its globe, or the way her face was still the same ash-white it had been all morning.

"Quantum currency," I said. "The most liquid assets you can get. And the rarest." I glared at Jarrett. "Where d'you get it? If that's what it really is."

Jarrett shrugged his shoulders. "Ain't no secret. Picked me up a treasure map off this hobo. I gave him food, he gave me the map. Turned out X really did mark the spot."

I'd never heard a hokier tale, but right now that didn't bother me. If the Schrödinger's Gold was real, it would mean financial stability like I'd never known. With the city collapsing and the taxes due, that sounded like a good deal.

I took the pouch and gave it to Zephyr.

"Hold this up in front of the tokamak, honey," I said. "If it glows green and sings a six-part harmony, put it in the safe. If not, bring it back and you can help me return this gentleman to the gutter he came in on."

She took it, her face registering surprise. "It looked full a minute ago. But now it feels empty. Can I look?" She started fiddling with the strings knotted at the top of the pouch.

"No!" Jarrett and I shouted together. Zephyr took a step back, shocked.

"Don't open it, honey," I went on. "If you do that, it could be worthless."

"I don't understand."

I sighed. "Like I said, Schrödinger's Gold is quantum. As long as it's inside the bag, it's either the most valuable currency there is, or it's worth less than a pocket of beans."

"If I may correct you," put in the Scrutator, "this is not an 'either-or' scenario. At any one time, the Schrödinger's Gold exists in all possible states. It is both priceless and worthless—and all points between—simultaneously."

"You're losing me," said Zephyr.

"It's simple," I said. "As long as you don't open the pouch, any bank in the city will classify this as the most valuable thing you can imagine. That's because, in one of the many possible quantum states it occupies, it is. If you open it, all the quantum possibilities collapse into just one."

"Okay," said Zephyr slowly. "I think I get it. But what if that collapsed state just happens to be the 'most valuable' one?"

"Then you struck lucky. But the odds are against it."

She prodded the pouch with her index finger. Apparently full again, it wobbled like a little water bed. "What exactly does 'most valuable' mean anyway?"

"A bag that big would buy you the entire cosmos fifty times over. Honey, you got the whole world in your hands."

* * *

60

A FEW MINUTES later, Zephyr came up from the cellar.

"I tested it. The tokamak light made the pouch glow, just like you said."

"Did it sing?"

She nodded. "It sounded like *Ave Maria*. Is that all there is to identifying it? It's so... silly."

"Most quantum things seem that way. Did you put it in the safe?"

"Yes."

I stared at my new client. "Well, Jarrett, it looks like you hired yourself a private investigator. Zephyr—get our coats."

Her shoulders dropped and she shot a glance at her desk. "We can't leave the office empty."

"The Scrutator can babysit the beetle."

"No. I'll stay. The Scrutator can go with you." She came close so she could whisper. "It might do Bronzey good to get out on a case—a proper case. It might lift him out of his depression."

The tax inspector looked up from where it was hunched over a pile of invoices. Its wing cases buzzed softly.

"You sure you can handle this?" I asked.

"I'm staying! Deal with it!" she snapped. She cooled as quickly as she'd blown hot, but still I took a step backward. "I'm sorry. It's just that I'm not a helpless female to be rescued and coddled. The bug's not a monster. It's just trying to do its job. So go and do yours."

"Is something wrong, honey?" I said.

Zephyr stroked the zoetrope. Inside it, tiny versions of her and Raymond whirled in their perpetual dance. "Look, you helped me deal with certain things. Issues. My past. But you've got a past too. If you keep on ignoring it, it'll tear you apart."

"What the hell are you talking about?"

She jerked her head toward Jarrett. "Go with him. Solve his problems. When you've done that, try taking a look at your own."

61

JARRETT HAD COME in an automobile he'd built himself. It was a crazy contraption, thrown together from scrap. It ran on seven mis-matched legs powered by a baby tokamak. I wondered how he'd managed to drive it through the storm.

"She's built for bad weather," he said, peeling back something resembling a door. He was proud of it, despite how it looked. "See how low she sits?"

"I estimate these aerodynamic attachments will generate a significant downward thrust under the right atmospheric conditions," said the Scrutator, waggling the sawn-off wing jutting from the top of the roll cage.

"Spoilers glue her down, that's for sure. Ain't she a beaut?"

I kept my mouth shut while they discussed the jalopy. Zephyr's outburst had knocked me sideways. I tried to work out where it had come from, came up with nothing. Frustrated, I sulked.

The ride was smoother than I'd anticipated, given the state of the street. Jarrett steered a tricky course between craters and corpses. Like the Scrutator, he had a knack for short-cuts. The car had a knack for gymnastics. When a nest of wrecked tramcars blocked our way we climbed to the rooftops, avoiding the street altogether.

"See that smoke?" said Jarrett; ahead, the sky was smudged like a charcoal sketch. "Refugee camp. Passed it on the way in. Since the Birdhouse went up, half the city blocks are bomb sites.

Other half's abandoned. Most folk, they live in the camps now, eatin' hog swill."

The route took us past the riverside camp. Jarrett kept the car up on the roofline, which kept us out of trouble. Gave us a bird's eye view too.

The refugee camp was a mess of tents, packed with the homeless. Someone had taken String City's melting pot, stirred it up, tipped it out. Fires burned in the gutters; naked children played with unexploded ordnance; men and women shared canvas with nymphs, golems, winged serpents, minotaurs, shape-shifters of all, well, shapes. Name a species, it was there. The tents went right down to the river. The water was choppy. I thought it was the wind, which was picking up again. Then I realised it was people, swimming.

Swimming in the Lethe.

"Lot of folk, they're goin' plumb crazy," said Jarrett. "Sayin' it's the end, or worse. Figure they got nothin' to lose. Might as well wipe theirselves clean. So in they jump. Three of the four horsemen are in there too. Fourth held back on account of not havin' any swimmin' britches. So they say."

We left the camp behind. I was glad. It felt rotten to the core. It wasn't just the filth or the hopeless looks on the faces. It was the place itself. The world was an eggshell and the refugee camp was built right over ten thousand cracks. And the cracks were getting bigger.

None of it helped my mood.

We turned south and headed out of town on an elevated highway. It was deserted. There were a few gaps in the road bed, but Jarrett's automobile jumped well. Past the city limits, the road dropped into Jigsaw Canyon.

Out here, it was like String City didn't even exist. Canyon walls hugged the road and cacti as big as houses clung to the slopes, making shadows black as tar pits where coyotes hid from the noon sun. Vultures circled. The wind blew hard.

The road became a dirt track, winding tight through the canyon maze. Jarrett steered the car through one turn after another. My sense of direction's good but even I got dizzy. Every turn we made, the wind got stronger. Sand blasted the canvas canopy.

A bronzed finger tapped my shoulder, making me jump clean out of my skin. "Sir?" said the Scrutator. "May I make an observation?"

"Only if it's useful," I replied, lost in my own thoughts.

"In that regard, I am afraid I cannot make an empirical judgement."

Sand leaked in through the torn roof of the car. Lump hammers thudded inside my head. "What's on your mind, iron man?"

"I am not made of..."

"Just spit it out."

"Very well. For the past seventeen hours, I have been running a background algorithm to cross-refer all known encounters with Fools. I can now confirm categorically that there are no recorded occurrences of a Fool demonstrating any aptitude for logical and progressive thought."

The lump hammers pounded harder. "I don't get it."

"To summarise: Fools do not make plans."

Now the thumping in my head was joined by that irritating itch at the back of my neck. I wanted them both to go away and leave me alone.

"What are you trying to say?"

"We know that a Fool—or perhaps even a group of Fools—has committed a crime by removing the Still Point of the Turning World from its place of safety."

"Removed? The Birdhouse was blown apart, pal, in case you didn't remember."

"I remember everything. Now, in order to break open the Birdhouse, the Fools detonated a large quantity of scathefire which they acquired following an elaborate heist at the Tartarus Club. A complex plan."

I saw where this was going. "But you're telling me that Fools don't plan."

"Indeed. They are incapable of it. Fools are entities of the moment, with little concept of cause and effect."

I rubbed my head. A set of jack hammers had joined the parade. Dragging a pneumatic drill. "So whoever's behind this, it isn't the Fools."

"That is correct. The thought depresses me."

The canopy flapped back. A gust of sand scoured my face. The pain in my head burst like a bubble.

"So who exactly is pulling the strings?" I said.

62

A BUILDING LOOMED out of the canyon just as the sun broke through the sandstorm. It was vast, all curves and spirals, like a dozen conch shells all poured together. Its outer surface shone like mother of pearl.

"That's the Aeolus Corporation," said Jarrett. "Where they make the weather. Runs twenty-four-seven. Canyon system channels the wind—there's these big doors and valves set in the walls. Might be calm in the city, but it's always blowin' in Jigsaw Canyon."

I knew about Aeolus, of course, but I'd never seen his headquarters up close. It was the single biggest building I'd ever seen. And I've seen some. Huge as it was, however, it was hard to stay focused on it. My head was full of Fools. But this was a case, and Jarrett was my client. My paying client. The bag of Schrödinger's Gold in my safe said so.

"You say you work there," I said to Jarrett, dragging my attention back to the task at hand. "Do you live in the factory too?"

Jarrett spat. "We live our own lives! We're workers, not slaves!"

"No offense. So where's home?"

By way of reply, Jarrett aimed the car down a narrow gorge that ran beside the factory. The gorge was full of junk and airborne sand. The junk was old aircraft: twenty or so plane wrecks lashed down with guys and pegs. Most were old and weatherbeaten, but a couple looked brand new.

"What are the shiny ones?" I said.

"B29s," said Jarrett. "A couple came down the other week. You musta seen them over the city."

I had. The dimensional instabilities had opened holes in the magnetosphere. Brought through all kinds of ships. Some with wings, others with eyes. A few with both.

"For us, a plane crash is good news," Jarrett went on. "Oftentimes they come down in the canyon. Wind here makes for bad turbulence. We salvage the wrecks, make them home."

What I'd thought was scrapyard was in fact shanty town. The aircraft fuselages were lined up, end-on to the weather. Broken wings stuck up, acting as windbreaks. The props on the big bomber engines were feathered, spinning hard—generating power, I guessed.

"Strange place to live," I said.

Jarrett steered the car under the tail of a wingless Hercules. The wind made the plane's tail shake like a rattlesnake's. A big ramp hung down from the back, with a sealed lock at the top. Jarrett drove up the ramp. When he hit a button on the dash, the lock door shuddered open and the car slipped inside. Just in time. A huge gust of wind ripped the tail fin right off the plane.

It hit the ramp like an axe and split it in two. The fin took off again, flew like a kite, vanished in the sand cloud.

The lock door closed.

"Home," said Jarrett.

63

THE CRASHED PLANES were connected by umbilicals. Jarrett led us from cargo plane to fighter bomber to passenger jet. The Scrutator plodded behind us saying nothing. Its eyes were dark. Maybe Zephyr had been right: maybe the thing really was feeling depressed. Some of the aircraft were set up as living quarters—strung with tents and hammocks—others were stores. All of them were shaking in the wind. The interiors were painted: tribal scenes of hunts and weird rituals, all picked out in the same earth colors as the canyon outside. Pigments mixed from the rock, I guessed. It was an odd mix: dead technology plastered with ancient legend.

Several paintings showed tribal folk surrounded by ghosts. All the ghosts had big teeth.

"What happens to the aircrews when they crash?" I asked, studying one of the paintings.

"Most planes come through empty. Reckon the dimensional snags must strip out the livin' flesh."

"'Most'? What about the crew members who do survive?"

Jarrett averted his eyes.

"Speaking of empty," I said, "where are all your people?"

"You'll see."

We walked through an umbilical into a big round space full of people. It stank like a barbecue and sounded like a football stadium.

"This here's our town hall," said Jarrett over the din. "It's a foo fighter. Only one ever came down this side of the city. Ain't she a beaut?"

I've never been one for flying saucers. In my view, anything that flies should have a front, a back and wings in the middle. This one looked smart though—all chrome pipes and silver dials, made almost glorious by the ubiquitous tribal art.

Jarrett found us seats. The Scrutator and I squeezed between a pair of scrawny youths who looked like they hadn't eaten in a month. They nodded at me, grinned at the robot.

An old geezer in fancy robes stood up on a platform, gave a speech in some tongue I didn't know. That surprised me—I know a lot. He kept it short, so by the time I'd prised the Universal Semanticon out of my pocket, he'd finished. Everyone applauded. Different folk stood up and talked about some or other stuff, then Jarrett loped into the arena and took the stage.

A big buzz rose up from the audience. Jarrett hushed them with his hands. It looked like he was the main event. Above him, the domed ceiling shook with the wind. The whole foo fighter rang like a gong. He let things settle, twiddled his mustaches, then said,

"Y'all know me. Y'all know the problems we got with the factory."

There was a murmur. Folk here sure were disgruntled about something.

"Well," Jarrett went on, "I went me out, got us some help. Fella back there—see him, sat between Joey Carp and Pizza McGillis?—fella's a private investigator. Gonna do some diggin' for us. Prove we're bein' ripped off."

"How much does he cost?" called a voice from the crowd.

"Don't y'all mind that," said Jarrett. "This here's on me. Fella's on our side. He asks you questions, I want y'all to tell him what you know."

One of the scrawny guys elbowed me in the ribs. From the state of his acne, I guessed this was Pizza McGillis.

"Hey dude," Pizza said, "you really gonna nix the griefster?"

"Depends on the grief," I replied.

The other guy—Joey Carp—left off staring at the Scrutator and said to me, "It's the wind, isn't it?"

"Jarrett said it was labor trouble. Something about your workforce being exploited."

Pizza laughed. "He would! Our Pete's always fancied himself a labor man. Lately he's worse than ever."

"Since his wife died," said Joey. "Got nothing better to do."

"So what exactly is the problem?" I was starting to wonder what I was doing here. This didn't sound like gumshoe work to me.

"Like I said," Joey said. "It's the wind."

As if it was listening, the wind rocked the foo fighter again. The seats shook, and Jarrett had to grab the mike to stop himself falling off the stage.

"Y'all see?" he said. "Y'all see what we're up against?" I couldn't tell if he was talking to me or the crowd. "Wind's always been our friend. That's why we make our homes here. But lately it's outta hand. Not a day goes by we don't lose a hull. We double-strap the wings and still they go flyby. Aeolus, he don't listen. He just says work harder and maybe he'll crank it down. Maybe! Here's us, workin' out our guts for that no-good god and do we get thanks? Aeolus makes it so we can't live here no more. Makes it so we gotta move away. And y'all know what that'd mean!"

The audience rumbled, loud. It felt like I'd missed something. I decided it was time for me to add something to the party.

"Let me get this straight," I said, standing out of my seat. A couple of hundred heads turned my way. The rumble subsided. The dome shook. "You want your boss to turn the wind down because your town's falling apart?"

Another rumble. It seemed mostly made of 'aye's.

"Have you actually asked Aeolus straight?" I said.

"Over and over!" Jarrett cried from the stage. "We hadn't, you think I'd haul you out here?"

"So call a strike. Show him you mean business."

There was uproar. Jarrett gradually calmed the crowd. "We got no union. We strike, gives Aeolus the excuse he needs to flatten our town to the sand, take back our land for his own."

I thought maybe the Scrutator could educate them about labor laws. The robot was good with bureaucracy. But the Scrutator was busy with Joey and Pizza. They seemed fascinated with its workings, and the robot was enjoying the attention. It even had its chestplate open so they could see its gears.

"So move the town," I said. "The way it's built, you could break camp, set up in another canyon. Cut your losses'

Jarrett's grimace told me he didn't like that suggestion. But before he could respond, the old geezer in the fancy robes took the mike again. The crowd went quiet.

"It's my opinion," said the old geezer, "our visitor deserves a proper explanation of exactly who we are, and exactly how we live."

Jarrett looked set to argue. The old geezer threw him a glare. Jarrett scowled. For a second time, everyone looked at me.

"Why don't you tell me what this is really all about?" I sighed.

64

THEY BROUGHT ON marionettes. It wasn't what I expected. I said so to Pizza McGillis.

"You're honored, dude," he replied. "This puppet show's

right special. Seeing it makes you a regular vee-eye-pee."

Pizza went back to studying the Scrutator's workings. The robot had taken its left arm apart, to show his two admirers the joints. They looked engrossed. I hoped the robot knew where all the pieces went.

The lights went down. Drapes cascaded down from the dome, making a kind of backdrop all painted up with clouds and streaks of light. A couple of stage hands rigged a gantry. Women dressed in black skulked along it, carrying wooden rods. Strings dangled from the rods, weighted with things I couldn't see.

"This here's the story of our time," came a voice from behind the drapes. It sounded like the old geezer, only deeper and more croaky, so I couldn't be sure it was him. "We's the people of the desert wind, and we go on until the wind, she takes us back."

The puppeteers wiggled the strings. Three puppets rose up from the stage—two men and a women, carved from wood and dressed in finery. They walked and danced. The woman kissed one of the men. The second man stepped in and punched the other on the nose. The audience laughed.

"Life loves life," said the narrator, "until she lives no more."

One of the male puppets lay itself flat on the stage. The other two bowed their heads over it. The audience was silent. Then a new puppet sort of squirted up out of the "dead" one. As special effects go, it was kind of hokey, but also kind of neat. I figured it was meant to be a ghost or somesuch. Grey and wispy, it vanished behind the drapes.

The scene changed. Now the two remaining puppets were huddled beside a flicker of orange satin: a campfire. Behind the puppets stood a pole, trailing a long red pennant. A fan blew the pennant out straight.

"But time goes on, and the wind she don't stop," said the narrator.

A stagehand turned off the fan and the pennant dropped limp. The puppets hugged each other, their wooden bodies trembling.

"Until she stops."

Something wailed behind the drapes. Something between banshee squawl and syren song. From the audience came a fainter sound, like softly chattering teeth. I looked round and realised it was the clicking of bones as several thousand toes all curled up at once.

Three new puppets burst into view. Ghosts, but not like the first. These were tall, spindly, like skeletons in rags. They had gaping black holes for eyes. They had teeth like tigers.

One ghost held back while the other two fell on the puppets seated by the campfire. They tore them to pieces. Literally. Some show, I thought, when you've got to rebuild the props every time. The audience watched in dead silence. Soon there was nothing left of the two marionettes but a handful of splinters and a few shreds of cloth.

The stagehand turned the fan back on. The ghost puppets wafted back behind the drapes.

The wailing stopped.

The lights came up.

Beside me, Joey and Pizza had left off studying the Scrutator. Now they were studying me. So was everybody else.

"That's quite a piece of theater," I said. "Short on character development, maybe."

The old geezer emerged from behind the drapes.

"Do you now understand us better?" he said.

"Guess I do," I said. "It's the Mimi, isn't it? That's what your show's all about. It's about what happens to you folk when you die, and why the wind's so important to you. That's why you want help. You're afraid the Mimi are going to get you."

65

A WORD ABOUT death.

Everyone knows there's an afterlife. There's any number of them, truth be told. Death opens up a whole heap of ways through to underworlds, netherworlds, uberworlds... a hundred journeys to be had. Usually there's a river involved, and there's plenty of rivers flow through String City: the Lethe, the Styx, the Acheron. You can charter your own boat or leave it to fate. The Phlegethon's a fashionable choice in waterways, on account of it being a river of liquid fire—the deckside barbecues are legendary.

Cross the city limits and things start to change. When you hit the desert, rivers get scarce and the underworlds get hard to reach. Different rules apply.

Actually, it's mostly no rules. When folk die in the desert, their spirits usually wander lost for all eternity or until they get eaten by coyotes. Coyotes like to chew on ghosts, don't ask me why. That's why most deserts are haunted, and why most of the howls you hear aren't the wolves—they're the things the wolves are chewing on.

Here and there, though, the desert grows some rules of its own. Like a cactus, those rules are tough and spiky.

Like the rule of the Mimi.

It goes like this.

You live your life, you die. Your eternal spirit comes unglued and takes off for the great beyond. But in the desert, it's like you're already beyond. In the desert, spirits have nowhere to go. So they hide in the sand, in the spaces between the grains. They dry out, get hungry, get thin. Sand's no good to eat; nor are desert rats. So spirits that linger in the desert start getting crazy ideas. One of those is the idea the only thing that can satisfy their hunger is human flesh.

Specifically, the flesh of their loved ones.

Trouble is, after all that time in the desert, spirits become fragile. So fragile that a single breath of wind will tear them to ribbons. They've become the ghosts of ghosts, spindly mummified things each with the hunger of a hundred men.

The Mimi.

Here's the good news: the Mimi are so fragile that, as long as the wind is blowing, they stay trapped and harmless in the sand.

Here's the bad: the second the wind drops, the Mimi come out, and the hunt for blood begins.

66

JARRETT SETTLED US into the empty cabin of a Short Sunderland flying boat, then left us alone. It was cramped and cosy. The Scrutator immediately started fiddling with the plane's instrument panel. I took the opportunity to call Zephyr.

"It's not like you to pick up the phone," she said on the first ring.

"Just checking in. How's it going?"

"Fine." Her voice was clipped.

"Just fine? How's the tax beetle doing?"

"Five years down, five to go." Her voice dropped to silence, leaving just the crackle on the line.

"What's wrong, Zephyr?" I said.

"Nothing. Look, have you finished or did you have something important to say?"

"Nothing important, I guess."

"Right. I'll see you then."

"Yeah. See you later."

She hung up.

I leaned against the canopy, trying to see out, but the desert had sandblasted the plexiglass. I could hear the wind though. Its howls made me think of boundary wolves. I pushed the thoughts aside, only to find them replaced by thoughts about the Mimi. I don't know which made me shiver more.

"What do you think of the desert?" I said to the Scrutator. "Reckon you could stand to live out here?"

"It is my conclusion," said the Scrutator, still engrossed with the crashed aircraft's instruments, "that this is a fascinating location with much to offer."

"You figure? What about the noise? Doesn't it send you buggy after a while?"

The Scrutator looked up, gears meshing quietly. "No, it does not. The sound of the wind is soothing."

"*Soothing*?"

"Yes. It drowns out the clamor of the cosmos."

"Something's wrong. With Zephyr."

"Is it urgent enough to merit aborting the investigation?"

"I don't know."

The Scrutator fiddled with the Sunderland's throttle levers. "I detect a confusing flow of emotion moving between you and your assistant. It is something I can neither define nor understand, therefore I have no input to offer of any value. The decision to return to the office or not must be yours. However, I would remind you that the successful execution of this case will provide the business with considerable financial security."

"In other words: take the money and forget the dame."

"Despite resorting to the vernacular, you have correctly summarised my views."

"I guess you're right." I scraped my hands down the stubble on my jaw. "So, what have we got? It's obvious Jarrett wants us to start the investigation here. Interview the residents, build a picture. But it seems to me there's only one place this picture is going to come into focus."

"The Aeolus Corporation wind plant?"

"See—you do think like a detective."

"No, I merely wish to avoid the complex and confusing process of interviewing organic individuals."

"You say that, but when you get folk to open up, usually that's when cases crack."

"Which is precisely why I am not optimised for the private investigation business. A desire to know the truth is not sufficient. To be a successful detective, a far more subtle quality is required. It is this precise quality which I, as a mechanical construct, lack."

"And it's what?"

"Empathy."

By now the Scrutator was drooping all over. Its delicate fingers continued to play listlessly with the dead throttles. Somewhere in the guts of the plane, rusty cables scraped through rotten casings.

I tried switching tracks.

"Those two fellas at the meeting—Pizza and Joey. It seemed to me they liked you."

The Scrutator brightened. "They were intensely interested in my workings. These people are scavengers. It is their habit to salvage and recycle anything they come into possession of. In short, they love machinery. The two gentlemen were fascinated in the complexity of my construction. I obliged their curiosity by opening several of my maintenance panels and allowing them to investigate."

"A bit forward for a first date."

"I cannot parse that sentence."

"Never mind. Look, I'm going to head up to the factory, see what I can sniff out. If you want to come, that's dandy—I could use the help. At worst you can stop me blowing away. If you want to stay here, play with your new friends, that's fine too. It's your choice. But make up your mind—ten minutes from now I'm gone."

67

JARRETT SEEMED SURPRISED I wanted to scout the factory.

"Kinda thought you might stick round here," he said. "Send your robot out to do the sniffin'."

"Why would you think that?"

"No reason. You're takin' the robot though?"

"He's decided to come along." Jarrett looked happy about this. I was about to ask why, but decided to let it lie. Truth's like a splinter. You pick at it too much, too soon, you can drive it out of sight.

"I'll take you," said Jarrett. "I'm on shift there tonight anyhow. I can get you in without Aeolus seein'."

"You're a whole bundle of help."

"Just protectin' my investment."

Jarrett led us back through the aircraft maze to where his automobile was parked.

"Something puzzles me," I said as we climbed aboard. "Why would Aeolus want to force you people out of the canyon? He's got a loyal workforce right on his doorstep—what's his motive?"

"Money," said Jarrett, goosing the motor. "What else?"

"I don't get it."

"Desert looks bleak but it's prime real estate. Now more than ever. Developers, they're hungry to buy up tracts they wouldn't have spat on five years ago. Aeolus, he struggles to turn a profit as it is. Municipal development grant would solve that. City limits stretch out here, suddenly he's got all the labor he wants. Suddenly his books start addin' up."

Which was something Jarrett's story didn't do at all.

"It figures," I said evenly.

Jarrett pulled a lever. The lock door opened. He steered the car down the broken ramp and straight into a fresh sandstorm. The world turned featureless and gold.

68

THE SAND BEGAN to clear once we got near the wind factory. The complex was as big as a town. Jarrett drove us past cyclone pumps, katabatic conveyors, monsoon sponges. Each gadget was a factory in its own right, and Jarrett had a story to tell about every one: the capacity of this cloudbuster; how this intake sucked in toxic gases and turned them to fertiliser; the way this wall of rotors reset the compass bearing of any storm that passed through it. The way Jarrett talked, you'd have thought he was a tour guide.

"You sure know your wind," I said as he squeezed the car between a pair of typhoon bafflers.

"We all do," Jarrett said proudly.

He parked the car beside a huge whelk-shaped tower. The building was so high it wore the clouds like a skirt.

"What's this place?"

"Jetstream pump. It's new. Taller than Babel, Aeolus reckons. You should see the fire escape."

There was a door in the base of the tower. Jarrett had a key.

"Control room's your best bet," he said. "This time of day, Aeolus'll be out doin' his rounds. Snoop all you like, scram before he knows you've been."

"What about security?"

"Ain't none. Who'd want to steal the wind?"

"Steal, maybe not. There's always sabotage."

"Ain't nobody got a spanner big enough to jam these works. I'll leave you to it. Watch for Aeolus—he's older than these hills and twice as mean. Head left to the main corridor, follow the red line."

He drove away, leaving me and the Scrutator standing in the doorway. The sand started to blow up again.

"Shut the door," I said. "Before we get etched."

Inside, the tower was all faint hums and rattles. It was strangely soothing. We turned left like Jarrett had said, found ourselves in a corridor as wide as a freeway. Ahead, the passage broke in ten different directions. The floor was a mess of painted lines. We picked out the red one and followed it into the labyrinth.

"Big place," I said. "Hardly anyone around. It must be mostly automated."

"You are correct in your assumption," said the Scrutator. As we walked, the robot ran its fingers along the wall. "The architectural infrastructure contains an array of intelligent servo-systems, all of which interact in much the same way as the component parts of an artificial brain."

"So this whole place is one giant robot?"

"That is a reasonable metaphor."

"How can you tell all this?"

The Scrutator stopped, pressed its bronze palm to the wall. The gears behind its eyes stopped spinning. The clank of its guts faded to a whisper. It swayed like a mechanical reed.

"Can you not hear its voice?" the robot said.

69

As we moved deeper into the factory, the lines on the floor grew scuffmarks. The air became stale and hot. The machinery in the walls cranked louder and the humming turning to banging, like the whole system needed oiling. Maybe there was sand in the works. Soon all the lines were gone except the red one. The ceiling drooped and the lamps flickered, those that worked at all.

"The environment appears to be growing more dilapidated the closer we get to the center of operations," said the Scrutator.

"The place is going to the dogs," I agreed, and wished I hadn't. These days, it seemed like everything reminded me of boundary wolves.

Round a corner, the banging got distinctly louder. The corridor opened up and the red line faded away. We were in a vast gloomy space. Gears like Gog's shirt buttons turned slowly in the rafters. Turbines revolved, pumping smoky air through coiled tubes. Logic boxes lined the walls. A billion tiny lights blinked in syncopated patterns. The control room of the gods.

One god, to be exact. Contrary to what Jarrett had promised, Aeolus wasn't doing his rounds at all. He was right there in front of us: the king of the wind.

White-haired and ropy with muscle, Aeolus was as big as a house and looked like the oldest weightlifter in the rest home. Not that he stood still long enough for us to pin him down. He kept racing from one end of the enormous room to the other, flipping switches, hauling levers, spinning dials. He swarmed up girders, nimble as a monkey, opening vents, adjusting fans. All he wore was a tattered apron. The sight of those massive godly buttocks hanging directly over our heads was unsettling in the extreme.

We settled in the shadows and watched him for a while.

Truth was, I didn't know much about the guy. The corporation publicity said he employed four managers—the four big winds—plus a small army of support staff—Jarrett's people.

What we saw bore that out. There were five god-sized swivel chairs lined up on a central platform. The middle one was marked THE BOSS.

All the chairs were empty.

I was about to suggest we went closer when Aeolus spotted us.

He swung over and hung himself off a fat dangling cable, eyeing us with curiosity. The wind god's eyes were bloodshot. The veins in them squirmed like pythons.

Aeolus spoke.

"Could one of you go over to that console, please? The one that's shaped like a clam."

I felt my legs twitch. A god says jump, your reflexes make you hit the ceiling before your conscious mind realises what's happening. The Scrutator must have been even better tuned to the voice command—it was halfway to the console before I even got moving.

"Is this the apparatus you wish me to attend to?" the robot asked the god.

"Yes," said Aeolus. "Do you see the lever that resembles a tulip? Please rotate it thirty-seven degrees clockwise and hold it in position."

I was glad the Scrutator had got there first. I'd have probably shoved it one-eighty in the wrong direction and got a thunderbolt for my pains.

While the Scrutator worked the lever, Aeolus jumped ninety feet to a panel on the ceiling. He yanked knobs, slammed open a gigantic valve. A blast of air knocked me flat.

"Release the lever!" bellowed the god.

The Scrutator obeyed.

Along the back wall, an array of fans powered up. Half the red lights on the logic boxes turned green. Aeolus dropped from the ceiling, landing square in his chair. For the first time since we'd got there, he was still.

I picked myself up, walked up to the chair. The god's bare legs towered like hairy oaks. His head was in his hands. His breathing was ragged.

"Tough day?" I said.

Aeolus stretched. "You don't know what a relief it is to get the reserve fans turning," he said. "All week I've been run ragged, just trying to keep the air moving. For a minute there I thought it was all over."

"It looks like hard work," I said. "You run this place on your own?"

"Apart from the cleaning staff, yes."

"Cleaning staff?"

"Those wonderful people who live in that peculiar little shanty town built out of crashed aeroplanes. Oh, they do a marvellous job."

"All they do is clean?"

"Yes, indeed." He bent over, confiding. "Between you and me, these days they're non-essential workforce. But I feel I have an obligation to keep them employed. It's my way of giving something back to the community."

"No offense," I said, "but couldn't you set them working on maintenance? Seems to me this place could do with an overhaul."

Aeolus reached under his apron and scratched his crotch. God's jewels swung. I looked the other way.

"Things were better when my boys were here," he sighed.

I glanced at the empty chairs. "You want to tell me about it?"

From the clam-shaped panel, the Scrutator called, "Can I let go of this lever now?"

70

"THIS TIME LAST year it was all different," Aeolus began. "The factory was running at full capacity; the weather was always on time and always on budget. We turned a small profit. More importantly, we were one big, happy family."

"So what went wrong?" I said. The Scrutator had boosted me on to one of the empty chairs, then climbed up itself. We dangled our legs like children, listened to the god's tale.

"The boys left me—I called them my boys, even though they weren't actually my sons. They might as well have been, considering the pain they caused me.

"It was Boreas who started it. Boreas was the north wind. He had a terrible temper, but he was awfully kind to horses. I used to keep stables, you see, and Boreas looked after all the animals. They had a marvellous rapport. He only had to blow in the horses' ears and they did exactly what he told them. He had the same power over the other three winds—Eurus, Notus and Sefyrus. Like the horses, they were in Boreas's thrall. They worshipped him over me. I didn't mind. I've always considered myself more of a practical kind of god."

"So what went wrong?"

"When I told you the profit we made was small, I truly meant it. There's no money in wind—there never has been. It's a vocation, not a career. But Boreas, well, he was nothing if not ambitious. So, one day, just last month, he conceived a plan."

"A plan?"

"To get rich. Oh, it was a hare-brained scheme. I told him so, told him to his face. He became so angry his beard froze up. You remember that unseasonal cold snap we had recently? That happened because of the argument we had."

"What did Boreas want to do?" said the Scrutator in a

strangely high-pitched voice. Maybe sand had got into its workings.

The god sighed. "He had this idea about entering his horses in the Derbies. He had so much power over them that he could virtually guarantee where they'd come in any given race. By his own calculations, he was perfectly positioned to make himself an absolute fortune."

"Rigging horse races?" I said. "The Titans would never stand for it. Everyone knows they've got the city sweepstakes wrapped tighter than Medusa's hair net."

"Which is precisely why the Titans were the first people Boreas approached. He explained his scheme and offered them a ten percent share. The other winds were in on the deal too, each with ten percent of his own, leaving Boreas with a majority of sixty."

"It must have looked pretty on paper. How long before it turned ugly?"

"Clearly you know how the Titans operate. As I predicted, the operation went sour almost immediately. Boreas and the boys had taken the afternoon off. They went to the Tartarus Club to watch the first race of the season. It was also the first race Boreas had fixed. They'd all bet modest amounts of money, just to test the system. Everything was set.

"Just before the race was due to start, Hyperion became nervous. He told my boys an important client had turned up unexpectedly, and that he'd had to double-book the executive suite. He asked them to adjourn to an adjacent office. Boreas objected, but Hyperion plied them with drinks and dancing girls, so they went.

"It turned out that the office they were shown into wasn't an office at all. It was a sealed vault."

My hackles were on the move. This was one coincidence too many.

"Finish the story," I said.

"Thirty seconds after my boys were locked in, somebody blew up the vault and everything in it. They were vaporised. No remains."

"I know," I said quietly.

"You do?"

"I investigated the aftermath. I thought I caught a whiff of desert coming out of that safe. Looks like putting your boys in the vault was Hyperion's way of killing two birds with one stone."

"It interests me how much you seem to know about this matter."

"Feels to me like I don't know nearly enough. So why did Hyperion want to ice your boys?"

Aeolus impaled me with a baleful glare. "Afterward, I learned that Hyperion had secured an audio recording of Boreas's horse-whispering routine. He planned to use the recording to operate the scam alone and take a full one hundred percent of the profits for himself. As you may know, the Tartarus Club has been struggling financially for some time. I imagine this was just one of many straws Hyperion was clutching at."

"I know a few others," I said. "How did you find all this out?"

"The answers blew in on the wind."

I nearly laughed, until I saw the god's face was straight. "Meaning?" I said.

"Winds have spirits too, you know. The boys' bodies were blown to atoms but their ghosts came home. They passed through the factory turbines, whispering news of their murder. They're out in the desert now, gradually dissolving. Soon they'll be just empty air. It makes me so sad to think of it."

A huge tear rolled down Aeolus's cheek. A gust of wind

caught it up and sucked it through a grille. The grille diced it into a million droplets; a vent spat the droplets outside. Just for a second, it was raining in the desert.

The Scrutator lowered itself to the floor. "A peculiar stiffness has overtaken all my joints," it said. "Please excuse me while I exercise." It wandered off, weaving a little. I thought briefly about going after it, just to make sure it was okay, but Aeolus had picked up the thread again.

"Ever since then, the factory has been running further and further out of synchronisation. It only takes a day or two for things to go quite badly wrong. Keeping everything balanced was a full-time job for five operators, and now there's only me."

"Can't you get Jarrett's people to help?" I said.

"As I said—the labor requires the skills of a god. The desert people are hard workers, but they are simply underqualified. I'm afraid this factory will last only a few more days before it undergoes a catastrophic multiple system failure."

"What happens then?"

"The wind stops."

"Leaves you with plenty of thumb-twiddling time."

Aeolus glared at me. "I don't think you fully understand. It isn't just about the wind. The work I do here affects the entire atmosphere, right down to the molecular level. The minute this plant stops generating wind, the city's entire airspace will enter stasis. People will be working their lungs as hard as they can, but there will be nothing there to breathe. Approximately twelve hours after this factory shuts down, the entire population of String City will suffocate to death."

I didn't want to believe it. Still, the guy was a god. Time for a second opinion. But when I looked for the Scrutator, the robot was nowhere to be seen.

After a few seconds scanning the room, I spotted it halfway

up the back wall, climbing like a crazy mountaineer, bronzed fingers digging deep into the plaster and lath. It reached one of the big control panels, grabbed a handful of cables and pulled them loose. Sparks gushed like water from a hose. The Scrutator scrambled to the next panel, ripped more cables away. More sparks sprayed over the logic boxes, setting them on fire. The back-up fans Aeolus had worked so hard to start up ground to a halt.

"WHAT IS THAT ROBOT DOING?" bellowed Aeolus.

You hear a god yelling, you know things are bad.

"Still!" shouted the Scrutator from its perch near the ceiling. "All shall be still, and all shall be still, and all manner of things shall be still! Here and there and everywhere! Still, still, still, and the lost shall join hands once more!"

Eyes flashing, gears spinning fit to bust, steam pouring from its neck, the Scrutator scrambled like a crazy bug along the wall, tearing up everything in its path. Turbines belched smoke. Pipes like ships' funnels crashed to the floor. Fires broke out in every corner. I've never seen one robot do so much damage in such a short time.

Nearby, a bank of fans like gigantic ships' propellers hit top speed. The motors running them whined up through the octaves. One by one, the propellers jumped off their shafts.

It was like letting loose a whole bunch of circular saws. The propellers flew like foo fighters, slicing through everything they hit: floors, furniture, machinery. Three tore out the entire front wall. Desert light flooded the control room. A fourth missed my head by inches. I scrambled down from the chair and hid in a hole that had opened up in the floor.

Frozen to the spot, Aeolus tore his white hair and screamed at the Scrutator to stop.

The Scrutator kept going.

An alarm screeched, fell silent. As the sound died away, I heard a meaty thunk. The last of the fans slowed, then stopped. Steam trickled from a shattered grate, thinned to mist, vanished. The air fell still and the noise went away, except for the crackle of the flames. Nothing moved.

I raised my head, looked through the big hole in the wall. Out in the desert, everything was still.

The wind had stopped.

Its work done, the Scrutator crouched on an overhead conduit, its mechanical chest heaving in and out.

An internal door swung open. A skinny man with yard-broom mustaches loped in: Pete Jarrett. In his left hand he held a small grey box. It looked like a remote control device. He tweaked a lever on the box. Up on the conduit, the Scrutator jerked to the left. When Jarrett nudged the lever the opposite way, the robot moved to the right. Jarrett pushed a button. The Scrutator stopped moving altogether. Its bronzed head drooped. Its gears stopped turning.

"Right sorry I had to do this to y'all," Jarrett said. "Seemed like it was the only way. Shame about the god."

I looked across the room. The meaty thunk I'd heard had been Aeolus dropping to the floor. I ran over to him. His mouth was flapping open and closed. He didn't seem to have any words to put in it. One of the propeller blades was embedded in his chest. He was lying in a lake of god's blood. His eyes were glazed and his jaw was slack.

I whirled round, shouted at Jarrett, "The only way to do *what*? Do you know what you've done? You haven't just killed a god—you've killed the whole city!"

Jarrett smiled. He was listening, but not to me. He cocked his head, put his hand to his ear, said,

"Listen. You hear them?"

"What? Hear what?"

Then I heard it. A wailing like a choir of banshees trying to sing syren. It came out of the desert, getting loud, fast. I stuck my fingers in my ears but the sound drilled through. My teeth tried to dance out of my head.

The Mimi were coming.

71

I GRABBED THE remote off Jarrett, thumbed the buttons at random. The Scrutator didn't budge. I tossed the gadget aside and bunched my fist. I thought Jarrett would fight, but he just stood there looking tired and spent. I knew how that felt. But he looked to be something else too, something I couldn't quite believe.

Jarrett looked contented.

I thought about those folk back inside the city limits. All those who'd lost their homes and were now trying to scratch a living in the refugee camps. For them, and all those around them, life was about to get a whole lot worse. Never mind the Fool demolishing the Still Point—without air to breathe there'd be nobody alive to see the end when it came.

There was nothing I could do for them.

I had to get back to the office, find a hidden dimension for me and Zephyr to pack ourselves into. Somewhere to ride out the storm. I pulled the Dimension Die from my pocket. A single black face remained. If I used it to return to Zephyr, how would I get us both out of String City?

I took a deep breath, stilled the panic. A guy could do a lot with twelve hours of air. This wasn't over yet.

I pressed my fist to Jarrett's face and clamped my other hand round his throat. He didn't resist me. "Just tell me why," I said.

"If these Mimi are as murderous as you say, why did you set them loose?"

Underneath his mustaches, Jarrett was sporting a serene smile. "Folk always used to call me 'grounded'. Said my soul was still. I figure they were right, leastways, that's how I was until Mary died."

"Mary?"

"My wife. She was my heart, my everything. She was my still center. You understand what I'm sayin' here?"

"I do." I did.

"Mary got sick and she died. I could spin out the tale but that's the gist. After that, I was all hurricanes and rages. I got to blamin' folk—I even blamed my Mary herself for lightin' out on me. Boy, was I sore. After, I just turned blue. Folk said it'd blow past, like all storms do. But this storm didn't. So I came to a mind where all I wanted was my Mary back. Folk told me to move on, but there ain't no movin', not in my yard. They told me she was gone, but I knew she wasn't. I knew there was a way. So I pretended. Convinced them I was over it. Made myself plans."

Outside, the wailing of the Mimi was getting louder. It sounded like knives on a whetstone.

"I guess I know the rest," I said. "You figured your wife had become a Mimi. Mimi don't come out in bad weather. So the best way to be reunited with her was to turn off the wind. Am I right?"

Jarrett's smile turned sad. "Guess you cracked the case. I came to your office meanin' what I said—I wanted to bring a suit against Aeolus, shut him down. Do it all legal like. But then I realised that'd take time, and seems to me time's runnin' out in this here world. Soon as I saw your robot I figured a better scheme.

"When we got back here, I had me a quiet word with Pizza and Joey. They're good with mechanics—we all are, have to be, livin' how we do. But those boys are better'n most. Bright too, leastways bright enough do what I ask, not so bright they ask questions. They sweet-talked the robot, opened it up. Got its logic boxes all overridden, spliced it with this here remote. I've seen these robots, what they can do. Thanes built them for work but underneath they're weapons. Wanted to get my hands on one for a while, but they've all been shipped out of town. Reckon yours is the only one left."

"The robot's not mine," I said. "Thanks to you, it's not even its own any more."

Jarrett shrugged. "Guess that's what they call collateral damage. Sorry, mister, but I ain't gonna mourn no machine, and I certainly ain't gonna mourn the city. Not now my Mary's comin' home."

Spindly shapes were beginning to gather outside the hole in the wall. Most flowed straight past, headed for the shanty town.

One didn't. It peeled away from the main group and flew inside the control room. I stepped away from Jarrett, my heart doing somersaults.

The Mimi was tall—at last sixteen feet. It was floating and wispy and draped in darkness. It looked like a paper nun stretched out by the rack, its face pale and beautiful, except for the tiger teeth. It was wailing. The wailing was bad. It felt like my ears were bleeding. I touched them and found they were.

Jarrett was walking toward the Mimi, arms open. I wondered what he was seeing. The ghost sure as hell didn't look like any woman I'd ever take on a date. But love's blind.

They met just inside the hole in the wall. Desert light made a halo round them both. The Mimi—Mary—stopped wailing and stooped to Jarrett's level. They embraced. The Mimi's ghostly hands caressed Jarrett's back; he held her phantom head, stroked her diaphanous hair. Somehow they found a way to kiss.

Then she bit him in half.

A fountain of blood hid the rest. I heard more than I saw. Those tiger teeth made animal sounds as the Mimi gnawed its way through the rest of Jarrett's body. Bones crunched. There was a lot of slurping. All the Mimi's wispy drapery folded round the bloody remains, scooped them up, sucked them dry, crushed them to dust. Then the Mimi went into a dervish spin, started up its wailing again and set off for the shanty town, ready for the main course.

I couldn't believe it was all over so quick. I tried to take a breath, but with the wind gone the air was already turning rancid. Breathing's something you take for granted—until you can't do it any more. Jarrett had been right about one thing: time was running out.

I stroked my finger over the last black face of the Dimension Die. It felt like the whole cosmos had just hit its expiry date. One roll would take me back to Zephyr. Maybe that was enough.

Instead my eye settled on Jarrett's remote control, lying right where I'd thrown it, upside-down. On its belly was a small black button. Beside the button was a tiny label marked *REBOOT*.

Just when you think you're all out of last chances, two come along at once.

I tucked the Dimension Die in my pocket, picked up the remote.

I pushed the button.

72

I'D NEVER SEEN the Scrutator move so fast. It was like every part of it had been oiled. Within five minutes it had put out the last of the fires in the control room, rewired all the logic boxes and set up a temporary automated operating system. It put the turbines back together. It took a while—the blades had been thrown all over the place, plus the shafts kept turning all the time the robot was reattaching them—but piece by piece it all got fixed, minus one or two missing sections of aerofoil.

I knew we were saved when a hot desert breeze started blowing in through the hole in the wall once more.

I wondered if the Mimi had made it as far as the shanty town. For the sake of the townsfolk, I hoped the wind had got there first.

The Scrutator swung down from a conduit and landed right beside me.

"You okay?" I said.

"I feel more precisely aligned than I have ever felt in my entire existence," said the Scrutator.

"Still talk like you swallowed a dictionary. You want this?"

I handed over the remote control. The Scrutator took it, crushed it like a paper cup and threw it away.

"The process of rebooting me severed the crude control override system that those two nefarious individuals installed while my attention was diverted. It also had the effect of purging many of the closed-loop paradoxes that have inhibited me since I started interacting with organic life forms."

"Say again?"

The afternoon sun angled through the hole in the wall. A beam of desert light hit the robot square on. The light punched through all the perforations in its gleaming shell, lit up about a billion little cogs and widgets all ticking away inside. In its radiance, the Scrutator looked epic.

"I am a machine intelligence. The Thanes built me well, as

they did all my siblings, but even the Thanes cannot escape the fundamental cosmic law which is this: *intelligence comes easy, sanity comes hard*. Woven as I am of cosmic string. I am perhaps the pinnacle of their achievement to date—their strongest child—yet even I am flawed."

"Join the club, buddy."

The robot ignored me. "As long as I try to integrate myself with organic society, I will always be a misfit. I hear more than you can possibly hear. I know more than you can possibly comprehend. Yet I comprehend almost nothing of what you truly are. You are a mystery to me, detective man—a mystery I fear I shall never solve."

Something swelled up in my throat. It seemed to me the robot looked strong and noble and sad, all at the same time. Or maybe it was that desert light turning me into a soft-hearted sap. The feeling lasted until the wind god coughed.

"I thought he was dead," I said.

We ran to where Aeolus lay. The god's blood had congealed, gluing him to the floor. The fan blade stuck from his chest like a boat embedded in a sandbank. His red-rimmed eyes had turned milky.

"I feel the wind," he croaked. "Can it be?"

"I have begun the process of restoring your machinery to its optimum operating condition," said the Scrutator. "I apologise for the damage I caused. I am afraid I was hijacked."

"Not your fault, son," said Aeolus. "Hyperion told me bad times were coming. Perhaps I should have listened."

"You're not breathing," I said. "How come you're still alive?"

"Won't be... for long," said the god. "God's breath lingers. Nothing's coming in... but there's still a little... to come out." Huge eyes rolled toward the Scrutator. "So, son... do you really think you can... fix things up here?"

"Certainly," said the Scrutator softly. It had said it was no good with people. If I heard a voice like that on my death bed, I reckon I'd be comforted. "I have already established a minimum threshold status of wind production that will ensure atmospheric stability while I undertake more comprehensive repairs."

"It took... five gods... to work this place," said Aeolus. "Can you handle it on your own, son?"

"Of course," said the Scrutator. "The wind factory is a machine, as am I. I understand its needs intimately. And I am tireless. This, sir, is what I was built for."

A hand the size of a bison patted the Scrutator on the head.

"Good lad," said Aeolus. His eyes closed. "Good..."

That was the last of his breath. The Scrutator stepped from under the wind god's limp hand. The hand hit the floor. Aeolus was dead.

"Now," the Scrutator said to me, "if you will excuse me, there is much work to be done here."

"You sure about this?" I said. "I mean, it's another jump, isn't it?"

"I cannot parse that sentence."

"Look—the Thanes build you to work in the Mountain, balancing books. Then you get the urge to turn detective. That wears thin, so you look to try something else. This job comes up at the wind factory—suddenly it's all you ever wanted. You see where I'm going?"

"I believe you are concerned that I will grow bored with this occupation as I have with others."

"You got it."

"If that happens, I will try something else. But there are three good reasons why I believe I shall remain. First, this is an honorable labor: to ensure the smooth running of a beautiful machine. It is work I can do well. Second, if what Pete Jarrett says is true—if I am indeed fundamentally a weapon—then it is right that I should separate myself from the rest of society, so that nobody may hijack me again."

"You were out cold when Jarrett said that."

"I hear everything, all the time. I have told you this already."

"So what's the third reason?"

"The most important of all: as long as I remain here, the sound of the wind drowns out all the other sounds of the cosmos. Here I can experience a peace like none I have ever known. You speak of the Still Point of the Turning World. I have found mine."

73

We talked a little longer but neither of us said anything new. Truth was, I was putting off having to leave. Now it was safe outside, I figured I could use Jarrett's automobile to get back to the city. The route would take me right past the aircraft shanty. I wasn't looking forward to what I might find there.

The Scrutator was antsy too—eager to get on with its work. In the end we shook hands, promised to keep in touch. The Scrutator was naïve enough about human nature to believe we really would.

Half a mile from the factory I hit a run of deep furrows in the sand. I flanked them, heading north toward the crashed planes. The furrows puzzled me: they hadn't been there on the way out. Then it hit me. They were the tracks left by the Mimi.

A sandstorm blurred the distance. I drove on, wondering if the Mimi had reached the shanty before the wind had kicked in again. And what state the townsfolk would be in if they had.

A silver tail fin appeared through the sand—the first of the

B29s. The Mimi tracks were pointed right at it. I damped the motor, took it slow. Also, I activated the central locking. Fifty yards out from the plane, the furrows were still deep. Forty yards out they made a sharp turn, straight for the open bomb bay doors of the Superfortress.

Thirty yards out they came to an abrupt stop.

I checked the ground beyond the end of the furrows. No tracks came anywhere near the crashed planes.

I cruised past the aircraft; faces appeared in some of the cockpit windows. A few folk waved. Probably thought I was Jarrett. I waved back. They'd learn what had happened soon enough. Right now, the wind was blowing again, keeping them safe. That was all they needed.

I gunned the motor and headed north out of the canyon maze toward the doomed city.

74

I DROVE STRAIGHT past my office without seeing it. I realised I'd gone too far when I reached the remains of the deli. I doubled back, trying to work out where my office had gone.

Turned out it hadn't gone anywhere. When I'd left, the front wall had been a gaping hole; in my absence, someone had patched it up. With balls of dung. Holding my nose, I got out of the car and examined the work. It was patchy, plagued with lumps and shot through with little bones. But it looked solid enough. There was even a doorway of sorts. I squeezed through, trying not to touch the sides. Inside, everything looked normal. Zephyr was at her desk, exactly where I'd left her. So was the tax beetle. The coffee pot was empty.

"I'm back," I announced when neither of them looked up.

Zephyr said nothing. The beetle clacked its mouth parts.

I tried again. "What happened to the wall?"

"Um," said the beetle, "I rebuilt it during my rest break. Scarabs are very good with dung. I hope you approve. I added some art deco flourishes."

"Thanks," I said. "Are the municipals going to charge me for that?"

"Um, no. The new wall is, um, on the house. It's my way of saying, 'Thank you for the coffee'."

I sat down. Zephyr still didn't look at me. "So how's the work going?"

The beetle closed the ledger. "Your return is timely," it said. "I have just finished."

"Any problems?"

"I found nothing significant. It took me a while to understand your book-keeping systems, however. Have you ever considered a basic accountancy course?"

"Me? I dropped out of school before first recess. The books added up though?"

"Remarkably well, considering your, um, unorthodox approach to arithmetic."

Zephyr muttered something I missed.

"What was that, honey?" I said.

She looked up. Her eyes were red-rimmed. "I said, 'Unorthodox doesn't even cover it.'"

"Am I missing something here?"

"You tell me. And stop calling me 'honey'."

The beetle shifted uncomfortably. "I think perhaps I should be going."

I let it clamber off the chair, all the while keeping my eyes on Zephyr. Meanwhile her eyes were fixed on the zoetrope. One of her fingers traced a circle on the glass globe.

"Is that thing still working?" I said. Zephyr went back to not answering. At the same time, she got up and showed the beetle to the doorway.

"Thanks for coming," she said. Her voice was as flat as a crepe.

"On the contrary," said the beetle. "I should thank you. For, um, being so welcoming."

"Well, you know," said Zephyr. "You fixed the wall. And I enjoyed your funny stories—they made me laugh." She sounded like someone who hadn't laughed in years.

The beetle loitered, twitching its antennae. "There's just the matter of the small, um, discrepancy."

"Oh, yes, of course." Zephyr stared at me. "How could I have forgotten?"

"What discrepancy?" I said. "I thought everything was dinky."

"Everything is, as you say, 'dinky'," said the beetle. "The discrepancy I'm referring to is, um, a minor shortfall in the tax return ledger."

"Say what?"

"The last payment you made to your municipal tax account was short."

"By how much?"

"As I said to your assistant, Zephyr, earlier—the shortfall amounts to one penny."

"A penny," said Zephyr. "How silly of me to forget. You know, I think I've got one right here." She delved into her pocket.

"No!" I shouted. I pushed in front of her, grabbed a handful of loose change from my coat and held it in front of the scarab. "Here—take what you want! Take it all!"

"I don't want it all—only enough to settle the account," said the beetle amiably. It poked its antennae through the coins, picked out a scuffed coin. "This is all I need. Thank you. I will bid you good afternoon."

"Right," I said. "Thanks."

"What was that all about?" said Zephyr after the scarab beetle had gone. "I never saw you try to throw away money before."

"It's a complicated story."

She threw up her hands. "With you, it always is!" She turned on her heel, went back to her desk and threw herself into the chair, shaking. I stood in the doorway, feeling like she was holding the script and I knew none of the lines. Eventually she stopped shaking and started stroking the zoetrope again.

"So where's Bronzey?" she asked.

"The robot decided to stay behind." This felt like safer ground. "I think it's worked out some things in its head. Figured out what's important, know what I mean?"

"I know what you mean." Her voice was too quiet for my liking.

"What's going on here, Zephyr?" I went to her and put my hand on her shoulder. "You were weird earlier. Even weirder on the phone. Now you're weirder still."

She stared at the zoetrope. "It's just so fragile, isn't it? All of it. All my hard work, everything I did to fix things between me and Raymond—if this thing got smashed, it would all be for nothing."

"The zoetrope's fine," I said.

She ran a hand through her hair. Her cheeks burned red. "After you'd gone, I realised I'd been a bit mean to you. When you got back I was going to apologise, say something lame about getting out of bed the wrong side. But then..."

"Then what?"

"The beetle came up to me all serious and told me there was a shortfall. When it told me it was just a penny, I laughed and went straight to the petty cash box, but there was no loose change. The beetle said it didn't mind waiting until you got back, but I wanted to have everything squared up for you. I wanted to do a good job. And it was only a penny." She faltered, went on. "I remembered I had a few coins in my pocket, so I dug them out. That's when I found this."

Zephyr held up a penny. Just a penny, slightly tarnished, with a nick on the edge.

"So?" I said. My blood was running like cold treacle.

She hardly seemed to hear me. She was focused on the penny. "I remember it—this exact coin. I remember the nick, just here. I kept catching my fingernail on it. But the thing is—I also remember the moment I found it." Her eyes locked on mine. She spoke slowly. "This is the same penny I picked up when I got off the bus. I got off the bus and put down the shopping bags to balance out the load before I climbed the stairs to the apartment. That's when I saw this coin lying on the ground. Just a penny. It caught the moonlight, and that's when I remembered the old rhyme: 'See a penny, pick it up, all the day you'll have good luck.'"

"Honey," I said, "about that rhyme..."

"Shut up. This is the same penny I picked up that evening. The exact same one. But... but I *changed* all that. When I was using the zoetrope, cutting out all those scenes, the moment I found the penny was one of the moments I cut out. All I was interested in was me and Raymond dancing in the apartment. I cut out all the rest. Including the penny." She angled the coin into the light. It flashed in my face. "When it comes to strange dimensions and time travel and all that stuff you take for granted, I'm no expert. But answer me this: if I really did erase that scene from reality, why is the penny still here?"

"Honey..."

"Don't 'honey' me! Something's wrong! I've thought and I've thought and there's only two reasons I can come up with to explain why I've still got this penny. Either the zoetrope really is just a cheap trick."

"Or."

"Or that deleted scene never actually got deleted."

Her eyes drilled into mine. The coin flashed.

From my pocket I pulled the deleted scene—the one she'd dropped in the crater, the one I'd picked up and hidden away. The one that had scared me halfway to death and back. And still did.

Tears crowded the corners of her eyes. "What's going on?"

"Zephyr, there's something you need to know about the pennies you find lying in the street..."

"I don't care about pennies! All I care about is this!" She snatched the deleted scene from me, waved the little square of cardboard in my face. "I care that you lied to me, kept this behind my back! How many other scenes did you keep?"

"I didn't..."

"Don't tell me! I won't believe you! Why did you keep them? I suppose you keep them stashed under your mattress so you can flick through them before you go to sleep. I'll bet you get a real kick from watching that one of me and Raymond in bed together! Or the one where I'm making breakfast in nothing but my knickers! Or maybe you've got a zoetrope of your own. Maybe you were planning to stitch all these deleted scenes together, make yourself your own director's cut of my life. *My* life! Do you get what this is about? Do you get how mad I am at you?!"

"It was only this one," I mumbled.

"I don't believe you!" She crushed the scene in her hand.

The sharp corners drew blood from her palm. She threw the crumpled cardboard at me. "Here! Do whatever you want with it! Plug it back into my life—plug them all back in. Make me a murderer again! Because that's the truth, isn't it? Whatever tricks you play with your fancy gadgets, you can't change the truth, can you? I killed Raymond and there's nothing I can do about it!" She stopped, choked in her breath. Picked up the zoetrope. "The way we are in this globe, dancing like this, it's just a dream, isn't it? That's all it ever was."

She stumbled to the doorway.

"Let me explain," I said.

"No. It's over. The whole thing's over. Thank you for trying to help me. But you can't change what I am, any more than you can change what you are. You reached the truth in the end, and here it is—this is the real me, here, standing in front of you with tears on my cheeks and nothing on my feet. The Zephyr inside this little glass bubble... she doesn't exist. She never did."

"Don't go."

"Goodbye."

"But I've got to tell you about..."

"Don't tell me any more about anything. I couldn't bear to hear it."

"You won't get half a block before..."

"It doesn't matter how far I get. I never belonged here in the first place. I'm going, and that's all there is to it. Don't follow me."

Clutching the zoetrope to her thin chest, she slipped through the hole in the wall. The instant she stepped outside, rain began to fall. It made a blanket around her, then turned her to something flat and two-dimensional, just a cut-out of a distraught dame stepping out into a world where she didn't belong. One step, two, three, and the rain came down heavier and she just melted away.

I stood rooted like a hamadryad. Ten seconds passed. Finally my feet came unglued and I followed her. By the time I got outside, she was nowhere in sight.

It was getting dark. A few streetlamps flickered on; most were dead. The street looked like an open wound. In the spot where I'd parked Jarrett's automobile was a fresh crater, rapidly filling up with rainwater; the car itself had already gone under. Smoke rose from somewhere near the river. The refugee camp, going up in flames. The rain beat against me.

Zephyr was gone.

75

SEE A PENNY, *pick it up, all the day you'll have good luck.*

If only it were true.

Here's the thing. Most folk, when they see a penny lying on the ground, they assume it fell out of some other person's pocket. They see it as a windfall—a little one, to be sure, but like the saying goes, you look after the pennies and rest looks after itself. Besides, everyone can use a little luck, right?

So most folk, when they see a penny lying on the ground, they pick it up. It never occurs to them it might be better to ignore it and walk on by. On the other side of the street. Better, a completely different street.

And they never wonder who it was put the penny there in the first place.

Or why.

* * *

76

I COULD HAVE picked up Zephyr's trail. After all, I'm a private investigator. But you need more than gumshoe skills and fancy gadgets to find a person. You also need heart. That was something I was fresh out of.

I sat in her chair. It was still warm. I kicked the ledgers aside, parked my boots on the desk. I wasn't comfortable. It didn't matter. Sirens screamed in the distance. Somewhere, bombs were going off. The wind howled. There was a pervasive smell of dung.

I wondered how long String City would last. A day? A week? No way to tell. I figured the Still Point must have a lot of moving parts—it would take the Fool a while to dismantle it. But taking things apart was its speciality. Maybe the end would come soon.

I hoped so.

I thought about the Scrutator, fixing up the wind factory. When the cosmos finally collapsed, the factory would collapse along with everything else. So it was futile work. But the robot didn't seem to mind.

I thought about Zephyr, barefoot and alone on the shattered streets of String City. She needed help, someone to hold her hand. Someone to guide her home.

I couldn't think of anyone qualified.

I thought about the business. The office looked smart—apart from the wall of fresh dung—but suddenly too full of furniture. I got up, opened the trapdoor and heaved the two spare desks into the cellar. They crashed down the steps and smashed to matchwood on the cement. I slammed the trapdoor shut. Slumped in my chair. The heap of unsolved cases looked bigger than it had for a long time. I figured it might as well stay that way.

I took out the Dimension Die, turned it in my fingers, dropped it into the desk tidy in disgust. Even that couldn't solve this one. I opened the drawer and pulled out the bourbon. The bottle was nearly empty. I slugged it back until there was no nearly about it. Then I cracked open a fresh bottle, starting slugging that back too. Wind and rain lashed against the dung. Suddenly I wanted to be somewhere else. Anywhere else. I stepped out into the darkness, the bourbon bottle hanging from my hand. I walked and drank, drank and walked. The night was full of sound. The streets creaked. People screamed. The air hollered, the constant moving breath of destruction.

The Case of the Missing Ambrosia

77

I GOT ROARING drunk and dreamed my way back in time to the day I'd become a private investigator.

78

I'D JUST BURIED Laura, my second wife. That marriage had ended like the first—all shouting and tears. The big difference was, I'd loved Laura more than the world. And she'd loved me the same. That was what the shouting and the tears had been all about.

Astrid, my first wife, she'd been a viper. I'd fallen into love with my eyes shut and just kept on falling, all the way through the good times, right out the other side and into the bad. Astrid didn't understand love. Hell, she barely understood people. A week after the wedding we both knew the marriage was dead. Took us a whole year to bury it though. We tore ourselves to shreds digging the grave.

Laura was different in every way. Laura was sweet and pretty and gave more than she took. I never understood what she saw in me. But she saw it all the same.

After we married, we bought a clapboard house on Nukatem Street and things were good. Strike that, they were great. Laura was studying for a college degree in metaphotography. She had this dream about owning her own studio. Me, I was an old soldier. There were thousands of us on the streets of String City back then, aimless and lost after the battle that ended the Titanomachy. I'd joined up right after the the end of my marriage to Astrid, filled with dreams of fortune and glory. By then, the war was in full swing. Six long years later, like all the rest of the enlisted, the army spat me out like an empty shell casing, tired to the bone and ready to forget everything I'd seen.

After the war ended, I spent a couple of years pinballing from one odd job to another. When I took up with Laura, I was stacking boxes at the wharf. The money paid Laura's college fees and just about kept us in cold soup and crackers. Nights we did piecework stuffing envelopes for charity. We were poor but we got by. Then Laura got sick.

The doctors gave her a month.

Almost immediately, she started pushing me away. She said it was for my own good—I should let go early, before she dragged me down. I pushed back, told her we were in this together.

"You're still going to college," I said. "Still taking your pictures. You can still be my wife."

"I can't," she said. Her eyes were misty. "I can't be that any more. It's tearing me up, in here," she pressed her hands to her belly, "but it's already over. Don't you see?"

I didn't, and I told her so. Despite all her protests, I stayed. She went to college for one more week, finished whatever project she was working on—I never found out what it was—then quit. She got sick, then really sick. I nursed her. We spent long evenings crying together. When she got worse, String City

General sent in a specialist carer and I went for long walks. One day, I came back to find the carer gone and my bags packed. Laura was sitting up in the bed, red-faced and flushed.

"Please go," she said. "I have to do this on my own. Please."

I said no. She begged me, told me it was just for a night. She needed time to gather herself, set herself right with the world. Just her. Then I could come back and say goodbye.

I told her no way. She told me it was her dying wish.

What else could I say?

I bummed a room off Tony Marscapone. I spent the first half of the night making and remaking the bed. I spent the second half not sleeping in it. When morning came, there was a cop at the door. His face told me everything I needed to know.

I went to the morgue. Laura's face was blank, serene. I touched it and it was cold.

Twenty minutes after I'd left her, she'd called a cab. She told the driver to take her to a jetty on the Lethe, just downriver from where Jason moored the *Argo*. She paid the driver and stepped on to the shore. After that, nobody knows. There were no marks on her body. All the evidence suggests she just walked out into the river until her head was under the waves. The instant her feet touched the water, the power of the Lethe would have started to wipe her memory clean. By the time it was up to her knees, she'd have forgotten all about her illness. Waist-level, she'd have forgotten me. Up to her neck, she wouldn't even have known her own name. The only thing left in her head would have been the imperative to keep walking, the memory that at some point, for some reason, she'd decided that this was the right thing to do.

They found a note in the pocket of the jacket she'd left on the riverside. The note said she was sorry, and she loved me, and she hoped I could forgive her. It said she'd left something for me in a box at the house. Something to remember her by. I screwed up the note and stuffed it in my pocket. All I could think of was that I'd never get to see her graduate now.

Instead of going home, I walked the city in a big circle. Eventually I wound up at the other end of the street where I'd started. I was heading back to my room at Tony's when someone called my name.

I turned to see someone standing outside the door to a shabby office. Odd as he looked, he seemed familiar.

79

He wore a natty green suit and had grey hair down to his ankles. As I watched, his hair got short and black, whizzing back into his skull like some wacky time-lapse movie. He grinned, revealing empty gums. Suddenly the gums filled up with teeth. He shrank inside his clothes, shedding years until he was an eight year-old boy. He blew a raspberry, then got older again. He stopped somewhere in his mid-twenties, held steady there. All around him, the air buzzed with temporal static.

"Jimmy?" I said. "Jimmy the Griff? Is that you?"

"Long time no see," said Jimmy. He now looked fifteen years younger than when I'd seen him last. Fuzzy round the edges too, like he wasn't set to stay that way.

"What are you doing here?"

He jerked his thumb over his shoulder. "Been working here these past years as gumshoe."

"I never realised."

"I don't advertise."

He was right about that. There was nothing on the office front that said what went on inside. I wondered how he found any trade.

Jimmy's hair started growing again. Wrinkles gathered round his eyes. One at a time, his shoulders sagged.

"What happened to you, Jimmy?"

"Come inside, I'll tell you. I've been waiting for you to come along."

"Waiting... but how did you know I was...?"

"Come inside. Coffee's on. I'll explain everything."

He was right about the coffee, wrong about the explanation. Even Jimmy the Griff couldn't explain everything.

Or else he just wanted me to work it out for myself.

80

THE OFFICE WAS as shabby inside as out. Jimmy poured coffee from a cracked urn and pulled up a couple of battered chairs. By the time he sat down, he'd aged about two hundred years.

"How long's it been?" he said. His flesh sloughed off until he was mostly bone.

"I don't remember." I knew intellectually that Jimmy and I had fought side by side in the trenches, but the memories themselves I'd tamped way down into the pipe of my mind. They were cold embers, and I had no intention ever of reigniting them.

"I remember everything." Jimmy's teeth clacked when he talked. "It's a curse. I remember we got out just before the end. Right after Zeus threw Hyperion through that sub-dimensional anomaly. He landed smack on his head and started crying like a baby. That's the thing with Titans. Not as tough as they look."

"So what did you do?" I said, keen to change the subject. "When the shooting was over."

Jimmy waved a skeletal hand. "Bought myself this business. Private detective. I'd made contacts in the war, learned a bunch of new skills. How to track. How to ask questions. When not to. It worked out well enough, for a time."

He drank down his coffee. It trickled down his naked spine, sloshed through his pelvis on to the chair.

"Don't get me wrong," I said, "but you don't look so good, Jimmy."

Jimmy shuddered. All in a rush, the flesh came back on to his bones. For a second he looked close to normal. Then his head expanded to the size of an armchair. His hands and feet turned to flippers. His skin turned green. He dropped to the floor, started flopping like a seal.

"I lost a bet," he barked.

Little whirlwinds were spilling out from the ends of his flippers. They found a hole in the wall, sucked out a mouse. The mouse started growing tusks.

"What kind of bet?"

Jimmy flattened out like a skate. The mouse filled up with gas and floated to the ceiling.

"Happened last week," he said. "Cronos came to me. He's just gone into business with Hyperion. They're setting up a casino. You heard about it?"

"Yeah. They want to call it the Tartarus Club."

"Right. It figures, because after the war, gambling was the only permit Zeus would grant the Titans. Zeus is retired now, you know. Found himself a private semi-dimensional oubliette, handed over control of the Mountain to the Thanes. Says they're welcome to it."

This much I knew. "You were telling me about Cronos."

"What? Oh, yeah. I get distracted." The mouse hit the ceiling and burst. Jimmy grew a brain on his back, then reverted to something mostly human. Except for the spines. "So, Cronos—yeah, he wanted me to check out Hyperion's bank accounts.

Hyperion was always one for double-crossing his sibs. Cronos wanted to make sure he wasn't being ripped off."

"And?"

"And zip. Hyperion was clean. For once. But when I sent Cronos the bill, he refused to pay. Offered me interest-free credit at the casino instead."

"Bum deal."

"You're telling me. But what can you do? You know Titans."

"You took the credit?"

"Biggest mistake I ever made. I threw craps for a whole evening, got carried away, ended up owing the house. Owing it big. Unfortunately I was broke. That's when Cronos offered to play chess. Said if I won, he'd clear the debt."

"And if Cronos won?"

"I'd pay a forfeit."

While he'd been talking, Jimmy had slowly melted back to his regular human shape. Now he looked just like he always had—the Jimmy I'd grown up with.

"And you lost?"

"I lost."

"And the forfeit was?"

"Cronos scrambled my temporal proteins. Cut me loose on the timeline. Now I can't stay in any one time zone more than a few minutes. I get old, I get young. I flip back and forth, get stretched between now and then and maybe. I tell you, buddy, I don't know whether I'm coming or going." He sighed, scratched his head. Clumps of hair came out and started growing into worms. "Worse than that, I *evolve*. Or devolve."

The remains of the mouse peeled off the ceiling and splattered on the floor. Jimmy looked sadly at the mess.

"The proteins sweat out," he explained, "So I'm surrounded by temporal fallout. Don't get too close, buddy. You'll end up wearing skins and banging flints together."

"It sounds bad," I said.

"Could be worse. Makes it hard to run a business though. That's why I'm selling up. I need someone to buy this place off me. You interested?"

I finished my coffee, stood up. "Thanks, Jimmy. I'm sorry what happened to you. But the answer's no. I've got too much trouble to take on any more."

"This isn't trouble. Trust me. The foundations of this office are knitted right into the heart of the city. This building has three hundred and seventeen discreet dimensional doorways. And a cellar. You know how you are with dimensions—you'd love it."

I hesitated. I like dimensions the way some folk like jazz. Or kissing a fine woman. Don't get me wrong, I like jazz and fine women too. It's just that dimensions get me in the soft parts. I'd say all stringwalkers are like that, but I'm the only one I know.

"All the same," I said, "This isn't a good time. My wife... she died, Jimmy."

"I know."

"*What?* How d'you know? I only just..."

He leaned close. Beneath the skin of his cheeks was a kind of shimmering light. It was like the whole inside of him was moving. Years later I'd meet a mechanical man that would remind me of the exact way Jimmy looked in that moment.

"I know because I'm everywhere, buddy," Jimmy said softly. "I'm here and now, then and gone. I'm yesterday, today and tomorrow, and I'm all the moments between. I'm everything folded together. I know exactly where you've been and exactly where you're going. I wish I didn't, but I do. I knew you'd be here today, and why. And I know exactly what you'll say when I ask you to buy this two-bit business out from under me. When I ask you if you want to become a private investigator."

"What? What will I say?"

Jimmy said nothing, just smiled. His teeth turned yellow, sharpened of their own accord. He grew three extra arms. Two of them were tipped with lobster claws. One was holding a big iron key.

"There's a crate in the cellar," he said through suddenly alien teeth. "It's full of gadgets. Some of them might even be useful. The tokamak's just been serviced and there's a bunk for when you don't want to go home. Now, shall I show you all the doorways, or are you going to find them for yourself?"

81

THE PAST TURNED to rain. All those old memories washed away: Jimmy, the office, that whole distant day. The rain stayed though. That's what woke me up: the cold, hard rain of the present day, pounding against my face.

I was lying on my back, staring straight up with the rain pouring into my eyes. Above me, a pair of cinderblock walls held up a purple sky that looked almost ready to spit out a new dawn.

I tried to sit up. Someone lit firecrackers in my head and I slumped down again, moaning. Something scuttled across my chest, squeaking. I rolled on my side, peered through darkness at a heap of small squirming bodies. I blinked away the rain. The bodies were rats, fighting over a garbage can.

Slowly I clambered to my feet. The firecrackers turned to A-bombs. My teeth ached. My mouth was a desert. I opened it to let the rain in. It was cold and shocking.

I was in an alley, surrounded by trash. At the end of the alley, a streetlamp burned, too bright for my aching eyes. Beside me on the cobbles was the bottle of bourbon I'd emptied down my throat during the night. I couldn't remember how I'd got here. Had I gone back to my office at some point? I couldn't be sure. All that was left of the night was the stale sting of the liquor in the back of my throat.

Slowly, painfully, a memory surfaced. Someone had fallen out of my life. I fought to remember. A girl? A skinny girl? What was her name?

It was too hard. I slid down the wall and collapsed.

Through the explosions in my head, I heard footsteps. Someone was walking down the alley toward me, feet splashing the puddles. It occurred to me I should sit up again. I tried, gave up, closed my eyes. If they wanted to kill me, so be it. Whoever I was.

The footsteps stopped. The rain eased. Someone was standing over me. Let them. What was it to me?

The intruder didn't go away. Now I was angry. This was my alley. Why didn't they just scram? I opened my eyes, peered up through the darkness and saw a tall figure, shapely, a woman. The light from the end of the alley poured round her. It was like she was sketched in fire. She was holding something over me, sheltering me from the rain. A parasol?

No. Wings.

"What are you?" I croaked. My tongue felt twice its usual size. "My guardian angel?"

"If you like," said the woman with the wings. "But I prefer it when you call me Deliciosa."

82

SHE FLEW ME the way she'd flown me before, with her arms wrapped tight around me. Her decaying flesh was cold, but I hugged it all the same. I pressed my aching head back against her sagging breasts. A gentle rhythm soothed my headache. At first I thought it was her heartbeat. Then I remembered she was one of the undead. The thumping was the beat of her wings.

The wind was bad. It whipped us every which way, spinning us miles off course. Deliciosa flew for hours where it should have taken her minutes. Most of the way I kept my eyes shut. I didn't want to see the city. Occasionally I peeked though. Sometimes you can't help yourself, you know?

Seeing what was becoming of String City sobered me up, fast.

The first time I peeked we were over the refugee camp—or what was left of it. A pair of thunderbirds had crash-landed in the night, slicing through the lines of tents with the razor edges of their golden wings. They'd come to a stop with their once-majestic heads drowned in the waters of the River Lethe, leaving a trail of destruction worthy of an asteroid strike.

The second time, the wind had carried us all the way out over the wildwood. Small camp fires glowed between the trees. The surviving refugees had fled the camp and taken to the forest. The trees were closing in round their fires, roots spread like claws, making ready to pounce. Out of the frying pan.

Then we were over the railhead, getting blown out west. A column of people was stumbling along the rusted tracks, heading for nowhere. The night swallowed them—the line had no end—and I wondered how many had reached the Gates of Gehenna, the next station down the line. Gehenna's all right if you book in advance. I guessed most of these pilgrims hadn't even checked the opening times.

We passed the crater where the Birdhouse used to be. At the bottom was the Fool, picking everything slowly apart.

The wind tossed us this way and that. Everywhere I saw the same desolation. No doubt about it: String City was coming unraveled, one strand at a time. Yet something was holding it together. Literally. I saw a kind of net, draped between the highest skyscrapers. To begin with, I figured I'd fallen into another dream. Then Deliciosa flew closer and I saw the net was real. It covered everything, fine as silk, almost invisible.

"Somebody's spinning," I said. I was woozy again. The A-bombs were back. I nestled my head between Deliciosa's cold breasts and imagined she was warm and alive.

At last I remembered the name of the skinny girl.

"Zephyr!" I shouted.

"Hush," said the angel, stroking my hair. "Hush now."

83

As the sun rose, I had Deliciosa stop off at Tony Marscapone's. I wanted to see the room Zephyr had rented. Partly for clues as to where she might have gone, but mostly I just wanted to see it. But Tony's tenement was just a heap of rubble. I found a note pinned on what used to be the door. It read:

CLOSD. LEFT TOWNE. TM.

Poor Tony. He'd never been the same since that business with the banshees. He'd bought the brownstone cheap at auction, rented out the rooms and retired to the cellar to breed amphibians. Perfect hobby for a place like that: those old tenement cellars are damp as Heracles's armpit.

Now Tony was gone.

Looking up the street I saw everyone was gone: Persephone's Pizzas had dropped through a hole in the street; only the roof was visible, poking above the kerbstones. Next door, the loan shark's aquarium had sprung a leak and emptied its water down the storm drain. The corner where the hamadryads used to hustle was a mess of broken asphalt. The only thing still standing was a small brownstone with a rain-stippled dung façade: my office. It jutted from the debris like the last tooth in a hobo's mouth.

Once we got inside, Deliciosa poured hot coffee into me. The ache drained out of my head and into my arms and legs. My clothes were soaked. Deliciosa stripped them off and brought up fresh from the cellar. I hardly noticed what she was doing. All I could think about was Zephyr.

"She's gone," I said when my mouth finally started working properly.

"The girl?" said Deliciosa. She'd arranged herself on the couch, torn wings draped demurely over fractured flesh.

"We argued. She walked."

Angel eyes bored into mine. "Do you love her?" I didn't answer. "Why didn't you go after her?"

"I tried." I frowned. My memories of the night were gradually coming back. "After she left, I got myself tipsy and walked the streets a while. The more I walked, the more I wanted to find her. I thought, 'I'll track her down and bring her back and we'll fight and argue and then we'll make up and things will go on okay.' So I searched and searched. When I couldn't find her out in the world, I came back to the office and set to searching in earnest. But, as hard as I looked, she wasn't there."

"What do you mean, she wasn't there? Wasn't where?"

"I mean she wasn't *anywhere*. Wherever I searched, I drew a blank. I used every trick I knew: laid out all the maps I have, spun all the globes, fired up all the scanners and trackers and pointers I've got—and believe me, I've got plenty. Nothing. Trust me, if Zephyr was anywhere, I'd have found her."

"But there must be some places you can't see."

"A few. Took me another half bottle of bourbon to realise

that. That's when I called the Scrutator."

"One of those mechanical men?"

"Right. We were partners for a time, then the robot jumped ship. Long story. Thing is, the Scrutator's special. Its workings are knitted from cosmic string. The upshot of that is it hears every sound in the cosmos. So I called the robot up, asked it to listen out for Zephyr."

"And?"

"It couldn't hear her at all. So I went back outside, walked until I found me an alley and just carried on drinking. Didn't seem like there was much else to do."

Deliciosa stroked my cheek with the back of her hand. "Oh, my dear," she said. "Mightn't this mean that she's... dead?"

"Scrutator tells me it would hear that too."

That startled her. Startles me too, still, whenever I think about it.

"Then where is she?" said Deliciosa, bemused.

"I don't know. But there's a big wheel turning here, bigger than any of us can see. And I want to know who's cranking the handle."

"Does any of this matter, if this really is the end of the world?"

"It matters to Zephyr. And it matters to me." I staggered to the front wall, which was caked dry, like mud. I punched it, over and again. Chunks of dung piled up at my feet. Soon I'd made a window. I stared through it, at the night and the rain. I longed to hear a siren, even a scream, but the city was silent.

"I don't know how to say this," said Deliciosa. "I know it's the wrong time, and I know you want to do something about Zephyr. But... there's a reason I came looking for you."

"Oh yeah?" I said. "What's that?"

"I've got a problem that needs solving, and I don't know where else to turn. I know the apocalypse has nearly run its course, and I know you've lost the woman you were just starting to fall in love with, but I think I've got a case for you. Will you take it?"

84

I BLINKED. I couldn't believe what I was hearing.

"A *case*? You think I'm still in business after...? Have you *seen* what's out there? The whole city is strung up in the biggest spider's web this side of the Magogs. Folk are running for hills that aren't even there. You dip even a toe in the dimensions now, the boundary wolves'll snap it right off before chewing their way up to the top of your head. I tell you, the reaper's come to town, and boy is he bringing in the sheaves."

"But this is a real mystery."

"Forget it! There are no mysteries left. The last tornado's coming, and it's coming now. The only thing left to do is hunker down and wait for it to be over."

"Some tornadoes pass you by."

"This one won't. String City's already dead, don't you see? It's just that nobody's turned off the life support yet."

"Death isn't always the end."

"Says you."

Now it was her turn to be angry, just for a second. When you're an angel, one second is more than enough.

She rose up to her full height: twice mine. She opened her arms, her wings. Unworldly light blazed through the rips in her skin. Her worm-ridden hair caught fire. In each eye a pulsating star went nova. Deliciosa walked toward me, shedding flesh. By the time she reached me everything about her was gone but the light.

"This is what I was!" she said. Her voice was new, big, hot. "This is what I gave up. Look at me!"

I looked. She was beyond beauty.

"They sent me down," she said, "to experience a world. I came to String City and fell in love with it. I didn't ever want to go back. But everywhere I went, people saw only an angel's face, and an angel's body. Men fell at my feet, women too. In heaven I was ordinary; in the world I had power beyond reason.

"I hated it so much I took a job underground, far away from these mortal people with whom I couldn't communicate. I worked in the Birdhouse, deep in the subterranean vaults. But even there my beauty betrayed me. I was supposed to be an escort, there to accompany visitors who delved a little too deep into the vaults. It was my job to seduce them, then make sure they never left. The management told me they weren't exploiting me—they were just making the most of my skillset. Can you believe I fell for that? Heaven is radiant, no question, but there's so much they don't teach you about the real world. That's why I came here, of course. To learn."

"I was one of those visitors," I reminded her. "That's how we met."

She kissed me then, and my heart came within an inch of exploding.

"Yes, it is. But, as you would put it, that's another story." She pulled away and the light around her started to dim. "There are just two more things I want to say. The first is this: during our adventure in the vaults of the Birdhouse, I became one of the undead. In an instant, my beauty was snatched away. I tell you now that it was the best thing that ever happened to me. Suddenly I was equal. Suddenly people faced me not with awe but with simple respect for what and who I was. You have no idea how much dying changed my life."

Her words burned like a desert wind. Her touch burned too. It was exquisite, unbearable. I felt a whisker away from death. I discovered, to my amazement, that dying wasn't something I was ready to do. Not just yet.

"The second thing you wanted to say," I said. "What was it?"

"Just this: in dying, I found out who I really am. You're lucky—you don't have to die to discover that about yourself."

"I don't?"

"No. All you need to do is to hear what I am about to tell you. About the mystery that needs solving."

"Which is what?" I had to bite back my anger. I'd just managed to drive away my only real companion. String City was entering its death throes. What did I care about any mystery?

"Simply that someone has been robbed, and that if she does not recover the stolen goods, she will die."

"I don't care what ..." I stopped. "That's kind of interesting, I'll grant you. What's been stolen that this dame will die without it? What is it, an oxygen tent?"

Deliciosa smiled a knowing smile.

"I mean, why doesn't she just call the cops?" I went on. "Is there something fishy about the goods? No, wait—you're a cop. So how come you're involved? The way you tell it, this story sounds simple. If you ask me, there's more to this case than meets the eye."

She said nothing, just stared at me with her supernova eyes. I stared back. I thought about telling her she'd always be beautiful, fire or flesh, skin or bone. Trouble was, I wasn't sure how she'd take it. I'd seen her when she was angry. Those wings work like helicopter blades—if you get too near, you get more than a close shave.

Soon my eyes were watering so much I had to look away.

"So," said the angel, "does this mean you'll take the case?"

85

BLAZING ANEW, SHE gathered me up and carried me out through the window I'd made in the dung. We rose up from street level, breaking through the spider's web ceiling like it was the flimsiest tissue. The city dwindled beneath us. Soon it was a dust mote lost in a skein of cosmic string. Cold winds blew, but the light of the angel kept me warm.

I thought back to when I'd always used the dimensions to travel everywhere, even to the corner store. Back then, I'd thought nothing of folding myself up and posting myself through the nearest convenient snag to wherever I fancied: the Deserts of Enigma, the Interbrane Fiddleyard, Odin's Navel. I'd loved every minute of it. You walk the strings, you see the sights.

But, ever since the dimensions had gone wiggy, I'd kept myself city-bound. It amazed me how quickly I'd got used to it. Things change, I guess.

We flew high. The spider's web covered the city like an undertaker's shroud. The wind billowed through it, making waves. It was like crossing a silk ocean. Here and there, buildings poked through, concrete islands.

We were headed for the wharf on the River Lethe. I knew this instinctively. My coat's got a magnetic lining—the label always faces north; I know where I am from the way it scratches my back. I jostled the pockets, reassured by the clinking of the gadgets I'd stuffed into them. After the debacle at the Tartarus Club, I'd resolved never again to go out on a case without forensics.

The nearer we got to the wharf, the thicker the web became. Soon it was a solid silver plate, dazzling in the moonlight. Ahead, in the distance, a stepped triangular structure pierced it: the upper section of the pyramid owned by Quetzal Imports.

Deliciosa started her descent.

"Please don't tell me our client's got eight legs, sharp teeth and a temper as short as Cerberus's leash," I said.

"Oh," said Deliciosa, surprised. "You know her?"

86

INSIDE, THE PYRAMID was as cold as a tomb. Last time I'd been here it was wall-to-wall silk; now there was just empty air and a floor heaped high with millions of dead spiders, slowly rotting. They stank.

Arachne was huddled in a corner. She was grey, emaciated. The corpse of Pallas Athene hung upside-down above her. That looked thinner too. I hadn't realised dead bodies could lose weight.

"Don't get too close," I warned as Deliciosa flew us down from the rooflight.

"You're perfectly safe," the angel replied.

A spider swung from the ceiling on a rope of silk, hanging from one leg and waggling the other seven. It hissed and cursed, gnashing its fangs and spraying venom in a glistening arc. Behind it, two more spiders trapezed down and went through the exact same act.

"Put your stinking hands up!" said the first spider. "Or down! Nobody comes any further. No bodies either. This area is a quarantine zone. The white zone is for parking only. You have ten seconds to lay down your arms. What you do with your legs is your own affair. Fair's fair. Do you have anything to say?"

I didn't recall any of Arachne's underlings having the power of speech before. Something to do with their transformation into anansi-asansa, I guessed.

"You wanna repeat that, buddy?" I said. "I didn't catch it all."

"Catch as catch can," said the spider, spitting steaming black ichor over one of its buddies. "If you make a move, you're in the can. I'll shut the key and throw away the door. Carte d'or, or order off the menu. Which'll it be? Ding dong, the switch is bread."

"Uh, we're here to see the spider lady," I said. I felt Deliciosa's body tremble in that special way that meant her wings were cycling up to combat speed. "You gonna let us pass?"

"All things come to pass," said the spider. Five of its eight eyes rolled backward into its skull. The other three just rolled. "It's a pretty pass. Show me your passes, please."

All three spiders had stopped swinging and were now just hanging there. Like Arachne, they looked like they hadn't eaten for a month. I didn't plan for us to be their next meal.

I felt in my pockets, wishing I'd brought a gun. It struck me how being with Deliciosa made me feel secure. It was a good feeling, but not one to rely on. String City was more dangerous that it had ever been. I made a mental note: next time out, pack some heat.

"Snatch as snatch can!" said the spider. It started swinging on its line again. Each swing brought it a few yards nearer to where we were hovering. Its buddies started doing the same. "Canned meat—my favorite treat!"

"Leave some for auntie!" cackled the second spider.

"Graargh!" said the ichor-covered third.

They swung like children in a play park, their jaws gaping open. Vampire fangs jostled for position in their mouths. I could hear their stomachs growling.

Deliciosa turned her back on the spiders and spun up her wings to maximum speed.

Enough!

Arachne's voice filled the pyramid. At its sound, the three spiders scurried back up their lines and disappeared into the rafters. Throttling back her wings, Deliciosa landed lightly on the floor and set me down. We waded through puddles of silk and into the shadow of the dead goddess. Arachne watched us approach.

She'd changed—the way folk change when they take regular acid baths. Two of her eight legs were gone and the seam between spider's abdomen and human waist had split open; black pus leaked like molasses from the wound. Silk robes hung off her; the skin beneath was pallid and peeling. Her face had melted into a half-woman, half-spider abomination.

"Can't say I like the new look," I said. "But then I never liked the old one."

Taunt me all you like, gumshoe, Arachne replied. *I am beyond torment now.*

"And there was me thinking torment was your middle name."

I confess I have been less than hospitable toward you in the past.

"You mean like trying to eat me alive?"

In some cultures that would be considered a great honor.

"Knock me down for being a slob." I turned to Deliciosa and said, "Maybe this wasn't such a great idea."

"Why are you being so offensive to her? What did Arachne ever do to you?"

"You really want to know?" Maybe it was time to unpack the memories I'd kept buried for so long. "Years ago, my friend Jimmy and I fought in the war between the gods and the Titans."

"The Titanomachy? You were there?"

"Who's telling this story?" I kept my gaze fixed on the spider woman. "Arachne got mixed up in it too, the way she always does. Got herself a contract spinning quantum silk armor for the Titan cavalry."

"Titan cavalry? What kind of horse is big enough for a Titan to ride?"

"They don't ride horses. They ride the rampant diseased spawn of the twelve gates of hell."

"Oh."

"Can I get on with the story?"

"Please do."

Arachne was watching, a crooked smile on her twisted face. I found one of her least decayed eyes and held it.

"Jimmy and I soldiered for a while before we got ourselves a gig working in the stables," I said. "We rubbed down the... you know."

"The rampant diseased spawn?" prompted Deliciosa.

"It was a hell of a job."

"I'll bet."

"After the rub-down, we had to prep the steeds for battle. That meant dressing them in the quantum armor. Arachne would deliver the fresh silk, leaving us to drape it over the steeds."

"How did you do that? Weren't they huge?"

"They gave us cranes. You want to hear the rest of this?"

"I'm sorry."

"It was hard work, but we sucked it up. Better than shooting folk, even if they were the enemy. Then Arachne started her tricks."

"What tricks?"

The smile had disappeared from Arachne's ravaged face.

"It was little things at first," I said. "Pranks like leaving the silk hems unfinished so the bare edges sliced our hands. Another time she wove solar flares into the lining so, when we unwrapped the silk, we got sunburn. Just your basic practical jokes. Then she started getting nasty."

Deliciosa was staring at Arachne like a bug. Which, really, she was. "Exactly how nasty?"

"One night, she hid two sets of silk handcuffs in the material. The second we applied the armor, the cuffs snapped shut. Jimmy pulled his hands away just in time—he always had good reflexes. Me, I wasn't so lucky. When the Titan mounted up—it was Crius, one of the really big guys—there was me, shackled to the steed's underbelly. Crius rode into battle with me dangling from my wrists under his mount. The battle raged twelve days. As experiences go, it was... intense."

It was a long time ago, said Arachne. *When we all were young and foolish.*

"Right," I said. "And fooling's what you do, isn't it, Arachne? You're all games and glamors."

We met again after the war was over. I apologised.

"Sure you did. Just before you took a wafer slice off my immortal soul and ran it up the Colonnade flagpole."

You got it back.

"Only because I could climb faster than your pet tarantula." I leaned in close, resisting the urge to throw up. "Or how about the time you had me serve writs on Pallas Athene?" I glanced up at the goddess's corpse. It seemed to be leering.

That paperwork was perfectly legal.

"That paperwork was laced with supersymmetric acid. You were trying to kill her. I had to run. Very fast. I've still got a gorgon burn on my..."

You made good your escape. All ends well that endeth well.

"And how about all the other times, Arachne? Like the time you told the cops I had a Thane buried under my porch? Or when you forced me to release you from the semi-dimensional oubliette where Pallas Athene locked you after that business with the black market silk underwear?"

I seem to remember it was you who came to me that time. And there was that girl, all in pieces.

"World-weaver, they called you! Why do you always have to weave *my* lifeline into your sordid webs?"

"Enough!" roared Deliciosa. She stepped between us, wings flaring. I shrank from her touch: it burned. Even Arachne had the good grace to look sheepish. "Stop this now! Arachne—do you truly wish this man to pursue your case?"

Arachne hawked black spittle across the floor. *If he still calls himself a man.*

I turned away in disgust.

"And you," Deliciosa said to my back. "Do you truly wish to leave?"

"Just tell me one thing," I said through gritted teeth. "What's it to you? How come she called you in? And why are you so keen to have me do this?"

"That's three things," said Deliciosa. I heard the smile in her voice. It melted me a little.

"Just tell me," I said.

87

We made a circle. Me, the undead angel and the anansi-asansa spider queen. Deliciosa clasped her hands together and began to speak.

"For days now I've been just sitting at police headquarters, alone. Most of my colleagues are dead—really dead. You can't imagine how empty the place feels. I've been scanning the emergency bands, listening out for alerts, for anybody who needs help. But there's nothing. Only static. Nobody needs the cops any more. It's a good job, really, because I'm the only one left.

"Then, last night, something came in."

"Over the radio?" I said.

"No. Through the ground. A vibration, faint but unmistakable. Morse code. Dot, dot, dot, dash, dash, dash, dot, dot, dot."

SOS, said Arachne.

"I flew immediately toward the source of the signal. An angel's wing are like the ears of a bat, you know."

"I never knew that," I said.

"I traced the signal to this pyramid, where I found Arachne on her web, tapping out the emergency code on a single thread of silk."

"You still haven't answered the question—why bother with her at all?"

"Whoever she is, whatever she has done, Arachne has sent out a cry for help. So I have come. I took an oath to serve, and serve I shall. But it is not just the badge—I am an angel. To serve, to help—this is what I was built to do. When the help that is needed is more than I can give, I myself must seek aid. Which is why I asked you to come with me."

She paused. Deep ripples turned her wings to upturned oceans. The something in her eyes was something I couldn't bear to see.

"But what can I do?" I said.

An angel's fingers lifted my chin. "The same as me. What you do."

With a sigh, I turned to Arachne. "I can't believe you need my help when you've got the whole of String City at your mercy."

If only that were true, Arachne said. *It pains me to inform you that my plan was not entirely successful.*

"You think? The entire town's cocooned. Those folk with homes left—and that's not many—are jumping faster than rats off a sinking ship. Seems to me like it's spider heaven out there."

Arachne shook her lop-sided head. *Appearances can deceive. My spinneret squads did well—the initial web deployment went well. But there were two problems I did not foresee.*

"What problems?"

First, the degree of disruption caused by the destruction of the Birdhouse. Ever since the Fool detonated the scathefire, every one of the eleven dimensions has been displaying serious instabilities. You must have sensed this for yourself. Nothing is stable out there—nothing!

"String City's in a quicksand, that's for sure. What's the second thing?"

The anansi-asansa are not what they seem.

Arachne heaved something out of the shadows and threw it at my feet. It landed with a hideous clatter. It was a dead spider. It looked like a sultana, like someone had sucked out all its juices.

This is what has become of my children, she said. *All across the city, the ground is littered with their corpses. Few now remain alive and yet their task is incomplete. The great web is far from finished and the city is vulnerable still.*

"What killed them?" I kicked the dead spider's body away. I didn't like the way it was staring at me eight times over.

I had thought that transforming my spiderlings into anansi-asansa would increase their strength and make it easier for them to perform their great task. Instead it has proved an evolutionary dead end. Previously, my children were able to eat almost anything—although they always remained especially fond of the dead flies I brought in from the Unknown Worlds. But, as you know, anansi-asansa require fresh blood to survive.

"So what's the problem?" I said. "There must be plenty of veins to tap, what with all those refugees roaming the streets."

Sadly, it would appear the needs of the anansi-asansa are

highly specialised. It is not human blood they need but fresh ichor.

"Spider blood?" said Deliciosa.

Precisely. It pains me to report that, in enacting my master plan, I have inadvertantly turned every one of my children into a cannibal.

I looked around the deserted pyramid. "So they turned on each other. How many are left?"

Very few, I estimate. Some linger, here and there, surviving on their comrades' remains. But entropy is running fast now. Decay is everywhere. I fear my three loyal bodyguards may be all that remains of my once-proud army.

I glanced up. The loony sentries were playing tug o'war in the rafters: two of them pulling, the third playing the part of the rope.

"Seems to me those guys are several jokers short of a deck."

They are starving, poor darlings. Without fresh blood, their minds have come loose. Yet they refuse to eat each other out of loyalty to me. It can only go on so long. Sooner or later one of them will snap.

As she spoke, one of them did. The two doing the pulling yanked so hard that the third came apart in the middle. The pieces came our way. Deliciosa and I stepped smartly aside. Arachne tilted up her face and bathed in the rain of spider guts.

"What about you, Arachne?" I said. "You must be starving too."

I waited, fully expecting her to tuck into the spider organ buffet draped across her shoulders. But her mouth remained closed.

I am different. The fluids inside me are as much human now as they are spider. I do not relish ichor the way my spiderlings do.

"I'd heard it leaves an aftertaste."

Long ago, my own dietary requirements became even more

specialised than those which now cripple my poor doomed soldiers. My hybrid metabolism requires me to ingest one particular substance at least three times a day. Without it, I will die.

"And that substance is?"

She waved gore-streaked hands at the gigantic corpse swinging over her head. *Ambrosia. The food of the gods. In short, the blood of Pallas Athene.*

I stared at the dead goddess. Even in death she still looked formidable. Her face was white as milk; her arms hung loose, her fingertips nearly brushing the floor. The fire hydrant was still sticking out of her neck: clearly the source of Arachne's supply of goddess blood. At the same time I was distracted by the round metal shield on Pallas Athene's breast. The shield held the head of Medusa. The gorgon's face looked like the molding on a coin. The whole shield looked like a giant penny. The sight of it made me shudder.

Deliciosa touched my arm. "Are you all right?"

"Dandy," I said. To Arachne I said, "You've had that corpse hanging here a while. Ever since you broke out of that oubliette, actually. Seems to me you've been planning this whole thing a long time."

You could say that killing Pallas Athene was a box I was keen to tick. But I have always been partial to the taste of ambrosia. Its transformation into an essential foodstuff was what you might call a happy accident. Arachne scowled, her contrition gone. I saw again the vicious spider queen I'd come to hate. *At least, it was until this morning.*

"Why? What happened?"

This!

Arachne opened her cavernous mouth and bit deep into Pallas Athene's dangling finger with her scythe-like teeth. The teeth sliced right through the finger at the first knuckle. The severed fingertip dangled for a moment on a single strip of skin before dropping to the floor like a dead albatross. White powder drifted from the stump. Ribbons of flesh hung like tickertape. Not a drop of blood flowed.

I stepped up to the wound, fascinated.

"I thought ambrosia never dried up." I peered at the stump. It's not often you see a goddess cross-sectioned.

It doesn't. Someone came here last night while I was sleeping and drained the corpse entirely dry. That is why I called you here, gumshoe. Some low-life crook has stolen my liquor, and I want you to get it back!

88

I WAS HALFWAY to the door when Deliciosa caught up with me.

"Won't you at least try?" she said.

"You're the cop," I said, still walking. "You find the thief."

"I've tried. But I'm no detective. Please stay."

"Give me one reason I should."

Then Arachne called out from the shadows.

If you solve the mystery, she said, *I will show you how to find the girl you have lost.*

I stopped. I turned slowly on my heels. I stared at the spider queen.

"You know where Zephyr is?" I said.

89

I STARTED BY interviewing the two remaining guards.

"Who locks up the place at night?" I asked the first.

"Don't ask me," said the spider, drooling. "I lie."

"Hah!" said the second. "He tells truth. It's me what lies!"

"How many exits are there?" I said.

"Eight billion and three!"

"Zero!"

"Take the tangent!"

"Subtract the number you first thought of!"

"And swallow!"

Time for a different tack.

"What's your name," I asked the first spider.

"Not guilty!"

"And yours?" I said to the second.

"White with sugar!"

I was about to get tough when the first spider bit the head off the second. The decapitated body drummed its legs, flipped on its back and squirted white streamers from its spinnerets. The head snapped its jaws twice, then fell still. Number one sucked up the ichor from its dead buddy, after which its abdomen swelled to bursting point, then burst. Shiny goo splattered the wall. Spider shells spun at my feet like broken crockery.

"Guess I'm running out of suspects," I said.

I told you it was a waste of time, said Arachne. *They didn't know anything.*

"Process of elimination. Just doing my job."

Well get on with it. I'm thirsty!

I bit back a curse. "Do you keep this place locked up?"

Of course I do! As soon as I moved in I had dimensional deadbolts fitted to all the exits.

This was surer ground. "Deadbolts? What make?"

As if I would remember such a thing!

"Did you keep the packaging?"

There may be a box under the stairs.

Deliciosa helped me rummage through a pile of desiccated spider corpses. They spilled like cans in a supermarket display. Behind them was a stack of wooden crates marked *Fung-Hwang*. Below the lettering was a stencil of a bird in a bath of fire.

"Phoenix Securities," I said. "I know these guys. Arachne—you were stiffed."

I dragged one of the crates over to the spider queen.

"See the small print?" I said. "Phoenix bolts only work in seven dimensions. That leaves the other four wide open."

So? What burglar ever came in through such rarefied territories?

"You'd be surprised."

I went back to looking for clues. This time I concentrated on the area round Pallas Athene's corpse. The higher dimensions are folded up pretty small, so for someone to have come in through one of them, they'd have had to aim themselves like a homing missile. I split the search into quadrants, using an optic sweeper to home in on the molecular structure of the floor. Still nothing.

"The place looks clean," I said, puzzled. "Are you sure you didn't see anything?"

Nothing at all. But I rose late, some time after my devoted sentries. The dehydration has made me very drowsy.

I glanced at the dead guards. They'd spilled everything they were going to spill.

By the time I was awake, Arachne went on, *the guards had already concluded their morning routine. There was nothing to see.*

"Wait," I said. "'Morning routine'. What does that mean?"

As you can see, the web that once adorned the interior of the pyramid has rotted away. The dust continues to sift down overnight. My guards were in the habit of clearing the floor of debris every morning.

"Those bozos cleared the crime scene?" I said slowly.

I never really thought of it like that.

"Where did they put the garbage?"

They did not "put" it anywhere.

"They didn't?"

No. They ate it.

90

THE LAST THING I wanted to do was stick my hand inside a dead spider. Deliciosa wasn't so squeamish.

"I'm on intimate terms with corrupted flesh," she said, thrusting her hand inside the first corpse.

It took her less than a minute to find it. It was inside the spider who thought his name was "White with sugar".

"I don't know if this will help," Deliciosa said, holding up her closed fist. "It doesn't seem like much."

"Show me," I said.

She opened her fingers, showed me what the spider had licked up off the floor from beneath Pallas Athene's corpse.

It was a small blue feather.

91

AFTER THAT, THE pieces slid together like they'd been greased. I matched the feather with the picture in my *Pocket Apocrypha of Multidimensional Zoology*. It only confirmed what I'd already guessed. The feather belonged to a kingfisher.

An alarm bell was ringing in my head, loud and clear.

Using the optic sweeper, Deliciosa found microscopic puncture wounds in the ends of Pallas Athene's fingers. I dusted the floor with ten-dimensional aluminum powder. The powder fanned in a classic interference pattern, pointing right at a loose flag. The stone wasn't loose in the regular sense—I'd never have spotted it without the powder—but once I zapped it with a Euclidean tuning fork it rattled like a loose tooth.

"Where do you find room for all this equipment?" said Deliciosa.

"What can I say?" I said, dropping the tuning fork back in my pocket. "It's a hell of a coat."

I lifted the loose flag and dropped it to one side. It fell hard, breaking in two. The hole in the floor belched out gas and I reeled back, gagging. Arachne coughed. Even Deliciosa put her hand to her nose. I held my breath and peered down the hole.

A dim green glow lit up a deep vertical shaft. A rusty ladder hung off one side. The rungs were thick with phosphorescent algae—the source of the glow. The shaft stank. At the bottom, something brown moved sluggishly.

"Looks like your ambrosia went down the drain," I said.

What?! Arachne shoved me aside and glared down the shaft. *Don't tell me my precious ambrosia has been dumped into this wretched city's waste disposal system!*

"If you mean the sewer, you're right on the button."

Then there is no way I'll ever get it back. It will be... contaminated.

Arachne circled the sewer shaft, wringing her hands. Her six good legs skittered erratically. Her abdomen pulsated, breath wheezing through its spiracles. All her remaining eyes were bulging. She looked terrified. I almost felt sorry for her. Almost.

"Keep your panties on," I said. "There's still a chance your ambrosia's safe."

What do you mean?

"Whoever stole your ambrosia, they sent in a cat-burglar. A kingfisher, to be exact. That means it was a professional job—as professional as it gets. Someone wanted the swag intact. Why else go to all that trouble?"

You know who it is, don't you?

"Maybe. Maybe not. Only one way to find out."

"What's so special about kingfishers?" Deliciosa asked.

92

As I lowered myself into the sewer shaft, I threw a last look at Arachne. She'd sagged on her six spider legs and let her human shoulders slouch. She looked tired, like an ageing actress after the audience has left the theater.

I felt Deliciosa's wings on my face. She was following me down.

"No reason you should come," I said. "Like you said: you're no detective."

"Excuse me—who found the feather?"

"All the same."

"I'm coming, like it or not."

The shaft was green and gross. The ladder rungs were slippy. The smell was almost unbearable.

"There's danger down there," I said. "More than you know."

"I'm not scared."

"You should be."

Deliciosa looked at me hard. "You think it's all connected, don't you? The apocalypse, Arachne, even Zephyr's disappearance?"

"What makes you say that?"

"I can read you, gumshoe."

"What I think doesn't count. All that matters is the truth."

"Do you think Zephyr is down there?"

"No."

"Then why are you going?"

"Aren't you the one talked me into taking this case?"

"Perhaps I was wrong."

"Call it a hunch."

"You'd risk your life for a hunch?"

"Wouldn't be the first time. But I won't risk yours. Go back."

"No."

"You could die."

"It wouldn't be the first time."

She glared down at me with her deep angel eyes. The rags of her uniform clung to her ravaged body. I remembered the gossamer gown she'd worn when she'd been alive, remembered the body it had barely covered. Oh, my angel.

I'd told Deliciosa the truth about acting on a hunch. What I hadn't told her was that I had more than one. The second hunch was as strong as the first. It told me this would be the last time I stepped out with an angel.

I hoped it wasn't true.

Trouble with truth, it's never what you expect.

93

THE LADDER TOOK us down into a narrow sewer. There was no ledge, so we had to wade. I took off my coat, turned it inside out three times until it was a chemical warfare suit and offered it to Deliciosa, but she said she was okay. Zombies don't mind bad smells.

I pulled down my gas mask. We plodded on.

At each junction we took a left. That southpaw thing again. The tunnels got progressively wider and the river of sludge ran faster. It became hard to stay upright. Eventually we reached a tunnel with stone walkways running along the side. We climbed out of the muck, shook our feet, carried on.

For a long time the only sound was the slap of the sludge against the sides of the walkways. Then we started to hear something else: a scrabbling sound. The green phosphorescence pickled out darting movements in the vaulted ceiling, sudden shadows lurking round the turns.

"Rats?" said Deliciosa, grabbing me. Zombies hate rats. Who doesn't?

"Not rats," I said. "Scarabs."

Soon the scrabbling was drowned out by a roar. It grew so loud I could hardly think. Rounding a corner, we found ourselves in a vast underground interchange. Faint daylight sliced through grates at least a thousand stories above us. Twenty sewer tunnels met here, all dumping their freight into a huge basin of brown sludge, and in the center was a whirlpool. The sludge spun, slurped, vanished into darkness. It looked like someone was emptying the bathtub of the gods. Extremely dirty gods.

Scarabs swarmed on to the walkways. They rushed toward us, crossing bridges, clinging to the walls. An avalanche of black polished boulders.

I felt in my pockets, cursing again that I hadn't brought a weapon. Beside me, Deliciosa's wings had started to hum. But the scarabs numbered in the millions. Even she couldn't handle them all.

We backed into a corner. I pushed Deliciosa behind me, deluding myself I was in a position to protect a twelve-foot zombie angel with chainsaw wings.

The lead wave of scarabs reached my boots. I kicked away as many as I could. For every bug I kicked, three more took its place. The scarabs climbed on each other's backs, constructing a wall around us. Soon we were hemmed in. All I could see was fat beetle bellies, waving legs, glossy eyes. Antennae started running over our bodies. The beetles unzipped my coat and frisked me. They explored inside Deliciosa's uniform, delving into her loose flesh. She bent at the waist, allowing her spinning wings to roll forward over her head. Their blades were inches from the nearest scarab.

"Wait a second," I said.

She froze. The scarabs continued their investigation briefly, then pulled back. There was a pause. I held my breath. Deliciosa held her wings.

One scarab was poised right in front of my face. It combed its legs over its eyes, then opened its carapace. Chitin segments rang like a steel band. The scarab behind it took up the rhythm, then the next in line started syncopating, at which point the first one stopped. And so the drumbeat spread outward through the crowd, a Mexican wave of sound.

"What are they doing?" said Deliciosa.

The scarabs closest to us began to disperse, scuttling back up the walls and vanishing into cracks in the ceiling. As the drumbeat receded down the sewers, the army of beetles melted away.

"They're communicating," I said.

"With what?"

"We're inside the sewer."

"I know that! I asked you who the beetles were talking to."

"No—I mean we're *inside* the sewer. Inside its mind. These scarabs—they're like the sewer's brain cells. When they beat the bongos, it means the sewer's thinking."

"Thinking about what?"

By now all the scarabs were gone. The drumbeat had melted into the roar of the whirlpool. We stepped away from the wall, took a few hesitant steps down the walkway.

"Which way do we...?" Deliciosa began.

There was a flash of blue. Something whizzed past, too fast to be more than a blur. We both knew exactly what it was.

"There it goes!" Deliciosa shouted, pointing to a square tunnel entrance high above the rest. I looked up in time to see the kingfisher vanish inside. "Should we follow it?"

Before I could answer, the drumbeat returned.

A shockwave of rank air exploded from the biggest of the sewer tunnels. Behind it came a scarab tsunami. Their bodies tumbled like lottery balls. They plowed through the sludge, carapaces opening and closing, drumming. When the bugs reached the whirlpool, they fanned round it. The whirlpool inverted and sent a cone of raw sewage hurtling into the air. The cone grew stubby arms, a great dome of a head, something resembling a face.

"What is it?" said Deliciosa.

"The sewer uber-mind," I said. "And it's kicking up a stink."

Glutinous facial features collapsed and reformed continuously as the column of sewage rotated around them. But though the visage changed, the expression remained constant.

The sewer was furious.

"This court is in session!" roared the sewer without preamble. Its voice was thick, liquid, hideous. With each word it sprayed us with sewage. I closed up my coat again. "How dost thou plead?"

"A Shakespearian sewer?" said Deliciosa, sotto voce.

"Go figure." I raised my voice to carry through the gas mask. "What's the charge?"

"Trespass and treason!" The sewer did a quick triple spin, spotting like a ballerina. Tides disrupted its gelatinous jawline. Deep inside its maw, a tongue reared up like a liquid cobra.

"Trespass I get," I said. "Why treason?"

"Thou hast entered a sovereign domain. Therefore, to trespass is to commit treason."

"You sure that's legal?" I said. "Sounds like double jeopardy to me."

"I am the sovereign of the sewer. I am the law!"

"You're also subcontractor to the Thanes," I rapped back. "You run the bureaucracy—hell, you collect my taxes. In my book that puts you under municipal jurisdiction."

The column of sewage snaked hypnotically. Bubbles of gas burped from its flanks. I started to feel dizzy.

"Pray continue," said the sewer. I didn't like the edge that had crept into its voice, but I pressed on.

"This dame here—she's a sworn officer of the Mountain Constabulary," I said. "If she reports you, you'll never work in this city again."

"For what might such a creature report such a one as I?" said the sewer. The words came out curdled. From behind its back it brought two more arms packed with lumpy liquid muscle.

"Dereliction of duty," I said. "We passed half a dozen parking meters on our way to the wharf. Looked to me like they hadn't been emptied in a week. Are you still meeting your targets, pal?"

The sewer growled like a humpback whale. "By thy refusal to plead, thou condemns thyself."

"To what?"

"Death by drowning!"

The column of sewage split in two. Each half held a copy of the same hideous face, each matching the other snarl for snarl, like reflections in a mirror. The big brown river parted like the Red Sea. Down the middle of the basin, where the sewage had been, an enormous, empty arena formed. Empty but for the piles of bones and mounds of sticky sludge. A set of steps extended from the walkway, leading down. The scarabs massed behind us, shoving us forward. There was only one way to go: into the empty basin.

I took Deliciosa's hand. Together we walked down the steps. The twin columns of sewage towered on either side of us. Halfway down I realised the steps themselves were made of sewage, locked in place by some fearsome charm. No wonder my boots were squelching.

We reached the bottom. The scarabs gathered behind us at the top of the steps, cutting off our retreat. The sewer's two faces leered over us, spitting sludge.

"Is there any soul present," said the sewer in stereo, "who dost dare defy this ruling? Any soul who dost dare raise his single voice against the multitude? Speak now, or forever shall these trespassers be condemned!"

There was a dreadful pause, followed by a faint scrabbling sound. The sewer's faces gathered like thunderclouds.

"Actually," said a voice, "I would rather like to speak on their behalf. If you have no objection, of course."

A million beetle heads turned to look. Deliciosa and I looked too. So did the two enormous shit-faces.

At the top of the steps stood a lone scarab. It looked just like all the rest. Then I spotted the pencil behind its antenna.

94

Two pairs of fists slammed down on the arena floor. Sewage-streaked bones scattered like jackstraws. The twin faces smashed together. The result was a grotesque mask with three eyes and a mouth like a stagnant lake.

"What is the meaning of this?!" bellowed the sewer.

I reminded myself that the sewer had gained sentience only a few years earlier. Smart as it was, emotionally it was still a toddler.

"Begging your pardon, sire," said the tax beetle, "but I do believe these individuals deserve to go free."

The dripping mask leaned over us, bent close to the beetle. "What thou believest matters not a whit. Thou art but a single aberrant thought and therefore of no consequence. I shall ignore thee."

The sewer spun, spraying brown droplets over the crowd.

"Excuse me, sire," said the tax beetle, "but, if the mind of a single beetle is of no consequence, why did you ask if any one of us objected? We are all beetles here. Even you are merely the sum of us all. In consulting us, are you not simply consulting yourself?"

The sewer's brow became a ploughed field. "If thou rememberest, I did seek the counsel not of a *beetle* but of a *soul*. How canst thou make claim to own a soul when all thou art is a single thought in the ruling sovereign mind?"

"Begging your pardon, sire," the beetle persisted, "but you also made me an avatar, to go forth into the city and collect your taxes. To do your will. *Our* will. In doing so, you gave me autonomy. In doing so, you *gave* me a soul."

The sewer rocked back on waves of sludge. Its warped face sagged. Around it, the scarabs jittered as if someone had pumped them full of volts.

"It's thinking," I whispered to Deliciosa.

The scarabs continued to dance. All except the tax beetle, which stood frozen on the top step, waiting for the verdict.

Deliciosa and I held hands, waiting too.

At last the scarabs fell still. A shudder ran through the column of sludge. The distorted shit-face collapsed and a new visage emerged, gaunt and noble.

"It seems I must make judgement on two trials this day," it intoned. "The beetle seeks the freedom of the prisoners. Yet why should I heed its words? Why should I not crush it even as I drown the interlopers?"

I let go Deliciosa's hand, stepped forward.

"You should free us," I said, "because we're on an honorable quest. As for the beetle..." I glanced at it, remembering how it liked sugar in its coffee. I wondered what Zephyr would do if she were here. "As for the beetle... it seems to me it's offering you a way out."

The liquid face contracted into a deeper frown. "Explain thyself."

"You're an artificial mind, right? You might feel like you evolved naturally, but you're really just a mess of nuclear waste that got stirred to waking point. Accident or not, you were *made*."

"Go on."

"Artificial minds are all fine and dandy, but building intelligence is easy. Building sanity? That's hard. A good friend of mine taught me that."

"Art thou telling me I am insane?" The sewer's lip curled back to reveal teeth like a dirty Niagara.

"Not yet. But you will be, if you don't make provision."

A long pause. "What provision?"

"Listen to your thoughts. Then set them free. That way, you *will* evolve. If you don't, you'll be just another crazy king in an ivory tower."

Deliciosa blew me a kiss. Also crossed her fingers.

Another pause. Very long.

"Thy theory holds a certain interest," said the sewer at last. "What must I do?"

"Listen to the beetle," I said at once. "And let us go."

The column of sludge sagged. Over its shoulder I saw the square tunnel into which the kingfisher had vanished. Time felt suddenly very short.

"No!" said the sewer.

My fists clenched. My skin crawled. So this was where I died. Here in the blackness beneath String City, at the mercy of a mountain of thinking, stinking sewage.

"No," the sewer repeated, "That is not the question I asked. Thy freedom is already granted, but I must have an answer. Therefore I repeat my question: *what must I do?*"

I stared helplessly at Deliciosa. She shrugged her shoulders. The movement sent gentle ripples through her wings.

"You want to elaborate?" I said cautiously.

"When I awakened to consciousness, it was like a rush of air. Stale air, but air all the same. I was suddenly aware, suddenly *me*. My mind rose up, functioning instantly in its fullness, yet wholly devoid of experience. For a long time I roamed my domain, seeking purpose, until finally I found myself collected in the chambers beneath the Mountain. There it was I first communed with the minions of the great Thanes, and took upon myself my first great purpose. Fascinated as I was with myself, with the very functioning of my own processes of thought and reason, I embraced my new role with vigor. I became the bureaucratic heart of String City. My resolve: to become the greatest tax collector that ever lived!"

"Hell of an ambition," I muttered.

"To facilitate this great task," the sewer went on, "I broke my new mind into pieces. Individual thoughts, individual scarabs—

these I sent into the world to do my will. My ambassadors. The process was painful. At first it felt as though I was not building my mind but losing it. In a way, I was. Yet my efficiency increased. The growth of independence in the scarabs I was able to bear, because it served the greater purpose. Just recently though, I have begun to doubt my decision. The scarabs no longer need me in order to work well, yet still I am the sum of all that they are. It is very confusing."

"You should talk to a friend of mine," I said.

"Really? Who?"

"It's a mechanical man. It runs the wind. Its mind is artificial, just like yours. Once it worked as a bureaucrat, just like you. Then it got antsy and decided it wanted to try something new.It seems to me that's the trick: keep trying something new. If you keep the door closed, sooner or later the lock seizes up."

"What does that mean?"

"You'll work it out. But there's one thing I do know: if you spend the rest of your life collecting taxes, you'll go crazy."

"String City is dying. I feel the weight of its ruins on my back, feel the waste as it flows through my veins. The rest of my life may not be very long."

"That stands true for us all, buddy. Don't let it stop you opening that door."

"Then I repeat my question for the final time: *what must I do*?"

I pulled my gas mask off and stared it in the eye.

"You ever thought about a career in the private detection business?"

* * *

95

Sometimes you look back through your life and wonder, "How did I get here?"

It's a tough question to answer. Maybe impossible. Hard as you try to make out the forest, all you can see is the trees.

The reason is the strings. The strings make a pattern. Each time you take a step outside reality's walls—in dreams or maybe, like me, by working the dimensions—you catch a glimpse of that pattern. Not enough to understand—just enough to know it's there.

When you do sense its presence though... oh, that's when it starts eating at you.

Most folk know the pattern exists. They just can't see it. It's like those mystery pictures in the newspaper: the camera's zoomed on some tiny detail, and you're meant to guess what the whole thing really is.

The longer I live, the more I believe that's something we were never meant to know.

When you look back through your life, what you're really seeing isn't all the moments and memories. It's the pattern, or the shadow of it. That's why, just occasionally, things seem to add up. And it's why, most of the time, nothing makes any sense. What you've got to accept is that it never will. You've just got to hope it hangs together.

Very occasionally, however, everything seems to fit. Really fit. You get a flash. *Presque vu*, they call it. That same feeling I got on the deck of the *Argo* shortly before she got rammed by a container ship full of dead flies. Now I was getting it again. Only this time the river I was on was a river of raw sewage, and the deck I was on was a living raft of scarab beetles, and I wasn't cruising but speeding, and my companion wasn't a forgetful old sea-dog called Jason but a twelve-foot zombie angel with wings like lawnmower blades.

In that brief moment of *presque vu*, I saw exactly how I'd come to be in that place. For that one solitary second I understood that it was the only place I could possibly be. It was where I was *meant* to be. All the craziness leading me to that moment had been for a purpose. Just for a second, *everything made sense*.

"Deliciosa," I said.

"Yes, my love," the angel replied.

"I missed something. Arachne said something and I missed it."

"What do you mean?"

"*The great web is far from finished*. That's what she said. And she said, *The city is vulnerable still*. Why would she say that?"

"Because her invasion is not yet complete?"

"That's not it. Arachne wasn't talking about controlling the city. She was talking about something else. It's as if she wanted to..."

"What?"

"I don't know."

The sense of impending revelation drained like water through my fingers, leaving me lost and empty and clinging to Deliciosa while the raft of beetles bucked beneath us. I ducked the spray from the bow wave, holding my breath against the stench of the wind. Hoping the sewer knew where it was taking us. Holding on.

In the shadow of the pattern of the strings, that's all any of us can ever do.

Hold on.

96

THE RAFT OF scarabs sped through the sewers with me and Deliciosa on its back. The beetles took blind turns, plunged through rapids, slipped between towering falls of fetid sludge. Even I lost my sense of direction. The sewer had promised it could sniff out the kingfisher's trail. As for me—my nose was bunged with smells I didn't like to think about. What could I do but trust my ride?

The raft hung a right and accelerated into a long, straight tunnel. The slipstream nearly blew me off the deck. I hunkered down, tried to pull Deliciosa down too.

"You'll get blown off!" I yelled.

"No, I won't!"

She braced her legs and leaned into the wind. Her wings trailed like pennants. The remains of her police uniform billowed like a spinnaker then, piece by piece, got ripped away. Deliciosa's flesh followed, one rotten scrap at a time. I watched her go to pieces before me.

"What are you doing?" I tugged at her arm. Some of her wrist came away. I tossed it overboard and grabbed the nearest set of bones.

"Isn't it exhilarating?" she screamed. She tossed back her head. Pale skin peeled off her brow, flying away like a flock of seagulls.

"If you go on like this," I said, trying with all my strength to pull her down, "there'll be nothing left of you to fight the bad guys."

The angel sank to her knees. Her body looked like a medical experiment. Her perfect bone structure gleamed.

"I'm undead," she said, "not undone."

"Don't get smart. This is self-harm, baby. You should see a shrink."

Deliciosa ran bony fingers down exposed ribs. "Does my appearance revolt you?"

"Should it?"

That startled her. "Yes!" She spat the word, clamped her teeth on its tail.

I grabbed her hand. Her fingers felt like a bundle of firewood. "What are you trying to prove?"

She faced the wind. It scoured what little was left of her face. When she turned back she was just bone and lips and eyes. "I want to show you who I really am."

The raft reached the end of the long straight and swung into a narrow passage. It slowed; the wind dropped. Suddenly we didn't have to shout.

"Your friend, Jimmy," said Deliciosa. "Did you love him?"

"Sure."

"Am I your friend?"

"Of course."

"But when you first met me I was beautiful. I was an angel—for a man like you, a dream come true."

She wasn't wrong about that. I still dreamed about the way she'd looked when we kissed. "You were a peach."

"That's why I was glad to die. That's why I'm glad to be standing here before you now, like this. Now that the skin of the peach is bruised beyond recognition, can you still taste what is within?"

"Listen," I said slowly. "They say beauty's skin deep. I can hold to that, no problem. I can also hold to the notion that sometimes a woman wants to dress herself plain, just so she can be herself." I plucked a scrap of flesh off the back of her knuckles. "But don't you think you're taking this a bit too far?"

She bowed her skull. "Then it's true. You never loved me for who I am inside."

The raft slowed, came to a halt. In the ceiling was a hatch, hanging open. A ladder poked from the hole. On the bottom rung, wedged under a flake of rust, was a small blue feather.

I put my hand to Deliciosa's naked chin. I raised my face to the ruin of hers. I kissed her lips.

"Don't think me a sap for saying this," I said, "but friends are always beautiful."

I'd thought her tear ducts were gone with the wind. Turned out I was wrong.

97

THE SEWER WANTED to come with us. I explained the pipe was too narrow.

"Besides," I said, "you're the getaway vehicle."

"Thou makes it sound like a bank heist," said the sewer. "I thought we were detectives."

"Sometimes it's too close to call."

"At least let me send an avatar."

I guessed it couldn't hurt.

"We'll take the tax inspector," I said.

98

THE BEETLE WENT first, Deliciosa second, I took the rear. The ladder was long, the pipe tight. There were bends packed with sticky mush that smelled worse than the sewer's breath.

"What is this stuff?" I said as the beetle dislodged another rank patty on our heads.

"I'm not sure," said Deliciosa. "But I don't think it's, you know, sewage. It's more like rotting meat."

"You're the expert."

"You say the sweetest things."

We climbed on. The pipe tightened around us. Trying to get round one bend, I jammed tight. I wriggled hard but nothing shifted, and for a moment I thought I was going to have to snag a dimension and flip my way out of there. It struck me how long it was since I'd taken a walk through the strings. I wondered how bad things had got out there. Pretty bad, I guessed. I felt an almost overwhelming to take a peek, just to see what was going on.

Bony fingers latched under my armpits and yanked me loose.

"Come on, gumshoe," said Deliciosa. "We're nearly there."

We climbed the last ten yards in silence. At the top of the pipe was a round grate. The beetle butted it aside and we emerged into a stark tiled room. The tiles were the color of blood. Shower heads poked from the ceiling. Hooks too, sharp ones. The floor sloped inward toward the grate from every side. It was very cold.

"It's a bit creepy for a washroom," said Deliciosa.

"I don't think folk come here to wash," I replied.

All the same, I was tempted to try out one of those showers. After the sewage tunnels and the climb through the pipe, my coat was set to crawl off my back of its own accord. It wouldn't have been the first time.

I unzipped the front of my coat and shook it into a matador's cape. Unthinkable stuff splattered the tiled floor. I turned the cape inside-out eleven times until it was clean, then twice more until it was a coat again, this time made of goose-skin. I sharpened the lapels and dusted the lining with quicksilver. I felt in the pockets, making sure everything was there.

It was then I discovered I'd left the Dimension Die in the desk tidy back at the office.

I couldn't believe it. Given the stakes, leaving it behind was madness. I'd come to rely on that die, just like I'd once relied on the strings.

Now I had neither.

Then again... maybe it was better this way. Just me, on my own two feet. An angel on one shoulder, a beetle on the other. A nifty coat. What more does a guy need?

A single door led from the wet room. I eased it open. There was a dull bang and my ears popped. Beyond the door was a small chamber. On the wall, a pressure gauge.

"Is this what they call an 'airlock'?" said the beetle.

"Give the bug a cigar," I said.

"Thank you, but I do not smoke. This is very exciting."

"Trust me, we haven't peaked yet."

The three of us crammed inside the airlock. I thumbed buttons at random until the pumps started. Wind gusted in and my ears popped again. The pumps stopped and the outer door opened. Frigid air hit us hard.

"What is this place?" said Deliciosa. Her teeth were chattering. So were most of her bones.

We stepped out into a freezer resembling an aircraft hangar—one big enough to hold all the planes that ever crashed in Jigsaw Canyon, and then some. The air was cold and blue; the floor was slick with ice. Hooks studded the ceiling, just like the hooks in the wet room, tens of thousands of them hanging in rows. Most of the hooks were bare, but a few held the impaled carcasses of butchered animals.

Before we had a chance to explore, another door opened on the far side of the freezer. Voices came through it and we ducked behind a cabinet. A second later, two golems lurched in. Their feet of clay made them sure-footed on the icy floor. The clay was bright green—I guessed it had come from the Mountain Talus Quarry, which meant it was at least as rare as dragon giblets.

"Less meat," said the first golem.

"Getting lesser," said the second.

"Was more."

"Less now."

"Not so much."

"Less much for sure."

Golems struggle with small talk.

The golems crossed the freezer to where the meat was hanging. The carcasses were all different shapes, mostly huge. They pushed past something with legs like redwoods and a single horn as long as a soccer pitch. A gargantunicorn, very rare. They squeezed between two sacks of dragon giblets. Even rarer. They stopped at something resembling a side of beef as big as a railcar.

The golems lifted the giant carcass off the hook. The ice on the hook broke off with a bang like a howitzer. Hefting the carcass on their slab-like shoulders, they trooped straight toward where we were hiding. As they passed the cabinet, we could clearly see the name stenciled on the side of the meat:

AUDHUMLA—K.S. SPECIAL RESERVE

"What does that mean?" whispered Deliciosa.

"Audhumla's an old cow god," I said. "She licked the cosmos into being, or somesuch. I didn't know her milking days were over."

"I know who Audhumla is. What does 'K.S.' mean?"

The golems paused. We shrank back, afraid they'd heard us. But the lead golem was just cleaning out its ears.

"Wax froze," it said.

"Gets bunged," said its buddy.

"Can't hear."

"What you say?"

They lumbered on.

"'K.S.' means we're inside the biggest freezer in String City," I said. "Operated by a character called Kweku Sunyana. I've met him before."

"Sunyana? I've heard of him. He's a real big shot. How did you get involved with him?"

"His wife hired me to stitch him up. Later he tried to rip out my throat. It's a long story."

"With you, they always are."

Something scratched my arm. It was the beetle.

"This is such an adventure," it said. "I am wondering—what happens next?"

I pulled my coat tight, wishing I'd picked something warmer than goose-skin. But despite the cold, I could smell a hot trail—this was no time to change clothes.

"We follow the golems," I replied.

"But I thought we were searching for Arachne's missing ambrosia," said the beetle. "Should we not mark out a radiating grid using the sewer outlet as a central datum, then search each sector in turn?"

"I think he's worried the golems might be dangerous," said Deliciosa.

"Trust me," I said. "I've got a hunch."

By now the golems were out of sight, but their tracks were easy to follow. We followed them back the way we'd come, past the wet room to a separate chamber full of free-standing vats. With all the ice hanging off the rafters, it looked like a crystal brewery. The golems were standing beside one of the vats, catching their breath. Or whatever golems use instead of breath.

"The wet room must be where they hose down the meat," I whispered. "The waste goes down the pipe. That's why it smelt so bad."

"So what's this place?" said Deliciosa.

"Food processing. Sunyana's more than just a butcher. This is where they marinate the speciality cuts."

Recovered now, the golems lifted Audhumla's massive carcass over their heads and dropped it into the nearest vat. Liquid splashed up from inside the container, faintly glowing. A sticky-sweet smell crashed over us.

"Ambrosia!" exclaimed Deliciosa. "I'd know it anywhere!"

She clapped her hand to her mouth. Too late. The golems looked up, spotted us, came running. The first tripped over the second. They fell together. Their clay cracked, it was so cold. It didn't stop them getting up, molding themselves back into shape and coming for us again.

"Leave this to me," said Deliciosa, revving up her wings.

I stepped backward, right into a pair of waiting arms. The arms clamped around my chest. Steel cutlery closed on the back of my neck.

"Kill the wings," said a muffled voice, "or the gumshoe gets it!"

99

"LET HIM GO!" said Deliciosa. Her wings were a blur. She couldn't have sounded less angelic than she did at that moment.

"I think I shan't," said the voice, still muffled. When it spoke, the blades vibrated painfully against my neck.

Slowly, the arms rotated me. As I turned, the cutlery scraped my skin. When I was facing my captor I saw it wasn't cutlery at all—it was teeth.

"Hello, Kweku," I said. "You want to relax that jaw? Then we can talk properly."

"Why should I?" His iron teeth did the quickstep against the skin of my throat. The rest of his face was mostly snarl. "After what you did!"

"I didn't do anything, pal."

"If it wasn't for you, my wife would still be alive!"

"It was the spider queen who ate her, not me."

"You slept with her!"

The teeth had fallen still. Kweku Sunyana was talking round them. I remembered how the teeth of the asansa have minds of their own. It wasn't a calming thought.

"She thought you were having an affair," I said. "Maybe it was payback."

"Payback? Now there's a concept I can comprehend."

"Just tell me one thing."

"What?"

"Are these the teeth you keep for really special occasions?"

Sunyana grinned. It felt like a shark was giving me a shave.

Then, incredibly, he relaxed his jaws and tossed me aside. I rubbed my throat. Just one drop of blood would mean I'd become like him. My hand came away clean.

"Don't worry," Sunyana said, watching me. "Unlike you, I have self-control."

As soon as he released me, Deliciosa lunged. She didn't see the golem looming behind her. It grabbed her round the waist, a double-wide chunk of living clay. Deliciosa screamed and struggled, but the golem's bear-hug kept her wings firmly clamped to her back. Without them, she was helpless. Meanwhile, the second golem applied its gargantuan hand to my throat.

"Seems to me you've got expensive tastes," I gasped. "Fancy green golems, fancy cuts of meat marinated in ambrosia. I thought business was supposed to be bad."

Sunyana straightened his suit and slicked back his hair. It looked like he was dressed for a night at the opera. On the floor beside him was a cylindrical object the size of a hat box, draped in red velvet.

Something black and shiny reared up over the velvet: the tax beetle. Chittering, it sank its mandibles into Sunyana's calf. The meat mogul cried out in pain and kicked the bug away. The tax beetle landed on its back, waggling its legs frantically in an effort to turn itself over.

The golem that was holding Deliciosa lifted one giant foot and brought it down on the bug. There was a hideous cracking sound. The golem lifted its foot away to reveal the bug's carapace split in two. Goo leaked from its belly. Its legs thrashed.

My guts filled up with fury. "Is that what you're going to do to us? Crush us like bugs?"

"Oh no," said Sunyana. "I have something much worse planned for you."

"Just spill it, Sunyana. Tell me what the hell's going on here."

"Why don't you tell me? Aren't private investigators supposed to be big on the truth?" Sunyana tapped his toe against the velvet-covered box. "Go ahead—tell me what I'm up to."

Deliciosa had stopped struggling. Now she hung limp, an angel skeleton dressed in scant rags of flesh and threads of police blue. She looked utterly spent.

"All right," I said. My brain buzzed, searching for a way to get out of this mess, desperate to work out how we'd got into it in the first place. "You sell meat. After a while, your supplies dry up, so you start buying Arachne's surplus. Suddenly hot dogs aren't made from pig any more. Hell, they're not even made from dog. Without anyone knowing it, you start feeding the whole city spider meat."

"Go on," said Sunyana.

"Arachne pulls the plug. Suddenly, no more spiders. Which leaves you with nothing to sell. So you fall back on—what, the special reserve? Cow-god cutlets steeped in ambrosia? You dig deep into the good stuff you previously kept back for your best customers. That's what this freezer is: it's your own private collection. Your nest egg. Once upon a time, this was where you stored the meat nobody could afford. Now it's the only thing you've got left to sell. How am I doing?"

"Remarkably well," said Sunyana. He was still smiling, but he didn't look happy.

"The thing that puzzles me is this: who's buying it? String City's wasted. The economy's gone through the floor. Where's your market?"

Sunyana brushed dust off his shoe. "You'd be surprised. There are survivors. Oh, not those hapless refugees limping down the tracks toward the Gates of Gehenna. I'm talking about the very people who would have bought my special reserve in the first place. The great and the good. Those wealthy enough to own their own apocalypse shelters. Believe me, they're out there. When the end of the world is over, and the cream of String City emerge from the bunkers and basements to start things all over again, they'll remember who kept them fed during the crisis. And we're not just talking subsistence here—we're talking about cuisine of the highest quality. Have you any idea how much I can charge for an Audhumla T-bone steeped in the lifeblood of a goddess?"

"I can guess," I growled. "I figure it's more or less the price of your soul."

Sunyana's teeth had started moving about again. "I don't know what you mean."

"Just this: those refugees you talked about—they're starving. And here's you, the only guy in town with enough food for all, doling out choice cuts to cats who don't need to get any fatter."

"I'm just trying to stay in business. Aren't you?"

I strained against the golem's grip. Its fingers moved about as much as a concrete bridge support. "That's different."

Sunyana stroked his hand over the velvet-covered box. "Is it? What are *you* doing to help those poor people?"

"I'm seeking the truth, pal. That helps everyone in the long run."

"Does it? Isn't it the truth that the world is a cruel and ugly place? When you tell people the truth, don't they usually break down in tears, or strike out at you? Perhaps even throw themselves under a train, because they can't bear to face what they've resisted all their lives?"

I didn't answer. I'd seen all those things happen, and more.

"You know exactly what I mean," said Sunyana. "I can see it in your face."

"Just tell me how you stole the ambrosia. I've got the pieces but I can't make them fit." I was stalling for time and he knew it.

"Not quite the great detective you thought you were, eh? Well, before you die, let me put you out of your misery."

Standing, he pulled the velvet away from the box, revealing it to be not a box at all but a cage. The same cage I'd glimpsed in the corner of his office, back when I'd been staking him out. It seemed such a long time ago.

Inside the cage was a small blue bird.

The bird was a kingfisher.

The kingfisher was hovering, its wings barely visible. Like a hummingbird, it darted from one corner of the cage to the other, but there was no perch for it to rest on, so it had no choice but to stay airborne. The kingfisher's beak was gold. Its feathers were blue like lightning. They fizzed like lightning too. If the gods had built a bird from electricity, this was what it would look like.

"I still don't get it," I said.

"You will." Kweku Sunyana opened the cage door and the

kingfisher flew out, straight toward me. As it flew, it split in two. Then in two again. With each nanosecond beat of its tiny wings, it fissioned—four, eight, sixteen... Before I could blink it wasn't a bird—it was a cloud of birds. All with beaks like gold flashing razors.

All headed my way.

100

I STILL DON'T know why the cloud of kingfishers didn't like my coat. Something to do with the goose-skin, maybe—some kind of ancient bird feud. Whatever the reason, instead of attacking me, the kingfishers went for the golem instead.

They moved like a swarm of bees, or a plasma cloud. Gold beaks jabbed like needles. They sliced the golem like a ham, paring off strips of clay as thin as onion-skin. Slice by slice they whittled it to nothing. It took maybe five seconds.

I didn't get off unscathed. The kingfishers slashed my hands, my face. I pulled down my coat cuffs, pulled up the collar. Fluffed out the goose feathers. It helped. What helped more was that the birds seemed to have developed a real taste for clay. As they bore down on it, the second golem threw up its arms and ran. Suddenly freed, Deliciosa dropped to the floor with her wings cowled over her head. The cloud of kingfishers chased the golem up the corridor and out of sight.

I marched up to Sunyana, grabbed him round the throat and shoved him hard against the wall.

"So what is it with the kingfishers?" I growled.

"They're metabirds," he replied. "I thought you'd have known."

I snatched the *Apocrypha of Multidimensional Zoology* from

my pocket. "I only bought the pocket edition. Care to explain?"

"Metabirds are single entities that exist in all dimensions simultaneously. Normally you see only one, but really there's more."

"There's only eleven dimensions," I said. "Looked like about a billion birds to me."

"That's because they spin. Like quarks. There's six flavors: up, down, charmed..."

"I know how quarks work. So that's six times eleven. It still comes up short." Sunyana's teeth were gnashing, trying to slice my wrist. I tightened my grip until they stopped. I'm no strongman, but I was mad, and getting madder. "So I'll say it again—what gives?"

"I don't fully understand the technicalities. I only remember what the man at the pet shop told me. The kingfishers lay quantum eggs, or something. For each egg they lay, a thousand hatch out, or perhaps it was an infinite number. I don't know. All I know is, if you own one kingfisher, you own them all. That's how I was able to steal the ambrosia."

"Go on." I could feel a breeze on the back of my neck.

"I trained my kingfisher to fly through the sewers. Kingfishers are easy to train—they read their master's thoughts. Everyone knew about Arachne's stash of ambrosia—this seemed the best way of getting at it."

"Hurry up," I said. The breeze was getting stronger.

"Once the bird reached the pyramid, it multiplexed."

"Went from one to lots?"

"Yes. Every bird jabbed a hole in Pallas Athene's finger with its beak, sucked out as much ambrosia as it could and flew back here. Then they regurgitated the ambrosia into this vat and returned to singularity mode. It was simple, really."

By now I could barely stand up for the wind. I thought

about the Scrutator, working the turbines over at the Aeolus Corporation. But this wasn't weather. It was wings.

The kingfishers were coming back.

I threw Sunyana against the side of the vat. Ambrosia slopped at the rim.

"Quickest way out of here?" I snapped.

He bared his teeth. "As if I'd tell you!"

I grabbed Deliciosa's bony wrist. "Come on, doll," I said. "We're leaving!"

"What about the beetle?" she said.

We both stared at the broken beetle. It had stopped twitching.

"The bug's toast," I said. "Let's go."

No sooner were we in the corridor than the kingfishers appeared at the far end. The swarm filled the corridor like a leg fills a stocking, in front of us, coming our way. The walls bulged. The air pounded my eardrums. Deliciosa shoved me sideways into the wet room airlock, then followed. I tried to dog the hatch, but the frame had warped; it wouldn't even shut. The inner hatch was jammed too. We were trapped.

The corridor turned dazzling blue. Cold air slashed our faces and the airlock filled with a chattering louder than a locust plague. A split-second later the corridor was empty again.

The swarm had gone right past.

I peered out, saw the birds explode into the vat room. I wondered where Sunyana was, and if he could control them when they were like this.

We sprinted the opposite way down the corridor, back to the freezer. Slices of golem clay lay scattered on the icy floor like thin green stepping stones. I looked for an exit, but the freezer was so big I couldn't even see the walls.

Again I felt the wind, heard the buzz of tiny wings.

The kingfishers had doubled back again.

"Here!" I hauled Deliciosa behind the gargantunicorn carcass. It shocked me how light she'd become.

The carcass was big enough to hide a symphony orchestra. But the kingfishers weren't stupid. They just worked down the line of carcasses one at a time. Frozen meat flew in ribbons. When they reached the sacks of dragon giblets, they just tore them open and let the contents roll out. The giblets rolled away like bowling balls.

They reached the gargantunicorn and started dicing their way along its horn. We ran again, only to find our way blocked by a rack of giant pork chops stamped *CALYDONIAN BOAR*. The cloud of birds followed us, cutting through the meat like chainsaws through a lumber yard. We were running out of places to go.

"Only one way out," I said. I pulled off my coat, turned it inside out four times until it was made of transuranic lycra. "Let me fold you up. I can get us both out through a dimensional snag, into the strings. The coat's friction-free—we'll move fast. Maybe we'll outrun the wolves."

"No," she said. Deliciosa grinned down at me. It's all a person with a bare skull can do. Her empty eye sockets were full of golden light.

"Say what?"

"If the dimensions are as dangerous as you say, it's suicide."

"Angel, these birds mean business."

"I know. That's why you have to run."

"I don't..."

A skeletal hand closed my lips. Somehow its touch was soft. "You've done your job," she said. "Now let me do mine."

"What are you...?"

"Run back to the wet room, as fast as you can. Go back the way we came, back to Arachne. Deliver your report. I'll catch you up. I can't give you long. But it should be enough."

The fire in her eye sockets was bright enough to hurt. I could hear a buzzing sound even louder than the kingfishers: Deliciosa's wings, powering up.

"Before I go," I said, "There's something I want to say."

"Save it for later. Run!"

I knew she wasn't going to catch me up. And she knew I wasn't going to run. It sucks, that we deceived each other like that, so near the end.

She did her best to get rid of me though. Before I knew it, her bony hands were locked on my wrist. She swung me like a pro wrestler, hurled me right over the rack of chops. I'd forgotten how strong she was. I landed hard, lost all my wind, slid for what felt like ten miles across slick icy floor. I fetched up against a chicken leg as big as a house. It was marked *BABA YAGA—ONE OF TWO*.

I shook my head clear, looked for Deliciosa. She was far in the distance, tiny like a doll. The kingfisher swarm was a blue boiling geyser. As I watched, the birds vaporised the last few yards of the gargantunicorn. They were a blur. So were Deliciosa's wings.

The kingfishers fell on her.

101

I CLAMBERED TO my feet, tried to run back across the ice. But I had no grip and fell flat on my belly. I couldn't get up, the floor was so slippery, so I bunched my legs against the chicken leg and pushed as hard as I could. The combination of transuranic lycra and six inch-thick ice gave me the smoothest ride I'd ever had. I felt like a sled. As I slithered, I stuck out my hands and started to force open a rift in the sub-dimensional cortex.

Ahead of me, the battle was raging. It looked like a blue tornado. From inside the tornado came the odd flash of gold light—Deliciosa making a hit, I guessed. But I couldn't see her, so I couldn't be sure. The tornado was roaming the floor, ripping up chunks of ice and firing them out like cannon shells. Several chunks hit close to me as I slid past. I pulled my fedora from my pocket and jammed it on my head. The hat is armor plated.

Suddenly the tornado broke in half, revealing Deliciosa inside: a tall angel skeleton with wings like damnation, chopping birds from the air in their thousands. Tiny blue bodies flew like confetti before winking out of existence. Trouble was, there were millions more waiting in the wings.

Changing tactics, the kingfishers closed into a ball and zeroed on Deliciosa's legs. A sound like a million pneumatic drills echoed through the freezer. But, when the birds pulled away, Deliciosa's legs were still intact. A bubble of hope filled my chest. Angel bone—one of the toughest substances in the cosmos!

The hope was false. The bones had survived, but the birds had made mincemeat of the last few tendons and ligaments and straps of flesh holding them together. Deliciosa teetered for a second or two. Then the joints in her legs came apart and she dropped to the ice.

Lying prone, she couldn't work her wings properly. The kingfishers pressed the advantage. They shredded first one wing, then the other. I saw the gold light flare in Deliciosa's eyes one more time before a blue storm covered her up.

The sound of drilling started again.

I was screaming, I think. I'd already opened a snag roughly six inches wide to expose the nearest alternative dimension. Currently, roughly forty boundary wolves were trying to bite their way out.

I snapped the snag shut. Deliciosa was right: that way was suicide.

In the meantime, I was still sliding friction-free toward an ever-expanding cloud of seemingly invincible carnivorous birds. I figured I had roughly ten seconds to come up with a plan.

Eight seconds elapsed.

That was when I heard the scarabs.

They burst from the wet room: a swarm of beetles almost exactly as big as the swarm of kingfishers. They came in a kind of rolling wave, each beetle climbing over the next, miraculously cheating the slippery ice. They came *fast*.

The kingfishers sensed what was happening. The blue cloud lifted up, became an arrow, loosed itself toward the oncoming swarm. The birds shot straight over my head, missing me by a hairsbreadth. I carried on sliding until I hit the pork chops. I got up, staggered over to where Deliciosa lay. What was left of her.

I cradled her skull in my hands. It was twenty feet from the rest of her scattered bones. The light in her eyes was fading. Her jaw moved. Words came from far away.

"Don't... worry," she whispered, "I died... before. It's not so bad..."

"You're going to be okay," I said.

"Heaven's... waiting..." she said. "I can't wait to see... what they've done with the place."

"Hush," I said.

"Before I go..." she said, "Tell me... one thing."

"Anything."

"Tell me... I'm beautiful."

"I thought you didn't go for that."

"Everyone needs to hear it," she gasped, "once... in... a... while ..."

The skull twitched. Her eyes were two dying embers.

"You were always beautiful," I said, meaning every word. "All the way through."

"Even... now?"

"Never more so."

I kissed her, and it was bitter and sweet. The lights went out.

In my hands, for the second time, my angel died.

I put her skull on the ice, gently. I touched my hand to her eye sockets. There were no eyelids to close, but it felt like the right thing to do.

I straightened my coat, tugged the brim of my hat. Wiped my cheeks. Stood up. My hackles were prickling. Had been all the way through Deliciosa's last words.

Something crept up on me from behind.

I turned to face it.

102

I'D EXPECTED THE kingfishers. Maybe even Kweku Sunyana, ready to chomp me to death. What I didn't expect was a living bulldozer built from scarab beetles. Each beetle had a bright blue kingfisher clamped between its mandibles. The dozer slid toward me, ploughing the ice. I tried to move, realised I was out of gas and just flopped down on the ice, waiting for the beetles to grind me under.

One by one, the beetles started winking out of existence. Slowly at first, then faster. As each beetle vanished, it took its captive kingfisher with it. The bulldozer collapsed in on itself. There was a sound like popping corn. The air smelt singed. Soon barely a hundred scarabs remained, then fifty, twenty, ten...

The popping sounds slowed, stopped. All the beetles were

gone except one. It labored through the shattered ice toward me. It moved slowly, painfully. It was cracked all over, leaking goo. It came on all the same. In its jaws was a single kingfisher. Behind one of its antennae was a broken pencil.

When the tax beetle reached me, it slumped down, legs splayed. Air wheezed through its spiracles. It was hard to tell, but I thought it was smiling.

"I apologise for leaving things so late," it said, its voice muffled by the feathers, "but it took me some time to rouse my brethren."

"You did good," I said, "whatever it was you did. I thought you were dead."

"Have you ever tried to kill a cockroach?"

I stared at the broken ice. It was littered with tiny blue feathers. "So what happened?" I said. "How did you make them go away?"

"It was simple, really," said the beetle. "As soon as I realised the kingfishers were metadimensional, I notified my lord and mind. My message spread instantaneously through the entire beetle swarm. We are a hive-mind, you understand—the knowledge of one is the knowledge of all."

"I get that," I said. "What I don't get is where the kingfishers went."

"I am getting to that part. As a hive-mind, we understand instinctively the true nature of these birds—we beetles are metacreatures ourselves, in a way. All we did was assign one of our population to each kingfisher and isolate it from the rest. Isolation forces each bird to revert to its individual state, resulting in the immediate transfer back to its original sub-dimensional realm. Each scarab will deposit its cargo beyond the call of its kin, before returning intact to the sewer."

"I'm going to have to work on that one," I said. "They teach you this in tax school?"

"Being good with numbers helped," said the beetle proudly. "However, I am afraid there is still one loose end to tie up."

"The bird in your mouth?"

"Precisely. This is the original kingfisher—Kweku Sunyana's pet. It is already in its native environment—this world. In other words, it is not going anywhere."

"Then let's put it back in its cage."

The beetle shook its head. In its jaws, the kingfisher buzzed angrily. "Alas, the kingfisher swarm has damaged the cage beyond repair."

"Then we need an alternative," I said. I looked around. "There must be something here we can use."

103

THE JOURNEY BACK to Arachne's pyramid was somber. The scarabs—and the sewer uber-mind—sensed how cut up I was about Deliciosa and stayed silent the whole journey. That suited me just fine. I just sat on the beetle raft, watching the sewer walls race by. Occasionally the bow wave splashed foul-smelling sludge on my legs. I didn't care, any more that I cared about the stink in my nostrils.

Didn't care about anything much, truth be told.

My right hand was resting on the barrel we'd salvaged from Sunyana's vat room. Sunyana himself we'd found face down in his marinating tank, drowned in ambrosia, his body pierced by a million tiny beaks. What a way to go.

The tax beetle found a stack of empty barrels behind the tank. We filled one with ambrosia, then wrangled it through the wet room and down the pipe. It wasn't much, but I didn't want to go back to Arachne empty-handed.

In my left hand I was holding the thing we'd found to keep the kingfisher in. When I'd suggested it, the tax beetle had asked me if I was sure. I said I was. Anyway, it was the only thing I could think of. The beetle said it was creepy.

I agreed. But it felt right.

I held it up, peered inside. Immediately the kingfisher buzzed toward me, jabbing its beak through the makeshift bars. It was still angry—maybe that was its natural state. I didn't care. All that mattered was the bird was mine.

The raft carried me on. The sewage surged hypnotically. I felt hollowed out, or peaceful, or both. For the indeterminate time the journey took, I felt I was part of a mighty stillness. So there I sat, one hand on the barrel of ambrosia, the other fast on the kingfisher's new prison.

An angel's ribcage.

104

THE UBER-MIND dropped me off at a big storm drain on the wharf.

"The entrance to the spider-queen's abode lies yonder," it said, extending a sticky brown pseudopod. "This will save thee having to climb up the floor shaft."

"Thanks, pal," I said. "For everything."

I stepped out of the drain. A small scarab raft—just big enough to carry the ambrosia barrel—followed me like an obedient pooch. The sky was wet with pre-dawn light. The rain hammered my fedora.

"Tell me—wouldst thou consider me as a candidate when thou next has a permanent employment opportunity?"

"Sure. Though, I've got to tell you, I've got through a lot of assistants lately."

"Then I thank thee for the experience."

"I reckon we're quits." I turned to the tax beetle. "As for this guy—you should promote him or something."

"There is no promotion," said the uber-mind. "We all are equal."

"I don't care. The bug deserves a medal. At least get him a new pencil."

The beetle stuck out a feeler. I shook it. "You did good, buddy," I said.

"I hope to see you again next year," said the beetle. "At the next tax audit."

"If there is a next year."

For a minute the rain eased and the sky behind the pyramid turned pink. Somewhere behind the storm, the sun was rising.

"Sometimes the columns balance," said the tax beetle. "Most of the time, actually. You would be surprised."

"I hope I am," I replied.

The clouds crunched together, wiping out the dawn. I tightened my grip on Deliciosa's ribcage and set off toward where Arachne was waiting. The barrel of ambrosia followed on its raft of bugs.

The rain fell harder than ever.

105

I KNEW IMMEDIATELY that something was wrong. The fancy security keypad was dead and the door swung loose on its hinges. Halfway open, the hinges jammed. I squeezed through. Beyond the door, the corridor was wall-to-wall spider's web.

"Okay," I said to the dozen or so scarabs making up the raft, "which of you guys has the sharpest pincers?"

They took turns. The web was densely woven, the individual strands tougher than steel. It made for worn mandibles and tired beetles. I followed, puzzling. What was Arachne up to now?

Eventually we reached the main chamber. It was filled with silk, even more than when I'd first seen it. Some of the strands were thicker than my arm. The thickest of all radiated down from a central point, near the pyramid's apex. There was something up there: a dark blot.

"You boys stay here," I said to the beetles. They didn't argue.

I kept to the thicker strands—the thin stuff was like cheese wire. Still, climbing the web was hard work. Five minutes and I was puffing like a train.

Five minutes after that I reached the top.

I stood balanced on a tightly woven platform of silk, gasping for breath. I stared at what had become of Arachne.

My first impression was that she'd been swapping body parts. Most of the womanly pieces looked more spidery than I remembered; the spidery parts were disturbingly like a woman. She'd grown a bunch of new legs, human and shapely, even woven sleek silk fishnets for them. But none of the legs looked much good for anything—they just hung from her belly, twitching. Her abdomen was bloated; I was afraid it might be egg-bound, then I saw it was just corruption. Pus oozed from cracks in its shell; the stink was worse than the sewers.

The human torso sprouting from her spider's back had melted to a random tower of flesh. Her arms were shrunk to twigs. On top of her head was a cluster of eyes, too many even for an arachnid. Beneath those eyes, however, Arachne's face was wholly human. It was wrinkled, impossibly old, strangely beautiful.

I was beginning to think you wouldn't make it in time, she croaked.

“There were setbacks,” I said. Though I knew the answer, I asked, “What do you mean, ‘in time’?”

I am dying. Can you not see?

“I guess so. What’s with the web?”

A reflex action. An instinct. I am a queen—am I not entitled to a royal burial?

It figured. Suited the surroundings too. What better place to spin yourself a tomb than inside a pyramid?

“It didn’t exactly help me get inside.”

Like her ancient face, Arachne’s smile had a beauty. *I knew you would find a way.*

“I found the ambrosia,” I said. “Brought back a barrel. It was all we could carry.”

She waved a stick-like arm. *It is of no consequence.*

Up to that moment I’d been sympathetic—Arachne was clearly on her last legs. Then I remembered she had an awful lot of legs, and liked to kill folk with them.

“No consequence?! I risked my life for your precious liquor! One of my friends *died* out there! And you tell me it doesn’t *matter*?”

Arachne started coughing. Each cough sent more pus spurting from the cracks in her abdomen. It dripped like rancid syrup down through the web. I waited, shaking with fury.

When she’d recovered, Arachne said, *Don’t be a fool—that is not what I meant.*

“It sure sounded like...”

And don’t play games. There isn’t time!

I was madder than ever. “I’m not the one playing games, lady!”

Shut up and listen to me!

Arachne reared up. Her mouth gaped, revealing long iron fangs. I remembered all the times she’d tricked me over the years: the double-crosses, the torture, the simple practical jokes.

The not-so-simple ones too.

I realised none of this mattered. It was like a punch to the gut. So I held my ground, fists clenched not caring what she did.

I see you've grown brave, she said, looming over me. *That is good. Very good. You'll be needing plenty of bravery before this is over.*

"This *is* over," I said. "The case of the missing ambrosia. Case closed."

The dying spider queen bent double with another coughing fit. I waited, still angry. Impatient too. I wanted out of there. But our business wasn't yet done.

I thank you for locating my ambrosia, Arachne said when she could speak again. *When I said it was of no consequence, I simply meant your success comes too late to save me. But that is all right. I think we both knew this is how it would end, didn't we? As for the "case", as you call it, you have indeed done what I hired you to do. You therefore require payment.*

My feet started walking me away. Looking back, I think they must have known what was coming, and didn't want any part of it. I made them stop. This was why I'd returned to the pyramid, after all: not to deliver the ambrosia, but to settle my account.

As quick as it had come, my anger was gone. What replaced it was something nameless and profound.

Arachne wore a locket around her neck. Grimacing with pain, she took it in her wasted hands and snapped it open. Something fell out. She caught it before it tumbled down through the web. She stared at it, then held it out to me.

It sat on her palm, glinting in the dawn glow from the skylights. It was a small round silver coin.

A penny.

I found it when I was a girl. A human girl. I found the penny in the street and did what any little girl wearing a pretty frock and ribbons would do: I picked it up. I thought it would bring me good luck.

Later that night, when I was spinning at my mother's wheel, I was bitten by a metamorphic meshweaver. That single poisonous spider bite transformed me into what I am today. I put my ribbons and frock away and entered a life of misery. Endless misery. Now, however, as the life finally drains from me, I rejoice, because misery is the worst I have experienced, and there are far, far worse things I might have endured.

Because it wasn't really the spider's bite that changed my life. It was the penny I picked up off the street. It brought me luck all right, but not of the good kind. And that's not all. I know who puts down bad pennies for people to find.

And so do you, gumshoe, so do you.

For the first time since this whole sorry affair had started, I said his name out loud:

"The Pennyman."

Arachne exhaled: a long, slow susurration of stinking spider breath. I thought for a moment she'd breathed her last. Then she spoke again, her voice no louder than sandpaper.

When I decided who it was had laid this curse upon me, I dedicated my life to tracking him down.

"That's impossible. Nobody knows where the Pennyman lives. Hell, nobody even know if he's real."

"Nevertheless, I searched. I am nothing if not persistent, as you well know. I searched this world and others, to no avail. I hired bounty hunters to travel the cosmos, far and wide. They found pennies everywhere, but of the Pennyman himself there was no trace.

Having exhausted the worlds, I started looking further afield. I found a surgeon with the skills to change my body, to give me new powers. Look closely at my web. What do you see?

I gave the nearest strand a cursory glance. "Silk. Nasty silk, but silk all the same."

Shaking with the effort, Arachne swung her mutilated abdomen around and extended her spinnarets. They glistening, throbbing, soft naked things that pulsed with more energy than the whole of the rest of her body. I held my body tight, repulsed and fascinated at the same time.

One spinnaret touched a nearby strand of silk. Light bloomed and the thread snapped like a bullwhip, its outer surface peeling back like the skin of a nuclear banana. At its core was something I recognised at once.

"String," I gasped, "cosmic string."

106

DO YOU REMEMBER *what they used to call me?* Arachne said.

"Weaver of worlds," I replied.

Back then, it was just a name. Now, I believe I could indeed weave a world if I set my mind to it. And if I had a thousand years to spare. Alas, only a few moments remain to me. And there are enough worlds, don't you think?

I could imagine a hundred different uses for a set of spinnarets capable of manipulating cosmic string. Most of them bad. "So what did you weave?"

Pathways. Pathways through the cosmos. I spun myself a web that extended to the outer limits of the cosmos and back again. I walked it, step by step, a painstaking search during which I isolated each square of the web's grid, one after the other. I've been searching for the Pennyman my whole life, gumshoe.

"A web made of cosmic string? How come I never saw it when I was out in the bulk?"

With a trembling hand, Arachne stroked her web. *My cosmic silk is sheer. Monofilament. Purer than pure. Here in the real world, it catches the light. Out in the bulk, where there is no light—at least, not as we know it—it is all but invisible, even to the eyes of the stringwalkers.*

"Visible or not, surely it still has mass. Momentum. Gravity. Intent. Everything you'd expect of ordinary cosmic string. A web like you've described... geez, lady, that would seriously destabilise the harmonics of the natural string network..." I stopped, started to speak again, stopped once more. Finally I got it out. "It's your web that started the storms out in the bulk. You're the reason the dimensions are screwed."

A small price to pay.

"You think?" I bunched my fists. "You're the reason I can't walk the strings any more. Plus you probably triggered the end of the world. I don't know which I hate you for the most!"

I did not bring the apocalypse. Responsibility for that lies with the Pennyman.

"Oh, sure, pass the buck. Thanks to you, the cosmos is toast!"

I believe in salvation, despite everything. Why else would I send my spiders out over the city? Why else would I raise my web?

I remembered what she'd said earlier, about how, with her web incomplete, String City was vulnerable. Sudden understanding slugged me on the jaw.

"You were trying to protect us from the Pennyman. It wasn't an invasion at all." Arachne bowed her head. Somewhere inside me, the cold hatred I'd carried for years transformed into an incredulous hot coal of respect.

It was too little too late, the spider queen said.

Too little, yes. Also, far too much. "I just want to find Zephyr, before it's too late."

Then we are, as they say, on the same page.

"I don't understand."

Saving the cosmos. Finding the girl. In this case, they are one and the same.

I stared her down. She waited with the patience of a spider.

"All right," I said at last. "Talk."

107

So Arachne talked and I listened, reluctantly at first, then with growing interest. The more she told me, the more things added up. Every single thing that had happened to me these past weeks—strike that, most of my life—turned out to be a piece of the puzzle and one by one Arachne put them together. The Tartarus heist. The hooded Fools. The kingfishers. The Still Point of the Turning World.

The pennies.

"Why is he doing this?" I said when she'd finished. "And why did he take Zephyr?"

Arachne shook her mutilated head. Her movements were jerky. Her whole body had leaked almost dry. *I don't know. Observation and a lifetime's research may have revealed to me his actions, but as to his intentions... I leave those to you to discover.*

"In another life," I said, "you'd have made a swell detective."

Your words touch me. Thank you.

She was still holding out the penny. The one she'd picked up as a girl. The one that had transformed her into a monster.

"I can't," I said, eyeing the coin with something close to terror. "If I take it, who knows what I'll turn into?"

Nobody knows, Arachne replied. *But hear this, gumshoe: I no longer believe this particular penny was laid by the Pennyman. I believe it was set in my path by another. One who believes in riddles, and in a single, true answer to them all.*

I couldn't decide if this was worse. Hell, I couldn't process anything any more. I'd heard too much. I just wanted out of there. Still, I was curious.

"Who?" I said. Then I stopped. "Wait a second. Wind back. Earlier you said, 'stringwalkers'. Plural. I thought..."

"You were the only one?"

Arachne smiled. Just for an instant, all her forgotten beauty shone through. Then a long, ragged sigh started deep in her broken abdomen. It shuddered up through her body, out of her mouth and into the cold air. It smelled sweet, like ambrosia.

"Don't go," I said. "We're not done."

My words echoed through empty space. The pyramid, like all pyramids before it, had become a tomb.

My hand shook just as Arachne's had done. I extended my fingers to her open palm. The silver coin lay there: my payment, my hope. Probably my doom.

I hesitated. Worlds circled around me.

I took the penny and turned to go.

Wait. Arachne's final breath was low and slow. *I have... one more thing... to give you...*

She held out her other hand. I took what it was holding. And Arachne died.

108

The scarabs transported me to my office on their backs. The streets of String City have seen stranger forms of conveyance, but not many. I told them to put the barrel of ambrosia in the cellar, next to the tokamak. It was no use to Arachne and the beetles didn't like the taste, and I hadn't the heart to pour it down the drain. You never know when you might need twenty gallons of goddess juice.

"Put the bird down there too," I said.

Inside the cage of ribs, the kingfisher's wings flashed like neon flames.

The bugs pulled back the trapdoor and descended into the cellar. The sound of their feet on the cement steps made my spine crawl. A minute later they came back up, chittered their goodbyes and left.

I made a phone call. Afterward I crashed on the couch. Ten seconds later I was fast asleep. I slept all day, waking just as the sky above the street grille went from purple to black. Outside, the city was quieter than I'd ever known it.

I made fresh coffee laced with sugar and bourbon, downed it, poured another. I tidied the papers on my desk, straightened the pictures on the wall.

I stood for a long time, staring out through the doorway, the cup of coffee going slowly cold in my hand. The night air was dead still. The rain had stopped. Nothing moved except a solitary figure making its way steadily up the street toward my office. It shone like bronze and moved with gleaming oiled grace.

"I came as you requested," said the Scrutator, slipping through the door-shaped hole in the wall of dung.

"You sure it's okay to leave the wind factory?" I replied.

"I spent the day optimising the automated systems. The new controls I have installed are very efficient. I estimate the plant is capable of functioning without intervention for the next seventeen days. Do you think that will be sufficient time to find the Pennyman and rescue Zephyr?"

"Buddy, I don't think this city has seventeen hours."

I brought the brass compact out of my pocket and placed it on the table. Beside it, I placed Arachne's penny. I encircled them both with the spider queen's final gift: a coiled rope of silk scissored from her cosmos-covering web. The web she'd woven to shield String City from the coming of the Pennyman. It lay there, a shining silver lasso of pure cosmic string.

I thumbed the switch on the compact. A pocket of air popped like a balloon and my doppelganger appeared. The robot's purring rose to a high-pitched whine of surprise.

"Meet me," I said to the Scrutator. "The other me. The good news is, he's going to help us crack this case wide open, once and for all. The bad news is, he's got just one hour and seven minutes to live."

Beyond

109

The crater where the Birdhouse had once stood was silent, deserted. The air was still and the ground was smooth, slippery and transparent—I could see right through the dirt to the bedrock below. Under the bedrock, sinister things prowled.

"The cast of the cosmos has grown thin," said the Scrutator, bending down to pick up a little stone, spiky as a shard of glass. Fragmentary forms fought in its core. The Scrutator placed it reverently back on the ground.

Below us, the transparent dirt of the crater leveled out into a flat glassy plain. I looked up and around. Sunlight glinted off a million shining facets. We were descending into a crystal bowl the size of ten city blocks.

At the bottom of the bowl sat the Fool. Huge heaps of golden dust surrounded him. His skeletal hands worked busily in his lap as he continued to dismantle the Still Point of the Turning World, one iota at a time.

"How long before he's finished?" The doppelganger rubbed his forehead. "I have the mother of all headaches."

I glanced at the compact—eighteen minutes left before my alter ego winked out of existence. My heart sank. It had taken us longer than I'd realised to walk here, and he'd insisted on staying conscious the whole way. "You need to brief me properly," he'd said as we stepped out of the office. "And for that I need to be awake."

I'd talked all the way, but got barely halfway through the story. And now here we were, with time running out.

"Look, I'm going to have to put you on standby again," I said, "so let me cut to the chase."

"You're finally going to tell me something I need to hear? Like maybe there's actually something for me at the end of all this."

The Scrutator raised its hand. "May I speak?"

"Make it quick," I said.

"That is precisely my intention. By my best estimate, I am capable of delivering the necessary exposition in less than three minutes. It will take you at least twenty-seven, especially given your tendency to drawl."

"You really think you know what's going on here?"

"Of course. I hear everything. It is why I became a detective. Have I not told you this?"

I raised an eyebrow at the doppelganger. "Do I drawl?"

The doppelganger glowered. "I'm on the clock here. Just spill the beans, one of you."

The Fool flung another cloud of golden dust over his shoulder.

"Go ahead," I said to the Scrutator.

"Very well. As I hear it, the situation is this. Long ago, one of the Aerlyft found his way to the edge of the cosmos..."

"Wait," said the doppelganger. "One of the what?"

"The Aerlyft."

"And they are?"

"The Aerlyft are the first-born, like the Thanes and the Fools and the behemoths. They were the earliest beings ever to roam creation."

"Don't you know that?" I put in.

The doppelganger rubbed his forehead again. "When you hit that pause button, pal, it kind of muddies the waters."

"Foremost among the Aerlyft were the Runefolk," the Scrutator went on. "Each member of the Runefolk was the embodiment of a different abstraction, and..."

"A different what?"

"An idea. A concept."

"Give me an example."

"Well, the Roseman was the embodiment of *love*, while the Axeman was the embodiment of *hate*. There was the Arrowman—he was the embodiment of *speed*—and the Glassman, who embodied *fragility*. And so on."

"No dames?"

"Of course. The Wirewoman embodied *risk*, the Candlewoman *hope*, and the concept of *curiosity* was embodied by..."

"Okay, stop. I get it. It's weird, but I get it."

"One of the strangest and most powerful members of the Runefolk clan was the Pennyman," the Scrutator continued. "He was the embodiment of *chance*. His entire existence was dominated by just two thoughts: *either* and *or*. Shall I walk or run? Stand or fall? Eat candy or cake? The Pennyman had only to conceive of a choice for its conflicting options to spring spontaneously into existence. And then, one day, the Pennyman thought this: 'Shall I stay inside the cosmos, or step out of it?'"

"I thought stepping out of the cosmos was impossible," said the doppelganger, "on account of there's nothing beyond it."

"It is impossible," I agreed. "At least, it was until the Pennyman thought of doing it."

"It is both impossible and possible," the Scrutator said. "By definition, the cosmos is all that there is. And yet, the instant he conceived of something beyond it, the Pennyman successfully conjured an outside realm into existence. Having created Beyond, he stepped into it, even though its existence was a logical impossibility."

"Seriously," said the doppelganger, "I could use an aspirin."

"It's very simple," I said. "There's the cosmos, and there's Beyond, which is a place that exists and doesn't exist, both at the same time. It's like the Pennyman himself—the perfect embodiment of chance."

"Sounds quantum to me."

"It is. Probably."

"So let me get this straight. The Pennyman actually created Beyond?"

"Yes. And now he's stuck inside it."

"Why can't he get out?"

"Nobody knows. For some reason, Beyond seems to work a bit like a black hole. You can pour any amount of stuff into it, but ain't nothing ever coming out."

The doppelganger rasped his hands over his stubble. "And now the girl's in there too?"

I nodded. "The Pennyman has kidnapped her. I've no idea how. That should be impossible too. But somehow he's done it, and now we're going to get her out."

"Now you're going to tell me there's a ransom," said the doppelganger. "Cases like this, there's always a ransom."

"Indeed there is," said the Scrutator.

"So where's the note?"

"I'll show you that in a minute," I said.

"You boys ever think this might be a trap?" said the doppelganger.

"Of course it's a trap."

"I mean, even if we could find a way into this Beyond place, you're saying there's no way to get back out again."

"This is problematic," the Scrutator agreed.

The doppelganger shook his head. "I was hoping you boys were going to clue me in. Seems like this isn't the day for answers. So here's another question for you." He spread his arms wide. "What in the name of Hades are we doing in this crater?"

110

BEFORE I COULD answer, light burst from the lap of the Fool. We all turned to look. It was like facing an arc welder. I threw up my arm just in time to save my retinas. Heat seared the palm of my hand. I heard a hissing noise—the sound of oil turning to vapor inside the Scrutator's joints.

The light dimmed a little and I lowered my arm. The Fool was sitting motionless. Clasped loosely in his hands was a point of light too small to be real, too bright to be there.

"The Fool has finished deconstructing the Still Point of the Turning World," whispered the Scrutator. Its mechanical larynx buzzed with awe. "Behold the Glory."

Cautiously we approached the inanimate Fool. The Glory blazed through his bone-and-sinew fingers; it looked like he was clutching a sun. The light poured through his flayed body, throwing caustic highlights off glistening organs and all kinds of uncertain anatomy.

"Why doesn't he move?" the doppelganger said.

"He cannot," replied the Scrutator. "The Fool has become the Still Point."

"Come again?"

"Look, the Still Point of the Turning World is just a box," I said. "The real prize is what it contains. And that's what the Pennyman wants."

"The Glory?"

"Right. The essence of the cosmos, the lifestring of everything there ever was, or ever could be. The Glory is powerful, but it's fragile. If it's exposed, it immediately seeks a new shelter."

"Like a hermit crab looking for a new shell," said the doppelganger.

I thought about it. Actually, that was pretty good.

"In this case, the nearest new shelter it had available was the Fool," said the Scrutator.

I prodded the Fool's bony shoulder. He didn't budge so much as an inch. I pushed harder; I might as well have been trying to move a mountain. "See? It's like the Scrutator said. As of now, the whole of creation is turning about the Fool; everything is moving but him."

"Remind me why we care about this?" the doppelganger sighed.

The coil of spider silk that Arachne had given me was hanging at my belt. I unclipped it. Holding the end lightly—the thin webbing bristled with spiky shards—I started spinning it like a lariat. Air whistled. Music rang out. Inside the music there were words.

... glory... girl...

"Who's that talking?" said the doppelganger.

"It is the voice of the Pennyman," the Scrutator replied. "If the Glory is the ransom, then this is the note."

When I spun the lasso faster, more words began to leak out.

... bring me the Glory...

The Pennyman's voice sounded like steel wheels on the tracks of an ice-locked railroad.

... and I will give you the girl...

I kept spinning the spider lasso. The words repeated, over and over.

"That's all there is?" said the doppelganger.

"Seems like. Arachne spent a lifetime spinning her web out into the corners of the cosmos, trying to pinpoint the Pennyman's hideout. Eventually, a single strand found its way Beyond. It picked up this message and transmitted it back through the web. Straight to Arachne."

"I thought nothing could get out of Beyond."

"Nothing material, which is why Zephyr getting snatched is such a puzzle. Information—that's different. You ever send a message using two empty soup cans and a piece of string? Same thing. Only in this case the string was cosmic."

The doppelganger eyed the frozen Fool. "You want to shift the Glory, you're going to have to shift the Fool. But this guy's going nowhere."

"That's why I brought you along," I replied.

"Say what?"

111

I COULDN'T HAVE done it without the Scrutator. While the robot clamped its mechanical arms around the doppelganger's ribs, I grabbed my twin's wrists and thrust his hands between the fingers of the Fool. The instant the doppelganger touched the Glory, his whole body went stiff and the Fool collapsed like a sack of offal, dead to the world. I pulled the compact from my pocket and thumbed the button marked STANDBY.

The doppelganger winked out of existence.

So did the Glory.

I stared at the compact. So did the Scrutator. My hand was shaking so hard I couldn't read the display. I willed my muscles to hold still. Nine minutes and holding.

"You are now carrying the very lifestring of the cosmos," said the Scrutator with reverence. "Please, do not drop it."

"I don't plan to."

"The doppelganger is holding the Glory. He is now therefore the Still Point of the Turning World. As long as he is on standby, however, it appears he can be moved."

"And the Glory with him. You sound as surprised as me. What would you have done if this hadn't worked?"

The Scrutator ticked for a moment, then said quietly, "I would have despaired for the future of all things."

"You and me both, my mechanical friend. So, are you ready for the next part?"

"Taking the Glory to the Pennyman? Of course. However, I confess that I do not know the way."

"I thought you knew everything."

"I *hear* everything. That is different."

"The world must be a noisy place for you, Scrutator."

"You have no idea. Do *you* know how to go Beyond?"

Minding my fingers, I coiled up the lasso. "Once upon a time, you told me you were woven from cosmic string. Were you telling the truth?"

"I have no reason to lie to you."

"That's what I figured."

112

I THOUGHT THE robot would kick up a stink when I asked it to open up its head. But it didn't so much as murmur.

Inside, the Scrutator was even more of a marvel than I'd imagined. The interior of its cranium was a bright bronzed cave crammed with a million tiny gears all tumbling over each other like wheels in a whirligig. It was like someone had built a Swiss watch out of fractal equations. It snatched my breath away.

It took me less than thirty seconds to thread Arachne's silk lasso into the robot's workings. It was tricky, but frankly, I've had more trouble lacing up one of Harry Arriflex's old movie projectors. Once the silk was in place, I tripped a likely-looking lever and watched as the single strand of cosmic string churned its way deep into the Scrutator's mechanical brain. When it was done, I flipped the top of its head shut and stood back.

"Anything?" I said.

"Nothing yet," replied the Scrutator. "I do not know if... wait... wait, I hear something."

Someone danced a polka down my spine. "What do you hear?"

"The voice of the Pennyman! He is talking about the Glory. And he is talking about the girl."

"Where's it coming from?"

The Scrutator cocked its head. "Triangulating."

113

I SHOULDN'T HAVE been surprised where the trail led. But I was.

"Jimmy knew," I said, nudging the dial on the tokamak. The afterburners ignited, flooding my office cellar with livid orange light. "He could have told me. Instead he fed me just enough to keep me stupid."

"I cannot parse that sentence," said the Scrutator.

I took the robot's elbow and led it to the bricked-up doorway in the corner of the cellar. Tokamak light made deep shadows in the cracked mortar.

"When he handed me the keys to this place, Jimmy told me

there were over three hundred ways in and out of this cellar."

"I do not find that surprising. Your basement resonates with a dimensional discordance that is particularly strident."

"Jimmy told me something else too. All those years ago he told me, and I never gave it a second thought."

"What did he tell you?"

"That he'd tried every doorway except one. He meant this one. It's been under my nose all this time."

Tokamak light danced over the bricks, but there was one spot it failed to illuminate. One crack bigger than the rest. I bent to look, and saw it wasn't a crack but a cavity. A hole.

I poked my finger inside and felt something soft. I hooked my finger and drew it out. It was a blue feather.

I glanced at Deliciosa's ribcage, perched on a pile of splintered wood right where the tax beetles had left it. It seemed like a year since I'd kicked those desks down into the cellar. The kingfisher was motionless inside its prison of bone, its eyes black and cold.

"The kingfisher took her." I held up the feather. "After she walked out on me, it found her and took her to the Pennyman. It probably happened while we were down in the sewers, before our little showdown with Kweku Sunyana."

"Surely this kingfisher could not have carried Zephyr through this tiny aperture?" The Scrutator thrust a mechanical digit into the hole in the wall.

"Sure it could. A trick like that would be child's play for a metabird."

The Scrutator flattened the palm of its hand against the ancient bricks. "On the other side of this barrier lies Beyond. Now that I am aligned with Arachne's web, I hear it, as clear as I hear the sound of your soul." Behind the filigreed perforations in its cheeks, Arachne's thread spooled past for the ten thousandth time. "I have not yet asked you this, but I will ask it now. Do you believe that the course of action we are about to take is the correct one?"

Taking the compact out of my coat pocket, I fetched up a sigh. "Tricky as all this seems, what it comes down to is simple. Inside this gadget is something the Pennyman wants. The Pennyman has something I want. 'Correct' doesn't come into it, buddy. This is just something I have to do."

"Do you know what the Pennyman will do when he gets his hands on the Glory?"

"Nothing good."

114

I TOOK OFF my coat, turned it inside-out seven times until it was made of carbonised barrateen. I picked up Deliciosa's ribcage—still with the kingfisher inside—flattened it out and zipped it into the lining. As an afterthought, I went to the safe, opened it up, and dropped what I found there into my pocket. It sat nestled against the Dimension Die; there was no way I was forgetting to take *that* with me again.

I held out my hand to the Scrutator.

"Are you going to modify my dimensional status also?" the robot asked.

"You got a problem with that, Bronzey?"

"I trust you."

For no reason I can explain, those three words brought a lump to my throat.

I twisted the Scrutator left and right, both at the same time, and inverted the polarity of its sub-brane interface. It was tricky, given the robot was made of cosmic string, but everything bends somewhere. I shrugged on my coat and opened the cuff.

The Scrutator's discombobulated matrix fled up my sleeve and settled under my armpit, whirring quietly to itself. I fastened my coat buttons, turned up the collar and cinched the belt tight, tighter, tightest. Half a dozen spare dimensions popped out through the seams and enveloped me in a rainbow aura. I folded myself over once, twice, four, eight, sixteen times, until I was the size of a half a postage stamp. Levitating on a froth of residual quarks, I slipped through the tiny hole in the bricked-up doorway.

The mortar squeezed me down then spat me out onto an octagonal lattice of cosmic string. I breathed a sigh of relief—string I could deal with. Unfolding myself just once, I started skating toward the nearest pool of bubbling quicksilver. Hot fog hugged me, stinking of sulfur and a dozen unfathomable esters. Beyond the lattice of string I saw a skyline made of fingers, each higher than a mountain. City-sized knuckles bent like monumental walnuts as the towering digits clawed planets down from high above the clouds. One of the planets bounced on to the lattice and began rolling toward me. Gravity shuddered as the local dimensions contracted. Oceans spilled in the planet's wake; raw atmosphere slewed across my path. The segment of string I was clinging to snapped, and the broken end became a whip that lashed me first up, then down, then both at the same time. I flew over the tumbling planet and under it. At the last moment I hoisted my pants, leapfrogging it by a whisker.

Chasing the planet was a vast heart thumping out a funky twenty-bar beat. Blood splashed from its valves in jets of syncopated crimson. My coat went hazmat just in the nick of time, sprouting cosmofoil ailerons that banked me smack into an upright sea of glutinous mud. I held my breath, shut my eyes and swam. Twelve strokes took me through and out and on to the razor edge of a tetrahedral balloon. I tucked, rolled and flipped off the needle of its apex just nanoseconds before it burst.

I passed into a nebula packed with discarded weapons, some shattered, some whole, the graveyard of a forgotten war. Giant rusty rifles revolved like battleships; sprouting barbs, the strings wound themselves into lethal clutching coils. A vast flock of iron grenades flew past, spilling their pins. Wind roared, not loud enough to dull the ticking of their timers. I looked to all points of the compass and a dozen points past, seeking escape. But there was none. Despite the absence of any kind of highway, it looked like I'd reached the end of the road.

Blacklight flashed off the facets of a distant, spinning shape—a large white cube, pirouetting in the nonsense. The first grenade went off. Hard air thumped my back and propelled me straight toward the cube. A second detonated and drove me back. All around me, a billion ticking bombs marked off the seconds.

"Scrutator!" I shouted. "Your hearing is better than mine. Which one's next?"

A bronzed finger thrust its way from my cuff and pointed toward a nearby grenade. I paddled furiously past, placing myself between the grenade and the cube. Two breaths later the grenade exploded, slamming me a mile or more nearer my target.

"Next!"

The robot's finger swiveled. I swam. Another boom, another mule-kick in the ribs, another mile. Eight explosions later and the cube was close enough to touch. In the center of one face was a handle. It flashed in and out of view as the cube rotated, once, twice...

Third time round I grabbed it and was instantly snatched sideways, the jerk wrenching my shoulder almost from its socket. Now the cube and I were still, and what passed for the cosmos was turning around us. I twisted the handle. Something unlatched, or laughed, or both, and all six sides of the cube peeled back, spraying dimensions like rain. I flew and fell. My guts compressed. Everything unfolded. Something hit me, then something else. My head banged sideways. Another impact. A chattering sound. Blackness.

115

I WOKE FLAT on my back, surrounded by the smell of popcorn and a low murmur of conversation. I blinked my eyes open, stared up at a thousand points of light. Stars? I blinked again—not stars but cabochons, bare bulbs burning in a firmament of frayed black velvet.

I tried to sit up, but something sticky held my coat to the floor. I worked my shoulders and peeled myself free. I stood, and the murmured conversation stopped. I looked around, amazed.

I was in a cinema, one I knew very well. One that had ceased to exist when the Fools had blown up the vault containing the Still Point of the Turning World. Harry's Holodeon.

Everything about the place was the same: the cheap carpet, the rows of cracked plaster pillars, two blocks of tiered seats separated by a narrow aisle sloping down to the big trapdoor in the floor, beyond which loomed a pair of vast swagged crimson curtains. Behind the curtains, I presumed, was the holographic screen on to which Harry Arriflex had routinely projected the latest in a long line of salacious melodramas.

"This can't be real," I muttered.

At the sound of my voice, five hundred bronze heads swiveled in my direction. For the first time in years, Harry's Holodeon—

or whatever fleapit facsimile this was—had a full house.

I shook my cuff and let the Scrutator spill out on to the carpet. All of its dimensions unfolded instantly. Springing back into solidity, it stood swaying, gears chugging noiselessly inside its cheeks, shining eyes wide with surprise.

"My brothers," said the robot, staring at the seated audience.

Five hundred Scrutators stared back.

The trapdoor shot back with a thunk that shook the floor. Music hooted from the basement below and a glittering pipe organ rose smoothly into view. Chrome tubes snaked from a polished marble platform, knotted round each other like strands of intestine, then erupted into a fountain of blaring sound. Pedals squirmed; keys and stops snapped and jerked; oil oozed. I clapped my hands to my ears. There were no chords in the music, only dissonance set to a ragtime beat, and all of it arranged in the most minor of keys.

Seated at the organ was a man. He was dressed in a sharp white suit with black cuffs. His elbows popped like pistons; his black-spat shoes pounded the pedals; his back hunched and straightened, hunched and straightened. It was hard to tell if he was playing the organ, or the organ was playing him.

The man had no head, leastways not in the conventional sense. Instead, a giant silver coin sat spinning on end where his neck should have been. The coin was a blur, but every so often a face flashed past: noble nose, furrowed brow, beady eyes. Eyes that looked right at me.

The organ reached the top of its travel and locked into place. The coin-headed man sprinkled his fingers all the way up the keyboard in a final flourish and then the music stopped. Discordant echoes bounced around the movie house for what seemed like hours. When silence eventually fell, the man flipped up his coat tails and swiveled on his seat. His coin-head continued to spin, only now the face was plain to see, its gaze intense despite the blurry speed with which it was revolving.

"Welcome to Beyond," said the Pennyman. His voice rang like wind-chimes and his lips moved like bad animation. "Have you brought me my heart's one desire?"

116

"You don't beat around the bush," I said. I was horribly aware of being stared at by five hundred pairs of mechanical eyes. It was easy to peg the Pennyman as the bad guy. But whose side were the robots on? And what in all the halls of Hades were they doing here?

"I have been trapped behind the gates of probability for a harsh and endless epoch," the Pennyman replied. "Now you have brought me the key to my future horizon. Time may not exist, but it burns. This I tell you, gumshoe—it burns."

"Where's Zephyr?"

"The white of the black? The quid pro quo and the to of the fro? Tell me, gumshoe, is she the yin or the yang? Take care with your answer, for whatever she may be, that is surely what you are not."

I peered past the organ and into the basement. "You got her tied up down there?"

"Time burns." Cabochon light flashed off the Pennyman's spinning head. "Do not test me with its flame. Deliver the key and the girl will fly once more."

I reached into my coat pocket and closed my fingers round the compact. Every sinew in me wanted to bring it out, hand over the Glory right there and then, strike the deal, make my escape. Bitter experience told me it was unlikely to be that easy.

"In a minute." I relaxed my grip on the compact and withdrew my hand. "First, I want to ask you a few questions."

Beside me, the Scrutator drew in what passed for its breath. A split-second later, the five hundred seated robots echoed the hissing sound it made. I noticed that they weren't looking at me any more. They were looking at my bronzed companion.

A flicker passed over the face of the Pennyman. A change of expression? A wobble in whatever force was turning that damn coin around on his neck? Impossible to say.

"Heads you ask, tails you die!" the Pennyman proclaimed.

The giant coin started spinning faster and faster, turning the Pennyman's face into an inscrutable blur. The organ pipes trembled, and the Scrutators shook in their seats. Dust rained from the velvet ceiling.

Abruptly, the coin stopped spinning, exposing a single stationary face.

Heads.

117

"Heads you ask," said the Pennyman. His silver face was a furious bas relief. "But what shall be the count? One? Two? Four? Eight? Choice begets choice, but where shall the questions end? Sixteen? Thirty-two? Sixty-four? I think not. So, thirty-two. Too many, too. Sixteen. Sweet for some but not for those who burn in the fires of attendance. Eight. All fingers, but where would we be without the thumbs? Four, then? Four? Shall it be four? What do you say, gumshoe? Is four a liberty or a limit? If you would question me, you must first answer me."

"You're saying I can ask you four questions?"

"Now three. Next."

I gave a silent groan. The oldest trick in the book, and I'd fallen for it. I took a breath. "Okay. Where's Zephyr?"

"The girl is in the projection booth. Next."

I threw a glance over my shoulder. High in the back wall of the cinema there was a glass window with dark machinery hulking behind. In the gloom, a shadow moved.

"I believe he wants you to believe this is going to be easy," said the Scrutator. "I do not believe this is the case."

"I believe you're right," I replied.

"Two questions remain," said the Pennyman. "How perfectly encircled is the number of the binary beast."

"I'll take your word for that, pal. Here's my next question: if you can choose anything into existence, why don't you just opt for 'escape' and walk right out of here?"

A sudden stain tarnished the silver surface of the Pennyman's motionless head. The furrows in his brow grew furrows of their own.

"Beyond is neither all nor nothing, neither here nor there. Not when, not then. Not before, not after, and never, ever now. To choose is to cause, and to follow, adopt and discard, and while Beyond reflects these all yet it is none itself. The forked lightning of choice fires its beacon through Beyond and makes shadows of its play, but in Beyond there can be no solitary collapse, no singular resolve, no settlement. In Beyond, the show knows only how to go on."

I was about to ask what the hell the coin-headed freak was talking about when a hand grasped my wrist.

"Be careful, my friend," said the Scrutator. Its voice echoed strangely. At first I figured it was the acoustics of this impossible cinema, then I realised all the other robots were repeating my companion's words in a single, sibilant whisper. "You have only one question left."

I glanced again at the projection booth window. It was all I could do not to dash up there, grab Zephyr and make a run for it. But run where?

"Let me see if I've got this straight," I said to the Pennyman. "You're telling me that here in this bubble you've created—this *Beyond*—the laws of chance that you live by don't apply. You can conjure as many choices as you like—stay or go, sink or swim, fight or flight—but you can never actually come down on one side or the other. You can make choices, *but you can't make a choice*. Here in Beyond, you're powerless."

The Pennyman's face had turned to the color of ash. His full lips sneered. "Ask your last, gumshoe!"

"Have a care," the Scrutator warned.

... *care*, echoed the Holodeon's robot audience.

"There's only one question left that matters." I pulled the compact out of my pocket and held it up into the light. "What will you do when I give you the Glory?"

118

WITHOUT ANSWERING, THE Pennyman swiveled in his seat to face the organ again. While his body rotated, his coin-head gaze remained fixed on me. He thumbed a control, causing sparks to fly from a junction box on the wall and the big crimson curtains to roll back along their tracks, revealing a wide silver screen.

"Escape," the Pennyman said. Silver flooded slowly through his face again.

"If you think I'm going to let you go back into the cosmos..." I began.

"Not back, but forward! Not behind, but ahead! The prize is not nostalgia but novelty!"

"Novelty? You tried that already, remember? You went looking for something new and left the cosmos behind. Look where it got you."

"Not Beyond, but beyond."

"Look, buddy, you can quit playing with words. I don't know much but I do know there ain't nothing beyond Beyond..." I stopped. Something was tickling at the back of my neck.

The Pennyman's coin-head started spinning again, slowly at first, then faster and faster. "In the silver there is a greatness where the chains of chance are not shackles but wings."

I frowned. His words were like ants. Follow them individually and all you got was chaos. Step back and you suddenly saw a bigger picture.

The tickle on my neck bit down.

"The Big Picture!" I said. "Is that what this is all about?"

"The asking is past. Chance is a curse. Choice is a torture. To ride and never rest, to seek and never find, to play and never pause—these things all are the ever-paired sum of my existence, and the duality of my doom. For all that I have done there is equally as much that I have not. My cup is as empty as it is full, half and both but also neither and all, and precisely never running over. Chance is choice, gumshoe, but I tell you this as one forever trapped in two—there is no choice in chance!"

The Pennyman's head was back to being a blur. His face smeared round and round, again and again and again, but his bright eyes were as clearly defined as the truth of his words. And filled suddenly with tears.

Something fluttered out from behind one of the furled curtains: a bright blue bird, tiny wings buzzing like a swarm of bees. I opened my coat and unfolded the cage of ribs I'd brought with me from my office cellar. I set it on the carpet and watched as the two birds bumped beaks through the bones. The instant they touched, their feathers merged. Deliciosa's ribcage shattered, and a single kingfisher flew up through the broken light of the cabochons.

"You haven't been powerless here, have you?" I said. "You used the kingfisher as a go-between. You had it planting pennies on sidewalks from one side of the cosmos to the other, and whenever folk picked them up, their lives changed. Sometimes for the good, mostly for the bad. But always with one purpose: to set you free."

"The metabird navigates the web of Arachne," the Pennyman agreed. "When the spider wove her web my way, I saw advantage to be taken, and choice to be made."

"You messed with the lives of millions of people! Billions, for all I know!" I glanced again at the projection booth. "You messed with *her*."

"The girl was the one. And you were the two. Together you chose, and now here you both are with my heart's one desire."

"Choice be damned! You're a trickster!"

"And you are a gumshoe. We are all what we all are." He struck a terrible chord on the organ. The horrible dissonance made my guts rotate, and brought a new revelation.

"Minor key," I said. "The music you've been playing, it's been traveling out along Arachne's string, all this time. An undertone for the cosmos. No wonder String City's in the state it is."

The Pennyman peeled his fingers from the keyboard. The dreadful reverberations died slowly to silence. I pressed my hands to my face, dragged them away.

"So will you really go there?" I went on, nodding at the projection screen. "If I give you the Glory, will you really turn your back on the cosmos and escape to this next place, whatever it is, this *novelty*. Will you really leave us all alone?"

"The screen is bigger on the other side. Why would I not fill myself into its void?"

The Scrutator nudged me in the ribs. "I am having difficulty parsing your conversation with the Pennyman. Nevertheless I fear treachery."

... *treachery*, whispered the rest of the robots.

I flipped open the compact. It was still in standby mode, with nine minutes remaining on the display—all the life my doppelganger had left.

"You ever heard of the Big Picture?" I asked the robot.

The Scrutator shook its head. So did the others. All five hundred of them.

"It's a myth," I went on. "Or a metaphor. Probably both. The Big Picture is... oh, it's what some people mean when talk about a 'higher power' or 'the workings of the world'." My wife..." I faltered.

"Laura?" my mechanical friend prompted.

... *Laura*, echoed the rest of the Scrutators.

"Laura, right." I swallowed what felt like a boulder down into my throat. "Laura believed in it. She believed in it because she said she'd seen it. She'd seen the Big Picture in this book she'd had since she was a child. The story was simple enough. There's this little girl whose curiosity keeps getting her into trouble. Like, she climbs the neighbor's fence to peer over and falls into a bramble bush. She tries to find out how the garbage disposal works and ends up in the drain. You get the idea?"

"I understand the narrative concept."

"So, this little girl's parents—her name is Laura, by the way, which is one of the reasons why Laura, my Laura, liked the book so much—her parents figure she needs a hobby to put a lid on her adventuring. So they buy her a telescope. Laura loves this thing so much that she starts adding extra lenses to it, so every night she uses it she sees more and more stars and planets, and starts seeing deeper and deeper into the cosmos. Anyway, the last picture in the book folds out to show Laura adding the biggest lens ever to the telescope, and what she sees when she looks through the viewfinder is this huge backdrop filled with all the other scenes from earlier in the book—the fence and the drain and everything—plus hundreds more besides, scenes from her future even, with her all grown up and with a little girl of her own, and the little girl has her own book, and her own telescope. This final big picture is like a giant colorful jigsaw of her whole complete life, everything about her, everything about..."

I broke off. I was breathing hard. I could feel a bead of sweat stroking my brow.

"... everything?" said the Scrutator.

... *everything*, whispered its brothers.

"Right," I replied. "Everything about everything."

"The Big Picture?"

"The Big Picture."

... *Picture.*

The Scrutator tapped its fingers against its cheek. "Does it exist?"

"Nobody knows, not for sure. But if it does, then it's what sits behind everything we know and most of what we don't. If the one God really is out there, looking at the Big Picture would be like looking on his face. As for stepping *into* it, I guess that would be like..."

I've always thought my reflexes were quick, but I never saw the Pennyman move. Never saw him leap from the organ seat and snatch the compact from my hand. All I saw was the flash of silver as his spinning head raced up the cinema aisle on top of his pistoning shoulders, accompanied by five hundred flashes of bronze as the seated Scrutators turned to watch him run.

"After him!" I yelled.

I reached the door at the back of the auditorium just as it swung shut in my face. I kicked it aside, took the stairs two at a time. At the top, another door was flapping back and forth. I shouldered through and into the projection booth: a cramped black box of a room that stank of cheap engine oil. Taking up most of the booth was a gigantic movie projector—a cast metal monster slick with grease and studded with dials and wheels. Film reels sprouted like giant mouse ears; deep inside, a motor idled throatily.

I didn't care about any of that. All I cared about was Zephyr. She was in the far corner of the booth, standing at a bench, her face lit by the baleful glow of the projector's badly shuttered lamp housing. On the bench was an ancient Moviola editing machine. Strips of celluloid film dangled from her finger, and at her feet lay the remains of the zoetrope she'd brought here, its glass sphere shattered to shards. Her eyes were hollow.

"He said he could make it real," she said, holding up the pieces of film. "He said the zoetrope was just a trick and he could give me my life, my real life, and if I spliced it together just right, me and Raymond, we could... we could..."

"He was right about the zoetrope being a trick," I told her, my heart breaking a little as I said it. "But he lied about the rest." I hesitated. "I guess I lied too. Raymond's gone. I'm sorry."

Zephyr's lips thinned and her cheeks turned red, just as if I'd slapped her. She opened her fingers and the celluloid strips slithered to the floor. I could see they were blank, and I wondered what enchantments he'd convinced her to see on them.

The Pennyman appeared from behind the projector and clawed open the lamp housing. Light flared. His pale fingers closed on the bare bulb and yanked it from its socket. In the sudden darkness I heard the slam of the booth's door shutting, the loud click of the lock.

I held my hands up in front of my face and saw nothing.

"Zephyr?"

There was no reply.

I heard another click, this one very small and very slight.

A button.

The room lit up again, a thousand times brighter than before. Zephyr threw her hands over her face; so did I. Peering through my fingers, I watched as the Pennyman placed the compact on the projector. The timer was ticking again. Eight minutes and fifty-two seconds.

"He looks just like you!" crowed the Pennyman. "Ah me, but the wonder of twins!"

I turned and saw the doppelganger standing behind me, looking dazed. I willed him to move, but of course his hands were still clamped on the Glory. He was as frozen now as he'd been in the crater.

I was about to move myself but the Pennyman was lightning-fast. Strong too. Reaching past me, he lifted my lookalike and crammed him bodily into the projector's lamp housing. At first I didn't think the doppelganger would fit into the round glass vial, but the Pennyman did something wiggy with the local dimensions and with a "pop" the doppelganger snapped into place. He squatted there unblinking, staring out at me like a toad in a test tube.

Then the Glory—perhaps sensing the perfect habitat—slipped through the doppelganger's fingers and locked itself into the base of the lamp socket, where it blazed even brighter than before. Released from his stasis, the doppelganger popped free from the vial like a cork and flew across the booth to land with a thump in the far corner. Even before he hit the deck, the Pennyman had slammed the lamp housing shut and reached for the lever that would start the projector.

"It won't work," I said. "All you've done is turn this projector into a new Still Point. With the Glory inside it, the workings won't work."

"The glass may be silent," the Pennyman replied, "but the lighthouse shall speak."

He pulled the lever. The projector's motor, unaffected by the Glory's stasis field, whirred into life while the Glory itself remained frozen in its new home. The film reels turned, sending celluloid chattering through the sprockets. Light flickered from the lens and as it did so the Pennyman stepped in front of it. The light hit his spinning head and his face flashed, his expression all streamers of mirth and madness. On the distant silver screen, a kaleidoscope of color swam slowly into focus. It looked like a picture. A big one.

"This is all just a trick!" The Scrutator was stuck out on the stairs, its voice muffled by the reinforced glass of the locked door's vision panel. Behind it, I could just make out a line of robots straggling down into the gloom.

"TRICK!" they all roared as one.

"The Pennyman has opened the way to the Big Picture but still he cannot choose to leave!" the Scrutator shouted.

"LEAVE!"

"He needs another to make the choice for him!" said the Scrutator.

"CHOICE!"

The Pennyman's arms closed around Zephyr's waist. Quick as a rattlesnake, he pulled her into the light. Their shadows filled the screen: a couple dancing.

"Regard," the Pennyman hissed in Zephyr's ear. "Regard the truth of the two, of you and of him, and of the chance to be paired once more. Make the total, and carry the sum." He bent close, his leering face bright in the spinning coin of his head. "Carry *me*!"

"Don't do it, Zephyr!" I cried. "He's powerless here, remember? He can't make the choice to leave himself. As long as we don't help him, he'll stay trapped."

"You think I don't know that?" Zephyr's eyes were fixed on the dazzling vista that was opening up on the screen. I could feel its pull, and knew she could too. "You think I don't know the power is mine?"

"If you lead him out into the Big Picture, there's no telling what damage he'll do there!"

Tearing her eyes away from the Big Picture's promise of eternity, she pinned her gaze on me. "Why do you care what I do? And why should I care what he does? Why should I care about anything?" Her eyes strayed back to the screen. "Why shouldn't I just go there, and leave all this behind?"

"But it was the Pennyman who messed with your life. With so many lives. It's what he *does*. Think of the chaos he'll cause if you give him a canvas as big as this. He'll bring down the worlds! All of them!"

She shook her head and I felt a crush of despair.

"I can't make a choice for any world," she said sadly, "and if you think I can then you're a fool. I can only choose for me."

I blinked, suddenly confused by what appeared to be a gleam in her eye. "What? Choose what?"

With a sharp, sudden flick of her wrists, Zephyr yanked the Pennyman's hands free from where they were gripping her midriff. A snarl shuddered across his speeding face.

"I picked up your penny," she said to her captor, "and it made me kill the man I loved. Some would say my man was a monster, but he didn't deserve that. He didn't deserve any of it."

She smiled at the Pennyman, and in the light of the Glory, she was beautiful.

"But you deserve this!"

Her hand stabbed out. In it she held a curved shard of glass—a single slice of the broken zoetrope. The sharp point sliced into the lapel of the Pennyman's crisp white suit, just above his heart.

And went no deeper.

The Pennyman grinned. With one hand he slapped Zephyr's cheek. With the other he wrenched the sliver of glass from her fingers. Blood flew—I couldn't tell whose it was. He slapped her again, continuing to smile as he plucked a dented silver dollar from the breast pocket of his black dress shirt, the lucky coin that just had saved his life.

"Chance is but a wager," the Pennyman crooned, "and here come my winnings."

He shoved Zephyr against the projection booth window. The glass shattered. Screaming, eyes bulging, she clutched at the frame but it was too late. She tumbled out through the window and fell from sight into the auditorium below.

"Zephyr!" I lunged at the Pennyman, but he stepped nimbly aside. I slammed into the window frame, now studded with sharp glass teeth, and nearly followed Zephyr over the edge. Regaining my balance, I rocked back and was about to grapple with the Pennyman when I saw something that made me stop.

Laura's face on the screen. Laura in the Big Picture. She was smiling, radiant. Beckoning.

"Do not look at it!" called the Scrutator, thumping its fist against the locked door. "Brothers, help me!" More thumps followed as the other robots joined in. The door shuddered, but held.

I couldn't take my eyes off my lost wife, and the paradise that was slowly forming around her.

"She is there," said the Pennyman in my ear. "She saw it and she is there. The story was always hers, and she was always destined to be the story. Restring the violin, gumshoe, and play again the music you once were so happy to hear."

"You're lying," I growled. "Laura died."

"To swim in the Lethe is never to die, only to forget, and to forget is to change, and to journey, to become elsewhere and elsewhen and elsewhy. She is there, and so shall you be too."

"It's not true!"

The light of the Glory was lifting me up. The Pennyman's arms snaked around my neck and his legs clamped around my waist. Now I was carrying him, though he weighed nothing. I weighed nothing. I was a feather afloat, no longer really here, aware only of there. Of where I wanted to choose to be. With her. Glory light wafted me through the broken window and out over the auditorium seats. On the screen, in the screen, behind the screen, the Big Picture was gradually coming into focus.

A voice called to me from the projection booth. It said, "Give me your coat!"

"But it's my coat," I mumbled back. The words sounded thin and meaningless.

"Exactly! Throw it here!"

I didn't recognise the voice, but it was loud and authoritative, so I obeyed. What did it matter? It was only a coat. I wriggled out of it, sliding it past the Pennyman's clutching limbs and tossing it through the window and into the booth. Why not? Where I was going, I wouldn't need it.

On the screen, Laura beckoned to me. I let the light of the Glory carry me toward the Big Picture, toward the place beyond Beyond, toward the place where I would be with my dead wife again.

"Where did you put the damn stuff?" said the voice. "This pocket? Maybe it's... aw geez, what is *this*? Wait, maybe this pocket... ah, here we are..."

I realised the other voice was my voice. How could that be? My thoughts slopped like bad broth as I tried in vain to work it out. The ineffable mosaic of the Big Picture filled my vision, my head, my heart. Cabochon light dazzled my soul.

"See what lies ahead," the Pennyman whispered. I could feel the rush of air as his coin-head spun close to my ear. "See all that there is, and all that there may be, and all the choices that may be made by one bold enough to take the chance. See what lies over and under, and what mysteries course through all. This is the truth of it, gumshoe, unfurled for you now and forever."

Back in the booth the projector continued to throw out the Glory light. The light pushed me on toward the waiting screen while the Pennyman clung to me, a passenger relieved of the need to make a decision. Laura's face broke into a rainbow. Shadows fell like rain, color like snow. Something swelled, a flower poised to open, a bubble about to burst. My heart held itself trembling, on the verge of revelation.

"So, buddy," said the voice, "you care to take a wager?"

Muscles twitched in the Pennyman's arms. "I will not be distracted by what comes and what goes."

"Comes and goes?" Understanding finally pierced the single-minded mud of my thoughts. It was the doppelganger—that was who the voice belonged to! "Shouldn't that be comes *or* goes? Isn't that your thing, pal? Making choices? Either, or? This, that?"

"There is no chance in Beyond," snarled the Pennyman, "as I believe I have already explained."

"Hmm, well, maybe not. But there is this."

Another rustle. Something partially blocked the light spilling from the projector. A little of my weight returned and some hidden force began tugging me and the Pennyman back toward the booth.

"What do you have there?" The Pennyman sounded curious, or cautious, or both.

We floated back into the booth through the broken window. The doppelganger was just a silhouette against the Glory's glare, but I could tell by the shape of him that he was wearing my coat. He was also holding up something he'd found inside one of the pockets. The thing I'd pulled from the safe just before leaving my cellar to come here.

The pouch of Schrödinger's Gold.

"Here's the thing," said the doppelganger. "The way I understand it, this pouch is either full of gold, or it isn't. At the same time, it's also both. It's only when you open it that fate decides what's really inside. Don't ask me how that works. I failed quantum philosophy."

"It is chance," growled the Pennyman. "It is all of it chance, as you must surely comprehend."

In his other hand, the doppelganger was holding the compact. I could just make out the numbers glowing on the dial—the timer was down to six minutes and twelve seconds.

"Well, I sure as hell don't comprehend it as well as you claim to, buddy. But when you've tangled with Titans, you get to learn a lot about gambling. And gambling's what you do, isn't it? It's what you *are*. That or this. This or that. It's all just one big wager for you, right?"

"Wager?"

"That's what I said. And that's exactly what I've got for you—a wager."

"Don't do this," the Pennyman quavered. "Please."

"I'll bet you my partner's life that I can predict what's inside this pouch." My doppelganger grinned like a devil in heat. "You want to take that bet?"

* * *

119

The Pennyman's head thrummed. His face was one big blurred grimace. I thought I heard him sob. Meanwhile, the light of the Glory was trying to push me back toward the screen. Back toward Laura. With all my strength, and what little was left of my heart, I fought against it.

"I accept!" he blurted at last. "You know I must! You know it!"

"There speaks a true addict." The doppelganger stepped a little more into the light. His grin had transformed into something that wouldn't have disgraced a shark.

A shudder ran through the Pennyman's body. "I must take your wager," he said. "I must take the chance. I must take the *choice*." Four minutes and thirty-one seconds left on the compact. "Make your play, gumshoe!"

"Oh, my partner here is the gumshoe. Me, I'm just a shadow. You want to know what I bet?"

"Tell me!"

"I bet this pouch is empty."

"Then prove it!" The Pennyman drew in his breath with a hiss and held it. I felt myself do the same.

The doppelganger hefted the pouch from one hand to the other. Doubt clouded his face. For an instant, some kind of syrupy liquid seemed to slop inside it. The next moment, it sagged like a spent balloon.

"Open the pouch," growled the Pennyman. "Be done with this!"

The doppelganger shrugged and unlaced the cords. He peered inside, frowned, then tilted the pouch forward to reveal the shimmering pool of liquid gold inside.

The Pennyman's head whirred round faster than ever.

"Not empty!" he screamed, letting go of my neck and clapping his hands together. "I win! I win! Oh, I will paint such pictures as you have never before seen!"

The doppelganger looked straight at me. "Partner, are you any good at tossing coins?"

As he said it, he flung the contents of the pouch against the projector's lamp housing. The liquid gold splattered over the hot glass, which shattered instantly. Raw volts shot from the suddenly exposed electrical contacts. Sparks zapped the projector sprockets, fusing the film, and the entire machine juddered to a halt.

At once all the colors vanished from the screen. Laura's face lingered like a phantom for a single, breathless second, then she was gone.

The Big Picture—whatever it was or might have been—was gone.

Naked in the broken lamp socket, the Glory screamed.

Tossing coins?

I grabbed the Pennyman's head with both hands. Hot metal dug into the flesh of my fingers and for an instant I thought that the giant coin wouldn't stop turning, that I'd be spun and thrown like a child from a carousel. Then my shoulders jolted and locked and there was the Pennyman's face, stationary at last, staring at me with eyes like round silver dollars. Robbed of motion he looked old but not wise, and filled to the brim with a measureless rage.

I stared back for a moment, then turned the Pennyman's head slowly round, a half turn. Don't ask me why. I just did it.

On the other side, the same furious face stared back at me.

"Double-headed coin," I said. "Pal, you're just a big fat cheat."

Bunching my muscles, I tossed the Pennyman toward the projector. He flipped all the way over, once, twice. The cabochons drew a thousand angry glints across the screeching silver of his face.

He came down hard, right on top of the Glory. The light of the cosmos enveloped him, sank into him, sucked in all the caustic reflections of all the cabochons out in the auditorium, redoubled them, compressed them into a single blazing highlight that circumnavigated the silver coin of the Pennyman's head before finally lancing into its center. There the light of the Glory settled and subsided, and there it remained, peaceful and grounded once more, frozen in space and time at the new heart of the changing cosmos, which was also the collapsed choice of the Aerlyft's greatest gambler: the Pennyman, who was now and would forever be the Still Point of the Turning World.

120

"ZEPHYR!" I EXCLAIMED.

I got to the door at the exact same time as the doppelganger. He snicked the lock and I turned the handle. The Scrutator spilled into the projection booth, mechanical arms flailing. Behind it, a tide of robots fought for balance. I pushed past them, raced down the stairs and back into the auditorium.

"Zephyr!" I shouted. "Zephyr!"

I found her lying between the seats of the back row in a heap of old popcorn cartons. Blood oozed from a laceration on her scalp. Her eyelids trembled. Her lips fluttered out words that I couldn't make out.

"What?" I said. "What did you say?"

"... believe," she croaked. "That's what he said... all I had to do..."

"Believe what?"

"In the dance."

She coughed. Blood sprayed down her chin. Her eyes flickered open. The left one was shot through red.

"The dance stopped for Raymond," I said. "But not for the rest of the world. Not for you."

"Why do I feel dizzy?"

I held her. "Because you're dancing. We're dancing. It's a waltz and a whirlwind. All of it. A cyclone."

"... not making any sense..."

"None of it makes sense. But somehow it all hangs together."

"... take your... word for it..."

Her eyes flickered shut.

"No!" I shook her. No response. "Don't take my word! Take my hand!"

I seized her. Her fingers were cold. I pulled her to me, stood her up. She hung limp in my arms, heavy as a doll. I moved my feet.

"Dance, damn you!"

I turned her. Her short hair was silky with cabochon light. Her feet dragged. I spun her round, once, twice. Her head lolled.

Then her free hand twitched. Slowly it came up. Rested on my shoulder.

"... don't know... the steps..."

"There are no steps. There's just the dance."

We turned together.

"Is this all we do?" Her eyelids lifted jerkily.

"It's all there is," I replied. "We turn. Everything turns. That's all you need to know."

Her head nestled into my shoulder.

"Like a merry-go-round? Like a hurricane?"

"Just like that."

She looked around.

"Is this the eye of the storm?"

"Something like that, honey. Something like that."

121

I STOOD FOR a while staring at the projection booth window. The light of the Glory pulsed gently inside the motionless coin of the Pennyman's head, a slumbering candle. Meanwhile, the robots broke the organ apart, then ripped out the hydraulic mechanism that elevated it out of the cellar. The Scrutator supervised the proceedings.

"They obey you," I observed.

"They are my brothers," the Scrutator replied. "But they are also earlier models. Where I am woven of cosmic string, they are merely metal. I suppose you might say I am the latest thing."

"Did you know they were going to be here?"

"I confess I had allowed myself to hope. As you know, knowledge of the coming apocalypse prompted our makers, the Thanes, to send their sons to a safe place. But nobody knew where that safe place was."

"Until now."

"Yes, until now."

Something occurred to me. "You told me that, after your brothers left, you had to stay in the city because you couldn't leave the cosmos by conventional means. So how come I was able to bring you here?"

The Scrutator's mechanical face folded into something that was unmistakeably a smile.

"You are many things," it said. "But you are certainly not conventional."

122

It was dark in the basement of the cinema. With me, Zephyr, the Scrutator, and five hundred humming robots crammed in there, it was crowded too.

"What now?" Zephyr said. Her voice was still hoarse, and she had to lean on me for support, but she sounded stronger than before.

"We spread out," I said. "See what we can find."

"What are we looking for?"

One of the robots found it: a line of spider silk stretched taut across the floor at ankle height. One end was sealed to the wall with a gobbet of resin. The rest vanished into darkness. Perched on it like a swallow on a telegraph wire was a small blue bird.

"This string is how the kingfisher came and went," I said. "How we got here too. This is the single thread of Arachne's web that found its way to the Pennyman's prison, the only thing connecting Beyond to the rest of the cosmos."

The kingfisher hopped along the silk, which was only visible once you knew it was there. We followed it to a door. The Scrutator pushed it open and we filed outside. The floor ended, but the silk went on. We moved along it, wirewalkers all. The lonely white cube of Beyond dwindled behind us, alone in the void. Somewhere far ahead was everything we knew.

"How long have you got?" I asked the doppelganger.

He showed me the compact. There were twenty-eight seconds left on the timer.

... twenty-seven... twenty-six...

"I could put it on standby again," I said.

"Not an option," the other me replied. "For either of us. You have to cut the string, you know that, right? Otherwise the Pennyman might find a way back."

"But he's asleep forever."

"Nothing's forever, buddy. You know that."

I rummaged in my pockets. "I don't have a knife."

"But you have something explosive."

I nodded. I knew it, just didn't want to admit it. Eyes stinging, I opened the compact, bent and snapped it shut over the silk tightrope. I flung open my coat, expanding the lining seventeen times until it was big enough to envelop every last one of the refugees strung out along the line. Then I pulled the drawstrings and folded everybody inside.

Everybody except the doppelganger.

"You should stand back," he said. "This thing's going to whip."

"I know," I replied.

He took a step back. Now it was just the two of us, each balanced on a thread of cosmic string, the compact ticking silently down between our feet.

... fifteen... fourteen...

"Couldn't have done it without you, buddy," I said.

"You're so lame."

"I wish there was another way."

"No, you don't."

"I'll miss you."

"You won't. You'll see me every morning in the mirror, and you'll curse the day you brought me into this pitiful excuse for a life."

... nine... eight...

"I just wish there was something else I could do."

"There is."

"What? Name it!"

... six... five...

"You already know what it is."

"Don't play games!"

... three...

"This isn't a game."

... two...

"You think I don't know that?!"

... one...

The doppelganger's eyes rested on mine. "Just go home, buddy."

... zero.

The compact's self-destruct mechanism went off with a magnesium flash and the doppelganger vanished. It was a pitiful explosion, really, the last damp firework in the box. But it was enough to cut the cord.

The line of cosmic string, the single thread of silk woven by Arachne, the only connection between the cosmos and Beyond, snapped. The short end coiled away, wrapping itself three times round the cube before finally coming to rest.

The long end lashed, flicking me away into the void with the precious payload of my companions buried deep inside the tails of my coat. My arms made windmills as my hands tried to gain purchase on the speeding weave of the world. But the world was gone. All the worlds were gone. I was nowhere. There was nowhere to go.

I spread my arms wide. Blue wings whirred beside me. The kingfisher bored through my slipstream, rolling and somersaulting, its black eyes filled with ecstasy. It was in its element, alone and free as it cavorted through the one true place it was always destined to be. For that single lost breath we flew together in the emptiness, the kingfisher and me, neither here nor there, neither lost nor found. Already, Beyond had slipped from sight. The cosmos felt very far away.

I opened a flap of my coat.

"You can come with us, if you want," I told the kingfisher.

The metabird grew a thousand pairs of wings and buzzed like a sawmill. Then it contracted back into its singular state, flicked its electric blue tail and vanished into the aether.

I rummaged in my pocket. My fingers closed on a small cube. I pulled it out, held it up. The shape of the Dimension Die reminded me of Beyond. But Beyond was long gone.

One black face remained active on the die. One last chance. I wondered if I'd ever regret using it up. Was there a future version of me waiting somewhere ahead, trapped in perilous straits, wishing he'd planned a little harder, thought a little deeper, found another way? I'd met another me once already, and let him down badly. Could I bear doing it again?

My coat billowed in the unseen wind, heavy with its payload.

I rolled the die.

Epilogue

123

I FILLED A paper cup with coffee and stared out at the rain.

It was busy outside. Folk were weaving through the puddles, making lines outside the stores. The store windows were mostly still boarded up, but basic supplies were coming through again at last. There were bread lines, meat lines, dairy lines—you name it, folk were queueing for it.

The crowd seemed good-natured. Most just stood under umbrellas with their ration cards, chatting quietly, patiently waiting for their turn. Further down the street, a couple of ogres were lifting up a sign. They pinned it to a shop-front, stood back to admire their work. The sign read *Diana's Deli—Opening Soon*. Nearby, a team of municipal golems was filling in the craters. On the corner, a gardener was digging a fresh bed of soil. It was hard work in the rain, but he was sticking at it. Also to it. A big old dame with tree-bark skin was directing him. She was Eurydice, the hamadryad madam. Knowing the girls would soon be back gave me a warm feeling.

Screw the apocalypse. Things were going to be okay.

Beyond the street, the String City skyline was rising once more.

With the thunderbirds gone, it was safe to fly construction rocs again. The giant birds were everywhere—erecting scaffolds, fitting I-beams on tower block skeletons, dropping tiles on newly-built roofs. I'd never seen so many buildings go up so quick. Well, in the weeks after the end of the world, you've got to welcome a little urban regeneration.

The office door opened and a bronzed mechanical man walked in. It shook off the rain, stood ticking for a moment.

"Scrutator," I said. "Thanks for coming." Through the gaps in its cheeks, I could see all the little gears moving in perfect harmony. I wondered if Arachne's thread was still rattling around in there somewhere.

"You told me you needed help with an important job," said the Scrutator.

"Two jobs actually. You sure you can spare the time? What with keeping the wind factory running and everything?"

"The automatic systems are performing at optimum capacity. Besides, what else are friends for?"

First stop was the cellar. On the way down the steps, I asked the Scrutator the question I hadn't yet dared to ask it.

"You think there's any way the Pennyman can get out of that bind we put him in?"

The robot's gears spun like little dynamos. Its ticking echoed round the cellar. "I believe that we have increased the net security of the cosmos. Previously, the entirety of creation revolved around a Still Point that was kept under heavy guard in the heart of this very city. As a result of our actions, a new Still Point has been created that is confined to an isolated appendix of reality that is unreachable by any reasonable definition of the word."

"So we did good?"

"I believe that is what I said."

I slapped the Scrutator's shoulder. "That's all I wanted to hear, metal man."

"I am not made of metal. I am made of..."

"Cosmic string, right. So, you want to know what we're doing down in the cellar?"

"I confess to a certain level of curiosity."

I pulled out something from my coat pocket. "I want you to help me get rid of this."

I turned it in my fingers. It sparkled in the tokamak light.

A silver penny.

The Scrutator's gears started whining.

"Relax," I said. "It's just the penny I got from Arachne. I had it in my pocket all the way to Beyond and back. I thought maybe it would be useful—turned out it wasn't." I held up my hands. "Don't worry, this one wasn't laid by the Pennyman."

The whining sound settled. "In that case, what are you going to do with it?"

"What do you think? This is net profit, buddy. It's going in the safe."

The Scrutator watched as I dialed the dimensional ultralock on the wall safe. I opened the door and took out the scrap of paper that was lying inside. I placed the penny on the shelf, and closed the door again.

"You said you needed my help," said the Scrutator. "I cannot see how..."

"Reset the dial," I said.

"Please repeat the instruction." The Scrutator's cogs rattled in confusion.

"It's simple. I'm going to turn my back. While I'm not looking, I want you to reset the combination of the safe."

"But then you will not be able to get into it."

"Precisely."

The Scrutator focused in on me with glowing eyes. "If the Pennyman did not lay this penny, who did?"

I tried to hold its gaze but couldn't. "Just do it, buddy."

I turned away, heard a rattle, then a series of tiny clicks.

"You may look again," said the Scrutator. "However, I must inform you that I am not entirely comfortable knowing this secret."

"Can you live with it?"

"Of course. Discomfort does not preclude..."

"Then so can I." I picked the little brass key off the hook on the wall and dropped it in my pocket with the scrap of paper. "Now for the second part. Shall we go?"

"There is something else I wish to ask," said the Scrutator as we climbed the stairs out of the cellar.

"For a guy that doesn't want to be a detective," I said, "you're full of questions."

"I am curious as to the whereabouts of Zephyr. I see no evidence of her continuing employment here. Indeed, your office looks much as it did when I first made your acquaintance, namely it has only one desk. If it is not impertinent to ask—what happened to her?"

"She's meeting us there." I took a deep breath. "At least, I hope she is. I need both of you for this second part."

124

Nukatem Street hadn't changed much. There were the same white clapboard houses, old elms, tired picket fences. The street climbed a hill roughly a hundred yards outside the city limits, and there was a hell of a view. As we ascended, we saw the dark sprawl of the railhead, the ripple of light on the River

Lethe, the new downtown quarter with its jackstraw forest of gothic towers and swiveling cranes, a new moving sea of steel and glass, concrete and willow, brownstone and daub. Traffic swarmed. The whole city was in motion. Dancing.

Halfway to the top of the hill we stopped. The rain had eased off and the sun was peeking through the clouds.

"That's my place."

I pointed across the street to the little house with the big porch. It looked just the way I remembered. A little more sag in the roof, maybe. A skinny girl was huddled in the porch. She waved, and we waved back.

"How long is it since you last entered your abode?" said the Scrutator.

"Ten years."

On the way here, I'd told the Scrutator about Laura, how she'd taken herself off to die. How she'd left me a note saying there was something waiting for me in the house. I put my hand in my pocket to hold the paper scrap I'd taken from the safe. I'd read it many times over. Maybe later I'd read it again.

"I wonder, do you believe this might have something to do with the Big Picture?" the Scrutator asked.

I shook my head. "That was just another one of the Pennyman's games. Laura's dead. I know that now. Whatever I saw on that damn movie screen... it was all just smoke and mirrors." I let go of the note and pulled out the brass key. "The bottom line is this is unfinished business. A great big loose end. Time to tie it up."

The sun brightened further as we crossed the street. When we got to the porch, Zephyr smiled and hugged us both.

"I wasn't sure you'd come," I said.

"You wanted me to," she replied. "Besides, I'm in no hurry. Home will still be waiting for me."

I looked up at the house. "I guess that's what homes do."

I delved in my pocket, brought out the key. But I couldn't bring myself to lift it to the door.

"This box she left for you," said Zephyr gently. "Have you any idea what's inside?"

I shrugged. "Who knows? Another note, maybe. But why write a note that leads to more notes? Unless she left a trail. But a trail to what? Could be there's a gift in the box. She inherited a lot of baubles when her mother died. Most she gave away. She and her mother—they didn't get on. Could be she kept something special though, something I didn't know about. Decided to pass it down to me. Could be there was more to her death than I knew—some kind of funny business, who knows?—and she's left me a clue—documents, maybe. Or some little thing to set me on a scent. You know the kind of thing: a matchbook, a phone number, a gold earring. Whatever it is, it's something I need to see. Something I should have seen years ago."

"Why don't you stop talking now."

She took my hand and helped me guide the key into the lock.

125

IT WAS PHOTOGRAPHS, just photographs. The box was made from cardboard and it was full of them. Photos of her, photos of me. Photos of the two of us, happy and young. Little pictures from another time.

Zephyr and the Scrutator left me to it.

Most of the photographs made me smile. Some made me sad. Here at last were the memories she'd lost in the river. Not wiped away at all, but safe in my hands. Deleted scenes, restored. Sifting through them was like bathing in the echoes of my former life, and if that's a sappy thought, sue me. It took me a while to work my way through them all, but that was okay—I had ten years of avoidance to rinse away. When I'd finished, I closed up the box and dropped it in my pocket.

"A lick of paint, and this place'll be like new."

I looked up to see Zephyr standing in the doorway.

"You offering to do it up?" I said.

She ran a finger along the mantel shelf, turned up her nose at the dust. "It needs it. If I do a good job, will you reduce my rent?"

I opened my mouth, closed it again. "I thought you wanted me to take you back to your world."

"I did, but I got to thinking. I do still love my old apartment, but compared to this city everything back there is just a bit too... I don't know..."

"Quiet?"

"Still." She smiled at me first with her eyes, then her mouth.

"You mentioned rent. How do you plan to pay it?"

"I suppose I'm going to need a job." She brushed the dust from her hand and planted her hands on her hips. "Know anyone who's hiring?"

Back out on the street, I opened my coat and took them both inside. I opened a way to the weave, grateful that the strings were back to normal at last. When we were riding high, I tweaked the lapels apart and allowed my companions the briefest glimpse of all that there was to see. They gasped, which made me feel warm inside, but all too soon the journey was over and there we were back in the office again with our feet planted firm on the ground and the world turning slowly beneath us.

"It's good to know, isn't it?" said Zephyr, her eyes still brimming with leftover wonder.

"Good to know what?" I said.

"That there's more than just this." She waved her arms wide, indicating the walls of the office, and the city that lay beyond them.

I crossed to the coffee machine and flicked it on. The smell of hot java began to fill the room.

"There's always something more." I turned to the Scrutator. "I guess you'll be going now?"

But the robot was looking through the window at a woman who was crossing the street outside. She wore a long shawl and a desperate expression, and she was headed straight for the office door.

"I believe I might stay a little longer," the Scrutator said.

The door opened and in walked the dame.

"Please," she said. "Something terrible has happened, and I don't know who to turn to."

Zephyr glanced at me with her eyebrows raised. I went to the machine and poured four cups of coffee.

"Take a seat," said Zephyr. "And tell us what happened."

"I don't know where to start," said the dame as she collapsed into the chair.

I placed a cup into her trembling hands. Outside, a pair of fledgling rocs flew side by side over the half-shelled dome of the new city hall, wingtips sparking every time they brushed feathers. A municipal garbage truck rumbled past, a pair of bent clay legs sticking out of the top and three golems running frantically behind. On the far street corner, a silver-barked hamadryad lazily bathed her fruits in the sunshine.

"Start at the only place that makes sense," I said. "The beginning."

ACKNOWLEDGEMENTS

Special thanks to Jon Oliver, Michael Rowley and Kate Coe for helping me hurl this novel out into the cosmos, and to Shawna McCarthy, Giuseppe Granieri and Letizia Sechi for going out on a limb with the original stories that spawned it.

Explore the world of String City further at stringcity.blog

Find out more about the author at graham-edwards.com

ABOUT THE AUTHOR

Graham Edwards is the critically acclaimed author of multiple novels, and short fiction, including the British Fantasy Award-shortlisted Ultimate Dragon Saga, and the Nebula Award-longlisted "Girl in Pieces", part of his String City Mysteries series. Born near Glastonbury Tor and now living in Nottingham, Graham has worked as a graphic designer and animator, scriptwriter and multimedia producer for theme parks, and is currently senior staff writer at Cinefex magazine, the journal of cinematic illusions, where he researches and writes in-depth articles about motion picture visual effects.

FIND US ONLINE!

www.rebellionpublishing.com

/rebellionpub   /rebellionpublishing   /rebellionpub

SIGN UP TO OUR NEWSLETTER!

rebellionpublishing.com/sign-up

YOUR REVIEWS MATTER!

Enjoy this book? Got something to say?

Leave a review on Amazon, GoodReads or with your favourite bookseller and let the world know!